PRAISE
for Mark A. Rayner

"Mark A. Rayner is just a terrific storyteller and one of the most imaginative and original writers you will ever have the pleasure of reading."

~Ian Ferguson, Author of *Village of the Small Houses*

"I know some very funny people. I've also met lots of writers. But I've only come across a few truly funny writers, and Mark A. Rayner is one of them."

~Terry Fallis, Author of *Best Laid Plans*

"Mark A. Rayner is an author with a fantastical sense of humor and a dangerous imagination."

~*The Next Best Book Club*

". . . a top pick for any humorous fiction collection, highly recommended."

~Midwest Book Review

"Rayner's flair for sustained humor, and compelling storytelling enhances his preposterous premises ..."

~Janet Paszkowski, *Flash Me Magazine*

THE FATNESS

~a novel of epic portions~

by Mark A. Rayner

markarayner.com

This is a work of fiction. Names, characters, places and incidents either are the product of the author's imagination or used fictitiously. Any resemblance to actual persons, living or dead, business establishments, events or locales is purely coincidental.

First Paperback Edition – Monkeyjoy Press
Cover Illustration and Design by Taryn Dafault
Book Design by M. Tundra

ISBN 978-1-927590-05-8

This manuscript is set in Adobe Garamond Pro, a tasty typeface that is wholesome and nutritious. Chapter titles are in Futura medium italics, which is admittedly, high in refined carbs.

None of the satirical ruminations in this book should be taken as medical advice!

monkeyjoy press

For Shazzer, who loves me no matter my BMI

Also by Mark A. Rayner

Novels
The Amadeus Net
Marvellous Hairy
The Fridgularity

Collections
Pirate Therapy and Other Cures

THE FATNESS

~a novel of epic portions~

Part I

"He must have a long spoon that must eat with the devil."

~William Shakespeare, *The Comedy of Errors*

Chapter 1 – Eat Your Cake and Have It, Too

The weigh-in was a disaster.

Keelan Cavanaugh stood at the mirror in his tiny room, a wad of belly fat bunched up in his meaty hands. He cursed the roll breathlessly. The skin bulged and turned red as his hands gripped tighter, as if he could – through force of will and enough manual pressure – make the band of fat tissue magically disappear.

But it just hurt.

And for some reason it also made him hungry.

Intellectually, Keelan understood that it was more than the obvious roll of pudge around his middle that was the cause of his continued stay in the Uxford County Calorie Reduction Centre (CRC-17). In his mind's eye, he could imagine the fifty-one bricks of malleable, white, soft butter-like substance that were hidden inside his body somewhere – a pound tucked underneath his liver like cocaine stuffed into a smuggler's arse; some nestled around the heart and lungs, slowly choking him to death; and the obvious subcutaneous blubber that made corduroy pants a fire hazard … Fifty-one pounds of pure fat that took him from a perfect, Adonis-like body weight, to his current state of crapulence, at 230 pounds.

It was his two-year anniversary in CRC-17. He'd spent that time trying to lose enough weight so that his body mass index – his BMI, which was a measure of his body fat, determined by his height and weight – would drop below the magic number. Thirty and over, and you were obese. A fat bastard, according to the Revised Canada Health Act passed five years before by the federal government. The Fat Act, as it was known to everyone in CRC-17, was an attempt to help citizens deal with their weight problems, because it gave them a simple choice: Stay at a healthy weight (i.e., not obese) or forgo your government-funded health care. (And in fact, any reasonably priced private health care policy, because obesity was listed as a pre-existing condition.)

The space structurally resembled a prison cell except there was a door, and a screen around the toilet/sink area. The decor was definitely not prison-issue: instead of a bunk, Keelan had imported a nice double bed. He'd decorated the walls with paintings he'd created in his years at art school, and he had a small workstation that ate up the rest of the free space in the cell.

A shadow appeared outside. Keelan could see the shape through the opaque plastic door, and he opened it.

"So you think you'll do it?" his visitor asked.

Wayne Falco was a large man – much heavier than Keelan, probably closer to a 40 BMI than 30 – who had been in CRC-17 since the Correctional Service of Canada opened it up five years before. Wayne had been in the first year of medical school when the Fat Act had been passed; he couldn't afford to pay for his own health care, and he knew he would need it. Plus the school had kicked out everyone who had a BMI higher than the normal range, part of a PR exercise supported by the College of Physicians and Surgeons.

He repeated his question: "So you want to do the surgery?"

It was tempting. Keelan had been diligent about losing the weight, but after two years, it was clear he was going to need some kind of special help to get out.

"Go over it again," Keelan said.

"No. I want an answer," Wayne replied.

"Please. I'm just worried about the side effects," Keelan said.

"Do you want me to do the amputation or not?"

Keelan had given it careful thought, and he believed the left leg was the better choice, even though it was the right leg that had been injured playing high school football. The right had a blown-out anterior cruciate ligament, but another (slimmer, less shady) surgeon had expertly reconstructed it fifteen years before (courtesy of the health care system), and it had been fine ever since. The left knee always gave Keelan trouble, and he suspected something was wrong with it anyway. Besides, he was right-handed, which meant right-legged, too, didn't it?

"I don't know," Keelan said. "Explain to me again why we

can't just suck the fat out."

"Because I don't have that kind of equipment. The only thing I can do – and not kill you – is a quick, relatively painless amputation."

Only that morning he'd told his buddy Greg Bestard he'd be an idiot to amputate a perfectly usable leg, but that had been in the morning, before he'd had his daily weigh-in. He'd somehow gained a pound overnight. And he'd snapped.

"And there's really no cost?"

"Unless you want some morphine. Which I *really* recommend. That's a hundred. The rest of the operation is free, provided I get to keep your leg."

"What do you do with the leg?" Keelan asked.

"What do you care? You're the one having it cut off," Falco said. He looked at his phone, as though he was bored by the whole conversation.

"Yeah, but that's just so I can get out of here."

"Then leave. Nobody is going to stop you," Falco replied.

"Don't be a douche. You know why I can't do that."

At the two-year mark of Keelan's stay in CRC-17, a couple of things happened. The first was that he reached a statistical milestone that meant his odds of ever getting out of the Fatness were very low. After being in the CRC for two years, fewer than 5% of inmates lost enough weight to escape. The other was that he would lose his job. He worked as a web designer for the local university's communications department. Under the act, employers were required to hold an employee's job for two years or until they lost the weight. After that, they were able to let the lazy, fat bastards go. So it was lose the leg or pay for his own health care. For his whole life.

"Lose the leg," Falco urged. "How much do you weigh?"

"Two hundred thirty at the morning weigh-in," Keelan said, keeping the despair out of his voice.

"Then your leg should be about … twenty-three pounds," Falco said, plugging the numbers into his phone. "And you're what, six feet?"

"Five foot eleven."

Wayne did the calculation on his mobile. "Hey, congratulations, man, that would do it. You'd be sitting pretty at 28.9 BMI! Well under!"

The BMI – the body mass index – ruled their lives.

Keelan looked a little sick to his stomach. He couldn't believe he was even contemplating this. He thought about all the things he would no longer be able to do: no more hiking, no canoe trips (sure, he could do the water bits, but no portaging), no jogging – his main form of exercise. There were probably a zillion other things, but they had pretty good prosthetics these days, right?

Wayne could sense his indecision. "You know, I don't often suggest this, but you have pretty good calves – lots of meat there."

"Meat?"

"I mean muscles. Lots of muscle. They're heavier, right? And all you really need to lose is what?"

"Up until my weigh-in, fifteen pounds. Now, sixteen, I think."

"Look, the calf weighs about a third of your leg weight. So let's say eight pounds. What if you lose eight pounds, and we just do the lower part of your leg? It's really easy to rock a prosthetic if you've still got the knee. I'll do it for you as a favour. I won't really be fully compensated for the surgery, but hey, I'm not exactly busy, right? And then you're out of here."

Keelan's friend appeared. Like the other two, Maximillan Tundra was overweight. Fat, actually (BMI 34.9). But he carried himself with a certain confidence, if not swagger. He had a medical degree and was once a psychiatrist before he'd lost his job for professional misconduct. Max was a bit out of breath, having learned from Keelan's friend Greg that Keelan had gained some weight and that he'd been talking with Falco. "Falco – you fucktard – get away from that lad or I swear to god –" he took a big gulp of air and finished "– I'll drug your ass back into the Stone Age."

"Max! Buddy! I'm just doing a bit of business here. So let's be cool, okay?"

"Let's be cool? You're talking about mutilating my friend. I'm not going to be cool, you ghoul. You pit-stained, long-pig-eating, pre-med wannabe."

"I'm close with Taggart, man. You can't talk to me like that."

Max flicked the guy's nose and shouted, "*Touché malinga!*"

Falco had no idea what that meant. Neither did Keelan, but Keelan *did* think it was kind of menacing and funny at the same time.

"Later, kid. Tell me your decision when this maniac isn't around," Falco said.

"No, it's okay. I don't want to do it. I just wanted to know if it was possible."

"Sure," Falco said, trying to be magnanimous at the loss of his patient. "Besides, it's only sixteen pounds. You could lose that in a couple of months."

Keelan's shoulders slumped, and Max waved his hand at Falco. "F-ffff."

"You're a fucking lunatic," Falco said.

Max grinned and waggled his eyebrows as the hobby surgeon walked away.

"What does *touché malinga* mean, Max?"

"Malinga is a Sri Lankan bowler, I believe. Cricket. Now, let's go for a walk, because, clearly, you need some cheering up."

Pre-med wannabe or not, Keelan thought there might be something to Falco's diagnosis of Dr. Tundra's mental health.

As they walked to the commons, Keelan asked Max if it was true about the cannibalism.

"Oh yes, the legs are eaten. They did the first one before you arrived."

Max had been in CRC-17 for nearly as long as Falco; in fact, Max had been in and out of CRC-17. He'd lost all the weight he needed to get under 30 BMI and, within a year, gained it all back plus some extra. So he knew all the stories about how Colin Taggart and his Heavy Hitters took over the institution. Nominally, the CRC was run by Corrections Canada, but in fact, the gang run by Taggart were the real power in the institution.

"I can't think of anything more repulsive," Keelan said.

"Kee, as you know, I'm not really into boundaries, but I agree. Anthropophagia always struck me as really disgusting. A taboo for the ages." Max paused, running his hand through his thinning red hair, and asked, "But have you ever smelled leg of human, roasted with garlic, honey, and loving care?"

"No."

"Then don't judge."

"Max, you didn't –"

"Of course not! I'm just saying it smelled pretty damned good. Plus, you know, it was like they were making a point."

"That they're disgusting pigs? That they deserve to be in a real prison, not just the Fatness?" There were many nicknames for the Calorie Reduction Centres: The Girth Gulag. Chubby Choky. Plump Prison. The Fatness. They all gave the impression, but not the facts: the CRCs were concentration camps for the generous of flesh. Sure, cushy, non-death-dealing camps with running water, full free Wi-Fi, and on-staff exercise coaches, but the facilities were designed to keep an unwanted population sequestered and out of sight of polite company.

"No. That they don't care about the rules. They're here and they don't care, and they are going to run things as they see them."

"Oh."

"Yeah. Which is why we have to fight them."

"Sure," Keelan said.

"What's that mean?"

"Max, I like you, and I know you've got your heart in the right place, but I'm not signing up for any doomed crusade. I just want to lose my weight and get the hell out of here. The only reason I'm talking to Falco at all is because I'm near the two-year mark. If I don't lose enough weight, I'll lose my job. I know you may not care about what you do for gainful employment, but I do."

"Fair enough. I'll be fighting the good fight alone until you get wise. Until then, I'll papadums alone!"

They didn't talk as they walked through the common areas, the parts of the CRC that were open to all the "patients". On the subfloor they passed through the small gymnasiums, cardio pens, aquafit centre (a pool, mostly shallow end), and resistance training rooms. These were known, collectively, as the Dungeons to everyone but the Neckheads, who practically lived in the resistance training rooms, i.e., where they stored the free weights. Keelan was a regular user too, though he didn't have the body-fat ratio of the bodybuilders.

On the main floor, the large gymnasium had actual stands, almost like those you'd find in high schools, except not quite as flimsy – they had to support more than the lissome thighs of teenagers, after all. The idea behind the gym was the "patients" of the CRC would form sporting leagues and better their physical beings by partaking in regular athletic competitions. This pipe dream never materialized, and the gymnasium had become an ad hoc gathering place. At first the CRC administration had been unwilling to let their charges use the room for non-exercise purposes. A rash of suicides and the ensuing glare of titillated media attention convinced them they should be using all methods possible to keep their fatties happy. Now the big gym was a market, coffee house, and occasionally, it was used to hold dances. These were cringeworthy, but helped stave off cultural ennui and, if nothing else, gave people something to talk about.

This commons area was flanked by four wings of residences – two for men and two for women. Married couples were allowed to "blend" their BMI scores, and if their net score fell into the obese range, only one member of the couple was legally required to lose weight. The designers of the Fat Act did not like this exception, but it was too expensive to create the facilities for entire families to live in the Calorie Reduction Centres.

Not coincidentally, divorce rates were up around the 90% range for thin-fat marriages and now had the social acceptability of an antebellum mixed-race marriage.

The cost of housing all this human flesh was also why there

was a strict age range on the act. Only adults between the ages of eighteen and forty-five were required to keep themselves trim. Outside of that range (even Baby Boomers, older Gen-Xers, and those on the cusp) were allowed to stack on as much weight as they wanted. Kids got a pass too, but only until they were old enough to vote. Then they were pretty much fucked.

There was a rumour going around CRC-17 that the Subcommittee on Obesity, which had drawn up the legislation, had other criteria for deciding who would be asked to go to a CRC. The word was out that less attractive persons who were overweight were more likely to be sent than the hotter fatties. Nearly twice as many men were sent as women, but that was because amongst fat married couples, it was unthinkable that children should be without their mothers.

As they entered the commons, Kee spotted his friend Greg sitting at the coffee bar in the gymnasium with Tracy Bloomfeld, one of the staff exercise coaches. He waved at Greg, who smiled, but didn't seem to want to be interrupted.

"Our young African-Canadian friend has discovered Tracy, it seems," Max said.

"What do you mean *discovered?*"

"Heh. I'll let you ask Greg the next time you scalawags get together."

"What are you insinuating?"

"I'm not insinuating anything. But don't you think it odd that Ms. Bloomfeld should choose to work in a CRC, yet maintain a body mass index clearly in contravention with the act?"

"So she's heavy – so what? Everyone here is."

"Yet she leaves the CRC every night to enjoy the world beyond the Fux." This was Max's personal term for CRC-17, Uxford County, but it had never caught on. Kind of like the way he kept trying to revivify his childhood saying "No guff."

"Maybe she's rich. Doesn't need the coverage."

"Or perhaps she's found a way to eat her cake and have it, too."

"Don't you mean the other way around?"

"No. I spoke correctly. It is the only logical construction of that banana. One can always have their cake and then eat it." Max held out one hand and pantomimed eating it. "One cannot eat the cake and have it, too. Because one has eaten it; it is consumed. Now, I'm going to head back to my capacious giraffe, where I plan to read for a while and try not to think of cake. Shall I join you and young Gregorovich for luncheon?"

"You give me a headache, you know that?"

"You can thank me for saving your leg by letting me eat some of your state-sanctioned Jell-O."

"Sure," Kee said. "I'm on a diet anyway."

FACT
The Fat Cell

The average human has forty billion fat cells. These tiny, glistening, oleaginous buggers are designed to store energy for when we need it. Along with the brain, the liver, the pancreas, and the stomach, fat cells manage our energy needs as well, maintaining constant communication through our blood system.

This system is highly efficient and evolved over millions of years, during most of which humans were worried about starving to death.

And long before the invention of the cheeseburger.

Chapter 2 – TEAM AWFUL

Kee met his new calorie supervisor, an enthusiastic, blonde, razor-thin woman named Brittany, later that day. Brittany was going to help him reach his ideal weight, or at least, something under 30 BMI. She was damned excited about it. She was accompanied by a gorgeous, curvy woman in an expensive red suit. Kee didn't know much about clothes, but he could recognize expensive when he saw it; more than that, he could recognize style. The woman in the suit was about his own age, around thirty-five.

Brittany noticed Kee noticing her and said, "This is Jacinda Williams; she's shadowing me today because she's working with the Subcommittee on Obesity."

"Actually, Brittany, I'm helping Christopher Ballard, a partner in my law firm and an advisor to the Subcommittee on Obesity. I'm just here to learn the ropes."

"The ropes?" Kee wondered.

"What this CRC business is all about."

"It's about getting the porkers, manatees, and jabbas out of sight," Kee said. "It's about putting young people in jail for no reason."

"The what?" Jacinda asked.

"Porkers, manatees, and jabbas," Keelan repeated. "The fat people."

"There are *classes* of fat people?" Jacinda said.

"Absolutely," Brittany said. "Obesity can be measured in many ways, but according to the Fat Act, BMI ranges from 30-35 are Class I, 35-40 are Class II, and people with a BMI over 40 are Class III."

"Yes," Keelan said. "Porkers, manatees, and jabbas. And the Fat Act is all about keeping that unsightly flab off the streets."

"Keelan, that is just not true, and those are terrible terms," Brittany said. "The act is about getting you to a healthy weight so that you can have a long, happy, productive life."

"And what's your BMI, Brittany?"

"It happens to be 17.3," Brittany said, obviously pleased with her stats.

"So you're underweight?"

"Of course not! Look at me. I'm tone, firm, and, and, frankly ... perfect." She smiled.

"You're skinny, I'll give you that," Kee said. "But did you know that being underweight is actually more dangerous to your health outcomes than being overweight?"

"Ah!" Brittany said, leaping like an anorexic salmon at the bait. "But not more than being obese."

"It depends on *how* obese. I'm just over. You're under the healthy range. Your health is at high risk too. Just like the really heavy inmates here. The only reason you don't have your own prison is because you're still seen as highly fuckable. God knows why. I'd probably cut myself on your hip bones."

Brittany had never heard this argument before. She was simultaneously flattered and offended – flattered that he could tell her hip bones were prominent, and mortified at the thought of coitus with her flabby client. Brittany's mouth opened and closed, much like a tasty salmon that had leaped out of the stream and landed on shore. Right before it was eaten by a large hairy mammal of the family Ursidae.

"Mr. Cavanaugh, you are being exceptionally rude," Jacinda said. "I know I'm only here to observe, but I'm not going to sit here and listen to you abuse someone who's here to help you."

Keelan was ashamed. His face flared red.

"You know, you're right. I've been in here too long. I am getting bitter. I *do* apologize, Brittany. I know you're just doing your job. I just don't know why they keep sending us so many young, tight, practically anorexic Hellmuth University grads."

"Did you go to Hellmuth?" Brittany asked.

"Yes, for my undergraduate degree. And I work there too, in the communications department. That is, for the next couple of months I work there. After that, I'm in danger of losing my job if I don't lose the weight." Kee thought for a moment. "I'm guessing you got the health sciences degree, or did you do kinesiology?"

"Double major," Brittany said. She could not keep the pride

out of her voice. "I had the lowest body fat percentage in my class, and I played on the varsity volleyball team."

Jacinda rolled her eyes, and Kee laughed.

"What's funny about that?" Brittany asked.

"Oh, I was just thinking how good BMI would look on a baseball trading card; you know, right between games played and at bats," Kee said, grinning at Jacinda.

"Well, I was very proud of that stat. We all got to see our exact body fat percentage using hydrostatic testing – which is incredibly accurate. You have to dunk your whole body in the water and expel as much air as you can. I did it correctly on my first try! It was *so* awesome," Brittany said, her eyes lighting up at the memory. "I do wish we had one here, but the best we can do is with calipers and a bit of pinching."

"We're not going to do that today, are we?" Jacinda asked.

"Oh, you wish," Kee said. "I know you're just dying to get a look at my spare tire."

Jacinda laughed again. So did Kee. Brittany decided it would be best if she did too.

"No, we're going to talk about the things that may be holding you back in your weight-loss regime. Think of me as a coach. I'm here to help you get the TEAM working together so that you can get out of here and back to your life in the real world," Brittany said.

"What team?" Kee wondered.

"The T-E-A-M for your weight-loss success. T is for training. You have to *train* yourself to resist your urges. You have to train your self-control. You have to train to control the rest of your T-E-A-M. Train yourself to control your E: eating! Train yourself to find the joy in A: activity. And train yourself to find healthy ways to keep up your M: motivation! Training. Eating. Activity. Motivation. That's the TEAM!"

Brittany was absurdly excited about this acronym.

Keelan was intensely aware of the presence of Jacinda. He'd dealt with someone like Brittany before. In fact, she was the third calorie supervisor he'd experienced. The first had been Jenny, who had a BMI of 18.5 and was a Hellmuth kinesiology grad (with a health sciences minor). The second had been Ashley, who had a BMI of 18.1 and a Hellmuth health sciences degree (with a minor in health communications). It seemed that there was a downward trajectory in his calorie supervisors' skinniness and an upwards trend in their enthusiasm and credentials. Jenny and Ashley, for all their annoying perfection and cloying fervour, had never *shouted* an acronym at him. Keelan gave Jacinda a quick glance and was not surprised to see a hint of shock on her face. She was hiding it as best she could, but he could recognize the slightly slackening jaw, the glazed look in her eyes.

"TEAM!" Keelan shouted back at Brittany.

"Yay, go TEAM!" Brittany clapped her hands together. So did Keelan. He grinned like an idiot at Jacinda. He nodded his head, inviting her to join in.

"Yay team," Jacinda said. She couldn't muster up the hand clapping, but her tepid participation got just *oodles* of gratitude from Brittany.

"Thanks for getting into the spirit of this, Jacinda. And if later you want to do a little session with me, I can help you get your bum issues under control too."

Jacinda said, "Uh, thanks."

"Now, let's go over our plan for the next couple of months, 'cause you've got some blubber to burn. I've got you set up with one of our best exercise coaches, Tyrell, who's going to meet with you three times a week and help you get that A in motion – I mean your activities," Brittany explained. She laughed at her own wit. She also produced a paper schedule, with exercise times and gym numbers listed. She produced a second sheet of paper and said, "Now, this is the E-exciting part. What you'll be EATING this month!"

Here it comes, Keelan thought.

"For the first two weeks, I'm putting you on the Freedom Fries diet, followed by a modified Paleo-Portions diet for the next six weeks," Brittany said, as though she were still speaking English.

"What's the Freedom Fries diet?" Keelan asked, hope creeping into his voice. "Do I get to eat French fries on it?"

"No, silly. It's Freedom *from* fries. Nothing fried. It's actually quite restrictive, but we'll take off some pounds quickly. Here's the menu for the first two weeks," Brittany said, handing Keelan a piece of paper that was about the size of a Chinese fortune from one of those cardboard cookies. All it said was apples, cheese, chicken, celery.

"Do I get these with every meal?" Keelan asked.

"Of course not," Brittany said. "That's ridiculous. For the first four days, all you eat is apples, then one day of cheese, followed by four days of chicken, and you finish off with a nice celery cleanse."

Keelan did the math. "So I'm going to be eating nothing but celery for five days?"

"Isn't it wonderful? We're having great success with it in CRC-16. Their gross tonnage is down by 1.2 percent."

Keelan was absolutely silent.

"Gross tonnage?" Jacinda asked. She was now taking notes furiously.

"Sorry, that's not the right term. Please don't write that down, Jacinda. That's kind of the, uh, colloquial term we have for it. It's actually called the aggregate weight figure under losses."

Jacinda worked out its acronym: "AWFUL?"

"We don't use that short form," Brittany said. "It's undignified."

"Can I clarify something?" Kee asked.

"Of course, Keelan. This is your time. Let's get that TEAM on the right track."

"How the fuck am I going to survive eating nothing but celery for five days?"

"I don't care for the F-word much either, but you'll survive. Don't worry, Keelan. I *know* what I'm doing. And if you're worried, I can set up an appointment with Dr. Fundarek if you want. I'm sure he'll be able to reassure you."

"No. No. I do not need to see him. I'm sure you're right. I

don't mean to question your plan for the TEAM," Keelan said.
Even the *thought* of visiting Dr. Fundrarek's office made him
squeamish.

Jacinda made another note.

"Okay, well, that's about it," Brittany said.

"What about the T and M? When does Kee get the training
and motivation?" Jacinda asked.

"We just did that, silly," Brittany said. "And that will leave us
a bit of time to talk, girl-to-girl, about your thigh gap."

"Thanks, Brittany," Keelan said, standing up. "I'm sure we'll
have great success together. And again, I apologize for my earlier
outburst." He shook her hand and said to Jacinda, "Good luck
with your session with Brittany."

Jacinda shook Keelan's hand. He thought she looked jealous
that he was leaving. Instead, she was going to get ten minutes of
uninterrupted "girl time" with Brittany.

Before he closed the door, Keelan looked in her eyes and said,
"Celery you later."

Jacinda smiled at Kee despite the desperate lameness of the
joke.

FACT

Goldilocks and the Bliss Point

Major food corporations ensure many of their products reach something they call the *bliss point*. This is the apex that gives a food optimum pleasure, and incidentally, the point which creates the most desire or craving for more of it. Not enough sugar, and you haven't reached the bliss point. Too much sugar, and you're on the sickly sweet wrong side of "maximum crave."

It's kind of like "Goldilocks and the Three Bears". In the fairy tale, Goldilocks gobbles down all the porridge that is "just right," that hits the bliss point, and then falls asleep. When the bears return, she runs away into the woods.

In real life, Goldilocks can't stop eating the delicious Delissio Pizza, becomes morbidly obese, and is unable to run away. She is fat enough that she, too, has reached her bliss point. The bears consume her and have to explain to their GPs why their cholesterol readings are so high.

1

Chapter 3 – Rascals

Colin Taggart guided his mobility scooter, a high-end Rascal Vision, into the office of Selwyn Seward, the director of CRC-17, for their regular meeting. Taggart was a "patient" of CRC-17, but as the leader of the Heavy Hitters, an important one.

Seward, as formal as always, stood up and walked around from behind his desk to shake Taggart's hand. "Can I get you anything, Colin?"

"No, thank you, Selwyn. Thanks for moving the guest chair to the side. It's nice not having to get out of my Pike-mobile." Taggart grinned at his own joke, knowing Seward would never get the *Star Trek* reference.

Seward's thin lips smiled back. "So how is the program going?"

"You mean my 'weight-loss' program?" Taggart asked. "Well, I suppose you could say there's no danger of my release from our fine institution anytime soon. My bimmi is holding steady at 39.3."

"Your BMI, you mean?"

"Yeah, I'm just picking up some of the slang from the fat kids. They call it their bimmi."

"Well, I'm sorry to hear that, but I'm confident that you'll be able to manage your weight with our help."

It was almost a form of kabuki theatre. Now it was Taggart's turn. "And how is the family?"

Seward smiled, a little more genuine this time, and said, "They're doing well. They like the weather here in Southern Ontario. Though there's talk of a few CRC directors being promoted to subcommittee positions in Ottawa." The bureaucrat had been the director of one of the first experimental CRCs in Northern Ontario, and he had successfully brought the AWFUL down by nearly 20% in his first year. When the flagship CRCs were built, Seward was tapped to run one of the biggest: CRC-17.

"And that would be good? Would they mind the move?"

"My family would be thrilled if I could get that kind of

promotion. So let's talk about the aggregate weight figure under losses, shall we?"

And the true purpose of their meeting was about to begin. Seward was the person in charge of CRC-17, nominally, but Taggart ran all the illegal activities in the institution. Seward knew that Taggart ran all the illegal activities in CRC-17. And Taggart knew that Seward knew. That was what made their meetings such fun.

"So how is the gross tonnage?" Taggart asked.

"The AWFUL is down, thankfully, but only by about 1.6%, Colin. You promised me at least a 2% reduction this month."

"But that's still much better than the national average, correct?"

"Much. That's beside the point, Colin. This is Canada's premier calorie-reduction institution. We need to lead the way by leaps and bounds, not just edge out the rest of the pack. We're trying to show that this system can work for Canadians."

"Point taken, but this is the first month since we started bringing McDonald's into the Fatness. It was bound to play with our numbers a bit."

"I told you, Colin …" Seward sighed heavily. "I told you I can't know any of the details. The only reason that I let you and your little gang of scamps bring in as much contraband as I do is because the economics work. If it ever got out that I allowed some inmates to eat Quarter Pounders while the rest dined on skinless chicken breasts and broccoli, my career would be over. Are we understood?"

"But we have these meetings every week, surely –"

"These meetings are down in my diary as 'client relations' and you are the chair of the CRC-17 Client Satisfaction Committee."

"Really?"

"Yes. I've had a brochure made, and I'd like you to distribute it amongst your people so they're all familiar with their roles as part of the committee," Seward explained. "Now, back to our gross ton – I mean, the AWFUL. What ideas do you have for this month?"

"Well, the latest products are very popular, and we're having a little trouble restricting them. I suppose we could raise the prices again."

"A good start. But I have a suggestion as well."

"I thought you didn't want to know anything."

"It's not specifics. But if we could help some of our patients lose enough weight to drop the aggregate, but not leave the facility, that would greatly help."

"And how do we do that?" Taggart wondered.

"I suspect you'll figure that out. Now, I have to get back to work on my regular report to the deputy minister," Seward said.

"Fine, but I had one other matter of business. A few of my colleagues would like permission for their own mobility scooters," Taggart said.

"Well, I can't grant that unless the doctor prescribes them as medically necessary." Seward frowned.

"Yes, I thought you'd say that. Here are the letters from Dr. Fundarek." Taggart smiled. The implications were clear: he had the CRC-17 doctor in his pocket now too.

Seward sighed. "Very well, but I tell you, if the gross tonnage doesn't drop significantly this month, those Rascals are going to be a goddamned necessity. Get it?"

Taggart smiled and put his scooter in reverse gear. It beeped annoyingly as he said, "All the best to your family. It would be a shame if you didn't get that promotion, eh?"

Jacinda Williams returned to her office in downtown Landon after a long morning attending "client" interviews with her new best buddy, Brittany. Not only had she learned quite a bit by watching Brittany encourage her charges in their quest to lose some weight, she'd also gotten a bit of that treatment herself. One of Brittany's patients had cancelled, so she had an unexpected forty minutes of free time to help Jacinda with her "largish butt".

"I'm not saying it's huge or anything," Brittany had said in complete sincerity.

"Yes, well, it's kind of the way I'm made, Brittany. Since I was a teenager, I had a little extra junk in my trunk," Jacinda said, attempting to make a joke of it.

"That may be, but we can do some exercises and cut back a bit on our calories, and before you know it, your trunk will be empty!"

Jacinda, like Brittany, had grown up in a world where the female form was not only hyper-sexualized, but under the kind of scrutiny that made relative butt sizes somehow appropriate conversation between otherwise mature women. Jacinda, unlike Brittany, was at a healthy weight. Her body fat percentage had varied throughout her life, from about 20-24%, which was quite normal and even a little towards the low end of average. Everyone wanted to talk about her butt despite the fact that she was perfectly fit and attractive the way she was.

And despite her attempts to deflect Brittany's "helpful advice" back to the topic of the effectiveness of the Calorie Reduction Centres, the morning had been a bummer, so to speak.

So she really wasn't in the mood to talk to her boss, Christopher Ballard, Esquire, and partner in Ballard, Ballard, and Bones, who was waiting for her in her office.

"Hey, babe, you're back from the Fatness, I see! How is life in the land of the lard?" Ballard chuckled.

"Hi, Chris. It was educational, that's for sure. I think I'll try to go at least a few more times this week before our trip to Ottawa to meet with the committee," she said. They were scheduled to leave for the capital on Thursday, for a Friday meeting with the Standing Committee on Health and the all-important Subcommittee on Obesity (SubOb), which reported to them. Since the rewriting of the national health laws, SubOb had tremendous power and influence, and Christopher Ballard wanted to sway that influence.

"Uh, about that, babe. I'm going to take this trip solo."

"What?"

"I've got them for an in-camera session, just me, and I don't want to spook them with your presence."

"Well, I can sit outside if you want …"

"Sorry, babe. Already changed the hotel and flight arrangements. You can come next time. But if you could write up your findings this week by Thursday morning, you'd be my personal hero." He smiled and Jacinda tried not to be persuaded. Ballard was the kind of charismatic, handsome man that always got what he wanted, even when he was obviously up to something. He squeezed her biceps muscle a bit more intimately than Jacinda would like, especially when she wanted to stay angry with him. He walked by her, brushing up against her hips as he did so, and he smiled. He turned at the doorway and ran his fingers through his thick, black hair. At fifty, you'd think he'd have a bit of thinning or grey, but he was blessed with the kind of genes that are just annoying to mere mortals. Jacinda knew that in addition to the perfect hair and teeth, Ballard's body was just as slender as it had been in his twenties – and he seemed to be able to eat anything he wanted.

"Okay, Chris." She smiled. "Next time."

"And we'll keep it strictly professional, I promise." He looked around and whispered, "Not like last time. Now, get back to work, and I'll see you on Thursday before I leave. Remember, I want to see that whole report."

"Sure, sure, Chris. By the way, how should I be billing this? This isn't exactly legal research I'm doing."

"There's a docket I've started with the initials PB-WWA. Put it all there."

"This is pro bono? What's WWA?"

"Yes, I'm paying for this myself, but someday we may be able to charge WWA. They're taking an active interest in our little experiment up here in the Great White North, and they're good clients from way back in Daddy's day," Ballard said. "Now, back to work! Don't make me get my whip."

Jacinda wished that she didn't find him physically alluring, but, alas, sometimes the fundamentals just work against you.

Fact

The First Law of Thermodynamics

Is don't talk about thermodynamics.

No, just kidding. We can rap. This law is the principle that says energy can be converted from one form to another, but that it can't be created or destroyed. So you can burn calories worrying about whether you left the iron on, but that energy would have to come from somewhere. It wouldn't be possible to worry about the iron and turn it off without burning any calories.

That would be telekinesis, and it would be awesome.

Chapter 4 – The Physics Of Your Waistline

"So here's how you lose weight," Dr. Fundarek said to Keelan. "You expend more calories than you consume. It's all about the calorie deficit."

"But I've been reading that it's a lot more complicated than that," Keelan objected. He didn't know why he bothered to argue with the CRC doctor, who was widely regarded as a quack by most of the inmates of the facility. He was meeting with Fundarek in the infirmary – a twenty-bed "state of the art" medical facility that was currently filled.

Fundarek was not a harmless quack.

In addition to its declining decrease in gross tonnage, CRC-17 had one of the highest rates of kidney failure in the entire calorie reduction system, mostly because Fundarek had failed the unit in renal care during his alleged career at the Grand Academy of Fine Arts and Medicine at Brno.

"It's basic thermodynamics," Fundarek explained. "Simple, really."

"Well, then why am I not losing weight?" Keelan asked, not wanting to get into a conversation that was going to lead to the depressing idea of entropy and the heat-death of the universe. He changed tack. "Honestly, do you think this diet is safe?"

"I'm sure if Brittany thinks it's safe, it will be."

"But, Doc, she's so skinny."

"That just proves my point." Fundarek smiled. He was a short man, probably just under five foot five inches, and he had dark predatory eyes that had a tendency to dart. His smile was shark-like and marred by his pack-a-day smoking habit.

"But they want me to eat nothing but processed cheese for one day. That can't be healthy!"

"Oh, really? And where did you do your nutritional analysis of that?"

"I didn't! But I've been doing a little research. According to

HealthWatch.com, the average slice of processed cheese product has almost 225 mg of salt. Brittany wants me to eat, like –" Keelan checked his menu "– twenty-two slices in one day. That's nearly 5000 mg of salt! And that's just one of the problems with it. Look. It's not even listed as a food, technically. It's called processed cheese slice *product*."

"Well, I will admit that 500 mg is a little high," Fundarek said.

"No, five *thousand*. It's, like, more than two times the recommended daily allowance."

"But it's only one day, boy. You're young and, except for your unfortunate corpulence, healthy, as far as I can tell. Your kidneys can take it! I'm sure Health Canada would never approve a food product that would be dangerous." Fundarek was pleased with that phrasing, turning the cheese product back into a food.

Someone in the ward groaned.

"Now, would you like me to take some blood?"

The groan turned into a long moan of what Keelan could only assume was existential agony. "I know how that guy feels."

"I seriously doubt it. The idiot had his leg removed by an amateur surgeon last week, and it's the worst botch-up I've seen since my internship in abdominal surgery. Do you know I once sewed up a patient's duodenum? Luckily we have access to some of the best generic antibiotics available." He and Keelan walked over to the poor bastard's bed, and the doctor checked his temperature, with a rectal thermometer, naturally. The patient's fever was so high Keelan figured the patient probably didn't even know he was there.

Keelan didn't see how antibiotics today were going to help a patient he'd butchered in his days at medical school, but he wasn't done trying to argue Fundarek out of Brittany's deranged diet. He had one more idea.

"Well, according to the Fat Act, I mean the Revised Canada Health Act, 'patients of a CRC are allowed to have at least 750 calories per day', no matter what. The act also says that 'proper nutrition is to be monitored at all times'."

"So?" Fundarek asked.

The patient became somewhat agitated, probably because he was suddenly aware of the cold thermometer in his butt. "What's happening? Am I out yet? Belinda, I'm coming for you, babe."

"Tsk," Fundarek said. "That's sad. Belinda is his wife."

"He's just delusional," Kee said. "That's not sad."

"No, it is. His wife remarried last week. That's why he did the leg."

"Oh," Kee said, remembering his own brush with this particular insanity that morning. But he was on a mission. "Look. I'm required to get 750 calories per day by law."

"That's true," Fundarek said. "And you will get them. In celery form, for five days."

"But that's crazy," Kee said. "There's hardly any calories in celery. How much would I have to eat?"

Fundarek consulted his datapad. "According to Brittany's kitchen instructions, you are allowed up to forty cups of chopped celery per day."

There was a stunned look on Kee's face.

"I took the liberty of figuring out how much that is, by the way, in gallons. It's just over 2 gallons, or 9.4 litres." He smiled his brown smile at Kee and pulled the thermometer out of his patient's ass.

The patient had obviously been listening to the whole exchange; he looked over at Kee and said, "You poor bastard."

QUOTE

"A journey of a thousand miles begins with a single step."

–Lao-tzu, *The Way of Lao Tzu*

Chapter 5 – Lao Tzu Didn't Have a Treadmill

Jacinda watched the display screen of her treadmill as she ran in the gym. She was jogging as fast as she could, getting nowhere. She'd been on it for thirty-five minutes, she'd run nearly five miles, and she'd burned 507 calories exactly. According to her new BFF, Brittany, she needed the kind of exactness her display had. To be precise, her butt needed it. Her posterior needed a guidance system, a measure, some method of quantification, and Jacinda was worried about what that might mean for her overall health.

She had been hyper-accurate before, when she'd been a young woman finishing high school and starting her university career. Her precision actually had a clinical name: *bulimia nervosa*.

It had started later in high school, when she began dating one of the most popular boys in the school, Joshuah Smith. Josh was the kind of dreamy guy that all the girls wanted to be around: he was athletically talented, playing varsity football, hockey, and soccer. He was also a pretty well-rounded individual, and he played guitar in a fairly popular band, The Knuckleheads, which had a following in the school and around town. She had started out as a groupie and then graduated to girlfriend status. She knew he played around with other girls. He always came back to her, but there seemed – to her, anyway – to be a congruence between her weight and the moments of Josh fooling around. Every four weeks or so, sometimes more, sometimes a little less, she gained anywhere from three to four pounds and it was usually during these time periods that Josh drifted. She never made a big deal about it.

But she did work extra hard to make sure her weight stayed down in those times. She'd see the scale tip up, and bang – it was time to get down and dirty with the exercise. She'd spend all her spare time working out, jogging mostly, to keep her weight down. When that didn't do it, she'd wear a garbage bag and bang away at her mother's treadmill in the basement. (God forbid someone see her running in a black garbage bag, even if it was at night.) If she ever slipped and ate a bit too much food – well, she'd take care of that with her finger and the toilet later.

Josh said he loved her when she was thin enough. She could tell you what the exact weight was when the love kicked in: 116 pounds. At 118 he didn't say anything. At 120 he drifted.

Jacinda later recognized this coincided, almost exactly, with her menstrual cycle, which was how she'd gotten her bulimia under control, more-or-less; occasionally, the old thought patterns would reassert themselves, and she would spend an afternoon over-exercising.

She'd managed to snag Christopher Ballard through a combination of good looks, sex, and wit.

She'd joined Ballard, Ballard and Bones as an articling student; she'd actually worked for Jeremiah (Jed) Bones, who was one of the most famous litigators in Canada, mostly because of the high-profile defense cases he took on. It quickly became apparent that litigation – arguing in front of a judge and jury – was not going to be Jacinda's métier. Her intelligence, acuity, and insight were obvious, which was why she was transferred over to Christopher Ballard's office. If the aging Jed Bones was the media star – the face of the firm – then C. Ballard was the intellectual force behind it and the black heart of the firm. Christopher directed who Jed should be defending.

His father, Valence Ballard III, had been the co-founder of Ballard, Ballard and Bones, but he had died before Jacinda joined the firm, so she never had a clear understanding of the part Christopher's father had played in this dynamic. The firm's gonads, perhaps?

Everyone in the firm knew they would take on another partner at some point, and this was the whip that helped BBB get so much out of its roster of junior attorneys, Jacinda included.

The treadmill beeped to tell her she'd been running now for an hour solid. She checked the display. Her pace had obviously slackened, and she frowned: 8 miles. 7:30/mile. 847 calories. She did the arithmetic. The average pound of fat contained 3500 calories, so that was less than a quarter of a pound. Her legs were wobbling. And she already felt hungry.

But she kept going.

Brittany's whole calorie-in-calorie-out philosophy was going to kill her. But then again, Chris had just bumped her from the Ottawa trip, which could only mean one thing – they were off again.

At first it had gone so well. She'd been transferred to his office and immediately made a great impression, not only because of how she filled out her sharply tailored Dior suit, but because she'd spotted an error in the documents they were about to present to Proctor and Gamble, one of BBB's many corporate clients. Corporate law was Ballard's expertise; he had developed a serious and deep expertise in health law and policy as well.

The trip to P & G's head office in Toronto turned into an overnight affair, with a shared hotel suite, champagne, and an "exchange of briefs". They loved spending time together, they worked well together, and the sex was fantastic. This provided the basis for an on-and-off-again relationship as she finished her articling year, passed the bar, and was hired by BBB full-time.

They'd been lovers for about three years now, but they didn't have a "relationship" per se.

Like Josh, Chris took a keen interest in Jacinda's weight, appearance, and even how she dressed herself. *It's kind of humiliating*, she thought as the sweat poured off her now. It sluiced down her back, between her breasts. She was panting, but she was damned if she was going to quit before she hit that magic 1500-calorie mark. That would be almost half a pound.

Since her undergraduate years, Jacinda's weight had been creeping up, slowly, year after year. It was natural, she thought, that she would fill out as she matured. She still weighed less than 140 pounds, which put her squarely in the "normal" category of the BMI. Her body fat was even slightly lower than average, and *it sits in all the right places*, she thought. But at 140, Chris was guaranteed to lose interest in her.

Just because Brittany had a flat ass didn't mean she should.

Goddamn it, Jacinda thought, *why the hell do I let skinny bitches like that manipulate me? Why do I keep taking that bastard back?*

"Fuck," she said, and hit the emergency stop button on the treadmill. She was exhausted.

And starving.

She looked at herself in the mirror and tried to imagine what they saw. She was wearing a black tank top and black Lycra running shorts. Her skin glistened with perspiration and looked healthy, glowing. She didn't like her arms. They were too fat. She would have agreed with Brittany about her arms, but Brittany never mentioned them. Jacinda turned and looked at her profile. There was nothing wrong with her ass. It was fine! It was fucking awesome. *Jesus, that skinny bitch is just jealous,* she thought.

Jacinda remembered how the patient – Keelan, that was it – had put Brittany in her place, and she smiled. Keelan seemed like a good man, even if he was a bit overweight.

But she had to admit, her thighs looked a little heavy.

She toweled off a bit and faced the mirror again. Yes. Her thighs definitely looked a bit fat. The way the Lycra cut into them. Maybe that was what the problem was with Chris. He always said he loved her legs, even though they weren't the long, willowy legs of a model. But he hadn't said anything recently.

She should lose some weight off her thighs. Definitely.

She turned the treadmill back on and began jogging again.

MYTH

Calories In, Calories Out

Talk to many medical professionals about how to lose weight, and they will explain that it is very simple: "You just need to eat less and exercise more."

Technically speaking, if this myth was true, you should be able to lose weight just by eating less than you need to keep alive. This calorie deficit would force your body to burn your stored fat and voila: weight loss! Of course, this is a myth. One that is so pervasive that maybe even your own doctor believes it to be true. The truth is actually much more complex.

There are pixies inside your bloodstream, and when you stop feeding them the calories they require, they just order in Chinese.

Chapter 6 – The Calorie Dispensing Hall of Shame

A lively crowd of jolly people gathered in the Calorie Dispensing Hall, known to the inmates of the Fatness as the cafeteria. But not tonight. Because it was pizza night.

The pizzas in question did not come from any of the major chains. Instead, they had been created by some of Corrections Canada's most talented nutritionists and chefs. They were designed for weight loss rather than taste. According to the two dozen participants of the focus groups who tested the pizzas, the overwhelming flavours attributed to them were "cardboard" and "despair". But those participants were all free to have a pizza delivered to their homes, or, in a pinch, they could put some kind of frozen pizza-like substance in their ovens. There were even hot pockets, which might come out of the microwave with all the nuance of lava, but they still didn't taste like "despair". But for the denizens of CRC-17, anything pizza-like was a welcome change from the usual boiled chicken and broccoli.

Unless you were on a special dining plan, like Keelan. As everyone waited anxiously in line for their slice, Keelan dreaded his meal. It was the first full day of the Freedom Fries diet. For breakfast, he'd been served some kind of applesauce served with a few slices of apple on the side. Lunch was simply two apples – one Red Delicious and one Macintosh. Everyone seemed genuinely interested in his lunch, because they didn't get to see fresh fruit too often in the Calorie Dispensing Hall. If he hadn't been so famished, he would have sold the apples to someone, but he was too hungry to even make it to his seat. He wolfed down both apples, cores and all, before he left the line.

He got to the "special diet" queue, which was for people like him, whose calorie supervisors were trying something new to help them lose weight. His buddy Greg Bestard was in line in front of him, waiting for his meal. They shared the same calorie supervisor, but apparently she was trying another tack with Greg. He had been in the Fatness a little longer than Kee. Greg was the same age as Keelan, thirty-five, but his BMI was higher than Kee's: 34. At five foot nine and 230 pounds, he was a bit farther away from that elusive goal of under 30, i.e., not fat. He was about to say something to Kee, when he was distracted by a flash of blond hair walking by the food line.

Kee was sure he'd seen the woman before, but he didn't know how. She was obviously not an inmate, as she was wearing civilian clothes. She was short, muscular, and Greg couldn't keep his eyes off her.

Kee was transfixed by the presence of Jacinda Williams, who was walking with the blond woman.

They watched as the inmates retrieved their pizza from the warming trays. Her eyes flashed with annoyance, and she said something – Kee thought it sounded like another language, but he couldn't be sure. She shook her head and stared out at the sea of jowly faces stuck into their government-approved faux personal pizzas. Something was wrong, according to this woman. Jacinda said something to her.

Kee was trying to catch Jacinda's eye, without looking too dorky. He succeeded at the former, not the latter, as he caught her attention with a wave. She smiled, and the two women approached Kee and Greg.

"Keelan, right?" Jacinda asked.

"Yes, and you're Ms. Williams."

"Jacinda, please."

"This is Greg," Keelan said, introducing his friend, who was trying not to stare at Cindy.

"Hi," Jacinda said. "I suppose you both know Cindy Vandenkieboom?"

"Pleased to meet you," Kee said to Cindy, who nodded.

Greg opened his mouth, but no discernable sound emerged. Jacinda covered the awkward moment and addressed Kee: "So how's the celery treating you."

"Ah, we haven't started on that yet. It's apples first. I've had applesauce, apple slices, and actual apples today. You could say I'm not at the core of the diet yet."

Jacinda smiled. Greg rolled his eyes. Cindy was still muttering to herself.

"Well, nice to see you again, Keelan. I suppose we better peel out of here."

Kee laughed. "You just made my day."

"Good luck with the diet, Kee. I'm rooting for you!'

As they walked away, Greg said, "Wow, she is just … gorgeous."

"I know," Kee replied. "And she came over to talk to *me*." He was unable to keep the surprise out of his voice.

"What do you mean?" Greg said. "She was just tagging along with that Jacinda woman."

"What?" Kee asked.

"I … Oh, you think Jacinda is gorgeous."

"Yeah. And obviously you have a thing for blondes. Who is Cindy anyway?"

"She's gorgeous!" Greg said. "Look. How can you not know Cindy Vandenkieboom? She's legendary."

Kee could see that Greg was truly smitten, so he was careful about what he said next: "Vandenkieboom?"

"That's her name. She's Dutch."

"Ah, well, that explains it."

"And she's …"

"Gorgeous?"

Greg nodded.

"Why didn't you say something?"

"Like what? I'm just another fat bastard to her."

"No, you're not," Kee said. "Just because you're a little over-weight doesn't mean you don't have lots to offer. You're a person. A good person. With, uh, emotions and thoughts and all the wants and needs and frailties that thin people have." He was trying to do better and added, "You're a nice guy, Greg. The best."

"You think so?"

"I know so. And you're kinda sweet and funny too, right? Women like that."

"Yes, they do like that," Greg said, unsure.

"And confidence. The right kind of confidence. Women like that too."

"Hmm. Well, I don't have that," Greg admitted.

"I wonder what she was saying?"

"Garbage," Greg said. "The Dutch word for fat garbage."

"Oh," Kee said. Maybe he was giving his pal some bad advice if Cindy was calling them fat garbage.

"She meant the pizza, Kee, not us. She's radiant and a really good person too. She's a calorie supervisor on the women's side of the Fatness. I asked Tracy. Cindy's well known. Even the women she treats like her."

"Really?" Kee wondered. He'd yet to meet any calorie supervisor that he liked. He remembered he wanted to ask Greg what the deal with Tracy was, but it was their turn to get their meals. Kee steeled himself. The server scanned the bar code on his wristband and said, "Keelan Cavanaugh? You're on the Freedom Fries diet?"

Kee sighed. "Yes."

"Here is your meal – apple pizza."

Kee looked down and was horrified to see they had constructed some kind of pizza-like abomination out of apples. Instead of a crust, the deranged chefs had created a lattice of apple peels. On top of that was what Kee assumed was some kind of applesauce, and the pièce de resistance, pieces of apple cut to look like pepperoni, mushrooms and green peppers. They even had the colours right.

"That took us nearly an hour to make," the server explained, obviously pleased with their effort.

Kee could see there were a couple of other cooks looking over, as if to see his reaction. He managed a smile and said, "Well, I'm sure I'll enjoy this. Thank you." The cooks looked pleased, and Kee kept the smile on his face. "Really. Great job."

He looked over at Greg's tray to see what he was eating. It looked like … well, it was a pinkish medium of some kind, and suspended within it were little pieces of corn, along with some kind of yellowish chunks. There really was no getting around it.

His buddy was just served what looked, for all intents and purposes, like a plate of vomit.

"Okay then," Kee said, nodding his head towards the rows of tables and chairs. "Let's get this meal over with, shall we?"

FACT

Fitness Can Trump Fatness

According to recent stats, the Canadian fitness industry has about $3 billion in revenue yearly. You read that right. Three. Billion.

Most of that is spent by consumers in January, right after the saturnalia of chocolate, cheese, and regret we call "the holidays". Shortly thereafter, a large majority of us give up our exercise regimes, which is too bad.

That's because there's growing evidence fitness is a better barometer of health than obesity. And also, because $3 billion is a lot to pay for a branded gym bag.

2

Chapter 7 – Stupid Human Tricks

The next morning Kee and Greg met their new trainer, Tyrell Taylor. Any "client" who had been unable to get their BMI under 30 in two years, using the facilities and the calorie supervisor-approved meal plan in the Calorie Dispensing Hall, were given more "help". Thus, they were both working out under the tutelage of Tyrell, another Hellmuth grad from the kinesiology department. Unlike all the other exercise coaches Kee had met in CRC-17, he immediately liked Tyrell.

Kee had encountered three of the other coaches: Bud Freeman, Magnus Pendergrast, and Tracy Bloomfeld. Freeman and Pendergrast were malignant mesomorphs who once had careers as high school gym teachers, and they ran the "group training" sessions, which were available to all inmates of the CRC free of charge. Freeman, especially, was a nightmare. He hated fat people. There was really no other way to put it, and he ran his training sessions like it was the last act of *Lord of the Flies* and everyone but him was Piggy. Pendergrast was a serious weightlifter – he'd once gone to an Olympics (Kee never found out if it was a Special or Regular variety) – and he naturally thought that the key to losing fat was to turn it into muscle as quickly as possible. That just seemed to drive up BMIs in the short-term, so neither Freeman nor Pendergrast had many people voluntarily go to their classes.

Kee had yet to hear Tracy Bloomfeld's story, but he had no idea how she'd landed a job as an exercise coach – her BMI was at least as high as Greg's and probably even higher. She got out of breath whenever she did the exercises along with her charges, and she would often come to the gym looking hungover. Sometimes she'd smoke, which was a clear violation of the CRC rules, but she never seemed to get busted for it.

Tyrell was cut from another cloth entirely. Like Brittany, and Tiffany before her, he was a fairly recent grad from Hellmuth – Kee guessed he was probably around thirty, judging from his looks. But Tyrell had a master's degree, not an undergrad, so why he was working as an exercise coach, Kee couldn't figure. But he knew his stuff.

The first thing Tyrell did was measure them both. This included the humiliating part, where the measurer had to grab a wad of skin in selected places (upper arms, legs, waist, love handles, man-boobies) and use calipers to measure the full scope of the blubber in his grasp. Whether this was as humiliating for the measurer as it was for the measuree, Kee was not sure. Nobody made any eye contact while this was going on. At least the measurer had something to concentrate on. Having a witness to the entire procedure would have made it worse, but Tyrell kept up a spate of banter the whole time, distracting both Kee and Greg from the slight physical discomfort and the indignity of the pinch test.

"So you guys have been in here for two years, eh?"

"Yep," Kee replied. Still careful not to make eye contact. Tyrell had two fingers and a thumb wrapped around Kee's left man-boob while they talked.

"I've been in even longer than Kee," Greg said, eyes wide. His big black moobies would be the next measured.

"Just three months," Kee said, oddly defensive.

"Hey, three months count, brother," Greg said.

"He's got you there, man," Tyrell said. "I wouldn't want to be here one day, so three months." His eyes crinkled a bit as he smiled. "That's serious time, in my book."

"Fair enough," Kee conceded the point. "Hey, if I'm the newbie, why am I getting the pinch test first?"

"Gives me a chance to limber up my fingers," Tyrell said, "before I tackle my brother Greg over there."

It was a risky joke, but both Kee and Greg laughed.

And then they got to the questionnaire. Tyrell asked them all kinds of questions: how much do you sleep every night? What kinds of foods do you like? He tortured them with a series of pin-point-accurate questions about the sorts of food that really made them lose their shit. For Kee it was potato chips. Greg agreed that chips were good, but ice cream was better.

"Now, what about stress? What's stressing you guys?"

"You mean, apart from living in a prison for fat people?" Kee asked.

"Obviously, that's stressful. What are some of the key things that stress you out about it?"

The list was long. The communal showers. The line-up for food. (Sometimes the Calorie Dispensing Hall ran out of meals before everyone was fed.)

"Really?" Tyrell asked. "That happens?"

"Yeah," Greg said. "About once a week or so. Seems to be on Fridays and Mondays."

"So you have to skip a meal?"

"Yeah, man," Greg said. "They tell us it's good for our long-term weight-loss plan, so not to worry about it."

"Unless you're on a special diet. Then you won't miss a meal, no matter how desperately you'd like to be able to skip it," Kee said. He was on day two of his Freedom Fries diet and was already sick of apples. He was dreading the celery cleanse at the end.

"Well, that's not good. Skipping meals is about the worst thing you can do for weight loss," Tyrell said.

"Really?" Kee asked.

"Yeah. The secret to losing weight is making your body think that it's got lots of food available to it so that it doesn't store everything as fat. As soon as you start skipping meals, your body goes into starvation mode. It says, 'holy shit, I'd better store this food away for when I really need it. Who knows when I'll get food again?' Skipping meals – especially breakfast – is the worst thing you can do. It will make you gain weight, long-term."

"Well, that explains why I gained five pounds after my last diet," Kee said.

"You're lucky it was only five," Tyrell said. "So no more skipping meals. Even if they are feeding you garbage."

"What?" Kee asked.

"Sorry. Shouldn't have said that," Tyrell said. "It's just that they aren't exactly doing what I know will help you guys lose weight on the nutrition front. But don't worry, we have lots of other things we can control, and that will help."

Kee could tell he wasn't saying something, but he didn't push him.

The measuring continued, and when they were done, Tyrell put them both on the treadmill. First he tested their overall fitness, and then he had them do another forty-five minutes of cardio. Kee had been jogging for a while, but Tyrell had the treadmill set to do steep elevations at intervals, so he was panting heavily by the end. Sweat sluiced off his face. He didn't even want to think about what all the moisture was doing to his crotch.

Greg was wheezing and practically in tears, but there was no way he was going to fall behind Kee's pace, even if he did feel like he needed to throw up his vomit-like lunch.

Tyrell encouraged them the whole time and, while they could answer, even asked some more questions – where they came from, what their families were like, and so on.

Maybe it was because Tyrell was black and had fought prejudice his whole life too. But they both loved it that he treated them like they were actual humans, not sacks of animated lard. And even though the whole session was a little humiliating, and hard work to boot, they left feeling a strange thing: hope that they could actually lose the weight.

FACT

Fat Rats & Cats

Experiments in rats have shown that processed, high-fat, high-sugar, high-salt foods can be as addictive as cocaine and heroin.

When given the choice, rats prefer to eat these foods, and their brains produce the same chemical, *dopamine*, that is released when drugs like cocaine and heroin are taken. Eventually, this dopamine overloads the pleasure centres in their brains, and they have to consume more and more of the drug or food to get the same amount of pleasure.

The same basic process works in any large corporation regarding the generation of profits versus what is good for society.

3

Chapter 8 – Lovin' Addiction

Colin Taggart, the head of the Heavy Hitters, recklessly drove his Rascal through the commons – narrowly missing Kee and Greg as they made their way back from the gym where they'd been training with Tyrell. They'd already showered and were looking forward to having a coffee, while Taggart blasted by them. He beeped on his Rascal horn the whole time, shouting at people to get out of his way.

"Hot stuff, coming through!"

It wasn't a boast about his dubious looks. Taggart was transporting heated food in a large insulated container on the front of his scooter. His route was planned to get him from the service entrance to the men's wing that held most of his "customers", as he thought of them. Considering his bulk, the limited power of the Rascal, and the dense throngs of large people he had to navigate around, Taggart wound his way through the commons in record time. He was also trying to set a personal best time in his daily delivery, because it was going to be his last.

A collective moan went up from the crowd as Taggart left the commons in his dust. The signature odour of McDonald's food wafted in the air, haunting the men and women gathered in the commons like a lover's perfume on one's pillow, but less with tender memories of a gentle touch, a sensual sigh, and more with the memories of stuffing several cheeseburgers into your face between brain-freeze-inducing slurps of a frozen chocolate concoction that was reminiscent of ice cream. A few individuals stood up and took a few steps into the redolent pathway left behind Taggart's scooter.

It should be noted that the crowd was as thick as it was because everyone in CRC-17 knew precisely when Taggart made his fast-food deliveries.

Taggart had no idea he'd had such an impact, of course, on the general morale of everyone in the Fatness. He was supplying a valuable service! In the more traditional facilities run by Corrections Canada, the inmates had a more difficult time smuggling items of high value into the buildings. Clever plans and ploys had to be used. Colons had to be packed with powdered materials. Things had to be thrown over walls. But Taggart had innovated the process quite a bit when he had learned that Corrections Canada did not intend to police their Calorie Reduction Centres with the same vigor as they did regular, nonfat, prisons. With that knowledge in hand, he had approached the CRC-17 director with a proposal that would light up the pleasure centres of any bureaucrat's mind.

Taggart proposed that he and his Heavy Hitters – a group of exceptionally corpulent and morally bankrupt denizens of CRC-17 – would help police "banned substances" if the gatekeepers would allow Taggart and his crew free access to the outside world. They would use this access to strictly control what came into CRC-17. Illicit substances, such as cheeseburgers, ice cream, French fries, chocolate bars, soda pop and so on, would only come in through the Heavy Hitters. Only the highest bidders would be able to get these things, thus strangling the supply of extra (sinfully tasty) calories to a few who could afford to pay. Sure, these few people would never lose enough weight to leave the CRC under their own steam, but the overall effect would be that most of the inmates would have to rely on the Calorie Dispensing Hall for all of their food needs – thus, the overall weight of the population of CRC-17 would come down. (In his original presentation, Taggart had used a deck of PowerPoint slides that illustrated this concept with both pie charts and other charts that looked suspiciously like cake.)

Oh, and Taggart hadn't bothered mentioning that the Heavy Hitters would bring in anything else that might make a quick buck: drugs, alcohol, and sex toys seemed to be the most popular items. That was a sideline that he and Director Seward had never really discussed, but with the fast food, the *principle* had been established.

He made it to the hallway where many of his customers resided, and started his deliveries. He'd made the run from service entrance to hallway in two minutes forty-five seconds. His best time yet, and a benchmark for his delivery squad. Now that he had Seward's agreement to let more of the Heavy Hitters bring in their own motorized scooters, he could hand off the delivery job to his muscle and number two in the organization, John Carver.

He scooted next to the door and knocked on it, still seated in his Rascal. "Your order is here, Bernie."

The translucent door burst open, and a mountain of a man grinned at Taggart. "Colin, you magnificent bastard. I thought you'd never get here. I've been thinking about this all week."

"Sure, but I'm not running a charity here. Where's the cash?"

Bernie handed over a fistful of bills – nearly fifty dollars, and Taggart gave him his order: a Big Mac, three cheeseburgers, and two orders of super-sized large fries, which would normally cost a fraction of that. Both men seemed happy with the transaction, and Bernie didn't stand on ceremony. He ripped the paper covering off one of the cheeseburgers and stuffed it into his mouth with animalistic satisfaction. As Bernie masticated, a low growl of pleasure emanated somewhere from deep within his body, or perhaps it came from his soul, that turned into a moan of contentment that could only be described as orgasmic. Taggart felt a little uncomfortable in the presence of such a private moment, but he said, "We've arranged to bring it in on Thursdays and Saturdays for now. Shall I set you up with a regular delivery?"

"Oh GOD, yes!" Bernie said, his mouth still half full of burger. "Put me down for this order on every Saturday. And two cheeseburgers on Thursday. Any more will break the bank. Now if you don't mind, I'd like to savour the rest of this McFeast."

"Of course. And next time it will be Carver delivering the goods. Have the cash ready, right?"

"Natch," Bernie said as he closed his door, his nose already deep inside the paper bag, scenting the glorious mix of salt, sugar, and fat that made the fast food so delectable and addictive. Behind the door, Bernie got his fix, his brain squirting dopamine as his mouth absorbed the refined food-like substances for which he'd just been grossly overcharged.

Taggart sparked up his Rascal, pleased with this new business venture. He did foresee a problem though: if he made too many sales, the gross tonnage of the CRC would definitely rise; there was no way around that. However, if he kept cranking up the costs, eventually he would only have the wealthiest inmates taking on the extra calories, so theoretically, the calories would balance out. There was an upper limit on what he could charge even the most well-to-do, though. If they had real wealth, then they would have stayed out of the CRC and just paid for their own health care costs out of pocket. (Though it would be impossible for obese people to get into a privately funded plan, because obesity was listed as a pre-existing condition precluding them.) It was a delicate balance, but he was working on an algorithm to help him maintain it. (In a previous life, Taggart had been a computer programmer.)

He pulled in front of Oscar Leclerk's room – one of the CRC's few openly gay men – and beeped his little horn. "I'm finally here, Oscar!"

The door burst open. "Quiet! I don't want anyone to know that I'm on the McDee, you bastard."

"Sorry. Discretion is my middle name. Cash?"

Oscar presented his fifty dollars. All he'd ordered was a Quarter Pounder with Cheese, large fries, and a small Coke. Still, it was nearly 1200 calories, or about half of his daily allowance under the Fat Act – what he should be eating to lose his extra weight. Strictly speaking, both he and Taggart were breaking federal law.

He opened the bag, stifling his own moan, and instead, flashed Taggart a grin. "I'm lovin' it."

But Taggart was already speeding away to his next addict.

QUOTE

"Thin people are beautiful but fat people are adorable!"   ~Jackie Gleason

Chapter 9 – Cooks and Normies

In one of the meeting rooms just off the commons, Kee nervously awaited his meeting with Jacinda.

She had booked the space after learning that she would not be going to Ottawa with her boss. Jacinda's plan was to interview some of the people she'd shadowed with Brittany, to get more unbiased opinions and data about the effectiveness of the calorie reduction centres, and the act in general.

Kee had been thinking about Jacinda since he'd run into her at the cafeteria. He got to the room early and tried to look nonchalant while he waited. He'd dressed in a pair of chinos and wore a dark blue golf shirt that hid his pit stains admirably – standard work clothes, but which, he hoped, looked nice. In any case, they were a huge step up from the shorts and grey T-shirt he'd been wearing to his interview with Brittany, and the baggy sweatpants and football jersey he'd been wearing in the cafeteria.

She appeared in the doorway a few moments later, exactly on time. She was wearing another tailored suit, dark blue like his shirt. She came in, and Kee stood up. "Hi," he said. She put her briefcase down on the table and sat opposite him.

"Hi, Kee," she said. "It's alright if I call you Kee?"

"I prefer it."

"Good. I prefer Jacinda. Some friends call me Jacs, for short."

"Jacinda is a beautiful name," Kee said. "Where is it from?"

"It's Spanish, I think." She smiled. "Is it warm?"

"We're right above the pool, and they didn't put in enough insulation."

She took off her jacket and hung it on the back of her chair. Her blouse was tasteful, but a bit more low cut than what Kee was expecting from a lawyer. He tried to be casual and hoped that it didn't seem like he was trying to be casual.

"So how are you?" she asked.

Kee contemplated his answer. He didn't know exactly what he wanted out of this interview, but he sure didn't want to sound like a whiny child. On the other hand, something about her made Kee feel like he wanted to be honest. And true. There was something about being in the room with her that made Kee feel like the interview really shouldn't be about him at all. It would be about helping her in whatever way he could.

"I'm doing okay, even if Brittany's new diet is, uh, a little extreme."

She consulted her notes. "Freedom Fries, right?"

"Yes," Kee confirmed. "I'm on the last day of all apples. We switch to cheese tomorrow. But compared to my buddy's plan, the Pink Protein Diet, it's a walk in the park." There, Kee thought. I gave her the problem without sounding like a punk.

"Oh, don't worry. I've got that one on my radar. Your diet is more potentially damaging, you know?"

"Really?" Kee asked. "I know the cheese day is bad from the salt perspective."

"And three days of nothing but boiled chicken is not going to be a walk in the park either."

"Boiled?" Kee said. He worked hard to keep the whiny out of his voice. "I wasn't aware it was going to be boiled."

"Yep. It's like they're trying to cook any possible nutrition out of the damn stuff," she said. "Cindy explained some of the problems you have with nutrition."

"Well, I'm sure the cooks will do what they can," Kee said, perhaps a tad more generously than he actually felt.

"The cooks are lower level war criminals, from what I can see," Jacinda said. "You know, the more I dig into the way things are run around here, the less I like. It's all going into my report for SubOb."

"SubOb?"

"The Subcommittee on Obesity for the Standing Committee for Health," Jacinda explained.

Kee's brow furrowed.

"In Ottawa. It's the parliamentary subcommittee that does the oversight on the CRC program. Big stuff. Lots of money and high-impact politics."

Kee wondered why Jacinda seemed to be speaking another

language, but he nodded attentively. It was like listening to a computer programmer talk. Every once in a while he heard some words that he didn't really understand, but the gist still came across. This was an important job she was doing. She was an intelligent, dedicated professional. Was it wrong to be staring at her eyes? He loved her eyes – they were a deep brown that verged on black, and he wondered what it would be like to stare into them over a romantic dinner. A dinner that didn't have any apples, cheese, chicken, or celery in it.

"So what do you think?" she asked.

"I think it would be great," Kee said, imagining them having dinner at a nice restaurant. Candlelight. He realized she wasn't asking about that. "It would be great to know more."

"Sure. It's basically like this. There are two approaches to government in Ottawa. One side wants to create governmental structures that solve problems, and one side wants to create governmental structures that enable free enterprise, and there's a few outliers, of course, that just want government to work for the people. And the problem-solving group is in power, so they've created this new system to help obese people lose their extra weight, so that the country as a whole will be healthier. Their projections show that if they're successful, health care costs will be reduced drastically, especially in the long term. The other side wants to show that it can't be done, or failing that, that the private sector can do a better job of providing the service than the government. Right now this battle is being fought out in SubOb, but we think that it may become an issue that escapes the Hill."

"We?"

"Oh, me and Chris. Chris Ballard is the senior partner of my firm and the lead on this file. I'm basically providing research and helping guide him," she said, careful to keep her non-professional feelings about her boss from creeping in.

"Okay," Kee said, sensing there was something here. Did she like or hate her boss? Was it both?

"So what do you think?"

"Well, I can't really speak to the system, but it's hard being in here. I know that technically I can leave whenever I want, but I'll be on the hook for my own health care the rest of my life, and I … well, that seems risky. So it's like being in prison. You feel stifled, and there are major stresses …" Keelan realized that he was veering towards whiny again, but he wanted to be honest.

"Look," he continued, "I know that my choices have led me here, even if there are mitigating factors. But still, it seems a bit harsh a punishment for being fat. I'm likely to lose my job if I don't get my bimmi under 30 soon. I'll be in real trouble, so I 'm doing what I can. Brittany's diet may be a bit crazy, but I think it's working. And my new trainer, Tyrell, is really giving me some optimism. I'd like to think everyone in here can do it, but I don't know. I think the system, as it is, isn't going to work," Kee said. "You know, only a small portion of the population is in here."

"Well, from that perspective, the problem solvers are right. A huge number of Canadians are now paying for their health care rather than come here to do so. It's been a boon for the insurance industry too, so even the free enterprisers are a little happy about that."

"But we won't be healthier, we'll just have a two-tier health care system, won't we? One for fat people and one for normies."

"Normies?"

"People with a normal BMI, it's what we call them in here. No offense. I'm hoping to be a normie one day myself!"

Jacinda laughed and said, "That's adorable. Well, if it's any consolation, I don't always feel like a normie either. My mother certainly thinks I'm not, at least. She keeps harping on about my weight like I'm, uh –" She was about to say fat, but she didn't think that would be right. For starters, she didn't really think of Keelan as fat. Overweight, sure, but he carried it well.

"BMI challenged?" Kee suggested. "Pleasantly plump?"

She laughed again. "Sure. BMI challenged. That's the politically correct way of saying it, I guess."

"I think the more preferred description is *big boned*," Kee quipped. "Though I'm trying to get everyone to use the term height-versus-weight challenged, because it's more accurate."

"It doesn't exactly trip off the tongue, does it?" Jacinda's eyes sparkled with fun.

"How about *calorie-surplused?*"

"And for the record, you're not a run-of-the-mill normie. You're too nice, understanding, and –" Kee's face went red. He'd almost said beautiful. He could feel the blood rushing to his capillaries all over his body. He was running the risk of really starting to sweat, so he changed the topic.

"And?"

"And how can I help you?"

Jacinda understood that he was totally sincere. He really wanted to help her. There was something sweet and funny about this guy. "Well, let's talk about all the things that are going wrong here at CRC-17, and then we'll see?"

FACT

Tall, Mark & Handsome

Research into online dating shows that women have a marked preference for taller men, and it is often the first stat that they check out. Men that are a mere inch shorter than the average will see a massive decrease in their chances of meeting – and mating – with women. The same research shows that men are more concerned about weight. Women that are twenty pounds overweight will see a decrease in their chances of scoring similar to those short men.

If this is evolution at work, why is the world still choked with runty men and chunky women? Perhaps it's because, as other research has shown, that more attractive people of both sexes will mate with those less attractive than them so they have more power in the relationship.

Or it may be that only shallow people are attracted to online dating. Or shallow scientists are attracted to studies about online dating. In any case, it's less of a bummer to blame the whole mess on the internet.

4

Chapter 10 – Skinny Bitches

They used up the hour they had allotted and then some. Jacinda cancelled the next meeting she'd had scheduled, and instead, Kee showed her around the facilities, doing an impromptu tour. They ended with a coffee at the commons, where Jacinda was stared at by both the male and female denizens of the CRC. It was unusual to see a well-dressed normie hanging out with one of their own. Most of the trainers and calorie supervisors were thin, but they all dressed in exercise gear, and casually if they weren't wearing sweats or Lycra. Jacinda's tailored suit stood out.

"So when do you think you'll get out?" Jacinda asked Kee.

"I'd like to leave before I lose my job."

"And you can't leave until you're under 30 BMI, right?"

"Not without forfeiting my health care. Unless I can get a compassionate leave, but those are only for circumstances like family emergencies or deaths," Kee said with a sigh.

"I suppose taking someone out for a movie wouldn't count, would it?" Jacinda joked.

"Not unless I had a really good lawyer arguing the case for me," Kee said. Did she just ask him out?

"Okay, I'll get on it. Expect your pass by the weekend." She smiled.

Greg came to their table and sat down. "They fired Tyrell."

Kee wanted to tell Greg to go, but it was bad news. Tyrell was the first decent trainer he'd had in the CRC. "What happened?"

"He put in a request for you and me to be put on a special diet, and our calorie supervisor lodged a formal complaint," Greg said.

"When?"

"Yesterday, I think."

"Well, that's a bit unlikely," Jacinda said. "Most bureaucracies don't move that fast."

"Well, he's a black man, and he got uppity. Oh, and he sent a letter to the *Globe and Mail* complaining about the nutrition available to patients of the CRCs," Greg added.

"Ah," Jacinda said, "racism aside, that would do it. They all have to sign confidentiality agreements."

"Isn't there anything we can do?" Kee wondered.

"To save his job? I doubt it," Jacinda said. "He would have known what he was doing though. He was probably trying to make a point. I *will* make sure I interview him for my report, okay?"

Kee thought about Tyrell. His perfectly sculpted body. He wasn't exactly happy with the thought of Jacinda interviewing him, but he didn't want to seem jealous. "Sure, that would be great. He's very knowledgeable too."

"And he's in great shape," Greg added, quite helpfully.

"Well, I'd better go," she said, standing up. Keelan did as well. "Thanks for this, Kee. I'll look into that day pass for you."

"Really? I thought you were joking."

"I never joke about the movies," Jacinda said. She then did something that really astonished the crowd in the commons, a crowd that had seemingly grown since they first sat down: she hugged Kee, who promptly turned red again. A collective mental "oooo" emanated from the calorie-surplused cheeks of the assembled inmates.

"Thanks," Kee croaked as Jacinda walked towards the exit.

Greg was staring too.

"What?"

"I don't know, dude, it's been a long time since I saw someone like you hugged by a normie," Greg explained.

"It was just a …"

"Professional hug?" Greg wondered.

"I think she's just a huggy kind of person," Kee said. "At least, that seems the most likely explanation." *And the day pass*, he thought. *Was that just a kindness to let him out for a day, or so that she could go see a movie with him?*

He watched her disappear through the doors and hoped it was the latter.

As Jacinda was leaving the CRC, Serena Lee approached it. She was an enterprising journalist, doing some groundwork on a story about possible corruption in CRC-17.

Lee was a pretty woman who'd never been overweight. In fact, she found fat kind of repulsive. She had been a model in her younger years, and she'd started her journalism career as a TV reporter, so she understood how important it was to look trim and attractive. It mattered. Not just for career, but for so much in life. Now in her late thirties, she was intensely aware of how much looks mattered, as her youthful glow had started to fade. She was still gorgeous, but she knew where she was headed. Her mother and grandmother were alive, and they were a template for what might happen to her – first the crow's feet, the slight heaviness that came with the years and childbirth. But even they were not fat.

At the visitors' entrance, she gave her credentials to the guard. *A guard?* she thought. *Why do we need guards at a health facility?* She made a note, softly, on her phone.

"Sorry?" the guard asked.

"Nothing. Just making a note."

"Oh, about what?" the guard asked. He seemed like a nice young man. Tall. A white boy, his face was flushed slightly, and Lee could see the telltale signs of attraction.

"Why the guards?" she asked. "It just seems odd for a health facility."

"It's regulated, miss. We have to keep track of everyone who comes and goes. And if a patient decides to leave, we have to enter it in the system," he said, happy to extend his conversation with Lee. He'd recognized her from when she was a regular on TV. "Now, I have to ask, do you have any food with you?"

"Food?"

"Yes, contraband food such as chocolate bars, candy, and so on. As I say, it's regulated. We can't have the patients cheating on their diets."

"Do you check everyone who comes in?"

"Absolutely."

"So no outside source of food is allowed?"

"No," the guard said seriously, trying to keep the quaver out of his voice. He tried to forget Taggart and his regular deliveries. "Nothing. No smokes, no alcohol, no drugs. It's all for the health of the patients."

"I see," Lee said, thinking that he would be an excellent interview if she did a video piece. He was young, handsome, and well-spoken. She also suspected him of lying. She was good at telling. He was attracted to her as well, but he was also lying. "Would you be willing to go on camera to talk about this sometime?"

"Sure, but you'd have to get the director's permission. And you'd need to brief me – us – on your questions. I believe that's the procedure."

"Excellent," Lee said, and was ushered into the CRC.

"Your appointment with Director Seward is in ten minutes. The administrative wing is along the entrance here, and you'll see signs for his office. The commons is also open to visitors," the guard said.

"Thank you." She looked at the name patch on his uniform and made a mental note of it.

Lee laughed and walked to the commons, wondering if all the guards were as charming. But she was more interested in seeing what everyday life in a CRC looked like.

The first thing she noticed was not a sight, but a smell. It wasn't really a bad smell – perhaps a whiff of body odour – but no, it wasn't overtly offensive. There was a stale sweetness in the air. The commons was still busy. The crowd that had been talking excitedly about Jacinda and Keelan and their impromptu coffee date was still mostly there. A few had wandered away, but the tables were all filled. A hubbub of conversation filled the air, which stilled momentarily as Lee appeared at the top of the stairs. The commons was a level below the entrance way and administrative wing, but open to the glassed-in ceiling.

Women glared at her openly as she descended. The men did not; their stares were open, but not angry. Compared to everyone here, she seemed emaciated. Ridiculously thin. She only had a few minutes until her meeting with Seward, but she thought she should do more than turn around at the unwanted attention. She was not going to be run off by a bunch of lazy fat people!

She opted to approach a table of women who were engaged in a heated conversation. As she approached, she could hear them chatting.

"So yes, I've heard you can get anything you want?"

"Like Häagen-Dazs?"

"Anything. If you've got the –" They noticed Lee standing nearby and were quiet.

"Sorry to interrupt," Lee said. "But I was hoping I could ask you ladies some questions. I'm a reporter with the CBC."

"We know who you are," one of the women said. She was quite heavy and had a hard-looking face as well. *An unfortunate mix*, Lee thought.

"It's not nice to eavesdrop, you know."

"Sorry. I didn't mean to, but I didn't want to just barge into the middle of your discussion, and, as a group, you don't seem quite so put off by my being here," Lee said.

"Why not talk to them?" the woman asked, pointing to where a group of the Heavy Hitters were staring at Lee with unabashed lust. *At least they aren't catcalling*, Lee thought.

"I wanted to talk to some women," Lee said. "I imagine it's particularly hard on women in here."

"It's certainly worse when a lot of really skinny bitches come for a visit in one day," the hard-faced woman – who seemed to be their spokesperson – said.

"I'm not the first?"

"Oh no, there was another here just a while ago. Some lawyer working with the government, the way I heard it. Plus she's poaching our men."

"Your men?"

"The chubby fuckers in here. They're ours, by rights."

This was an interesting notion, Lee thought, but not the story she was following. "Well, I'm here on business. I have no designs on your men." She smiled. "In fact, I thought I heard you say something that I am interested in."

"Did you?"

"Yes, about ice cream. Is it true you can get ice cream in this place?"

"It's true," another woman said. She was quite pretty, in her way. Without the extra pounds, she would be kind of gorgeous, with her dark eyes and long lashes, her long black hair with a sheen of auburn. "You can get Häagen-Dazs if you've got the money."

"Quiet," the hard-faced woman said.

"Oh, right," the pretty one said.

"It's okay," Lee said. "I won't say anything. I do protect my sources, you know."

"Not from them," the hard-faced one said, nodding at the Heavy Hitters. Taggart was there, holding court from the seat of his Rascal, and keeping an eye on Serena Lee. The reporter decided he wasn't just looking at her with lust. His gaze was calculated and, she thought, dangerous. She'd once done a story about the biker gangs who ran the pot business in Landon, Ontario, and he reminded her of their kingpin.

"Okay, I'm sorry to bother you, but do you mind if I ask you one more thing?" she asked. She had a hunch. "Who is that, on the scooter?"

"Colin Taggart," the hard-faced woman said quietly, and added loudly, "Now move it, you skinny bitch!"

Lee's face flushed with anger and embarrassment, but as she climbed the stairs, she realized the woman had not been trying to hurt her. Instead, she was protecting all the women at that table. She was now five minutes late for her interview with Seward, but she had every confidence that the story had legs.

Fleshy legs with plenty of cellulite.

FACT

Drinking It All In

Is alcohol good for your health? It depends on the study you read, and even the science funded by the good people of Booze. com will always say that it depends entirely on how much alcohol you consume.

But will it make you fat? The answer to that is surprising. Many studies have shown that drinking up to two glasses of wine in the evening will actually reduce your chances of gaining weight, despite the extra calories taken in. (About the same as a slice of cake.) Let that sink in. So should everyone be pounding the merlot each night?

Only if you are an animal. Please, merlot?

5

Chapter 11 – Weight Winners

Christopher Ballard was pleased. He'd just met with the Subcommittee on Obesity and secured a regular consulting contract for his law firm. He made a mental note to congratulate Jacinda on her report, because it had had quite an impact on the committee, particularly the section on "rumours and unsubstantiated allegations". For the next year at least, Ballard, Ballard and Bones would be making quarterly reports on the "progress" of the Calorie Reduction Program. This was perfect, as far as his client was concerned. The client that he was on his way to meet.

They'd picked an out-of-the-way bar to have their meeting – a basement establishment off Frank Street that was well known for its microbrews and curries – Ballard especially liked their pulled-pork sandwiches and he figured that nobody from the SubOb would be hanging out there at midday. He got there about twenty minutes before his client was due to arrive, to secure a nice private seat and instruct the server on how to treat him and his guest. He did this everywhere he went, promising a glorious tip to his servers for pretending that he was a regular or more famous than he was. Here, his prep was all about setting the mood. He knew the establishment would make his client feel uncomfortable, and he wanted the service to be warm and friendly to compensate.

He had told the committee that he was doing all the survey work on the CRCs for free, on a volunteer basis, but he was actually charging his client, Weight Winners, for many of the hours spent on the project.

His principal contact, Melinda Handle, appeared in the doorway, looking uncertain. She was American, or at least a species of American. She was from Texas. She saw Ballard and walked over, looking every bit the Texan beauty contest winner that she was – it was the second thing she'd told him after they'd met, that she'd represented Texas in the Miss America pageant. Right after her name. She was pretty, but Ballard didn't make the mistake of taking her lightly because of that. She was a driven and intelligent woman; the fact she had perfectly coifed hair and legs that went to her ears just had nothing to do with it. She was VP of External Relations, which was the polite way Weight Winners America had of describing company expansion.

"Well, you just found a place that's safe as Granny's snuffbox, didn't you?" she asked as Ballard stood to greet her. She pecked him on the cheek and took her seat. "Afraid people were going to see us together, were you?"

"There's no fooling you, Melinda." Ballard grinned. "Plus, they have a pulled-pork sandwich that even a Texan will love."

"That's high praise, and we'll see. Not that it's on my diet." Handle smiled. "And you're going to ply me with your strong Canadian beer too, aren't you, you wicked man?"

"It may lubricate our discussion."

She raised an eyebrow and said, "So let's lubricate."

He couldn't help but feel attracted to her. He was built that way. And she certainly seemed to like him, he thought. He had definitely made the right call not bringing Jacinda along. Who knew where this meeting might lead? They'd have to be careful not to be seen together, but big hotels were helpful that way.

The server brought them drinks and menus, and they got down to the business of discussing how they were going to make Weight Winners a huge amount of money.

"So how did it go with your little committee?"

"Famously. I'm reporting to them quarterly, so I'll definitely have a seat at the table if anything changes. Plus, we can influence how the committee evaluates the progress of our little socialist experiment here in the Great White North. I'm also going to make a big PR push about the volunteer work we're doing as a firm, as well, so that when you do decide to make an official presentation at some point, we'll be able to do so without risk of exposure," Ballard said.

"So I'm paying you directly?"

"Yep. WWA pays you. You pay me – here's the numbered account, by the way – and not the law firm. And you should know that I'll be declaring all the income." Ballard handed over a slip of paper.

"So, then, darling," Handle began and leaned over to touch his knee, "what's your plan for putting socks on this rooster?"

Ballard smiled despite his confusion at that particular idiom. Was it a reference to cock? He put the issue to the side for the moment.

"Well, to tell the truth, the whole set-up is a disaster. I don't know what they were thinking when they got the same bureaucracy that runs the Canadian prisons to set up a system to help regular citizens lose weight. The socialists have no idea what they're doing, even if they claim that they do. At this point, they're still measuring success by the amount of weight that their inmates have lost in aggregate, not individually."

"And that's loading the wrong wagon?"

Ballard stared at her for a moment. She smiled her perfect smile at him, as if to say, "What, don't you find my folksy sayings charming anymore?" He smiled back and took a long draught of his beer, a nice craft-brewed ale. She sipped at hers, and her eyes widened.

"You can't beat that with a stick," she said. "Chewy."

"It's a beauty, eh?" Ballard said, full of irony. "But to get back to the point. They should be measuring individual successes. They should be showing the people who successfully lose their weight and get back to being productive members of society. The thing is, it's just not happening. Sure, every once in a while, through sheer willpower, one of the poor bastards escapes the Fatness, but most of the people who leave are just opting out of the system."

"The Fatness?"

"Oh, that's my favourite euphemism for the CRCs."

"I've heard some people call it the Lard Lockup." Handle grinned. "I like that one. Poor fatties."

"You've never had weight issues?" Ballard asked.

"Well, I'll be. Here I was thinking you were a gentleman, and then you ask me a question like that. I watch my figure, as every lady should. But that's it. Never been even a pound overweight. I'm an inspiration for all our customers. Our poor pudgy customers."

"You seem real broken up about it."

"Well, I can only imagine what it's like going through life as fat as the town dog, but it must be hell. Especially when it's hot," Handle said. "Yes, absolutely, I feel lower than a gopher hole when I think about our customers trying to lose weight without our help. And we show results on an individual level. None of this aggregate hokum."

"I knew you'd be a perfect fit for the situation," Ballard said. His eyes widened as she finished her beer in one gulp.

"I could do with another of those," she said, sitting back, her legs crossed ladylike at the ankle. "It does make me feel loose as a bucket of soot."

Ballard could only interpret that one way, and he turned to get the server's attention, but she was already there with two more pints.

He loved it when his planning paid off.

FACT

Parts of Your Body Contain NO Fat!

Every part of the human body contains fat cells except for:

- the eyelids
- ironically, parts of the oesophagus (the tube from your throat to your stomach)
- the brain
- the penis

From this we can learn three things:

1. the term "fathead" is grossly inaccurate, scientifically speaking
2. people who fetishize eyelids and oesophagi are probably on a low-fat diet
3. porn dialog needs an update

Chapter 12 – Let's Eat at the Hop!

Every Friday the denizens of CRC-17 had the specter of all the ignominies of their high school years inflicted on them again. Like many of the people in the Fatness, Keelan had fought a weight problem for his entire life. Even in high school. Of course, when he was in his teens, Keelan had not been technically fat. If anything, he was practically slender during his high school years, as he gained height and mass. His BMI, if he had known what that was back then, would have probably been in the "normie" range or, at the most, just slightly overweight.

But in comparison to the rest of his classmates, he had still looked downright chubby. That combined with a gentle and shy nature had made the high school dance a regular and cringe-inducing experience until he realized that he didn't *have* to go and it wouldn't really matter. Sure, his chances of getting a girlfriend had dropped to practically zero, but when a regular night of humiliation only bumped those chances to one in two million, who cared?

But in the Girth Gulag, things had turned on their head. Keelan, at just *over* a 30 BMI, was practically svelte. He was taller than average. And Keelan liked dancing, even if he did get all sweaty and felt even more loathsome. So he went. And he dragged his buddies Max and Greg along.

They appeared at the commons just after the lights had been lowered and the music began. The CRC social coordinator, Regina Partridge, looked on the scene with great satisfaction. The dances had been her notion when she had been hired, and were among her more successful events. Less impressive had been her "Diet Fact Bingo" nights and "All You Can Eat Shuffleboard" in which the winners of each game could scarf down as much arugula as they wanted between games. (With no dressing, of course.)

The women had already arrived, and it was kind of sweet to see that they had gathered at the far side of the commons, waiting for some of the men to work up the courage to ask them to dance. A few men had formed small discussion groups and were goading one another to ask for a dance.

"The women have congealed already," Max said. "All in one fatty lump over there."

"Shut up, Max," Keelan said. "You're as corpulent as most of them."

Max shrugged, but crossed the no-man's-land between the two sexes and asked someone to dance. It seemed almost as though he had done so at random. This broke the ice, however, and other men started crossing the floor. Even a couple of the women did the same, and one of them, a pretty woman named Tina, asked Keelan to dance. He smiled and joined the others on the dance floor as the band played an anemic version of "At the Hop". There was much jiggling, and sweat-stains started to appear under arms almost immediately, but everyone seemed to be having fun.

Greg noticed that Cindy Vandenkieboom was actually attending the dance, along with Tracy Bloomfeld. Cindy was thin and looked incredibly fit. Unlike the other women, she was not dressed for the occasion. She was still wearing her work clothes – a combination of yoga pants, a sports bra, and an Adidas tracksuit top, which was unzipped. Greg watched her for a moment, thinking, *Confidence. Women like confidence.* He had been thinking about it ever since Keelan had mentioned it in the cafeteria.

"Right," he said. He strode across the dance floor and stopped in front of Cindy. "Hi, my name is Greg. Would you care to dance?"

Cindy looked genuinely shocked. She'd just dropped by to see if any of her patients were dancing. She'd encouraged them all week to participate in activities that got their bodies moving.

"Uh," Cindy said.

Greg forced himself to put out his hand, rushing out farther on the branch of imminent humiliation. Now, would it break? Or would it hold him? He pointedly ignored the daggers Tracy Bloomfield was shooting at him.

Cindy looked like she was about to say no, but she looked at Greg, saw the immense vulnerability there, and realized there was no way she could. She took his hand and said, "Sure. Just one, then I have to go."

A tsunami of whispering engulfed the room, and the guitar player, who had been watching the whole thing, missed a chord. One of their own dancing with a "normie"?

It was unheard of.

The smile on Greg's face was so bright it could have been spotted from space.

"Way to go," Keelan said as he danced with Tina. The song ended, and he and Tina stayed on the dance floor.

Cindy thanked Greg and beat a hasty retreat, her face beet red.

The dance continued, and Tina danced with both Greg and Kee until about an hour later when Jacinda arrived.

She had dressed for the occasion, putting on one of her little black dresses, even though she was afraid it made her arms look fat. She wore a scarf around her shoulders so they were not too exposed. She took some video with her phone and went over to the punch bowl to get a drink. She'd cleared her presence with the director, saying that she was going to record the event to get a better sense of how the patients spent their leisure time, but she was there for another reason.

Keelan and Tina finished Twisting, and Keelan thanked her for the dance; though Tina could see that his gaze was fixed on Jacinda. It was the first dance she'd attended since she'd moved into the CRC. And she could hardly blame him for staring at Jacinda – the woman was gorgeous. Exotic looking. Dressed beautifully. And skinny to boot. Of course, Tina's judgement on the latter fact was somewhat skewed by the gravitational curve of the Fatness. At a 24.8 BMI, Jacinda was on the high end of the normal range. A couple of pounds shy of overweight, the truth be told, but in comparison with the vast majority of the people in the room, she looked downright skinny.

Keelan walked over to Jacinda at the punch bowl and asked, "What are you doing here?"

Jacinda sipped her punch. Her eyes widened and she noted

that she shouldn't drink too much of it because it had clearly been spiked – probably by the group of chubby rapscallions gathered over by the bleachers, who were pointing at her and laughing.

"To taste your punch, of course. Rumour has it that it's spiked."

"You are well informed." Keelan grinned. "The Heavy Hitters have ladled at least two bottles of alcohol into it. Don't ask me what kind. It's probably been distilled in someone's toilet."

Jacinda did a spit take, a tiny jet of atomized "Pure Passion" punch filling the air around Keelan. She covered her mouth and looked horrified when she saw a stream of red liquid running down Keelan's face.

"I probably deserved that," Keelan said.

"Oh my God!" Jacinda said, reaching for her purse. She pulled out a tissue and offered it to Keelan. "Never in my life have I ever …"

"Spit in a man's face?" Keelan asked as he wiped his face. "Pity. I'm sure you must have met someone who deserved it. Probably more than me."

She laughed. "I've met men who deserved much worse. I'm so sorry, but I just wasn't ready to hear the words *distilled* and *toilet* in the same sentence."

"Nobody ever is. But are you ready to hear: 'Would you like to dance?'"

Keelan was even more charmed when Jacinda smiled shyly.

"Sure," she said. "I don't see the harm in that."

Keelan almost missed her response, because at that very moment, the Calorie Services team arrived with the "evening snack" promised to anyone who attended the dance. Despite the fact that it was only cheese whip on celery, a phalanx of heavy bodies rushed in as the travesty was laid on the table near the punch.

Keelan and Jacinda escaped the crush, but had to wait to get their groove on, as even the band members abandoned the dance for a chance at a few extra (delicious) calories.

They danced to something fast-paced, and then the band attempted the romantic – yet incredibly cheesy – "Lady in Red".

The singer didn't quite have the range of Chris de Burgh, but it wasn't a total disaster. Keelan didn't care, as he held her as close to him as he dared. He wasn't sure why she had come to the dance and was lavishing this attention on him, but surely it wasn't because she liked him. Not in *that* way.

It was as though she were reading his thoughts. "I came to observe the dance for my report."

Ah, Keelan thought, *so this is part of her work.*

"But it's more than that too," she added.

Keelan dared to hope that meant she came to see him.

Part II

"Who ever hears of fat men heading a riot, or herding together in turbulent mobs?"

~Washington Irving

Chapter 1 – Bread & Circuses

Keelan, Max, and Greg looked about them, marveling at the size of the crowd and the elegance of the space. The meeting room was as humid and close as usual, but for the moment, they and the other inmates of the CRC were transported to faraway France. Posters decked the walls. There were French vineyards, famous French landmarks like the Arc de Triomphe, the Eiffel Tower, and the Moulin Rouge; mind-numbingly delicious placards of baguettes and wheels of cheese cavorted with grapes and ancient bottles purple with promise of sweet fermented love. The meeting table was covered with a giant French flag, and a banner hung at the end of the room, welcoming all with a hearty *"Bienvenue en France!"*

They were gathered for the first-ever "Virtual Wine and Cheese" hosted by the CRC social coordinator, Regina Partridge.

Now, the description of this event in the CRC-17 *Wholesome Standard* (the weekly "newsletter" circulated to inmates via email, social media, and on paper for the confirmed luddites) had been less than transparent in its description:

"Come to the first of a series of 'Virtual Wine & Cheese Tastings' at Calorie Reduction Centre Seventeen. Join Regina Partridge as she walks you through the major wine regions of France and complements each wine she has chosen for this event with a scrumptious French cheese. Bring your notepads so that you can take tasting notes for when you reach your goal weight and can take a real trip to France to recreate first-hand all the delicious, sensual experiences that Regina will share. Please tell your calorie supervisor you would like to attend, and you will be invited to the event."

Except for the week that some inmates were arrested for cannibalism, this was the most downloaded edition of the CRC-17 *Wholesome Standard* ever. The notice went out two weeks before the actual event and was never repeated. It was talked about. Argued about. The main bone of contention being, what was the better aspect of the wine and cheese tasting: the wine or the cheese? A certain segment of the CRC population, who could not afford to pay the Heavy Hitters for illicit alcohol, felt that the prospect of getting to taste actual wine was going to be as good as sex. Greg was firmly in this camp. Better than sex, he said. (Max counter-argued that Greg and all the other misguided fools who thought this would be better than sex weren't doing sex right. But Max had never had a 1990 Musigny from De Vogué.) For those who had access to more cash, or who were willing to drink toilet alcohol – it was made using the reservoir of the toilet, not the bowl, by the way – the prospect of cheese was the thing that approached the apex of orgasm. (They didn't fall into the same hyperbole as the wine lovers.) Max was a committed cheese eater. Keelan might have been on the fence, because they both sounded damned marvellous when he'd read the article, but since then he'd had an entire day of eating cheese, so he was tending towards Greg's viewpoint, even if he recognized on an intellectual level that processed cheese was not the same thing as a nice Gruyere.

It didn't seem to matter much what side of the argument the potential wine-and-cheese-tasters fell on, because roughly ninety percent of them seemed to miss the part about securing an invitation to this event by telling their calorie supervisors they wanted to go. Luckily Keelan had spotted the fine print in the article, and the three secured their invitations through the proper channels. (He had been worried that Brittany would object, based on his special program, but she was happy to indulge him, it seemed, for this special event. That should have been a clue, Keelan later thought.) Enough inmates had followed the forms, so the room was filled. The inmates shuffled in, clearly awed by the change in the meeting room's presentation.

"It looks nice," Greg said.

"I have to admit it; they didn't screw it up," Max agreed.

"Look at all the glasses," Keelan said, pointing to the rows of wine glasses lining the long meeting table, which was covered with the tricolour flag.

"It's practically classy," Greg whispered. "I'm worried about the mime though."

Keelan nodded. He hadn't noticed the mime at first. He was standing in the back corner, pretending to be a statue. This must be part of the presentation – more French "culture," Keelan thought.

"Okay, let's close the doors if everyone is here," Regina shouted at the guard, who was stationed at the doorway. "Mr. Powers, please ensure nobody bothers us."

The guard, Will Powers, tried to smile, but it came out as more of a grimace. He was already worried about the large congregation of angry fat men and women milling outside; they had been prevented from entering because they were not "invited" and they were not happy about it. Half, upon hearing that it was their fault they weren't invited, had meekly walked away, disappointed in life once again. The other half were hanging around. There were subdued, bitter conversations going on amongst the crowd. Powers decided to cross his arms and look large and threatening, but the fact was that even though he was in great shape, proportioned like a lumberjack from the Heroic Era, and well trained, there was little he could do to keep an army of tubby wine connoisseurs out of the room if they were really committed to getting in. He checked his Taser and radio to ensure they were on.

"Welcome to a magical evening," Regina began. Keelan noticed Tina was in the group. She smiled at him shyly, and Keelan smiled back in a way that he thought was friendly, but not flirty. His mind was replaying the dances he'd shared with Jacinda. The hope that she might actually – you know – fancy him.

The only reason that everyone in the CRC wasn't replaying this deviant exhibition of normie-fattie love was because of the virtual wine tasting.

Max put an elbow in Keelan's side and said, "Pay attention. This is going to be hilarious." Keelan gave Max a questioning look, but the defrocked psychiatrist had an inscrutable expression on his face.

"Tonight I'm taking you all on a breathtaking virtual tour of the wine regions of France. For our first wine, we're going to try a Burgundy, a famous wine-producing region. This is a pinot noir, a variety that produces some of the finest wines, but which is notoriously fussy to turn into a fine wine …"

As Regina painted a truly delectable picture with her words, Keelan watched with a growing sense of horror as the mime started to move. Instead of a statue, he now seemed to be some kind of waiter. He thrust out his chest and butt comically, arm cocked in front of him. He slowly and exaggeratedly pretended to open a bottle of wine. He handed the non-existent cork to Tina, who played along graciously, smelling it and nodding her head. The mime did a super-happy face and proceeded to pick up an empty glass and pretended to pour a glass of the Burgundy into it. Tina took the glass and held it daintily by the stem.

"Yes, that's exactly correct, Tina. Do you know why we hold the glass by the stem and not the bowl?"

"Where's the wine?" Tina's hard-faced friend Barbara asked.

"It's in her glass, silly. Now, the waiter will pour you all a glass and I'll explain the process of tasting. First you put the rim of the glass up to your nose and give it a smell. This is called, appropriately, the bouquet. Can you smell the notes of cherry?"

"There's nothing in the glass!" someone at the back of the room cried.

"What is this, a joke?" Barbara asked.

"I hate mimes!" someone else shouted.

Ignoring the mime-hater, Regina said, "Of course there's no actual wine. It's a *virtual* tasting. Just because we're on a diet doesn't mean we can't enjoy the good things in life. We just have to use our imaginations."

Keelan looked at Max, who was quietly laughing. Greg looked subdued. Actually, Keelan thought he looked about as despondent as he'd ever seen him.

"I can't believe I fell for it," Greg moaned. A tear welled up in one eye.

"Oh, come on, Gregorovich," Max said. "You knew, deep down, they weren't going to let you drink wine and eat cheese. Admit it. Now, let's have some fun."

"Fuck it," Greg said. "It's bullshit."

"I agree," John T. Carver, the mountainous lieutenant of Colin Taggart, said. "You shouldn't play with people like this." He threw down his glass and shouldered his way to the mime. At six foot five, he towered above the little man, who didn't help the situation by pretending he was in a tiny glass box at Carver's feet.

Regina, sensing that she was about to lose the crowd in a spectacular way and worried for her mime, said, "But I've worked very hard on all these descriptions and pairings. And later we're going to do a little pantomime about making wine! It's very droll!"

"You know what would be droll?" Carver asked. "If we destroyed this place. Let's do that, shall we?" He spoke to everyone in the room, but nobody seemed interested in destroying anything. He picked up the mime, who pretended he was a helpless beetle, waving his arms and legs frantically above him.

"Hey, let's not get crazy here," Keelan said. "Sure, it's disappointing there isn't actual wine and cheese, but let's get into the spirit of this."

"What we need is actual spirits," Carver said with an evil grin. He tossed the mime on the table, which was still covered with mockingly empty wine glasses. They shattered and the mime rolled off it, landing on his feet, and despite the wine glass sticking out of his thigh, managed to stay in character. He waged an admonishing finger at Carver, even though it looked like the wine stem was cutting pretty deep, judging by the drops of blood already hitting the floor.

Keelan was actually pretty impressed by the mime's professionalism. He hadn't cried out at all.

Regina looked sick and afraid, but she bravely made a last attempt at getting the situation under control. "Let's do the pantomime now, shall we? Let's learn how they make wine the traditional way in France!"

Carver opened the door and shouted, "There's no wine! There's no cheese! It's a big joke to them."

The mime was indicating there was plenty of wine. There was a whole cask of it, he seemed to be showing them all. That was when Barbara smashed him over the head with a very real chair.

The guard heard the crash and knew there was trouble. Powers had enough time to turn on his radio and say, "Uh, I think we have a problem down here at the meeting room," before Carver cold-cocked him in the side of the head. As he collapsed, Carver grabbed his radio and Taser and shouted, "Let's show these fuckers what we think of their little joke!"

Given that most of the people milling outside were Heavy Hitters, the crowd took that as an order.

And that was how the first-ever, full-on CRC riot began.

FACT

A Surfeit of Cheeses

Changing eating habits are a major cause of the increase in obesity. These altered patterns have multiple causes: Corporations trying to make more money. Governments giving us bad advice in the form of public health policies, such as the food pyramid. And overproduction of foods that are bad for us. One of these is cheese.

Cheeses are roughly seventy percent fat. A gram of fat contains nine calories, versus carbohydrates and protein, which contain four. So that makes cheese a high-calorie food – roughly 3400 calories per pound of cheese. According to the Physicians Committee for Responsible Medicine: "In 1909, the average American consumed only 3.8 pounds of cheese in a year's time. Today, that number is pushing 34 pounds." If you break that down into calories, that's an extra 102,000 calories a year, enough to gain 29 pounds!

And don't even get started on what this has done for the laxative industry.

Chapter 2 – Newton's Second Law Of Motion, Or Why You Should Never Get In a Fight With a Fat Guy

The riot was an impromptu thing, but when it started, it occurred to Colin Taggart that it might be useful. He thought, *Sure, there will be some damage, but it's a chance for us to get rid of some of the competition.* There were several toilet-booze makers who had recently expanded their operations. These entrepreneurs were producing a decent grain-like alcohol – by decent, Taggart meant that it had yet to blind or kill anyone. It seemed they had secured several large brightly coloured balls from one of the exercise rooms and were using the equipment as makeshift carboys.

He also thought that if the riot got just a little bit out of control, and he and his compatriots helped to get it under control, that might score him some points with Seward and win him even more influence.

It didn't require any help to get the riot out of control, however.

As soon as the virtual wine tasting broke up, Wayne Falco started the very plausible rumour that there was actual wine and cheese in the kitchens by the cafeteria. Falco, who'd had nobody to do amputations on for some time, was keen to take out his frustrations. The crowd waddled over to the cafeteria at their best speed.

Falco led them, his meaty fist held high, chanting an impromptu protest: "What do we want?"

The crowd was still split on this. Some shouted "cheese" while others said "wine". It sounded, en masse, like the crowd wanted either "chine" or "weese".

Falco was not deterred. "When do we want it?"

"Soon!" they all shouted back. (They were obese, but in aggregate, they were a bright group, and they knew that it was impossible to have it until they got to the cafeteria.)

As they pulled away, Taggart gathered a few of his men and

told them to get the rest of their crew. Their job was to ensure the riot really got out of control. Carver was already heading with the crowd towards the cafeteria, but Taggart stopped him and said, "I've got a special job for you."

"No way, boss. I have a bone to pick with these people," Carver said. "These fucking bureaucrats. I hate being in here. I used to play in the goddamned NFL! I don't deserve to be in here!"

Taggart could use Carver's anger. "Think of it this way. If we play this right, this will get us even more control over their laughable system. Not only will you get some revenge, but we'll get richer in the process."

"Huh," Carver said, clearly unconvinced. "Will I get to wreck anything?"

"Of course! There's at least a dozen brightly coloured, alcohol-filled exercise balls that need to be trashed, and if their owners get in your way, well, who says you can't rough them up a bit in the process."

And so Carver was sent on his mission of Swiss ballicide.

Keelan and Max stayed behind the crowd to help the mime and the guard. Carver was a pretty big guy and he'd hit Powers right in the soft part of his head. The guard was unconscious, but stable otherwise. Regina was helping support the mime as they walked to the infirmary. Greg was already heading back to his "room".

"Greg, stay and help."

"Do you need help?"

"I think we'll be okay," Max said. "I suspect he just has a minor concussion."

"I don't think you should be alone during all this," Keelan said. He'd heard enough of Colin Taggart's rabble-rousing speech to know that things might get rough.

"I'll be fine," Greg said. "I'm just going to lock myself in my cell."

"Okay, I'll see you at breakfast."

"Whatever," Greg said. He'd pretty much stopped eating because of the weird diet that Brittany had put him on. The wine had been his last hope. Now he had nothing but pink barf to look forward to for another whole week.

"Poor guy," Keelan said. He was into the boiled chicken phase of his diet, but at least it was still recognizably chicken. Nobody – not even the cooks – knew what Greg's rose-tinted vomit substitute was made out of.

"Yeah. He's having a better night than this fellow though. Here, let's get him to the infirmary."

"Will that be safe?"

"I think so," Max said. "I have trouble imagining a penitentiary full of porkers is going to riot for very long. It requires quite a bit of sustained effort to have a real riot, and look, most of the women are heading back to their own wing."

Keelan noted that Tina and Barbara were heading off with the others to the cafeteria.

"Good luck, Tina," Keelan said.

"You know you had a real shot with her," Max said. "I don't know what's wrong with you sometimes, man. She's pretty, and except for her propensity to join corpulent ex-surgeons and Oakland Raiders in a bit of mob violence, she seems pretty nice. Did you see how she played along with the mime? Adorable! She has really clean Flabometrics too."

Keelan didn't want to know what Flabometrics was. He really didn't. "Maybe, but I've got a real connection with Jacinda."

"The *normie* you were dancing with?"

"Yes!"

"I don't know. Intra-body-type relationships. Seems taboo."

"All the more reason to pursue it," Keelan said. He knew his audience. Dr. Maximilian Tundra lived for taboos. Not cannibalism, he drew the line there, but lots of other stuff was interesting to him.

"Okay, I'll condone it, but only because it's so far off the social norm here in the Fatness."

"Great. And stop calling it that."

"Never. Now, let's take this fit fucker to the infirmary," Max said.

It took them a while to get there – because of his impressive level of fitness, Powers was muscle-bound. Muscle is heavy. And a human body, while unconscious, is awkward to carry. Keelan and Max lugged him to the infirmary. Dr. Fundarek happened to be on duty, and Max scowled at him.

Keelan wanted to avoid this confrontation – the two disgraced doctors had little like for one another – so he volunteered to tell the guards on duty that a riot was under way. They both grunted their assent, and Keelan ran to the front entrance.

The guards were stationed there. Keelan didn't like going there, because, frankly, he was always tempted to leave the CRC and let the consequences be damned. Recently, he'd only been accompanying Greg, who seemed to spend at least a few minutes there every week, debating about whether he should leave or not. Keelan could hardly blame him. Greg had been in the Fatness for three months longer than Keelan, and he'd been much less successful at losing weight. Keelan had some prospect of actually getting out of the place. Brittany's crazy Freedom Fries diet seemed to be doing something.

Keelan had never met the guards on duty, but he introduced himself and said they had a problem.

"Everyone's a little upset about the virtual wine and cheese," Keelan said.

"Why tell us?" asked the guy sitting at the duty desk. The other was actually leaning up against the wall by the door.

"Because I think it's going to turn into a riot. The crowd is very worked up about it. John Carver stabbed the mime and knocked the other guard, Powers, I think, out cold."

The two guards laughed. "Good one, man. That's funny."

"Seriously, there's a riot going on. And Carver did punch out Powers. Call down to the infirmary if you think I'm making it up."

"Will Powers?" the guard sitting down at the duty desk asked. He seemed to be their spokesperson. "That guy is ripped. How did some fatty knock him out?"

"Hey, don't be stupid," the other guard said. "I used to work as a bouncer, and you always got to watch the fat men. You never fight with a fat dude if you can avoid it."

"What?"

"Oh, yeah. They are strong. They have to be to carry around all that blubber, and then if they grab you, or god forbid they get a run at you."

Keelan wanted to say, "Come on, guys, I'm standing right here." But he just put up with the insulting conversation. In fact, he decided to add his own two cents. "It's true. Newton's second law of motion is a bitch. Let a big guy build up a little inertia and you're fucked," Keelan added. "The only way to beat us is to tire us out."

"Hmm. Never thought of that," the guard at the desk said. "Okay, so there's a riot. What should I do about it?"

"I don't know," Keelan said. "Don't you have some kind of procedure?"

"For penitentiaries, sure, but not some glorified fat farm. You people aren't supposed to be violent."

"You know, I would really appreciate it if you stopped calling us 'you people'," Keelan said.

"Oh, right. Shit, sorry."

"Yeah, man. You'd think you weren't at that sensitivity training seminar," the other guard chided his colleague and said to Keelan quietly, "He was hungover."

"What?"

"Nothing. Look, I think this kid is right. We gotta do something. Why don't we call the cops?"

"Yes!" the desk guard said. "It's still something they should handle."

So they called the cops.

While they waited, Keelan asked, "Don't you guys have any CCTV or anything? Didn't you notice the trouble starting?"

"Good point," the guard at the door said. "They're in the booth. That's where I'm supposed to be, actually." He got up and went to the door just down the hall. Keelan tagged along, and the guard didn't object as they both entered the small room. It was bathed in the illumination of twelve screens showing a variety of places within the CRC. They seemed to be on a timer, as the screens changed regularly, displaying more than twelve locations in aggregate.

"Right there," Keelan said, pointing to one of the screens showing what looked like Wayne Falco directing a dozen other inmates as they used a dining table as a battering ram against the door to the kitchens.

"Wow," the guard said. "They seem angry."

The police arrived while Keelan and the guard watched Falco and his erstwhile assault team take down the door and get into the kitchen. What followed on the screen was hard to make out, but they clearly were finding food and eating it. Some even seemed to be organizing the kitchen.

As they watched, Keelan said, "I think that's Rita making pasta." His stomach rumbled at the mere thought of all those carbs. Delicious, delicious carbs. Rita and Barbara were acting as a dynamic duo of chefs, instructing the other rioters on what to do. Falco and a few of the others had since grabbed stuff from the massive wall of fridges and were sitting in the cafeteria, eating.

Keelan felt a presence and saw the cops were standing behind him, watching the screens.

"Weird kinda riot," one of the cops said. "Most rioters don't start cooking things."

"Most rioters aren't being systematically starved by their prison."

"Look, there," the guard said, pointing to one of the other screens. Taggart sat on his Rascal, smoking a cigar and watching while Carver and a large group of Heavy Hitters – all extremely fat men – fought a pitched battle in one of the weight rooms with three of the Neckheads. It seemed like the weightlifters were trying to protect the equipment from the Heavy Hitters, who were trashing weight machines with loose barbells and taking away dumbbells. The Neckheads were muscular and motivated, but badly outnumbered no matter how you measured it.

"He's not allowed to smoke in the building," the CRC guard said.

"Screw the cigar, they're going to kill those weightlifters. What the hell are weightlifters doing in here anyway?" the female cop said.

Keelan was about to explain and the male cop said, "Never mind, that's none of my business, but I think we'd better get in there before someone gets killed. We're calling for backup first!"

His partner, a strong-looking woman with a pretty face, poked her head in the door and watched for a while. "Tell them to call the riot squad. We're going to need a lot of people to deal with that!" She cringed while Carver and one of the Neckheads battled with twenty-pound barbells like they were two-handed swords. If either of them landed a blow on the head, there was going to be a fatality.

Keelan was fascinated. Meanwhile, Rita and her friend had finished their culinary insurrection – it looked like they had cooked roughly one hundred pounds of pasta with some kind of sauce. (Keelan guessed bolognaise, but it was hard to tell on the black and white screens. His stomach rumbled again.) They were eating some of it and dividing the rest into smaller pots and giving them to the other women who had accompanied the guys. Luckily, Falco and his buddies had finished gorging themselves and were already lying around the room torpidly, looking like hippos that had eaten one too many tourists, so they did not try to steal the pasta from the women. The women left the cafeteria and returned to the women's wing with their ill-gotten pasta, where they were clearly going to share it with their friends.

"Too bad there was no real wine to go with that," Keelan said wistfully.

The cops had trouble convincing their supervisor that the riot squad was going to be needed at a Calorie Reduction Centre, but eventually the panic in their voices made the argument for them.

They unholstered their Tasers and the male cop said, "Remember, this won't work as well on the really fat guys."

"Great," the female cop said. "What are we supposed to use, then? Harsh language?"

"Heh. *Aliens.* Good pull."

And they were gone. Keelan was almost afraid to watch the video to see what happened, but by the time Keelan saw the weight room screen again, the melee between the Heavy Hitters and the Neckheads was all over. Carver had broken the arm of his opponent, and this took the wind out of the sails of the other two. Exercise machines were destroyed, and weights were spirited away by the Heavy Hitters on their Rascals. What they planned to do with them, Keelan had no idea.

The other guard, who had yet to leave his post at the desk, shouted, "You are recording all this, aren't you?"

The other guard looked at Keelan, put his finger on his lips, and said, "You bet!"

He pressed the record button.

QUOTE

"Today, 'fat' has become not a description of size but a moral category tainted with criticism and contempt."

~Susie Orbach

Chapter 3 – The Unforeseeable Effects of a Low-Fat Diet

Fat wasn't catching, was it?

It seemed like a relevant question to Jacinda. Since she'd started working on the CRC project for her firm, she'd gained five pounds. It was probably water, but there had to be some connection. She'd been there four times, so maybe the exposure to fat was rubbing off on her. Not like it was an infection, of course, but maybe she was just getting more used to the sight of grossly overweight people. Even after a five-pound weight gain, she was still relatively thin. Not that her mother would agree. She grimaced as she guided her shopping cart towards the produce section.

Jacinda was trying to keep to the outside edges of the supermarket. All the diet books had this advice, but she'd noticed of late that the strategy might not be as safe as one might assume. Before she got to the vegetables, there was a wall of displays selling "healthy", yet calorie-dense drinks like pomegranate juice and "freshly squeezed" orange-mango concoctions. "How do you squeeze mangos?" she wondered aloud. Still. It sounded tasty.

She kept pushing. The juices might be healthier than a bottle of Coke, but were still filled with sugary calories. After the juices came a display of prepared salads and dressings that were no doubt loaded with fat and sugar and salt. (This is the magic combination that makes even salad delicious – and fattening – she knew.) The vegetables started to make their appearance. She picked up a few things for a stir-fry and grabbed some apples from the middle of the aisle for her afternoon snacks.

Next came the fresh pastas – also on the outside edge of the store. It took every erg of her willpower to guide the shopping cart past the fresh fettuccini, its hard-plastic container glistening with attractiveness. She imagined how easy it would be to cook. Just a bit of hot water, and she could get one of those pre-made blush sauces. She could just pop that in the microwave if she didn't feel like getting another pot dirty. Jacinda loved pasta, but she knew that it was her enemy, in the same way that a dormouse knew that big friendly-looking cat was its enemy. Sure, it might just want to play at first, but there would be blood. Her gnosis was instinctive now, but it hadn't always been. At one time, she'd run towards the pasta, the bread, the potatoes, desperate to fill her belly and avoid fat.

Fat used to be the enemy. Any kind of fat in your food was bad. Fat begat fat, at least that was the received wisdom of her parents. Her mother followed the prescriptions of the medical profession, who had long said that fat was the problem. Fat caused weight gain. It caused heart disease. Diabetes. Death. Moral decay and Communism. The low-fat diet craze became institutionalized by the mid-80s, back when her parents were fighting their epic battle with middle age and entropy. Institutions throughout North America recommended low fat consumption. In her house, any kind of fat product was an abomination. Her father thought her mother overdid it, but he was able to trot out a verse of the Bible to support the position: "It shall be a statute forever throughout your generations, in all your dwelling places, that you eat neither fat nor blood." (Her dad was not a religious man, but his reading and memory were prodigious.)

And the food industry helped them with their quest to slay the Dragon Fat. They produced fat-free and low-fat items galore. Some of them even tasted good, because the producers replaced the fat with the right combination of sugar and salt.

But something weird happened. It happened to her mother first. And then it happened to her. It happened to society at large. Society got larger. At least the component parts of society – the individuals – got larger. Despite the fact that they were doing what the medical authorities told them to do, society's gross tonnage was going up at an alarming rate. But her mother wasn't going to allow that. She had always been thin, and she would continue to be thin, no matter what life threw at her.

Her daughter would be thin too.

They managed it in different ways. Her mother abandoned the state religion, the low-fat, grain-based diet, and found a new seer – her prophet, Dr. Atkins.

"And lo, the truth was known. And Satan was revealed. And his name was carbohydrates," Jacinda muttered. She realized that somehow she was standing in front of the carbs – *I mean pasta*, she thought.

And so pasta, bread, cakes, cookies, even potatoes were banished from her house. It was a traumatic time for Jacinda, those last two years of high school. She'd grown up on those things, the low-fat versions of them anyway. They were her comfort food. So her solution had been to binge on them – only occasionally, when her mother was accompanying her dad on a business trip, or at school. And when she knew that she'd overdone it, she would purge them later. Jacinda tried barfing, but she didn't like that, so her chosen method of purging would be to over-exercise. She'd go out for a jog and return hours and hours later, drenched with sweat, exhausted and filled with a desperate rectitude, ready for her next binge. She would miss classes so she could burn off all the calories she'd just binged. She recognized it was not necessarily a good thing, but it kept her mom off her back about her weight.

As far as Jacinda could tell, her weight seemed to reflect, somehow, on her mother. If she gained a pound or two, her mother acted as though *she'd* put on the weight. Every pound off her perfect form was an indictment of her mother's figure.

"Are you trying to kill me?" she'd scream at Jacinda. "I can't eat any less."

The screaming matches they'd have. Her father would often intervene with these set-tos, but just as often he would be the one who instigated them with an offhand comment about how either of them might have gained a couple of pounds, only to break up the fight later. While they were self-regulating, they had no need to be: if there was any appreciable change in their figures, the paterfamilias would be sure to mention it.

Her dad had been an executive in a major food-processing corporation and so spent much of his time away from the house – inspecting facilities, overseeing food-testers and product line designers throughout North America. Despite all the time on the road, he maintained a trim, athletic figure throughout Jacinda's younger years. Her mania for exercising came from him. He didn't seem to be that careful about what he ate, but he always exercised – each morning he'd go for a jog and he worked out in their home gym whenever he was around. She'd always presumed that he did the same in all the hotels that he stayed at too. When she was fourteen, he had a massive heart attack during a corporate retreat dedicated to redesigning a major line of soft drinks. (They reformulated the syrup, mostly by increasing its sugar content, and it was wildly successful.)

He'd noticed the chest pains earlier that day, during his regular morning jog, and the pain had intensified throughout the presentations by food scientists, who were explaining how they could find what their lead scientist called the "bliss point" – the absolutely optimal amount of sugar in their soft drink. Despite the agony searing in his chest, he was fascinated by this concept and wondered if they could apply it – scientifically – to all their other product lines.

"I don't see why not," the scientist had said.

"Excellent. Then let's get into the bliss business," her dad had replied. Those were his final words, and they made him a legend in the industry.

Of course, the impact on Jacinda had been less mythic. She and her mother were left to their own devices, and without the buffer of her dad, they argued constantly.

Mostly about *her* weight.

"Fuck it," Jacinda said, returning to the present and grabbing the package of fresh fettuccini that had been taunting her the whole time.

She thought about Keelan at that moment and guessed that he would *never* criticize her about her weight. Could she do the same?

Still, the package of pasta taunted her during the rest of her voyage around the outside of the grocery store as she passed the baked goods, milk products, frozen food and then had to run the gauntlet of ice-cream freezers and stand-alone displays of all kinds of highly fattening snack foods like "X-treme Cheese Bangers" and "Ultimate Choco-Diet Bars".

Her willpower bent to the breaking point – the Ultimate Choco-Diet Bars had actually almost broken her with their promise of "real chocolate taste with a quarter of the fat", but pretty much the same amount of calories, she noted as she checked the nutritional information. She approached the cashier, feeling exhausted and filled with self-loathing. As it turned out, the technique of just shopping on the perimeter of the supermarket might not be the safest way of getting her groceries after all. She tried to ignore the lurid covers of the tabloids and magazines promising her diets to help lose thirty pounds in thirty days, the best sex ever, and the secrets to killer abs.

She couldn't get the thought of that fettuccini out of her head. It was going to taste so good. It had been so long since she'd had pasta. She deserved it, damnit!

As she placed it on the checkout belt, it felt like the glistening plastic package of pasta was flashing with lights and signaling a crime. She looked around to see if anybody noticed her groceries, she felt so guilty about the goddamned fettuccini. The lady in line behind her seemed oblivious, which was *hardly* a surprise. Her shopping cart was filled with all kinds of fattening (delicious) shit – compared with the Delissio pizzas stacked in the bottom of the cart, Jacinda's pasta was practically health food.

Jacinda chided herself for judging. She was becoming her mother.

This thought obsessed her while she made chit-chat with the cashier. Things had not been good with her mother for some time. Not as bad as they had been during her teenage years, for sure, but not well. Her mother had warned her against dating her boss, Chris Ballard, and it didn't help that her mother had been right about that. And the discussion of Jacinda's weight was just constant. Especially since Jacinda had hit her mid-thirties, and it became more of a challenge to maintain her figure. Her mother had somehow maintained the same weight she'd had her whole life – a svelte, gorgeous, and yes, infuriating, 103 pounds. Even in her sixties, the damn woman hadn't gained any weight.

She paid for her groceries, noting which bag the pasta was in, and took it all out to her car. At least the rest of the stuff was pretty healthy. Fruits, vegetables, some nuts, and some skinless chicken she planned on cooking with her pasta. Her mouth watered as she thought about it. She'd skipped lunch and was starving.

And she realized she hadn't purchased her blush sauce to go with the pasta. She was going to have to go back in there.

She sighed and girded herself for battle once again.

FACT

Fat Is a Plague!

There *is* a growing body of evidence that shows chubbiness is catching. A study by the Harvard Medical School in 2007 showed that close personal friends were 171 percent more likely to be obese if they had fat familiars. A more recent study by Brown University demonstrated people who were overweight or obese were more likely to have romantic partners, best friends and casual friends who were also overweight.

Why would this be? According to Miriam Nelson, author of *The Social Network Diet: Change Yourself, Change the World*, having heavier friends and lovers normalizes the oversized. "I believe that these changing norms have had a profound influence on the rapid spread of obesity."

The solution is obvious: wearable tech that makes everyone look thin.

7

Chapter 4 – As Addictive as Cocaine

For the first time in the five-year history of the Fatness, everyone's door was locked from the outside. This happened at five a.m., when most people were asleep, but Keelan happened to be half-awake. He hadn't even known that it was possible for the door to be locked from the outside, so he had no idea what the loud *K-THUNK* meant. He thought someone might have knocked on it, so he went to open it, to no avail.

He was about to experience a moment of panic when his computer chimed at him to let him know that he was getting a call. He turned it on and saw Max's face staring at him. His fire-red hair looked extra crazy today.

"What's up, Max?"

"You locked in too?"

"Yep."

"I have to say I'm surprised," Max admitted.

"Really?"

"Yes, I didn't think they'd had the foresight to be able to lock us in. I wonder what happens to the early risers who managed to get outside of their rooms first?"

"They'll probably round them up and gas them in the meeting room," Keelan joked weakly.

"Not yet, not yet," Max said. He looked worried.

"What's up? You claustrophobic?"

"Not really. I'm afraid I'm running low on *supplies*."

"You mean –"

"Don't say it," Max interrupted. "They're probably monitoring everything."

"Really."

"You didn't read the terms of service form, did you?"

"No, I'm a real person, so I just clicked 'accept'."

"Well, you don't know that they can monitor our communications any time they want to do so, to 'ensure our compliance with their nutrition and exercise guidance'."

"Shit."

"Hey, it's not a problem if you're not doing anything illegal, right?"

Keelan recognized that Max was quoting their buddy Greg. They'd been arguing about the nature of government surveillance the day before, and Greg had been surprisingly sanguine about it.

"Speaking of Greg, let's get him in on this call."

"I tried when I called you, Keelan. He's probably sound asleep or got his devices turned off."

"So now what?"

"Well, the lack of *supplies* is a problem, I must admit. If we're locked in here for long, I shan't be held accountable for the state of the room."

"I thought you had lots?"

"I keep them all in my lab, where I have been working on a new diet compound as well."

"Lab?"

"The custodian's room. I pay them a small rent. And they don't mess with my lab equipment at all. I've been making great progress on my Flabometrics, but I'm really excited about the DC – the Diet Compound."

"Like a pill?"

"Yes, exactly. I have been spectacularly unsuccessful. Everything I've come up with so far would help us lose all of our extra weight, but we'd also probably be dead. I've got something that can help us lose a little, though, and I've got an excellent notion. I was thinking we could sell some weight-loss powder to generate a little juju."

"Oh, Max."

"Just hear me out. With the Heavy Hitters controlling the Fux with their underground junk-food railway, we've got to do something to generate some goodwill for us. I was just going to sell enough to help people lose a bit of weight, and make a bit of cash for, uh …"

"Your *supplies*."

"But mostly it's about the goodwill. And we need to counter-act the extra calories they keep bringing in."

"That's not our job, Max. Our job is to get the hell out of

here. I have to get out of here."

"Oh, Keelan, you're adorable. You know I've been out once already, right?"

"No, I didn't."

"Yes, my first year here was hellish, and I worked really hard, and I got under the 30 bimmi. I was back in within a year."

"Why?"

"I put all the weight back on, like I always have, plus a few more pounds," Max said.

"I'm sorry."

"So am I, but the reality is, while it's hard to lose the weight, it's nearly impossible to keep it off. I know of only a handful of people from the Fatness who've lost the weight and stayed out."

"Well that's a bummer. I guess if I ever do get under the thirty, I'll have to be vigilant," Keelan mused.

Max was about to say something, and he stopped himself. Instead, he said, "Besides, they're not going to let us out of here en masse."

"What do you mean?" Keelan asked; the intimation of panic returned.

Max hesitated.

"Come on, Tundra. You can't just start saying something like that and then, then, not complete the thought!"

"Well, my reading of history is that as soon as you have a system like this set up, it will want to continue until it's too detrimental to the society to do so, or until a revolution destroys the system. Prohibition in the '30s. Nazi concentration camps. The war on drugs."

Keelan could think of some arguments for how they weren't the same thing, but he got the point. His head reeled with the knowledge, like he'd been sipping on one of Max's peyote milkshakes. Was he trapped here? Forever, no matter how much weight he lost? Surely, that wasn't the plan? People wouldn't have voted for it if they'd known. They'd demand that it be repealed if they found out.

To think he'd almost had a leg amputated to get out. He'd

been that close. A wave of despair washed over him. How was he ever going to go out on a proper date with Jacinda if he couldn't get out of here?

"Ah, don't listen to me," Max said, now worried about Keelan. "It's just the lack of *supplies* talking. I'll call you later when Greg is awake and we can make a plan for what we'll do when they unlock our doors."

"Okay," Keelan said, his voice flat.

When the call ended, he checked his email and saw that he had an official communication from Hellmuth University. It was worded awkwardly and probably had been vetted by a dozen lawyers, but, essentially, it told Keelan that his employment would end with them unless he could be at work by the start of the month. (The letter also directed him to check out the relevant passages in the Fat Act that allowed employers to terminate employees who had been in a CRC for more than two years.)

Keelan wondered why they had waited nearly two weeks to fire him for being obese, but realized that it was the start of their monthly pay cycle. No doubt it wasn't kindness, but a bureaucratic nicety. He sighed. He knew it was coming, but it was still depressing. Having nothing else to do, he turned on the TV.

And CRC-17 was headlining the news.

FACT

Keeping the Weight Off

So here's the dirty secret. You can lose the weight, but keeping it off is hard. Especially when you're a caveman. Biologically, we are really no different from our ancestors.

A study published in the *New England Journal of Medicine* showed that there are two major hormonal changes that occur in the body during a diet. The first is the drop in body fat messes with the hormones that tell you when you are full, so after you've lost some weight, you're prone to overeating. The second is weight loss increases the hormones that tell you you're hungry, so you're prone to overeating. The end result is that 90 percent of people who lost 10 percent of their body weight were *so* prone to overeating (let's call it *proneating* for short) they gained all their hard-lost weight back and then some. Their bodies, in a bit of biological perversity, makes this new slightly higher weight their new "normal." This evolutionary response is a survival mechanism that helped keep humans alive during droughts, famines and ice ages.

But it does no good when you've got enough freeze-dried ramen in your cupboard to feed a Paleolithic village for a month.

8

Chapter 5 – O Trespass Discreetly Urged!

Serena Lee was reporting, live, from outside the Fatness. She'd been planning to go to the CRC later that day, in another attempt to get something useful out of the warden about how cheese-burgers were making their way into a federal facility where every calorie was supposedly accounted for. Instead, her producer had dragged her out – much earlier than she'd planned – to cover the story of the riot that had taken place inside the CRC overnight.

Actually, it wasn't the earliness of the hour as much as it was the idea that she would cover the story like some kind of common news grunt. And her august presence wasn't doing much for the story, she had to admit. So far the CRC administration had yet to tell her anything more substantive than what the police media relations officer had told her when she arrived.

There were two bits of good news for her. The first was that her only TV competition was the local news crew, and they weren't nearly as telegenic or well-known as she was, so the world media was picking up her feed, not the swarthy, vaguely un-washed local reporter that was repeating the details to his viewers for the three microseconds allotted for local news. So even though she hadn't done much actual news gathering, she'd now played her report for the BBC, CBS, NBC, CNN, and a number of other major world players. In fact, she was doing a live interview for BBC, which her own network was also running live.

The second bit of good news was that it was clearly a slow news day, so this riot was actually getting coverage. Probably because there was already a bit of fascination with the Canadian solution to the obesity epidemic, and secondly, the thought of Canadians – even chubby incarcerated Canadians – rioting was a bit of a puzzler. Especially when hockey wasn't involved.

"So how many casualties were there during the night, Serena?" the BBC reporter asked in his plummy Oxbridge accent.

"The reports are still coming out, but from what I've been

told by the local police, one of the CRC guards was concussed, and two weightlifters were also hurt, one of whom broke his arm. There is speculation that some of the rioters may have pulled some muscles and there could also be scratches and bruising from their assault on the kitchen facilities. Oh, and a mime had some lacerations from a broken wine glass."

(That last bit of actual news she'd gathered by overhearing two of the CRC guards discussing it before their warden had arrived on the scene.)

"Nobody was killed? Not even the mime?"

"No, Alex. Though we suspect the kitchen may be out of commission for several days at least."

The crawl underneath the interview was adding helpful details, such as where Landon, Ontario, was in Canada (in relation to Toronto, of course) and how many people lived in the city, according to Wikipedia. It also noted that the famous actor and hunk, Ryan Duckling, was from Landon.

Serena could tell that the BBC anchor was quite disgusted by the lack of actual news in this news report, and she could see he was being told to wrap up the interview, so she added, "We also have unconfirmed reports that this riot was started because of fast food."

Now THAT was interesting to the anchor and her producers.

"How so, Serena? Our understanding is that the Calorie Reduction Centres are junk-food-free zones, and that any foods are carefully monitored to help the inmates—"

"Patients," Serena said. "The citizens living in the CRCs have not broken any laws and are free to leave whenever they want."

"Except not now, obviously."

"Yes, they have locked the facility down while they clean up. I should also say that these reports are unsubstantiated, but I have personally talked to several *patients* of CRC-17 who say it is possible to get ice cream if they have the wherewithal to pay for it."

"And how could this have resulted in a riot?"

"Any answer I could give would be pure speculation," Serena said, doing her best "serious face" for the camera, "but I would guess that it probably began as a fight between patients about some food and then spilled into the general population. Or perhaps the guard who was injured was trying to remove the ice cream when it got out of hand. That's conjecture, of course."

"Of course," the anchor said.

The crawl now read ICE CREAM CAUSE OF RIOT IN CANADIAN FAT PRISON.

"Well, shit," Keelan said when he saw the crawl. "We're gonna be locked in forever now."

His evaluation of the situation was pretty accurate. As he'd guessed, the warden, Selwyn Seward, was loath to unlock the room doors until they'd figured out a decent public relations response to the situation. As it turned out, the best thing for them to do was to tell the truth. At least part of it. By lunchtime, Seward had done an impromptu media scrum outside the CRC entrance way, explaining there was nothing to the rumour that Serena Lee had started. He did explain that the "unfortunate mishap" occurred at the Virtual Wine and Cheese. The employee responsible for the event would be disciplined, the mime would be blacklisted, and the "patients" responsible for attacking the guard and the two weightlifters would be caught and apprehended.

Keelan watched with amusement as the director tried to explain why none of the CCTV footage had been recorded, so they would have to investigate who had attacked the victims and who had damaged the kitchen.

"Good luck with that," Keelan said to the TV.

His Skype dinged, and he assumed it would be Max and Greg on the line, but he was excited to see that it was Jacinda.

She was calling him from her office downtown and the sun shone through the window behind her. Not that Keelan was paying attention to her view (which was lovely), but to her, because he thought she was *gorgeous*. And wonderful. And scrumptious. And all kinds of other adjectives that spring to mind when your brain is being washed and rinsed in dopamine. In Keelan's case, the dopamine was the result of seeing Jacinda, not because he'd just bitten into a Pop-Tart specifically designed to goose his brain's bliss point.

Jacinda did it for him, just by calling. That's what dopamine is supposed to be for.

"Hey ... you," Keelan said. (Extreme pleasure can make you seem like an idiot.)

"Keelan, how are you? Did anything bad happen to you in the riot?"

Aw, she cares about me, Keelan thought. *That's gotta be a good sign, right?*

"No, I'm cool. They've locked us all in our rooms. I suppose 'cell' is a better description of it; I'm starting to understand Max's point of view a bit better now. How are you?"

"I'm worried about you." She smiled. "I guess that seems a bit, uh, presumptuous to say ..."

"No, it's sweet."

"Well ..."

"Thanks again for coming to the dance," Keelan said. "I wish we'd gone out to that movie before this lockdown happened. Who knows how long it will take for things to get back to normal."

"I checked into it. There is a way to get a pass, but they're only issuing them for emergencies, and first dates don't count," Jacinda explained. "It's ridiculous."

"I'm not surprised. They really are trying to control everyone's access to calories. Of course, it's absurd, when you know what's going on in here."

"What do you mean?"

"The Heavy Hitters."

"You mentioned them at the dance. What the hell is that? Some kind of punk band?"

"I didn't tell you about that in our interview?"

"No, you were being very circumspect ... and charming."

"Oh, well, there's a group of inmates that are smuggling in high-calorie foods like McDonald's. The afternoon of the riot they did a run of Dirty Bird. I almost lost my mind."

"You scamps do have a lot of nicknames. What the hell is Dirty Bird?"

"Oh. Kentucky Fried Chicken."

She laughed. Keelan loved her laugh. Was it possible he loved her? That was crazy, wasn't it? He'd only just met her. How could he think he loved her?

"So when will I get to see you?" she asked.

"I have no idea. They haven't even explained how long we're going to be locked in our cells at this point, so it could be …"

"Too long." She leaned in a bit towards the screen, and for a moment Keelan thought she was going to kiss the camera or something, but she sat back in her chair and joked, "I don't know about getting yourself locked up. Seems like it's going to be hard to go out for that movie."

"Yeah, I've always found it best to play hard to get," Keelan joked.

She smiled. "So we're on for that date?"

"Yes, but how?"

"Well, I do have this law degree. Maybe that will help."

Keelan laughed. He felt hope blossom in him again. It had been all but crushed, and Max's theory that systems like the CRC were designed to keep him in there had nearly finished it, but it would not die. Now there was Jacinda. And she seemed to like him as much as he liked her. *Like* wasn't really a strong enough word. Across the pond, in the UK and Ireland, they had a much better phrase for it, he thought. *She fancies me. And I fancy her right back.*

I should tell her, he thought. *No, that's insane.* How could she possibly respond to that? He was fat. She was gorgeous. He was in the Fatness. She lived in the real world. But if he didn't say it, he would regret it. He would look back at this moment, and if he never got a chance to see the movie with her, or even to talk again using Skype, he'd regret it.

Sometimes in life it's hardest to recognize that even though we live in the present tense, evolution, the Universe – God, if you skew that way – has given us the ability to think in other tenses.

We have to project ourselves forward and imagine the thing you didn't do because you were too scared of it, or afraid of failure, or somehow unable to grasp the truth in front of you, in real time. It's one of the great ironies that to be present, to truly live your life to the fullest, you have to imagine this present moment through the lens of a future self. To cast your mind forward to a hypothetical you and judge your actions from a tense we don't inhabit, and translate it to one you do.

"I fancy you," he said.

"Really? I could barely notice."

"Seriously. I *really* fancy you."

"And I fancy you," she said. She was flirting. Her tone was light, joking, because she was unused to the word. But she liked it.

"So now what?" Keelan asked.

"Now we get you out of there."

FACT
Fried Food, Fried Wiring

Anyone who's ever struggled with their weight will have tried to diet to get rid of the excess pounds. Especially if they have a doctor. And in fact, diet is the best way to shed weight. If you try to do it with exercise alone, your chances of long-term success are slim. (Pun intended, and really, isn't it a surprise you haven't read it before now?) That's because intense exercise burns calories and makes you hungry. That makes you want to eat more.

So here's the bad news. If you gained those excess pounds because you've got a taste for fat – and you should, because all hominids do – a diet may not work either. That's because fat rewires your body's messaging system. It actually messes with the nerve endings in your stomach and makes you feel hungry unless you get it in you! That's right. If you got fat because of fat, studies have shown that you can't feel full without it.

So those deep-fried mozzarella sticks are staying with you, and even if you run for the Metamucil, their legacy will remain.

9

Chapter 6 – Salad-Bar-Crossed Lovers

The lockdown ended later that day, right after Jacinda called the CRC administrator to explain that what he was doing was actually unlawful incarceration. There was no provision in the Fat Act for CRC-wide lockdowns, similar to what could happen in an actual prison. There was a provision that said "patients" of a CRC could not leave without giving up their medical coverage, but that was as far as it went.

In other words, just because they didn't want to lose their health coverage didn't mean the "patients" had to give up habeas corpus.

But both of these facts were unknown to Keelan, who was dying to tell his buddies Max and Greg what had happened. The coffee bar had reopened despite the fact that some enterprising individual had expertly dismantled the espresso maker during the riot. No doubt it was now helping to produce a finer vintage of toilet alcohol than heretofore produced by CRC-17, Uxford County. They did have an old drip-coffee maker, and there was Sanka too. (Both were favoured by the CRC "clientele" for their diuretic and laxative effects, essential to weight-loss sanity. There's really no way to accurately measure one's weight, if you know you're carrying around a half pound in your lower colon.)

So Max and Greg sipped on their Sanka while Keelan relayed his conversation with Jacinda on Skype. Greg, with rapt attention, and Max with a growing agitation and skepticism. He barely let Keelan say, "I think she's the one, guys," before he interrupted.

"Mark my words, Keelan, this is going to end badly. She's a NORMIE."

"I think we should stop using that word, Max. It just divides us further and makes us feel like there's a fat world for us and a regular world for everyone else."

"Fuck that naivety," Max interrupted again. "You're just setting yourself up for heartache. I've heard it all before. 'Oh, Max,

I love having a bit extra to hold onto. Oh, Max, you're so funny, I don't care about your double chin. Oh, Max, it's your giant cock I love, not your massive spare tire."

"Oh, really," Greg said, arching an eyebrow. Almost all the denizens of CRC-17 had seen one another naked at one time or another despite their most heroic efforts not to.

"It's a grower not a show-er!"

"Well, Max's pathetic member aside, I disagree. I think the whole idea of Fat Pride is just wrong-headed," Keelan said.

"Shhhhh!" Both Greg and Max shushed him.

"You want to get us killed?" Greg asked. "Barbara is just sitting right over there."

"We have a Babs?" Keelan asked.

"No! She's only Babs to her friends. And I've only heard Rita call her Babs," Greg said, "you know, without damage."

"I don't know what you're so afraid of, guys. I just don't think Fat Pride is a good plan."

"Well, you don't want to mess with it, man. That shit will fuck you up, yo," Max said. He made a peace sign just to show he wasn't being ironic. Greg glared at him and Max shrugged.

"Okay," Keelan said. He dropped his voice to a whisper and said, "I think it's a bad idea though. It makes the separation even more obvious."

"Like this place doesn't?" Max smirked.

"Granted. But we need to change our own thinking first. Then the world's."

"What about the obesity epidemic?" Greg asked.

"You think that's a real thing?" Max scoffed. "You're as naïve as Kee here. It's a set-up. It's a fucking MacGuffin."

The other two looked at him blankly.

"A MacGuffin? You know, a story device that is a distraction, that you think is the point of the plot, but really doesn't have much to do with it. Like Rosebud." He looked at the blank expressions on his friends' faces.

"Oh, for fuck's sake! *Citizen Kane*? The name of the guy's sled. Spoiler alert!"

Keelan twigged. "Oh, like the briefcase in *Pulp Fiction*."

"Thank god, you're not an idiot at least," Max said. "So yeah, the obesity epidemic. It's a fucking distraction. The whole thing isn't real."

"What?" Greg wondered. "It seems like there are more overweight people than when I was a kid. And the numbers don't lie, do they?"

"You know what they say about statistics," Max quipped. "But no, you're right on that count. There are more fat people. There are more humans. And humans are getting heavier. So that's true. No, the thing that is a lie is that it's an epidemic. In medical terms, an epidemic is when there is an infectious disease that affects an unexpectedly high proportion of a population in a short amount of time. People have been getting heavier for years and years. Since the '80s. But does this mean really bad outcomes for health? That's what I'm saying."

"Sure. Diabetes. Heart disease," Keelan said.

"But is that just because of fat, or are there other factors? There are lots of thin people with diabetes. Let me ask you, what makes people fat?"

Greg looked at Keelan. "Shall I take this softball?"

Keelan smiled and nodded.

"I'd say, in order, eating too much, not doing enough physical activity, and genetics –"

"Let me interrupt you there. If you ate too much cruciferous greens, that could possibly make you fat, but I doubt it – by the way, have you started the celery phase of your diet yet, Kee?"

"It begins tomorrow when they reopen the cafeteria. I've been eating soup and sandwiches like the rest of you. Glorious sandwiches."

Greg nodded his head, then looked depressed. He was thinking about the return to his pink goo.

"Anyway," Max continued, "it's not the excess of food that is the problem. It's poor nutrition. There's lots of evidence to show that even if someone isn't overweight, an excess of sugar can cause problems like diabetes, metabolic syndrome, and so on. But I'm getting sidetracked. All the original estimates of the health costs of the obesity 'epidemic' were based on data that lumped it all together."

"I'm not sure I follow," Keelan said.

"They didn't distinguish between overweight, obesity, nutrition, and physical activity in the figures at all. Hell, some of the studies they looked at only included women, or really small isolated populations with potential genetic factors. There was one study that looked exclusively at little people with high IQs who taste-tested chocolate-covered pretzels. The science, in other words, was bad," Max said.

"That's horrible."

"I know. Can you imagine a job like that, if you're real smart?" Greg said. "But I don't see how that makes the science bad."

"What?" Max got red in the face. "All this –" he gestured to the prison-like facility around them "– is created because of questionable science and all you can say is 'so'? Aren't you outraged?"

"I think you got it covered for all of us," Keelan said.

Max got quiet for a second, running his meaty hand through his wild red hair. "Okay, let me put this another way. You and Jacinda can't even go out on a date because of this bad science. This whole system is a sham. It's built for economic and political reasons, not for your health."

"So everyone here is lying to us?" Greg said. He was thinking of Cindy Vandenkieboom and how it would crush him if she was knowingly in on it.

"No, of course not. The beauty of a system like this is that everyone buys it, including the oppressors. They really need the ones being oppressed to buy into it. If you can't fool your victims into thanking you, then you're not a competent tyrant."

They were quiet for a moment, and Keelan realized that other denizens of the Fatness had been listening to Max.

"So what are you saying?" Keelan asked. "That we're just pawns in some elaborate chubby chess game?"

"Taffeta pudding wheels!" Max cried.

"Oh no, no absurdist bullshit. What does it mean?"

Max looked at Keelan and the other people sitting in the auditorium of the prison for fat people. The tension in the space was palpable.

"It means that I am a penguin … Bork."

The crowd moved away, returning to more sensible conversations, and when it was clear they were no longer paying attention to them, Max said, "Yes. We're pawns. But just because we're pawns doesn't mean we are powerless. Now, who wants more Sanka?"

"I'm not prepared for what may happen if I have another," Greg said.

"But what about Jacinda? How will we get together?" Keelan said, trying to keep the despair out of his voice.

"As far as I can see, you've got two choices. You can either get your fat ass out of here, which isn't nearly as fat as it was when you arrived, so you might actually succeed at that. Or you can help her make the system work better so that we can all leave without having to change our body composition."

"Or do both," Greg added.

"There you go," Keelan said. "I'll do both."

"Assuming you can survive five days of eating nothing but celery," Max said.

"If Greg can eat the pink vomit for a week and not lose his mind, I can hack a few days of celery."

"Who says Greg hasn't lost his mind?" Max asked.

"Yeah," Greg said. "Besides, it's not that bad once you get used to it." He tried to sound convincing, but nobody was buying it.

"Well, there's only five more days for both of you, and then you'll be back on the regular old low-nutritional-value crap they feed the rest of us cattle. So, moo, boys! Moo like you mean it!"

QUOTE

"If you live in rock and roll, as I do, you see the reality of sex, of male lust and women being aroused by male lust. It attracts women. It doesn't repel them."

~Camille Paglia

Chapter 7 – The Shining One

Jacinda walked into Christopher Ballard's office, feeling great. Not because she was going to meet with the man himself, but because she had a new-found purpose and drive. She was going to get Keelan out of the Fatness, and they were going to have a great, healthy relationship. For the first time in years, she was excited about her whole life. Work was fascinating. Her love life had actual promise, unlike her earlier dalliance with Ballard, or as she thought sarcastically of him now, "The Shining One".

And she didn't have to worry about her weight anymore.

It had been nearly two weeks since she'd last seen Ballard, so she was intrigued to see if she was as over him as she thought she was. Ballard's executive assistant waved Jacinda into his office, and she went in. He was standing at his window overlooking the city and talking into his s-phone. The late afternoon sun glinted through the windows and highlighted his perfect hair. He was wearing an expensive bespoke suit – probably something he'd had custom-made on his yearly sojourn to London, or Milan, or whichever European city was "the" place for power suits that year. She hated herself for noting how good his bum looked in the pants.

So maybe not completely over him. She sat down and waited for him to finish.

"That's great, honey. Yes, the plan is in place. I loved seeing you in Ottawa too. Next time we should plan to make a weekend of it. *Ciao.*"

He took off his earpiece and smiled at Jacinda.

"Thanks for coming in." He paused for a second and regarded her thoughtfully. "What's happened?"

"What do you mean?"

"You're glowing, Jacs. Positively glowing. And you've gained about five pounds, I'd say, which doesn't jibe with glowing. Unless …"

There was a pregnant pause.

"No, I'm not expecting," Jacinda supplied. "I'm just feeling good. As are you, clearly. So who's the honey?"

"Ah, my nickname for our client. She's a folksy one and prefers to keep the honorifics to a minimum."

"Honey?"

"Like I said, she enjoys it rural," Ballard said, smirking.

The Shining Douche, Jacinda thought, revising his nickname.

"So, my weight and your love life aside, why'd you need to meet with me?" Jacinda asked.

"Ah, to business. I guess it's best that way, isn't it? But I am intrigued by this glow of yours. It's very sexy, I have to say."

"Chris, you know that's sexual harassment."

"Oh, Jacs, please. I'd just have to show them the tape. Pre-existing relationship."

"I'm kidding."

"Of course you are. But seriously, what's up?"

"What do you mean?"

"First, I've never seen you dress so casually at the office before. And secondly, the glow. What's going on?" He stopped talking and looked at her for a long, uncomfortable moment. To Jacinda it felt like he was trying to see into her soul or something. It was beyond douchy. It was creepy.

"I got it. You're in love. Or at least you think you are."

"What?"

"You're in love. I knew I recognized that glow. So who's the lucky guy?"

"There is no guy."

"A woman? Now I *have* to know."

"There's nobody. Can you please just tell me why you wanted to meet? I have work to do."

"Wow, you really aren't as much fun as you used to be," Ballard groused. "But you're a damned good lawyer, so let's talk about our obese friends. How are they? I mean, apart from rioting because of Ben & Jerry's Chunky Monkey?" He watched her with bright eyes that Jacinda worried about immediately.

"So you caught that?"

"It was all over the news. I even caught Landon's own Serena

Lee on the tube, telling us the tele-tubby details. How does this help our client?"

"I'm not sure, really, because you won't tell me who our client is. But if you're asking how this is going to affect my report, I can tell you, not positively. I've learned some things that are kind of shocking. In fact, I think Lee may be trying to track down the same story. Did you know there is an organized crime ring in CRC-17 that smuggles in contraband?"

"I figured," Ballard said. "How else could you explain the general lack of weight loss in these facilities designed to help people lose weight?"

"Oh, there's lots of explanations for that. The first is that the calorie-in, calorie-out model is highly flawed. There's lots of evidence to suggest that all calories are not created equal too, and that it takes more than just a diet to really lose weight."

Ballard's eyes started to glaze over. "Science, yeuch. So messy."

"Like law isn't?"

"Granted. But human nature isn't. Very easy to manage as a lawyer if you've got human nature figured out. But I'll take your point. So the thermodynamics approach to weight loss is a bust. But surely an illegal pipeline of Ho Hos and Frito-Lays isn't helping people lower their BMI?"

"Of course. But here's the part that is kind of amazing. I had several inmates –"

"Wait, did you just say 'inmates'?"

"Yeah. Because that is what they are. They are residents of a prison/hospital for fat people. I think we need to stop being so cute about what we call them."

"I don't think our client is going to like that term. Do a find and replace when we're done this meeting, okay? Use the word *client, customer,* or even better, *guest.* Definitely. *Guest* is best there. They'll love that."

"Okay," Jacinda said. Ultra-douche or not, Ballard was still her boss. *And goddamnit,* she thought, *why the fuck am I thinking about him naked?* "Anyway. Several, uh, *guests* said that the CRC administration was in on the deal to allow contraband food into the institution. The deal between the crime syndicate – they're called the "Heavy Hitters", by the way – the deal with them and the administration is that if CRC-17's gross tonnage continues to drop, they'll let in the food."

"Clever. So if the aggregate weight of the ... *guests* ... continues to come down, then the director will look good, even if very few *guests* get to leave. That is pretty frickin' smart."

That was high praise coming from an angle-cutter like Christopher Ballard, Jacinda thought.

"Interesting. I think we'll have to get this information to the SubOb folks as fast as a frog in a frying pan," Ballard said.

"A frog in a frying pan?"

"Just trying to be folksy."

"I would avoid it, Chris. It's not your strong suit. Witty and erudite is more your thing, assuming you remember to flash that smile," Jacinda said.

"Look at you. Edgy."

"So what shall I do?"

"Write it up and then send it to me. The local CRC isn't enough though. We need to be able to demonstrate this is happening in other places. So you're going to need to dig elsewhere."

"Okay," Jacinda said. She didn't want to get too far away from Keelan though. "Any idea how I'll do that? I just got lucky finding out about this locally. I have a good source."

"You said Serena Lee was working on the same story? Let's tell her what we know, on the condition that she doesn't go on the air with it until we have proof that it's happening elsewhere. Sound good?"

"Okay. I'll set up a meeting with her."

"Damn, I'd love to see the two of you in the same room, but I'll have to stay out of the meeting, okay?"

Ew, Jacinda thought.

"Okay," she agreed, and headed to the door.

"At least you put most of that five pounds in the right place," Ballard said as she left the room.

MYTH

Negative Calories

Many dieters like to believe that celery has negative calories –
that is, human beings burn more calories chewing the vegetable
than they actually get from ingesting it. Unfortunately, this is a
myth.

Celery *is* a powerful choice for dieters in other ways.
Celery is sexy. The veggie is loaded with androstenone and andro-
stenol, two pheromones associated with arousal and attraction.
(This only makes one attractive to women, so if you're trying to
attract a guy, it won't work.) Celery has a low glycemic load and
has lots of great nutrients, like riboflavin, vitamin B6, magnesium
and phosphorus. It's a good source of dietary fiber, vitamin A,
vitamin C, vitamin K, folate, potassium and manganese.

On the downside, it tastes like celery.

Chapter 8 – You Deserve a Break Today

It was day five of the celery fast, as Keelan was now thinking of his trips to the Calorie Dispensing Hall. Sure, he would eat some of the celery they gave him, but after a couple of days he really couldn't be bothered eating it. He suspected he was burning more calories by chewing than he was actually taking in via the vegetable. If not for the two days of sandwiches he'd eaten after the riot, he suspected he might be starving.

He was in trouble, no doubt.

It felt as though he was in some kind of weird dream. Everything he did progressed so slowly and, at the same time, it was as though the world had accelerated. He still met with Greg and Max for their morning coffee, which Keelan was not allowed to have. (The attendants did acquiesce to a bit of hot water with a slice of lemon in it, so he had something to drink.) He couldn't tell you what they'd talked about over the past week.

The only moments that seemed to have any reality were the evening conversations he'd been having with Jacinda over Skype. He looked forward to them the way a five-year-old anticipates the arrival of Santa. His attention could be diverted momentarily, but his focus always returned to the moment of truth, with similar thoughts as a five-year-old. *When will it happen, exactly? I hope I don't fall asleep before it happens. Did I do anything wrong? OMG, I'm So excited!*

But it was only mid-afternoon. He'd fallen asleep in his cell and awoke to the sound of someone opening his door, which he'd left unlocked. A person sat next to his sleeping form and gently shook his shoulder.

"Keelan," a tiny voice said.

"What?" Keelan replied, still mostly asleep. In fact, was he dreaming this?

"You need to wake up and talk to me."

Keelan opened his eyes. His vision was covered with a skein of gauze. The form sitting on the bed next to him was opaque, and something about it was odd. A charge of adrenaline spiked the hair on his neck, and he woke up.

A tiny figure stood in front of his face, filling his field of vision. It was white. And kind of chubby-looking, though it was hard to tell, as it was so close to his eyes. Keelan could see that the only form of clothing the … thing … was wearing was a tiny little chef's hat and a scarf of some kind. It was aggressively white. Except for two piercing blue eyes – which weirdly didn't have any pupils – and some kind of blue circle in the middle of the chef's hat.

"Wake up, Keelan. We've gotta talk," the creature said, in a voice that could only be described as insanely high-pitched and deliciously friendly.

Keelan lifted himself up on one elbow, and the creature rocked with his movement. It really was tiny, probably standing only about seven or eight inches tall. As he pulled back, Keelan could read the tiny letters in the blue badge on the creature's toque: Pillsbury.

"What the fuck?"

"Nothing says lovin' like somethin' from the oven," the figure piped.

"Oh boy," Keelan said. "I've snapped."

"No, you haven't, Kee. You're just hungry for some love!"

"In the form of, uh, corporate mascots?"

"No, silly. Baking! You love it! Everybody does. How about a crescent roll? Or even better? Some toaster strudel. You'll bust a nut over my strudel, slut!"

"What? No, the Pillsbury Doughboy doesn't … what's happening?"

"Now poke me in the stomach, you frickin' pansy, or I won't make you some nice buttery biscuits."

"I say, I say, did somebody say biscuits?" another voice said. It sounded eerily familiar, and Keelan looked around the room. From behind the screened-off toilet area of his cell, he could hear the voice say, "You know, boy, I say, boy, do you know how good biscuits would taste with a bit of chicken?"

"Who are you?" Keelan said.

"I'm your fortnightly friend, boy!"

From behind the screen, Colonel Sanders appeared. He was wearing his trademark white suit, with black tie and glasses. He stroked the chin strip under his mustache and said, "You have been hiding from me for too long, boy."

"What?" Keelan could not keep the terror from his voice. He didn't remember Colonel Sanders being quite as menacing as he was. He wasn't exactly a tall man, but there was something predatory in his gaze.

"That's a joke, I say that's a joke, son."

"He doesn't realize how serious this is!" the Pillsbury Doughboy said.

"Serious? But you're the Pillsbury Doughboy. How serious could this be?" Keelan squeaked.

"Call me Poppin' Fresh, you mutherfucker! What's it going to be, buns or crescent rolls? Now, poke me in the stomach and we'll get started."

"I can't just –"

"Poke me, bitch!" The little white mascot advanced menacingly at Keelan.

The Colonel came forward and gently pulled Poppin' Fresh back. "Stop, I say stop it, boy. You're doin' alot of choppin' but no chips are flyin'. Let me talk to him."

"Is this a dream?" Keelan wondered.

"No, this is not a dream, boy, but this is not exactly reality. Now, are you sure everyone is here?"

"I'm … uh …" Keelan looked around the tiny room. Apart from Poppin' Fresh and Colonel Sanders, there didn't seem to be anyone else there.

"What I mean to say, boy, is: are we neglecting anybody else that you miss?"

Keelan just looked confused.

Colonel Sanders turned to the diminutive pastry chef and said, "That boy's about as sharp as a bowling ball. I keep pitchin' 'em and he keeps missin' 'em."

"He's a fuckin' retard," Poppin' said. "Worse than my brother in the tire business. If he doesn't poke me soon, I'm gettin' my hurt on."

"Let's not go there again, son," Sanders said. "You'd better give him what he wants. You don't know how violent he gets when he doesn't get his due."

Keelan just nodded and poked his index finger into Poppin' Fresh's doughy stomach. "Hoo-hoo!" Poppin' said.

"Wait a minute," Keelan said to the Colonel. "You don't talk like that!"

"Sure I do, boy. You're just not a-membering the way you should." He whispered to the doughboy and twirled a finger next to his head. "Nice mannered kid, just a little on the dumb side."

"Foghorn Leghorn."

"Got me, boy. But you only have yourself to blame. Can't re-member what I actually sound like, come to think of it! Now that we're done with the bona fides, let's get to my last question – who are we missing? Oh no, not him!"

The clown appeared just at the end of the bed and lifted a giant red shoe onto the mattress.

"Hey, buddy, how's it going?"

"Not so good, Ronald. They keep feeding me celery."

"Uh-oh. Not so good. Yeah, not so good."

"Don't pester the lad with your hare-brained impersonations, boy! He's starvin' to death," Colonel Sanders said. With the clown in the room, the Colonel seemed a lot less threatening. Keelan's eyes widened as he watched the face of the clown darken, which was quite a trick given the pancake makeup he was wearing. The clown frowned, and despite the exaggerated smile drawn on his face, Keelan could tell he was angry.

The makeup looked almost like blood at that instant, and Keelan wondered what was going on. He used to love all of this food. He remembered some of the most incredibly happy mo-ments of his childhood, opening up that brightly coloured box. The smell of French fries was the smell of love. Now the beloved purveyor of Happy Meals was doing what Keelan thought was an impersonation of Dustin Hoffman as Rainman and looking positively murderous.

Keelan wasn't lovin' it.

"I can't believe I have to be in the same room as you … again," the clown rumbled at the Colonel.

"It's those eleven herbs and spices, boy. They are addictive."

"Maximum crave." The clown nodded. "Just like my fries. Nice." They high-fived one another.

Other things started to appear in the room. A giant peanut wearing a monocle and a top hat. Some kind of disembodied head with an old-timey mustache. A cheetah with an oversized head and white sneakers.

"Oh, fuck," Poppin' Fresh said. "He's really on a roll now."

"It'll get worse, I've seen it before. He hasn't even thought of breakfast foods yet," the Colonel observed.

"Don't give him ideas," the clown rumbled.

But it was too late. All the favourites started to appear. The chocolate vampire. The pink Frankenstein's monster. A leprechaun materialized next to Poppin' Fresh on the pillow, and they immediately got into a fistfight as it said, "I'm magically delicious!"

"Pull them apart, would you, Chocula?" the Colonel ordered.

"I'm outta here," Ronald said. "I don't share time with these lowlifes. Especially the cereals. That's just … I mean, they are just so supermarket."

The giant peanut twirled his cane and asked in a Virginian accent, "Did anyone else think it was weird that I was basically promoting a form of cannibalism? I mean, that's what it is when you eat your own kind, even if we are perfectly roasted and salted?"

Keelan's eyes got wider as the old-timey mustache figure swirled and looped around to a weird kind of popping sound. This seemed to spur a similar activity in all of the other mascots – they couldn't help themselves. They just fell into their patter. Poppin' Fresh became even more foul-mouthed in an attempt to have himself heard. The Colonel and the clown just stepped back, watching the mayhem.

There was a rumble, and all the mascots stopped talking as the room started to shake.

"What now?"

"Ah, the drinks," the Colonel said. "Bound to happen."

The wall burst open, masonry flying through the room, crushing the small mascots completely and causing all kinds of horrific injuries to the others. The peanut with the monocle was decapitated, and a disturbing jet of blood came out of its neck. As the dust settled, Keelan saw there was a giant glass jug of red liquid with a happy face standing there.

"Oh yeah!" it said.

Mercifully, Keelan passed out.

QUOTE

"They are as sick that surfeit with too much as they are that starve with nothing."

~William Shakespeare, *The Merchant of Venice*

Chapter 9 – When the Chips Are Down

As he ate his second bag of all-dressed, extra-crinkled chips that day, Colin Taggart reflected on how great a month he was having.

The riot had just been the start of something really big for the Heavy Hitters. Once the lockdown was over, the pent-up demand for junk food had been higher than normal, and the ad hoc diet of sandwiches and soup plus no Mickey Dees imported into the CRC meant there was a noticeable drop in the gross tonnage. He got the figure on a monthly basis from Seward, and they agreed upon the amount of food and alcohol Taggart could bring in based on that amount. It wasn't exactly scientific, but it had worked so far. CRC-17 still had the best gross tonnage of any facility in the entire country!

And of course, Taggart had taken the opportunity of the riot to have a go at the major power centres that still opposed the rule of the Heavy Hitters. With two of their leaders in the infirmary, the Neckheads were no longer a concern, and all the major toilet distilleries in the Fatness were taken out. (One enterprising individual was still cranking out a drinkable rice wine, somehow.) There was a disproportionately large population of aboriginal Canadians in the CRCs, just as there were too many in the regular prisons – but they tended to keep to themselves, and they liked their smokes and junk food too. They called themselves the FBI, and Taggart gave them a discount to keep them bloated and relatively docile.

And his connections with organized crime had finally paid off – in addition to supplying him with drugs that CRC inmates wanted, they'd helped him set up a network of Heavy Hitters in CRCs across the country.

He was building an empire. As an enterprise, the Heaver Hitters were making way more money for him than the mostly legal porn sites he owned. He had enough to bankroll the required "lubrication" to get HH chapters going in other CRCs, whether that simply be a taste of the profits for administrators (unlikely, because as a class, the fear of getting caught outweighed their love of money), a bit of friendly "persuasion" or simply a well-marshaled argument with scientific and bureaucratic background showing how they could lower their gross tonnage too.

He chuckled to himself and wiped crumbs off his chest. He was lying in his bed in his plus-sized cell (he'd asked Seward to tear down the wall between two regular sized cells). His laptop was open, and he was looking at sales projections. His meaty hand went into the "party-sized" bag for another handful of the delicious, salty, absolutely necessary chips, and the rotund fingers only found crumbs. He'd already eaten his second bag? *Holy shit,* he thought. *What's going on? I'm having a good month here, not one where I need two bags of chips in a sitting.* Compounding the sadness he felt at having finished the bag, which included enough calories to keep him going all day if he had to, was a tickle of something approaching conscience. Not guilt, exactly, but a form of self-loathing that he sometimes felt when he went overboard.

He determined to feel better. He had a bag of chocolate-dipped pretzels that he'd been saving for just such an occasion.

Besides, things *were* going well. He even had that pain-in-the-ass doctor, Tundra, talking to him on friendly terms.

That had been a real coup. He knew Tundra hated him, but he also knew that his friends really wanted to get out of the CRC without having their legs removed. The answer was obvious, if extremely illegal: diet drugs.

As yet, the Canadian health authorities hadn't approved any of the newer weight-loss pharmaceuticals. Even herbal supplements like hoodia were forbidden. Certainly nothing as dangerous as ephedra. According to the lawmakers, weight loss was about a healthy lifestyle and good science. No easy fixes.

He heaved himself out of the bed to look for those pretzels. Taggart was a big guy, in stature as well as girth. At six feet, he carried his 290 pounds remarkably well. But he was still obese by any measure. His calorie supervisor, Brittany, was forever encouraging him to at least bring his BMI down from a ridiculous 39.3 to a number that would take him out of the second class of obesity. But since the ascendancy of the Heavy Hitters and the amount of junk food they smuggled into the facility, Taggart had only gained weight. He had to be careful he didn't gain too much though.

CRC-17 was not rated for anyone in the "morbidly" obese category, so really, they didn't get much wider than Taggart in the Fatness. And if he gained ten more pounds, he would reach that morbidly obese category.

I remember when we were all just fat, Taggart thought as he stood, his legs wobbling a bit under his weight. *Now there are levels of obesity,* he thought, *and I don't want to become a jabba.*

He breathed heavily as he bent over to pull out his personal locker under the bed. It had a biometric scan – he swiped his fingerprint to open the lock – and it also had a refrigerated compartment in it for drinks and such. All the Heavy Hitter ice cream was stored in the Calorie Dispensing facilities by mutual agreement with Seward. (If this stash was ever discovered in a raid, Taggart had arranged for one of the guards to say it was his, so that Seward et al. would not lose their jobs.) The locker opened with a hiss and Taggart was transported by the wide variety of snacks available. There were several such lockers in the facility, controlled by those whom Taggart trusted, but this was the best stocked.

He groaned as he kneeled down in front of the food locker, looking for the salty-sweet pretzels that had got him out of the bed.

Taggart could see the appeal of being a bed-bound jabba sometimes, he really could. 39 BMI was a number to the system, Taggart realized. And 40 would just be another number. But that number would take him out of the CRC and into one of the facilities designed for the morbidly obese, where they would watch his food intake very carefully and possibly even cut out part of his stomach. He did not want the surgery. Once a patient had the gastric surgery, it was extremely dangerous to eat too much.

Of course, Taggart could afford to pay for his own health

care, if it ever came to that, but he liked being a big man in the Fatness.

As his hands rummaged in the locker, he considered his health. He was getting older. Most of his hair was gone, and though he thought his bald head looked okay, he knew that it was only one sign of his impending death. A death that his morbid obesity was surely going to bring about faster.

He started breathing heavily. For a man of his weight, the simplest tasks, like hauling your fat ass out of bed, could make you short of breath. Standing for a few minutes, let alone hours, felt like you were running a marathon. *Everything makes me sweat. Just being alive makes you sweat when you're a manatee,* Taggart thought. Stairs were a crucible, if not an outright mortal threat.

His fingers found the bag of pretzels, and though every cell in his body was crying out for the snack, he let go and slammed the locker shut. *What was the point of being the head honcho if you died too young?* He stood there, sweating. Part of him desperately wanted the pretzels, and part of him knew he had to get the overeating under control. But he was just so ... hungry. He got back on the bed and stared at nothing.

Up to that moment, he'd been having a great month.

FACT

The Moving Target of Morbid

It says something that we never had the term *morbid obesity* until the 1960s. In 1969, the *American Journal of Surgery* declared:

> "We identify morbid obesity as existing in any person whose weight has reached a level two or three times his ideal weight and who has maintained this level of obesity for five years or more."

Since then, the definition of morbid has gotten more stringent, from twice ideal weight (no time limit) to 40 BMI. Today's definition is more rigorous. Morbidly obese people have a BMI of 40, or a BMI of 35 along with other problems such as sleep apnea, diabetes, and cardiac troubles. This reflects a greater understanding of extreme obesity's dangers, and also the increase in population that would fit this designation.

And there's no joke that can be made here. At least not tastefully.

Chapter 10 – A Mother's Love

"So, I see you're eating again."

"What?"

"Well, it's obvious that you've been eating carbs, based on what your posterior looks like, my dear."

"You mean my butt?" Jacinda said. Her father had been born in Toronto, but moved to New York and fallen in love with her mother, who was a blue-blooded Yankee. The word *butt* was not in her vocabulary, and Jacinda knew it.

Jacinda was visiting her mother in Rosedale, an older, yet upscale part of Toronto. Their house had once been owned by the founder of the Toronto-Dominion Bank, and her parents had purchased it from him in the early seventies when Rosedale was the *most* upscale part of TO. All of Toronto's "old money" had lived there and they wanted to cash in on that cachet. Like the neighbourhood, Jacinda's mother had experienced a general decline in her expectations, but she was fighting the trend as far as her daughter went.

"That is not a word a young lady uses."

"Mom, I hate to break it to you, but I am not a young lady. I'm a woman. I'm not even young anymore. I'm middle aged. When you were my age, I was ten. Reagan was still president."

"And who was the prime minister? You're Canadian, young lady."

"I'm a dual citizen. And it was … uh, Brian Mulroney?" Jacinda hated that the answer came out like a question, even though she knew she was right.

"Correct, young lady."

"Mom!"

"Fine. You modern girls are so hard to figure out."

Jacinda sighed heavily. She didn't want to have this particular conversation again, because she really couldn't take it right now. Her mother had the luck to be born into a generation where women still had a choice between working and raising a family, and the misfortune that their husbands expected the latter and resented the former. Her dad had been so successful that there had been no question – her mother wouldn't work. But in the past few years, Jacinda had wondered if that had been such a great decision.

Sure, her mother had bridge clubs, book clubs, and a short-lived, esoteric club devoted to books about bridges, to occupy her time, but was it enough? Her family was all in New York, and though she'd been accepted by the hoi polloi of upper-crust Toronto (in fact, she was well regarded by the blue bloods of Upper Canada), she'd never flourished there. Truth be told, she looked down on the idea of "old" money in Canada. It was undemocratic, and she'd been raised to believe that worth was not inherited. (Even though, in her case, it manifestly was.) It was an attitude of superiority that really had no basis in fact, but it was so real that Jacinda had never really questioned it.

Until now.

"We're really not hard to understand. Imagine that you have complete control over your life, and then do things that you think will make you feel fulfilled and happy. That's what we do. We get it wrong, but that's the underlying motivation, Mommy dearest."

"So you think that I never wanted to be happy or fulfilled?"

"No, I'm not saying that." Jacinda sighed. "But your parameters were so different from mine. Why can't you see that?"

"Don't shout at me. I understand that you grew up in difficult circumstances. Your father's passing made life hard. Can you imagine how bad it would have been if I'd had to support us afterwards too?"

Jacinda didn't say anything. She loved her mother, and the last thing she wanted to do was hurt her. But Jacinda really believed that if her mother hadn't had their father's life insurance policy and her family's deep pockets to support them after his death, they would have been better off. She would have had to get a job. And she might have been able to understand her daughter, just a little bit.

So Jacinda just stood there in the kitchen, holding her glass of sherry, trying to understand where her mother was coming from.

But her mother just ruined it all and said, "Your bust is bigger
too. Are you dating a negro?"

"What?"

"I understand they enjoy large breasts and posteriors, so it just
stands to reason."

"Mother!"

"Oh, please. I'm not racist –"

"Says every racist before they utter something unspeakable.
But you're right. I've gained five pounds. I'm not dating an
African-Canadian man, but it would be okay if I did."

"Of course," her mother said. She held her breath.

"I am in love though," Jacinda admitted.

"And you've GAINED weight? Normally women lose weight
when they meet someone."

"What?"

"Men won't like you if you pork up after you start going out."

"Pork up?"

"I'm sorry, dear. That was crass. But you know what I mean.
Your figure is your best friend, man-wise. It is the only thing you
have control over, after all. I mean, you're lucky that you've got
a fine mix of genes working for you – more of your father's than
mine, thank God – but your face will only get you so far. Men
say they love eyes and smiles and … but they're terrible, my dear.
Men are just terrible …"

Jacinda realized that she had been a bit late turning up for
her biweekly lunch with her mother and she asked, "How much
sherry have you had?"

"Just a glass."

Jacinda didn't believe her. "Would you like me to serve the
lunch?"

"No, I'll manage. But you should know, my love, that men
care about your body more than your mind or even your pretty
face."

"I've been around a bit."

"But your body …"

"What's wrong with my body?"

"Nothing. But you've inherited your father's genes there. You got his fine features – you are so much like him – but you also tend to fat, my love. You have to fight it!"

"Or I'll end up alone?"

"Yes!"

Jacinda was shocked to see her mother start weeping. They were not histrionic tears, either.

"I'm not going to live forever, Jacinda! You have to find a man and make a life for yourself."

"But I've met someone."

"You have? Really?"

Jacinda was touched by how happy her mother seemed. She'd never felt it before, though she knew, intellectually, that her mother loved her. But it was gratifying to see it.

"So tell me about him," her mother said.

"Ah." Jacinda stalled. "He's wonderful."

Jacinda experienced a moment of exquisite pain. The kind of pain that comes when you realize the truth of something. She realized that her mother would never understand her attraction to Keelan. This was an understanding that her mother's approval was conditional, even if her love was not. And like every child, Jacinda resented her parent for this withholding of approval. For above all, what every child craves from their parents is not love – that is expected and normal and right – what every child wants, in the depths of their soul, is the commendation of their parents.

And she knew that she was not going to get it.

"What does he do?"

"He works at Hellmuth University," Jacinda said.

"Oh, that's nice. An intellectual."

"He's a web designer there, on staff."

"But still, he works in an intellectual workplace. That has to rub off, doesn't it?"

"He is quite bright. And funny. And he's so sweet."

"How did you meet him?"

"While I was working," Jacinda said.

"On campus? I didn't know you had the university as a client, my dear."

"We don't. We're working for the government, and that's how our paths crossed."

"But where? My dear, I won't be satisfied until I hear the whole thing."

Jacinda sighed. She knew what her mother was going to think, but she told her the truth. "He's in the CRC. I'm doing work for Ballard there, learning all I can about the system for a report to the subcommittee in charge of it."

"He's fat!"

"Technically, yes, but he carries it very well, Mom. If he wasn't in the CRC, you'd never guess."

"How could you? It catches, Jacinda, you know that, right? Fat is contagious. I read a story about it. No, don't say anything. Let me find the article. I clipped it out of the paper to show to you."

And true to her word, her mother produced the article, which quoted medical studies that suggested that there was a correlation between having overweight friends and romantic partners increased the possibility that their subjects would also be overweight. It made a certain amount of sense, Jacinda had to acknowledge. If you were surrounded by heavy people, that might tend to skew your perception of what a normal weight would be.

A tear formed in her eye, and she said to her mother, "But he's so lovely. He's kind and funny and not like any other man I've ever been involved with, Mom. I don't care that he's overweight."

"Obese. He's obese if he's in there."

"Barely! His BMI is just over 30. He's going to get out."

"Oh, really, just like that fancy lawyer of yours was going to propose to you? Or how that married man you had adultery with was going to leave his wife?"

Jacinda grimaced, preparing herself for the long litany of failed relationships that her mother seemed to enjoy flogging her with. But the list ended there, thankfully.

"I don't care. He's going to get out. I'm going to help him get out."

"Oh, you're not going to support him, are you?" her mother asked. The look of horror on her face was so genuine that Jacinda couldn't help but laugh.

"Would that be the worst thing in the world? I can afford it."

"No! You can't do that, Jacinda. He would never thank you for that. Besides, what if the relationship doesn't work out? Do you want to be stuck with paying for his health care for the rest of your life? That's what you're talking about, isn't it?"

"That's the only reasonable point you've had. But you're missing the important one – the thought of him makes me happy, really happy."

Her mother stared at her and shook her head. She tossed off the rest of her sherry, and said, "Well, let's have some lunch, and at least let me try to dissuade you. You can be as stubborn as your father when you have an idea in your head, but I have hopes. Dreams. I see you with a handsome man."

"Keelan is handsome. He's quite striking, actually."

"But fat."

"Yes, but he's getting thinner. And he's healthy. Healthier than a lot of skinny people, I'd bet."

"That doesn't matter. It's all about appearances, Jacinda, don't you get that?"

"I reject that idea."

"I know you do." Her mother started to cry. "And it terrifies me."

QUOTE

"I believe in karma. That means I can do bad things to people all day long and I assume they deserve it."

~Dogbert

Chapter 11 – Time's Arrow and InstaKarma

Brittany was giddy with glee. Keelan had lost nearly six pounds, bringing him ever closer to his target weight.

"It looks like the Freedom Fries did a good job," she gushed. "You're less than ... ten pounds from your target weight, Keelan. Great work! And that's even with the two-day break in the plan. Can you imagine how much you would have lost if not for the riot?"

"Brittany, I have to ask you something though."

"What, Keelan? You can ask me anything."

"Is it normal to hallucinate when you're dieting?"

"No. That is not a side effect you should see." Something happened to Brittany's face at that moment. Kee couldn't tell quite what it was, but he interpreted it as her trying to look serious. She just looked confused. Or constipated. "Tell me what happened."

Keelan relayed the thrill of having some of the most famous corporate food mascots come and taunt him during a mild psychotic break.

"Oh, you're pulling my leg," Brittany said. "Seriously, stop pulling. It's not going to get any longer."

Keelan wondered what the hell that meant. Brittany had the strangest way of taking a cliché and making it her own. Keelan briefly wondered what she might be like in bed. Probably athletic and afraid to put anything in her mouth. He shook the thought away and tried to respond honestly.

"No, I'm not. I really had the experience. I think I may have been half-asleep while it happened, but I wonder if I shouldn't talk to someone."

"Like a psychiatrist?"

"If you think I should."

"Well, I don't, you silly goose. And even if I did, we don't have access to a psychiatrist. If you think the stress of living here is an issue, I believe there is coverage for you to speak with a psychologist once every six weeks or so."

"What's the difference?"

"Between a psychologist and a psychiatrist? One has a PhD and the other uses drugs, but I think I may have misspoken myself," Brittany said, using her "serious" face again. "We don't have access to either professional group. I can get you into see the therapist though!"

"Therapist?"

"I think she does talk therapy, like a psychologist would, but she has a social work degree, not a psych degree. She's super healthy and her BMI is the same as mine!"

Keelan wasn't sure that skinniness was a great recommendation for mental health. Sometimes it felt like Brittany was another species than him. *Homo slenderins.* Or perhaps the porkers and manatees in the CRC were the other species, but it seemed to Keelan there was a massive gulf between the two groups, and it made it hard for one to help the other. It took a special quality to be thin and help the fat lose weight: humanity.

Tyrell had it. He saw Keelan and Greg as just a couple of guys who had a weight problem. As opposed to Brittany and most of the medical profession, who saw a weight problem that just happened to be attached to a couple of guys.

"Let's put a pin in that for a moment. So what's the next strategy?"

"Oh, good. I love to move forward," Brittany said. "Moving forward is the best way to move, isn't it?"

"Well, when it comes to the passage of time, we have no other way to go," Keelan replied. "I agree it's good to move towards a goal; and mine is to get the hell out of here."

"I don't blame you. This place is great. But, you know."

Keelan didn't reply to that. She was clearly not supposed to say anything bad about the CRC, even if she was massively creeped out by the fatties inhabiting it.

"Do you like working in the Fatness?"

"Oh, we don't call it that. And yes, I love helping people become healthy."

"Even the really fat ones that don't want to do anything? I mean, I like to exercise. But what about all the manatees that won't get off their fat asses and do anything to burn some calories."

"I'm not sure what you mean by manatees."

"The really fat ones. The plus sizes in the 35 plus range."

"Oh, you mean the class II obesity cases," she said. The serious face again. "That is a dangerous weight class to be in. At 30 BMI you run a certain number of risks, but they aren't too horrible. But at 35 plus, things get more serious. Your chance of complications like diabetes, high blood pressure, and other issues increase. And your lifespan drops by at least four to six years in that class."

"And how do you feel about working with them?"

"I feel great," Brittany said. Though her body language said the exact opposite. Something like: "I'd rather claw my own eyes out than look at them."

"Yeah, they're kinda hot when they get that big, aren't they?" Keelan said.

The look on Brittany's face was priceless. He thought she might throw up, or perhaps she just did, a little bit, in her mouth.

"Uh, no. Being spectacularly unhealthy is not a turn-on," Brittany said. She brightened up and said, "But let's keep your good trend going, shall we? That will turn on the ladies!"

"Even you?" Keelan just couldn't help himself.

"Okay, let's get to our plan!"

"Brittany, I think you should know that I think about you a lot. A lot. You know how lonely it gets in here, right? And we're not allowed to go into the women's wing, and vice versa, so really all we can do is –"

"So here's the plan," Brittany interrupted Keelan, who was trying not to laugh. "It's all about calories in, calories out. And we're going to really bear down on the first part of that equation – I see you're doing a lot of exercise."

"Yes, let's bare down," he said, waggling his eyebrows. What she said was true. Except for the days of the lockdown and the last few days of his celery cleanse, when he felt incredibly weak, Keelan had stuck to his workout regime.

"Seriously, Keelan," Brittany said, doing her serious face again. It really did look like she needed to use the toilet. "I think you're a wonderful man, but I'm a professional calorie supervisor, and I can't get involved with my patients, can I? I'd hate to resign from your case, especially now that you're doing so well."

Keelan saw an opportunity to get rid of her, then. Not that it had been his intention when he'd begun the interview. He was just having some fun, and, yes, a small measure of revenge for the celery cleanse. But could he really make her feel so uncomfortable that she had to put another calorie supervisor on his file? And besides, he might find her skinny perkiness annoying, but she was getting results.

"I understand, Brittany. I'm sorry I even mentioned it. I knew it was … forbidden."

"Actually, it's not forbidden, but it's not professional. And I am professional. Now, let's talk about your poops!"

The upshot of his meeting with Brittany had been that they were trying a new approach – a high-fiber approach that sounded … just awful. Though that was the goal, wasn't it? Reducing the AWFUL. His new diet was going to be high in fiber. Excessive in fiber. Ludicrous in fiber. If she had been allowed to legally force him to eat cardboard, Keelan was sure that he'd be chowing down on the boxes that contained the generic rice-puff nightmare that his compatriots ate for breakfast. (Not that it would taste much worse.)

So Keelan was dropping by Colin Taggart's cell, hoping to do a little business.

At the very least, he was going to get a crate of super-soft toilet paper delivered to him – this was not an illegal item, but the TP that was provided by the CRC was a bit on the rough side, and Keelan was expecting that he'd need something a little gentler for the foreseeable future. He looked at the menu plan Brittany had drawn up for him and shook his head. The first day alone was a nightmare:

Breakfast – one cup bran with a half-cup skim milk. (He read that again. Yes, it was bran, not bran flakes or something with added bran. He would be eating raw bran.) One-half orange.

Snack – ten almonds and a small apple.

Lunch – cabbage, ten cups, chopped. Raw.

Snack – chick peas, raw. (Half cup.)

Dinner – bean medley, three cups. (The menu did not describe what beans would be making up the medley, but Keelan was pretty sure what kind of tune would emerge from him after said repast.) Broccoli. (Raw, of course.)

"I gotta get out of here," he said, his eyes tearing up as he started to scan the details of day two and saw that lunch would include a repast of raw celery. He knocked on Taggart's door.

"What?"

"I've got a business proposal," Keelan said.

Keelan heard the man wheeze as he got out of bed and shuffled to the door. It slid open a crack and Taggart said, "You? Where's your crazy commie friend?"

"Max? He's no commie."

"He doesn't seem to like business."

"He just doesn't appreciate your monopoly. But I'm here without him and I have some business I'd like to discuss."

"Okay, come in."

Keelan entered Taggart's cell and was surprised at the size. He'd never heard that the criminal had a double cell all to himself.

"Nice," Keelan said, trying to ignore the smell of body odour and what was clearly a bag of Doritos that was sitting open on Taggart's bed. "You've got Diabetos," Keelan noted.

"Funny," Taggart said. "And you can't have any unless you have the cash. I'll give you a handful for ten bucks."

Keelan thought about it, but he knew he was in a similar situation as a heroin dealer offering him some for free. "I'm here for two things. The first should be easy to get – some soft toilet paper."

"I probably have some on hand," Taggart said, "but why

should I sell any of it to you?"

"Because of the second thing I want. And what I'm willing to do for them."

"Okay, now you have my attention. But I don't go in for any gay stuff."

"No, not that," Keelan said, trying not to say, "Ew." He was mildly shocked by the insta-karma for teasing Brittany just earlier that day. "I want some diet pills, and I'm willing to help you sell them too. I'll even see if Max will help."

"Really?"

"Yes. Colin – can I call you Colin? I have got to get out of here. Look at what they've got me eating." Keelan showed him the menu and Taggart started laughing. It went on for a minute.

"Okay," Keelan said, "that's enough."

"Hahaha." Taggart's laughter trailed off. "You're going to be super-popular on this mix! Remind me never to get downwind."

Keelan bit off a quip about Taggart's body odour and said, "Please, I need to get out of here. They're going to fire me next week. Maybe with diet pills I can lose the last bit."

"If you help me out, I'll make sure you can ignore these menus from now on."

"No, I'll go with this nightmarish menu, because it's so extreme it *has* to work. But I want to ensure it. What diet drugs can you get?"

"Nothing safe," Taggart said. "Well, maybe I can get a lead on some phentermine. Would that do?"

"Will it help me lose weight?"

"Of course. But there are side effects, not least of which, you work for me from now on. Unless you've got the money to pay."

"You know I don't."

"Then welcome to the Heavy Hitters."

FACT

A Disgusting Bullet

Humans have been searching for the magic bullet – a pill or simple remedy they could take to help them lose weight – for centuries. Probably the most horrifying of these was the tapeworm diet, which was popular in the early twentieth century. There were plenty of ads advertising pills that would – purportedly – give the dieter a tapeworm. Your new best buddy would take up residence in your gut and start absorbing the calories you ate. Voila! Weight loss.

Of course, there would be side effects if a tapeworm did start growing in you. First, it would not only absorb calories, it would absorb the nutrients you need to survive. And you might be able to manage this for a while, but when they start to grow (they can become thirty-five feet long) and shed eggs and cysts throughout your body, then you've got a raft of other things to worry about. Here are some in descending order of severity:

- death
- dementia
- epilepsy
- abdominal bloating
- anal itching
- being grossed out *all the time*

10

Chapter 12 – A Pound of Hope

Keelan was surprised he enjoyed working for Taggart. All in all, he was actually one of the better bosses he'd had, and this helped him understand why the Heavy Hitter crew was happy and, apparently, satisfied. They certainly didn't lack for anything. Most of the crew, guys like Wayne Falco, were in the group primarily for the food, but some of them were interested in other things like alcohol and drugs. Keelan thought of the latter group with a little distaste, but he realized that was hypocrisy.

He was in it for the drugs, after all. The fact that they were weight-loss drugs didn't make any difference.

And his worry that Max would never forgive him for making a deal with a pudgy devil was a false one too.

One of the upshots of the riot was that the Heavy Hitters had a chokehold on all illegal substances in the Fatness, and Max had lost his connection.

"I don't want to say that I need this," Max said as Keelan handed him the package of psychotropic drugs, mostly magic mushrooms, mescaline, and peyote, but I do want to continue my research, and it would be impossible without them."

"Sure. But you still have to pay."

"Oh, I can pay. Don't worry. Now, let's check your blood pressure, okay?"

Max had once been a licensed psychiatrist before he'd had his "epic freak out" during grand rounds at St. Dymphna's hospital. That meant he had a medical degree, and he often helped his friends with their medical conundrums, particularly since the CRC physician, Dr. Fundarek, was, in Max's words: "A quack and a human rights violation waiting to happen."

"You're okay. A bit hypertensive, but who the hell isn't in here? Your heart rate is a bit high though. How long do you plan on taking these pills?"

Taggart had procured a bottle of phentermine; Keelan hoped the appetite suppressant would help him survive Brittany's latest torture diet, which was all about fiber. Phentermine was fairly

safe, but it was an amphetamine-type drug and had a list of side
effects that was hilariously long – if you weren't taking it. Slightly
terrifying if you were. Of most concern to Keelan: convulsions,
hallucinations, violent outbursts, and sexual dysfunction. He was
pleased to see that "heart-bursting-out-of-chest-like-an-alienitis"
was not on the list.

"I dunno, Kee. I should run some tests on the pills. You can't
trust Taggart. Next time you're near him, just look at how his ass
jiggles in those track pants he's always wearing. And his gait. One
look at his gait tells you he's a pathological liar.

"Max, we both know you can't tell that."

"Yes, we can. There is some interesting work being done in
gait-pattern recognition and how it relates to moods. I've been
practicing it for years, and there's quite a bit of evidence for it.
But I've been expanding that into an analysis of how rolls of fat
can indicate psychopathologies as well."

"Psychopathologies?" Keelan wondered. Max was so strange
most of the time that it was easy to forget he had been trained as a
doctor and psychiatrist at one point.

"Psychological pathologies – abnormalities in brain function,
mental disorders, those kinds of things. But my approach is one
that I have been developing since they incarcerated me here. I
believe that adipose tissue can be a way to diagnose mental illness,
and if we can get to the root causes of that illness, we can figure
out what is causing the excess fat."

"Without other interventions?" Keelan wondered. "No exercise. Dieting?"

"Of course. There's still biology to deal with, but my take is
the underlying mental problem prevents us from losing weight,
even if we work at it really hard, like you have. The fact that
you have managed to drop your weight so much, in a stressful
environment like this, is frankly amazing. You must have in-
credible willpower. I will have to check my notes about your
Flabometrics."

"Flabometrics?"

"It's the ad hoc term I've been using for this new science."

"Oh god," Keelan said, not wanting to hear about this line of inquiry. It was bad enough Max was taking drugs, did he have to be insane too?

But the pills worked. Not fast enough to save his job, but enough that he lost more weight.

The one side effect that seemed somewhat positive to Keelan was mild constipation. Normally that would be a negative side effect, but given that his diet was composed mostly of cabbage, beans and other intestinal rocket fuel, it was balancing out nicely. Most importantly, he was able to stick to his diet, despite the fact that as a member of the Heavy Hitters, he now had ready access to all kinds of delicious, non-fiber-packed, fatty, salty and sugary wonders created by modern science.

He'd lost another pound. It didn't seem like much, but it got him one-tenth of the way to his goal, which was to get him the hell out of the Fatness and into the arms of Jacinda. It was a pound of hope.

Both Keelan and Jacinda looked forward to their evening Skype conversations. They shared everything, so Keelan felt guilty that he hadn't told her about the phentermine or his deal with Taggart yet.

"Ballard has me leaving in two days for another trip. I've got a lead on another group like the Heavy Hitters in Edmonton," Jacinda said.

"That's great, Jacinda."

"What?"

"Nothing."

"Seriously, Kee. I know we haven't spent nearly enough time together in person, but I am getting to know you pretty well. What are you hiding?"

"Okay, I have to tell you something. I'm just not sure if it's safe to do this way."

"Fair enough. What about in person?"

"They're still not allowing visitors."

"But what if you could come out with me?"

"Seriously?"

"Yes." Jacinda smiled. Keelan's heart was pounding, and he could hear the blood rushing in his ears. He wasn't sure if it was love or his diet pills about to kill him, but he couldn't be happier. So he almost missed the news she relayed: "I've arranged for you to have a compassionate leave pass. Two whole days. Now, I know you have to spend a little of it visiting your parents, but I'm hoping that most of it you can spend with me."

Keelan's head reeled. The news was so good, he was going to pass out.

"I don't know what to say."

"Say you'll spend most of it with me!"

"Of course, Jacs! I want to be with you so bad."

"The feeling is mutual," she purred. This was the part of the Skype call where they turned the lights down in their rooms and told each other what they would do when they were together.

Tonight was no different, and Keelan was relieved to see that "sexual dysfunction" didn't seem to be one of the side effects he was suffering. Though he was a little worried about Poppin' Fresh appearing again, making a threesome of it.

"Hoo-hoo!"

Jacinda was nervous. She hadn't seen Keelan in person since the night of the dance, but since then they'd been having long talks via Skype. What she was feeling for him was real, though she had her qualms. Her mother had certainly sown as much doubt as she could. She had never really been with anyone who was overweight before, and she wasn't sure if it was going to have an impact on her. She didn't think she was prejudiced, but Jacinda had worked with people enough to know that sometimes one's own biases are the hardest to spot.

She thought about all the times they'd talked. Really, their evening Skype was the highlight of her days. She looked forward to them more than anything she'd ever looked forward to – and that included sex with Christopher Ballard.

She tried to shake the image of her boss and ex-lover out of her mind. Why did he always pop in there just when she was waxing romantic about Keelan? She didn't really want to answer that, because she knew that somehow she was still attracted to her boss, even if she found him emotionally stunted and morally repellent.

But that ass.

Keelan appeared. She was waiting for him just outside the CRC, as the director was still not letting anyone but the staff into the facility.

Keelan looked … thinner. There was no other way to put it. She could tell he'd lost weight. She'd known, intellectually, that he was losing some pounds, but now she could see it on him. His face, especially. He was wearing a pair of jeans, docksiders and a button-down dress shirt. He was nervous. She could see that from a distance.

He got through the door and smiled at her. Tentatively, he opened up his arms for a hug.

Jacinda stepped into his arms, and she felt her skin flush. Her breathing picked up, and she looked up into his eyes. She'd never noticed how startlingly blue they were before. They kissed. Gently, at first, and then with a passion that felt like a bone-deep hunger to her. As first kisses go, it was a doozy.

They came up for air, and she noticed that the guards were watching them, smiling.

"Get a room!" one of them yelled.

Both Jacinda and Keelan laughed, and Keelan whispered to her, "My thoughts exactly."

They lay back in Jacinda's bed, exhausted.

Keelan smiled, feeling like he could drift into the best sleep of his life. He experienced a strange emotion. *What is that?* he wondered, and he grinned some more. *Right, that's the feeling of being truly happy*, he thought. He was drained. The anxieties about if his weight-loss pills would allow him to perform, and whether Jacinda would be disgusted by his flabby body, and if he would be able to last long enough … they had melted away, and he felt wonderful. Jacinda snuggled into him, her head on his chest.

"Whatcha thinking?"

"How happy I am."

"Me too," she said. "Isn't it funny how banal pillow talk can be? But so meaningful at the same time?"

"Yep," Keelan agreed, but he was having trouble remembering the last time he'd had pillow talk. Or heard the word *banal*. Certainly at least since he was in the CRC, and probably before that; it was possible that Max had used the phrase *the banality of evil*.

"I agree, but it's kind of theoretical for me at this point."

"What's that mean?"

"Just that it has been a long, long, long time since I last experienced pillow talk."

"Of course," Jacinda said.

"And not just 'cause I'm in the Fatness. I haven't exactly been a Don Juan."

"I have trouble believing that," Jacinda said. "You're so yummy."

"Really?"

"Yep."

"Even with the gut?"

"Women aren't as shallow as men when it comes to looks."

"Thank god." Keelan grinned. "Because you are gorgeous, and I wouldn't have it any other way."

"Well, just so you know, I think I look fat."

Keelan was quiet, the smile disappearing from his face, the feelings of anxiety returning. What could that possibly mean? Jacinda was perfect. Sure, he was in love with her, but even if he wasn't – before he was – he recognized that she was sexy as all hell. Jacinda was short, and she had what he would describe as a buxom figure, but fat? That was ridiculous.

Keelan knew he couldn't say that though.

They'd been talking every night for a month. He knew her well enough that if she was telling him this, now, while they both lay there naked and covered in one another's sex, there was a truth here he had to acknowledge. Even if he disagreed.

"It's hard to imagine you feel that way, especially after you've been working in the CRCs. Those places are filled with real fat. Heck, I'm practically thin compared to some of the people in there. But if that's the way you feel, that's the way you feel. I'm just here to tell you that I don't see you as fat. You are beautiful."

"And that's how I feel too," Jacinda said. "You might just see the flaws in yourself, but I don't. I see the person."

Keelan thought that was the best thing he'd ever heard, even if it was a cliché. Especially if it was. That meant it was true. Dare he tell her how he really felt? What about the Heavy Hitters and the phentermine?

He was quiet for a moment, contemplating, and she said, "What?"

"There's something I have to tell you," Keelan said. He decided. "I've been taking diet pills."

"Really?"

"Yes, I hope – I hope that doesn't make you think any less of me."

Jacinda gazed into his eyes and said, "I know why you're doing it, so how could I?"

"Well, there's another thing."

"What?"

"I've had to start working for Colin Taggart to get them. I couldn't afford them."

"Oh, Kee, I could have –"

"I know. And I would have asked, but I wanted to do it on my own. I hope you don't think that's too proud."

"No," Jacinda said. "But I've had relationships where money was a real issue. That's not going to be a problem, is it?"

"Of course not!" Keelan said. "I'm just worried about you thinking I'm some kind of criminal or something."

"No. No, you're doing what you need to do to get out."

"I wouldn't do it if I didn't want to be with you so badly, Jacs. I want this. All the time."

"Would you be willing to take it further?"

"How can we take it further?" Keelan joked. "Is there something we've left out?"

"I can think of a few things," Jacinda purred. "But I was thinking about the Heavy Hitters. Would you be willing to help me get more information about how they work? Tell me if they're expanding? It may help you get out faster, and everyone else too. Would you be willing to rat out the Heavy Hitters to that reporter? Serena Lee? I think it's the best way to damage the reputation of the system."

"Tell me something I don't know. Of course I'll help. Whatever you want." Keelan was quiet for a moment, and he switched subjects. "By the way, I've been eating nothing but cabbage, bran, and beans for the past week, so please don't judge me too harshly on the flatulence front."

Jacinda laughed.

"Seriously, the whole set-up is basically designed to fail," Keelan said. "The only reason I've lost any weight is because I've worked so hard at it. And it's kind of silly that a few pounds keep me away from you." He kissed her, and he felt her passion return. He whispered, "I'll do anything I can to help you, Jacinda."

"Hmmm," she murmured, and pushed his head down.

"Especially that," Keelan said, smiling.

FACT

Pudgy Paramours

That six-pack may look great, ladies, but it comes at a cost.

Researchers at Erciyes University in Kayseri, Turkey, have shown there's an inverse relationship between the body mass index (BMI) of a man and his ability to, um, "hang in there until you get your cookie". Their study showed that men with an obvious belly and higher BMI lasted 7.3 minutes on average. And the slender fellas only lasted about two minutes. Yep, you read that right, two minutes!

Not to mention the fact that bigger boys tend to be more interested in … er … snacking.

11

Chapter 13 – Frozen Dinner

She met with Ballard the day after Keelan had to return to the CRC or risk losing his health coverage. A part of her wanted to tell Kee to forget about it – she would cover his health care – but she knew that he would say no. Perhaps if they could arrange another "intimate" visit, she could convince him that she would take care of him, no matter what happened. But she knew it was dangerous territory. Even well-adjusted and enlightened guys could take umbrage at the idea of a woman "taking care" of them. That was *their* job. At least, that was what they had been trained to believe; the exception had been younger men raised by their mothers alone. They seemed to have less of a problem with it, in her experience, but that came with another whole raft of issues.

She was wearing her least revealing outfit for her meeting with Ballard. She really didn't want any more sexual attention from him, even if her mind did occasionally drift to the subject of his well-formed gluteus maximus. He was sitting at his desk, writing something longhand. The archaic form underscored their age difference, which she'd been willing to overlook before.

"Jacs, what's up?"

"I think I have the way to get the proof we need."

"That's great!"

"It is. I just wanted to be sure you want to do it. Once we do, who knows what will happen?"

"What do you mean? And please, sit down, Jacs."

She sat down and, for the first time, saw the age around his eyes and mouth. It wasn't unattractive, but it reinforced how good it was to be with someone her age. She and Kee shared all the same pop culture and musical references, while her on-and-off-again relationship with Ballard had sent her running to Wikipedia on a regular basis to decipher what the hell he was talking about.

"I'm just worried that when we reveal the corruption in the system, the government will fall."

"That could happen." Ballard smiled. "Would that be such a terrible thing?"

"I'm not really political, so I don't care, personally," Jacinda replied. "But what about your mysterious client?"

"Let me worry about it. I say we reveal the truth, and let the chips fall where they may."

But Jacinda could see by the grin on his face that it was exactly what he wanted. So she made the call to Serena Lee, the nosey reporter from the CBC, so she could tell her what she'd discovered.

Keelan was hiding in the pool. The day had been terrifying. There was no other way to put it. The night before, Serena Lee's documentary, *Trimming the Fat*, was aired on national television.

Not only did she unearth the illegal trade in Mickey Dees and Doritos, she also discovered, with Keelan's help, the connection the Heavy Hitters had to organized crime. She was able to prove that these criminal organizations were able to operate without interference because individual CRCs were run without direct oversight by Corrections Canada. The institutions were essentially little fiefdoms, controlled by their directors, like Selwyn Seward.

An epic shit storm was about to descend on Seward and his compatriots in other jurisdictions.

In the documentary, Seward actually came out looking pretty good compared to some other CRC directors, who were taking a cut of the profits. Seward seemed to be doing it out of a realpolitik evaluation that criminals would figure out a way to get food into the CRCs anyway, so at least he would control it so that it had an overall good effect on the CRC's "gross tonnage."

One of the best things about the documentary, from Keelan's perspective, was that Serena had taken up his suggestion that she interview Tyrell. Out of the whole hour-long piece, he came off as the most sympathetic character, as he outlined how the system was failing the people it was supposed to be helping. The worst? Well, Colin Taggart wasn't an idiot, and he figured out pretty quickly that a lot of the insider information that Lee had used to dig into the story had been provided by Keelan.

Keelan felt kind of stupid that he hadn't realized that would happen when he'd agreed to help Lee with the story. Though really, he was doing it because he knew it would make it easier for Jacinda to improve the CRCs and get him the hell out of there.

That was, if he survived the night.

The Heavy Hitters were on a rampage, tearing apart the CRC, looking for Keelan. He'd managed to make a quick call to Jacinda before he decided to find a place to hide. He hoped the cavalry was on the way, but he had no idea what was really happening. He wasn't even sure what would happen if they found him. A lot of the Heavy Hitters were pretty good guys, and they'd become friends of Keelan, so he had trouble imagining them killing him. However, if Taggart's bodyguard, Carver, got a chance, he knew it wouldn't be good.

He had a piece of tubing Max had given him, and he was floating in one of the darkened corners of the pool. The lights were on a timer, so there was no way for the Heavy Hitters to turn them on, which was his best hope. In the shadows of the pool, underwater, he would probably be hidden, especially if he "made like Rambo", as Max had suggested, and used the tube to breathe while he kept his head underwater.

What Max hadn't told him was how cold he was going to get.

The door opened again, and Keelan dipped his head under, making sure that his breathing tube was above the water. Flashlights played on the surface of the pool as he watched from underneath. Keelan's heart seemed to be making an escape attempt; it was hammering so hard at his chest. He knew it was the damned phentermine doing its thing again, but it didn't make things any more comfortable. The lights flickered over his corner and moved on. He closed his eyes, and in his mind's eye he saw Jacinda's face rapt in pleasure. They'd only spent forty-eight hours together, but in the past two weeks, each of those hours had been a retreat for him – particularly the hours they'd spent making love or simply holding one another.

As he shivered and his breath rasped in the tube, he shook his head slightly. He felt like a complete dork. He'd always thought it was a bit precious for lovers to describe having sex as "making love", but now he understood it. There was a difference. Sex is awesome, but sex with someone you love is transformative. Keelan understood that there was chemistry going on in his brain that made him want to feel that transformation – that deep and all-engrossing emotional connection he had with Jacinda while they, you know, did it. But he didn't care if it was largely hormonal. Something happened to him when she came, and he knew she experienced the same when he did too.

The lights disappeared, and he brought his head out of the water cautiously. He shook, his body starting to really get cold, and he wondered how long it would take Jacinda to get the police to visit the CRC.

"You're whipped, boy, I say, you're whipped," the Colonel said to him from the deck. He was standing in the dark shadows, holding a cane and wearing his trademark white suit with that stupid bow tie.

"I know," Keelan whispered, "but I'm happy. And so I'm going to ignore you."

"Nice kid, but not the smartest crease in the pants," the Colonel said to someone else in the shadows.

Keelan thought about how nice it would be to put on pants, and shook again before the clown had a chance to say anything …

He awoke in the infirmary. Max was sitting on the cot next to him, looking worried. He grinned when he saw Keelan's eyes open.

"Thank the great hairy monkey gods," he said. "You have been out for a whole day, you wanker. You know you could have died!"

"Hey," Keelan croaked, "the pool was your idea."

"I'd forgotten they'd stopped heating it. If I knew it was that cold, I would have come up with something better."

"But it worked. They didn't find me?"

"No. And somehow you had enough sense to pull yourself out of the water before you passed out and drowned."

Keelan had a vague notion that it had been the clown and the Colonel who pulled him out of the pool, but it wasn't really a solid memory. He suppressed it with a shudder.

"You're bloody lucky on two counts. First, if you weren't such a well-built fellow – that means fat, in case your brain is still frozen – you would have died from the cold. And it's a good thing you've been taking those diet pills. If not, I suspect your heart might have stopped beating. You were down to 82 degrees, you fucking idiot."

"So what happened?"

"A *major* fustercluck. The Mounties arrived at about three in the morning and arrested Taggart and his cronies. They didn't put Seward in custody, but he's on administrative leave while they investigate. They want to talk to you too when you're up to it."

"They're gonna arrest me?"

"No, I think they'll want you as a witness. Lots of the guys have agreed to fess up. A group of the manatees is saying they won't say anything unless the RCMP guarantees the junk food keeps flowing."

"Really? That's gutsy."

"Har, har. I think your sense of humour is still in suspension. Here, let me take your temperature again, and if it's anywhere near normal, we can get the hell out of Fundarek's infirmary before he explodes your liver or siphons a kidney out of your urethra."

Keelan resisted the urge to tell Max his hands were cold.

Part III

"They are all but stomachs, and we all but food; They eat us hungrily, and when they are full, They belch us"

~William Shakespeare, *Othello*

Chapter 1 – Here Come the Cons

Keelan was standing on top of a tall building in New York City. It was one of those Gothic numbers the robber barons were fond of constructing around the turn of the twentieth century. There were three guys wearing what looked like tan coveralls with huge backpacks. The backpacks not only seemed *really* heavy, but they had some kind of weird noise coming from them – like a high-pitched humming, but *much* more ominous. Pretty much like they were about to explode at the speed of light.

Keelan realized he was in the final scenes of *Ghostbusters* – the first one with Bill Murray. It was a movie that he'd been exposed to at a young age, kinda like *Star Wars*, which he loved, even though it was his dad who'd first seen it in the theater, not him.

"Choose!" the Babylonian god told them.

"What do you mean, choose? We don't understand!" *Hey*, Keelan thought, *that's Dan Aykroyd. Cool.*

"Choose! Choose the form of the Destructor!" said the Babylonian god, which now that he thought about it, was kind of sexy, Keelan thought. Sorta like David Bowie with tits.

There was a terrible, high-pitched roar coming from the distance. The crump of heavy footsteps as the building shook.

"I couldn't help myself," Dan Aykroyd said. "It just popped in there. I mean, there's just something creepy about the guy."

"Oh no," Keelan said. "Ray, you didn't …"

"It's the Leader of the Conservative Party."

He was hundreds of feet tall, wearing a sweater vest, but he still had those dead shark eyes filled with detached malice. He looked like he was either about to make a policy announcement that would send everyone to sleep, or eat a bus filled with school children.

This is a dream, Keelan reminded himself. *Nightmare, more like.*

Before they could get a chance to cross the streams, he woke up.

The nightmare wasn't too hard to interpret. The politician was due to tour the CRC that day, and Keelan was going to be on display again. As the "whistleblower" of Taggart's Heavy Hitters and the corruption in the CRC, he'd achieved a level of fame that he'd never had any interest in. In many ways he was one of the most famous fatties in all of Canada. And that myth about the camera putting on ten pounds was definitely not true – it added more like twenty or thirty.

It all made him feel like a prized pig.

The only good thing about this celebrity was that he'd been allowed out of the CRC twice to get some help on the legal, PR, and fame-management fronts. That had meant that he'd been able to spend two more glorious nights at Jacinda's apartment. He hadn't enjoyed the afternoon he spent with the image consultant Jacinda's law firm had paid to make him seem less like a bloated mayoral figure straight out of an editorial cartoon. He especially didn't like the way the (really in-shape) gay man had cluck-clucked as Keelan was made to try out several different outfits, including an unfortunate attempt to stuff him into a girdle of Shatnerian proportions. They ended up with a nice dark suit that was "naturally slimming" and was about as comfortable as day seven of a week-long upper-colon cayenne pepper cleanse.

He got out of bed and made his way down to the showers to slough off the unpleasant dreams. The wait to get his shower wasn't too long, and his fellow inmates seemed to have gotten over their relative jealousies, resentments, and pride at his activities with the Heavy Hitters. Apart from the attention of the outside world, he was returning to his persona as regular old Keelan – the guy that everyone liked, even if they couldn't really explain to you why they did.

Greg stepped out of a shower stall and smiled at Kee. "All yours, buddy. You're lookin' good."

Keelan smiled and took the compliment for what it was – a statement of fact. Despite being put into extremely stressful circumstances, Kee had managed to stick to Brittany's gastrointestinal workout regime of heavy-fiber meals. He was approaching the magic 30 BMI. Soon, all this would be behind him, and he'd be able to begin his life with Jacinda.

"You too, Greg," Kee said back.

"Well, it's nice of you to say, but I think Brittany's given up on me. I'm back on the regular diet in the cantina, which is just fine, 'cause it's pizza night."

"Don't give up, Greg. You can't give up."

"No, but I can get used to the idea of being in here. I can make a life in here, I think."

Greg had recently started "dating" Tina, the cute maker of pasta during the Wine-and-Cheese Riots. The look on Greg's face was so bittersweet that Kee wanted to give him a hug. But they were both partially naked, and Keelan suggested that neither of them were really keen to join the Bears – the enthusiastic, heavily bearded men who seemed to be the only people in the CRC who had any fun.

After his shower, Kee made his way to the Calorie Dispensing Hall of Shame for his "breakfast", which he ate with Greg and Max and a few others who had supported Keelan after he turned on the Heavy Hitters. Many of these guys were active in the resurgent activity of making toilet whiskey. To call it whiskey was actually a bit grandiose. For the most part, the liquor they managed to create was based largely on whatever fermentable foodstuff they could smuggle out of the cafeteria.

Since the breaking of the Heavy Hitters story and the cashiering of Seward, the new director of Calorie Reduction Centre 17 had instituted a "no food outside the cafeteria" policy. So, except for milk and sugar at the commons coffee shop – items that were strictly guarded and handed out by a couple of thin unpaid interns from the kinesiology program at Hellmuth University – there was no source of sustenance allowed in the CRC proper. This was a restriction, of course, but many of the denizens of the CRC were quite heavy and this allowed for no paucity of places to hide a slice of whole wheat bread or some strands of rice pasta. To wit, the folds of fat amongst the manatee population were excellent ways to smuggle out the seed stock needed to create some kind of toilet liquor.

Except for Keelan, whose love for Jacinda had helped him find hitherto undiscovered sources of willpower, the others all seemed to be gaining weight.

Keelan was also on Brittany's special diet, which was enforced by the cafeteria staff, while all the others were eating the recommended daily allowances of grains, vegetables, and fruits. The grains, in particular, Kee suspected of causing the weight gain. He'd noticed his table-mates were getting more pastas and breads than before, and less protein. Possibly this was to save money, though there might be some kind of crackpot diet plan behind it all.

After breakfast, he went back to his cell and strapped himself into his dark suit. The political visit was due to begin at eleven and he had been instructed to be ready.

He didn't mind participating. He'd held out for another two-day pass in exchange for spending time on camera. The Conservative communications team had even given him some talking points for his meeting with the leader, Richard Sneer. Keelan wasn't nervous about meeting a potential prime minister of Canada, but he was worried about how fat he was going to look on camera. He knew Jacinda would be watching it; she'd seen him naked, so of course she knew *exactly* how fat he was, but the thought of looking *more* fat made him feel sick. Perhaps that would be enough for her to realize she'd made a horrible mistake.

He never voiced it, but he was always worried that she would have this realization. It was always with him, this fear, like the feeling of hunger he had even when he was full.

The minutes until they called on him for the interview seemed like hours. He stayed in his room while the politician visited "patients" of the CRC, had coffee with some of the calorie supervisors and trainers, and glad-handed his way around the centre. Finally, they fetched Keelan, and it was nearly his turn to be in the spotlight again. Sneer was wearing a standard politician's dark blue suit with a yellow tie; his hair looked a bit unruffled, and he had a kind of smirk that showed off his dimples to good effect, as Keelan approached. They had a mini-studio set up in the commons, with about half the population of the CRC sitting in the bleachers, waiting for the show to begin.

"Sit down here, offstage, while the Honourable MP from Regina – Qu'Appelle – makes a few remarks first. Then we'll have you up to discuss your courageous acts during the Calorie-Gate Affair," one of the Conservative leader's flacks told Keelan.

"Calorie-Gate?"

"That's what we're going to call it. Listen."

"Calorie-Gate? Isn't that kind of a cliché?"

"Shhh."

Keelan shook his head and sat down, as asked. He just kept reminding himself that he was going to get to spend two whole days with Jacinda after this ordeal was over. The politician began his speech, which was pretty much what Keelan had expected. The Conservatives would dismantle the CRC system and replace it with something better. The experiment would end if they were elected to govern.

This received rapturous applause from the audience. It was all caught on camera for the evening news, and Keelan thought that the election was probably over. In combination with the taint of corruption the Liberals had all over them because of the affair, the Conservatives were likely to at least form a minority government, despite the fact that their leader was a smirking homophobe who was resolutely anti-choice and a virtual unknown.

Keelan spotted the look of expectation on Max's face, and he felt a sinking feeling. What was Max going to do?

Sneer smiled. It was a big, wide grin. The kind of overt pleasure you'd expect to see on the face of a hockey dad who'd just polished off a two-four with a buddy and then watched their son's team win the championship. It was kind of endearing, actually.

The staffer looked equally pleased. He wobbled a bit as he got on stage with Sneer, who gave him a huge hug. The kind of hug that the bears gave one another in public or in the showers. There was a round of applause, and a little laughter from that part of the stands, actually.

"Kiss him!" one of the bears cried.

The staffer ignored them and explained that Sneer would now invite one of their own up to the stage for a little discussion.

Sneer waved Keelan up. Sneer hugged Keelan just as warmly as he did his staffer, and Keelan really didn't have any choice but to hug back.

What the hell is going on? Keelan thought. He saw the grin on Max's face and he knew it was the mad doctor's doing, somehow. Keelan later discovered Dr. Tundra had spiked the morning's coffee with sodium thiopental. Among its other uses, sodium thiopental was sometimes given as a truth serum, even if the veracity of things said while under its influence was disputable. What wasn't disputable was the effects the drug had on high cortical functions. It made those dosed a bit more compliant, friendly, and loquacious – three things that were not exactly in Richard Sneer's wheelhouse.

"You are a big boy, aren't you?" Sneer said.

Keelan was a little offended. It wasn't like the politician was svelte himself.

"Um," Keelan stalled. Humiliated, he could feel the blood rushing to his face. He reminded himself that two days with Jacinda were on the line, so he played along as best he could manage. "That's why I'm in here, but I'm nearly under 30 BMI."

"And how difficult has that been?" Sneer asked.

Thank god, Keelan thought. *We're back to the script.*

"Very. The methods used by the staff are well meant, of course, but hardly set up for optimal success. The food, for example, is heavy on refined carbohydrates, which some researchers –"

"Plus potato chips? AmIright?" Sneer slurred. "They're my weakness too, and I bet you and all those Heavy Petter scamps were scarfing down chips every chance you got, amIright, big boy?"

"Uh, you mean the Heavy Hitters?"

"Pitters!" Sneer shouted. Something occurred to the politician, who seemed drunk. "You can really smell the pit in here, can't you?" The would-be PM raised his arm and shouted,

"Armpit!"

Everyone in the crowd was roaring with laughter, and even though Keelan was totally humiliated, he couldn't help himself. He laughed along.

"You should smell it in summer. Woo," Keelan agreed, waving his hand in front of his nose.

"I bet it's like a hockey bag you left in the trunk all week, amIright?"

"Worse. Imagine if you had the jockstrap lashed over your nose too."

Sneer held his nose and said, "Yeeeeee!"

Keelan felt some responsibility to get back to the talking points. He didn't want them denying him his pass just because Sneer was drunk. Keelan glanced at Max. Or drugged. "So how do you think you will overhaul the system, sir?"

Sneer looked seriously at Keelan for a second. "I'm going to change the laws. Gonna really put those –" he looked around and whispered conspiratorially "– *sinners* in their place."

That wasn't a talking point either, and potentially very damaging.

"And the CRCs?"

"Better food and better air conditioning would help," Sneer said.

"I thought you were going to dismantle them."

"Oh, yeah, that's the plan," Sneer said, winking exaggeratedly. "Gimme another hug, you fat fucker." Keelan was really shocked when the would-be PM kissed him on the mouth to cheers from the bear gallery.

That was when the Conservative campaign manager finally got to the commons. He'd skipped the morning coffee klatch and had been watching the feed from the director's office. He jumped on stage and whispered something to Sneer, who shook his head.

"No, I like it up here. These are good fatties," he said. He pointed to the bears and said, "But I think they may be a bunch of poofters up there."

Luckily for the Conservative Party of Canada, the mics didn't pick up the last comment, and the campaign manager thought of something to say to get him offstage.

Keelan couldn't be sure, but he thought he heard something about "making *The Handmaid's Tale* look like day camp" and "those fuckin' immigrants," but the campaign manager got his candidate the hell out of there before he could really get on a roll.

The meltdown didn't have a negative effect on the campaign. If anything, having Sneer appear to be an affable drunk created a huge amount of buzz around the unknown candidate. In a funny way it made him more likeable and more of a regular joe. As though his socially conservative leanings weren't as scary. As the campaign continued through the spring, culminating in a win for Sneer's Conservatives, it became clear that the moment when he'd asked Keelan for a hug and kissed him had been a game-changer. Everyone seemed to forget that as he was making this friendly gesture, Sneer called Keelan a "fat fucker", but that didn't matter. He could hug another human being. He could even kiss a man, so how homophobic could he really be? He wasn't just some smirking giant baby-man intent on turning the country into some kind of Fundamentalist Christian theocracy. (Even if he really was.)

Keelan regretted not putting Sneer more on the spot. Especially when he discovered that Max had drugged Sneer. He could have got him to reveal whatever nefarious plans he had for the country. But he'd wanted his two days, and he knew if he made a stink, they never would have let him out.

And whenever he thought of those two days, he smiled. They had kept him on his diet for the past six weeks.

While they watched the returns come in, and they predicted a Conservative majority, Keelan turned to Max and said, "This is all your fault, you know."

"I know," Max said, putting his face in his hands. "I'll never forgive myself."

QUOTE

"They say the camera adds ten pounds. OK. So I figure I must be standing in front of ten cameras."

~Al Roker

Chapter 2 – Total Protonic Reversal

Ballard was back in Ottawa, meeting with Melinda Handle. It was early May, and the capital was experiencing a taste of summer. Despite the fact that Ottawa is the most northerly capital in the world and regularly clocks in as the coldest capital city on any given day in the winter, in the summers the city could get downright stinky. And one such heatwave was gracing O-town now. Landon was also experiencing it, so Ballard had packed appropriately and was wearing a nice summer-weight suit for his meetings on the Hill.

Handle hadn't got the memo, but she was bearing up well, despite the extreme humidity. Her dark wool suit was not comfortable. They were meeting at the same pub where they'd had such a successful initial rendezvous, and, clearly, she'd come straight from the airport. She had a small suitcase in tow, with a parka tucked under one arm. Her face was flushed, but otherwise she seemed as composed and professional as before.

"Well, isn't it just hotter than whoopee in woolen?" she asked Ballard as she sat down. The waiter appeared (Ballard had pre-tipped as usual) and she said, "I need some water, darling. And one of your fancy Canadian beers."

"Nice to see you again," Ballard said.

"And you too, honey. I wish I'd checked the weather report before I got on the plane this morning. I thought you got cold weather up here?"

"Only when it's not as humid as a jungle." Ballard smiled. He'd forgotten how much he loved her drawl and long sexy legs.

"We have to work on your idioms, darling. That was pedestrian." The waiter arrived with her drinks. She downed the water and said, "Another, please." Her eyebrows rose when she had a sip of the beer. "This really is excellent. Now, let's talk turkey."

"Well, the government is ready to hear your pitch, at least. They campaigned on dismantling the system. We'll have to see who is put on the SubOb committee, but I imagine the chair will be someone I already know."

"Don't worry, darlin'. We're ready to go. All the data you've gathered for us is going to make this easy as pie. In fact, I'm talking with the new minister of Health tomorrow."

"Really?" Ballard said. He was expecting that Weight Winners would require a bit more help before they were ready to get to that stage.

"Don't fret. When we get the contract, we are going to need a lot of legal help. Our usual stable of attorneys won't be able to handle it all, and your firm will get most of it."

"That's good to hear," Ballard said. He knew this day would come, but he wasn't quite prepared for it to be so soon. He'd enjoyed the chase.

"You know I'll have to come up to Canada on a regular basis, and we're thinkin' that Landon would be a fine choice for our regional headquarters – assuming, of course, we could get a bit of a tax break from the municipal government. And I'm lookin' forward to a little bit more of that enthusiasm you showed before?"

Ballard smiled. "I'm sure we can help with the local government too, and I was hoping the same, Melinda. I enjoy our 'high-level' discussions."

She winked at him and said, "But let's get another one of your strong brews first."

Ballard signaled the waiter as Melinda put an unladylike hand on his thigh.

Keelan watched the announcement with Max and Greg and about a hundred other denizens of CRC-17 from the stands in the commons. The rostrum, which had so recently featured Keelan and the leader of the Conservatives, was now occupied by the same politician, who was now the prime minister, his new minister of Health, and Melinda Handle, who had been promoted to the position of president of Weight Winners Canada. In front of the stands there were seats set up for the guests of honour.

There was a sense of excitement in the room. The Conservatives had campaigned on a platform that described the Liberals as corrupt and incompetent, and the CRC system was the prime example. Keelan hoped they were going to announce its end. He figured that must be the case, if the acting director wasn't there. The massive amount of security present in the building hadn't even alarmed him. He smiled to see Jacinda, who sat next to her boss, Christopher Ballard, as one of the guests of honour. The mayor of Landon was also there, in addition to a few other local luminaries whom Keelan could not name. Except for the mayor, who was obese (but wealthy enough to pay for his own health care, apparently) most of them were thin or in shape, and they all wore fancy clothes. About half the audience members in the stands were wearing their workout clothes, and the other half were dressed casually. And they were all fat, but invitations to attend the ceremony had only gone out to those with a BMI of 35 or less, so the contrast was not quite as stark as it could have been had the audience been stuffed with manatees as well as porkers.

The program began. The health minister introduced the prime minister. The PM began with his usual soft-spoken, doughy delivery of a policy announcement.

"We're here today to begin a revolution in Canada's health care system," Sneer began. "It is a change long overdue. A change that will correct the mistakes of the past and usher in an age of better health outcomes for Canada. We will finally become leaders, not just in health care, but as the healthiest population in the world."

Keelan joined in the polite applause for these motherhood statements.

Here it comes, he thought. *They're gonna let us all go.*

"While the approach the previous government took to health care was flawed at best, and criminal at its worst, there is some sound thinking in the underlying idea that every person should be responsible for their own healthiness," Sneer said.

What's this now? Keelan thought.

"We've done a careful examination of the relevant data, including reports from the ministry and well-qualified outside experts, and we believe that the CRC system should not be dismantled. It should be enhanced. It should be run properly. Efficiently, but with a compassionate care for the individuals struggling to lose weight, correct their unhealthy behaviours, and rejoin society as productive citizens and consumers. The Government of Canada does not believe this is a goal that old-style bureaucracies can achieve. We firmly believe – we know – that this is a policy objective best accomplished with a private sector-public sector sharing of responsibilities. The Government of Canada will provide the policy objectives, the revenue, and the measurement capabilities, but we have asked qualified health care providers in the private sector to actually deliver these services."

There was more polite applause to this announcement, most of it coming from the guests of honour, but a smattering from the stands as well.

Keelan had a bad feeling.

"We have asked contractors to bid on this important new direction and we are proud to announce that as of today, Weight Winners Canada will be running the CRC system. I now will ask my colleague, the minister of Health, to explain how the changeover will work, and then Weight Winners Canada will have a few words. Thank you."

The PM left the stage and headed out of the building, flanked by his security detail, as the minister got up to explain the changeover would take place during the week. Keelan kind of lost track of what she was saying, actually, as his head reeled. *They lied. They said they'd dismantle the system, but they're just handing it over to their corporate buddies.*

As if reading his mind, Max whispered in Keelan's ear, "I told you they weren't going to let us out."

The minister finished her spiel. Basically, the changeover was immediate and there were significant alterations to the routines. But that would be overseen by Weight Winners Canada. She introduced the tall, blond, ridiculously pretty president, Melinda Handle.

"First of all, let me thank everyone here in Landon for being so kindly. As you might have heard, Weight Winners Canada recently set up our headquarters in your lovely town, and it's fine to be here. I especially want to thank your mayor and Ballard, Ballard and Bones for all the work they've done making us feel welcome," Handle said. She toned down her Texan drawl to an absolute minimum, but it was still there.

"Weight Winners has a fifty-year history of helping North Americans lose weight and keep it off. How do we do that? We offer guidance on what to eat, how to exercise, and how to develop healthy habits that will serve you throughout your life. Most importantly, we help our clients develop the willpower they need to stick to these healthy habits. It's that simple. And I'm not just saying that because I work for the company. Studies show that if you're with Weight Winners, you're more than three times more likely to lose weight than if you try to do it any other way. And now we're in charge. So that is good news. You're going to lose your weight and get on with your lives!"

This was met with some enthusiastic applause. Handle believed her rhetoric and she was able to convince everyone who heard her too.

"We've looked at the numbers, and we believe that it's just not realistic to get you down to 30 BMI and let you go. That just wouldn't be responsible. An important part of our program is reaching a healthy weight, not just under the line of what is obese and what is overweight. It's the right thing to do."

"What?" someone cried.

Keelan's whole body felt like it had in the pool. His brain slowed down. He couldn't even form the thought that was seething inside him.

"Yes, this is a Canada-wide decision, isn't it, Minister? Perhaps I should get her to explain this part, as I'm a relative newcomer to this fine country, and I don't want to sound like I don't know a widget from a whangdoodle."

The health minister got up and clarified the point. The act did not stipulate the actual BMI number, but that those admitted to the CRCs should reach a "healthy weight" before they were released back into the general health care system.

"But we can still leave if we want to, right?" someone asked.

"No," the minister clarified. "We've decided to revise the voluntary nature of this program. If you are over a BMI of 30, then you can still choose whether to enter the CRC or pay for your own health care. But once you've chosen, you must get to a healthy weight to return to the Health Canada rolls."

"And what's a healthy weight?" Jacinda asked. She voiced it so quietly, the minister almost missed it.

"We've decided to drop it, for now, to 29 BMI. That should allow people to get their habits under control, and it will definitely prevent some of the long-term issues such as diabetes and heart disease, which will have a huge impact on the health care system if we don't address it now."

Twenty-nine. The number reverberated in Keelan's head. It felt like his consciousness was breaking apart at the speed of light. His brain slowed enough for him to do the math. That was 208 pounds. He'd have to lose 12 pounds to get there. In one stroke of the pen, they'd taken him from being 5 pounds from his goal to 12. "That's twelve more pounds!" he cried.

Other audience members made their own calculations, using apps on their smartphones or, for those who lived the numbers, in their heads.

People groaned. Some started crying. Keelan was just shutting down. He couldn't believe it.

Melissa Handle saw that she'd lost the audience's goodwill and tried to save the day. "But don't worry, we've got plans to make it so much easier to lose this weight. Like my pappy said, 'There's more than one way to break a dog from sucking eggs.'"

"Did she just call us dogs?" Keelan asked.

"You know, I could really go for some eggs," Max replied.

Keelan started salivating, and he hated himself for it.

MYTH

Skipping Breakfast Makes It Hard to Lose Weight

So if you skip breakfast, received wisdom tells us that you'll have a harder time losing weight. But a study by researchers at the Department of Health Behavior at University of Alabama Birmingham showed that eating breakfast had no impact on weight loss.

In a large randomized trial, the results showed that breakfast-skippers and breakfast-eaters lost roughly the same amount of weight, demonstrating that breakfast had no impact on weight loss. But a caution: other studies show that skipping breakfast can lead to other negative health outcomes such as high blood pressure and links to coronary disease.

The main takeaway is that even if you waffle on this issue, you shouldn't let the conflicting studies egg you on too much.

12

Chapter 3 – The Unbearable Heaviness of Being Beautiful

Jacinda sat in Christopher Ballard's office and seethed.

She had been angry since the announcement at CRC-17, when she'd discovered that all the work she had been doing for her firm had actually made it even harder for Keelan to get out of the system. She had heard him shout, and she understood what an extra seven pounds meant to him in terms of weight loss. At best, it would take him another month or two to lose that much more. At worst, he might not ever reach it. She knew he was at a breaking point, and it made her angry. *Seething* angry.

It didn't help that since the announcement, she'd been unable to set up a meeting with Ballard to discuss it. Apparently Ballard had been spending most of his time with Melinda Handle, that Mary Kay Texan tart, in important "discussions", but clearly they were spending most of their time having the kind of sex that she wished she were having with Keelan. Was she jealous of Handle? No, she thought, that was ridiculous. She loved Keelan and didn't feel anything but contempt for Ballard. Even if he had certain qualities that Keelan didn't …

She shook her head and returned her thoughts to the important activity of seething. She had to maintain a level of outrage and anger that was going to be easily communicated through her body language, without affecting her ability to make a good argument.

She'd been waiting for Ballard for nearly an hour, when his executive assistant popped her head in the door and said, again, "Really. I will let you know when he comes in. There's no need to wait."

"I'm okay here, thanks." Jacinda smiled.

She folded her hands in her lap, which was more capacious than it had been for some time. Since starting to date Keelan, she'd gained weight. She tried not to worry about it, but she did. Her mother had noticed it at their biweekly lunch. In total, she'd gained just over ten pounds. It was enough that it showed a bit in her bust, her bottom, and even her face. In the moments when she was being kinder to herself, she had to admit that she actually looked sexier with the extra padding, and even by the standards of the BMI, she was still in the healthy weight range, at 22.3.

Still, her mother's voice sounded in her head as she sat in Ballard's office, trying to maintain her seethe: "You'll even lose the fatty if you gain too much, my dear. Mark my words. That's all men care about! Your shape and your *fooffle*."

She wanted to scream at that voice, to silence it with irrefutable proof, but part of her feared there was some truth to it. Even Keelan, who was so sweet and non-judgemental about everything, it seemed, loved to tell her how beautiful she was. How sexy. How he loved her hair, her eyes, her smile, her breasts, her legs, her bottom, her hands, her fingers, her lips, her ears, her stomach, her tongue, her … she blushed a bit at the litany of things he loved about her, physically. He did, indeed, dote on her genitals, which would be hilarious if she hadn't found it such a turn-on. Jacinda got up from her chair.

The seething wasn't going very well all of a sudden, and she hated that she had no idea when she would next have Keelan in her bed.

Of course, Ballard appeared at that very moment.

"Hey, babe, I hear you've been waiting to talk with me." He seemed tired, almost as though he hadn't been sleeping well. There were dark circles under his eyes, and his hair, though coiffed, did not seem as perfect as usual. She was standing near the edge of his desk, and he brushed by her as he went to his seat. Jacinda was able to look at his butt, and it did nothing for her, the first time in ages. She felt sad about that. Why would she feel loss because she didn't find Christopher Ballard attractive anymore? *I should feel happy*, she chided herself.

"Yes, I'm here about the file with Weight Winners America. That pro bono work you had me doing?"

"Ah." Ballard smiled. "You figured that out, did you?"

"Kinda hard not to, since we've all been working with Weight Winners Canada since they set up shop in Landon, and since

I've been pulled off everything to work with them on CRC regulations."

"You're the expert, babe."

"Don't call me babe, please. It's demeaning."

"Well, sorry. So what's your beef? Or is it just that you've been eating too much beef?"

"What?"

"I can't help but notice you've put on a few pounds," Ballard said.

"So what? Look, Chris, you really don't want to make any more mistakes at this point."

"Mistakes? What mistakes?"

"All of that research was going to Weight Winners America, right? Not the government?"

"It went to the government first. If Weight Winners America got access to your work, it wasn't through me." Ballard smiled.

"Even though you're having an affair with the president of Weight Winners Canada?"

"Hmm. I didn't know anyone had figured that out. We've been careful."

"You have a few tells, Chris. Anyone who hasn't endured sex with you probably wouldn't realize."

"Endured? You seemed to enjoy it at the time."

"Don't flatter yourself. You don't understand women nearly as well as you think you do."

Ballard's smile disappeared, and he said, "Be careful, Ms. Williams. You're still my employee."

"And that cuts both ways. You do know I have records of *our* affair."

"Blackmail?" he asked.

"No. Just protection. And that's nothing compared to the shit storm that would hit this firm if the world knew you'd been feeding government reports to your other clients."

"You can't prove that."

"I don't have to."

"Shit, you have got to be kidding. You can't go public. That would destroy you too. Nobody would ever hire you again."

"Well, then we have to find a way to ensure that it doesn't happen. We have to reverse the takeover of the CRCs by Weight Winners," Jacinda explained.

"What? That was the whole point! Do you have any idea how much money they are going to make running those fat camps?"

"They're not camps. They're prisons now," Jacinda said.

"Don't be such a drama queen. They can get out anytime they lose some fucking weight. It'll be good for those fat bastards to have some proper incentive. Before they knew they could leave any time and there was no stake to staying fat. Now they have no choice," Ballard said.

"But it's not that easy. Have you ever tried to lose weight?"

"Never had to. I have self-control," Ballard said.

His smugness reignited her seethe; in fact, it flared into outright anger. "Self-control? You've never had to control yourself in your life. You can just take whatever you want, or you have had it handed to you. Ballard, you're such a pompous, arrogant, entitled one-percenter you wouldn't know what to do if you had limits!"

"Get out of my office," he said.

"Or what?"

"Or I'll have you removed. Permanently."

"Are you threatening me?"

"With dismissal, certainly."

"It sounded like more than that to me," Jacinda said. Her face was flushed and she could feel pricks of perspiration appearing under her arms. She heard a faint ringing in her ears and she realized that she'd never been so angry. Or frightened. She'd long suspected that Ballard had a dark side, and now she was starting to see it.

"Get out."

"I'm leaving, but this isn't over," Jacinda said.

"As far as I'm concerned, it is."

She turned to leave, and he said, "Yes, your ass is definitely spreading from shapely to stout, babe."

She ignored him and slammed the door behind her.

Ballard's assistant stared at her as she made her way back to her office. She grabbed her coat and left, her face aflame as her anger lost its seethe and turned to shame. She hadn't helped Keelan or all the other people stuck in the CRCs at all.

     If anything, she'd just made it worse.

FACT
The Brown Liquid of Life

Much like alcohol, the research on coffee is mixed. Some coffee is okay, but too much can be a problem. Especially if you use sweetened creamers and sugars in it.

There is a frightening 2013 seventeen-year study of more than forty thousand people published by the Mayo Clinic that discovered an increased risk of death – from any cause – for drinkers of four or more cups a day.

But caffeine can help you get more out of a workout. And let's not forget the diuretic benefits of a cup of Joe. Maybe that's why Canadians call a coffee with one sugar and one cream a "regular".

13

Chapter 4 – An Extra-Large Timmy's Existentialism

Keelan hadn't seen much of Greg since his friend had started dating Tina, and even less since the Weight Winners takeover of the CRC.

They'd met that morning for coffee in the commons. As usual, Keelan was just drinking some green tea – he'd read somewhere that the antioxidants in the tea might help ramp up his body's metabolism – and the trainer that had given him some of his best weight-loss advice also thought that the "fake" energy of caffeine was counterproductive. But he couldn't help but look longingly at Greg's extra-large Tim Hortons coffee, topped up with sugar and cream, and wonder if just one wouldn't be okay?

"God, I missed this," Greg said as he had a sip. "Are you sure you don't want one? I can spot you the cash if you need it."

"No, I'll stick with the green tea. I'll deny myself … again."

"You know, I didn't think Weight Winners was going to be a good thing at first," Greg said, "but they really have made the place much more livable. Letting Timmy's do the coffee was a good step, that's for sure. Turning the cafeteria into a restaurant was good too. And I really like their new policy regarding fraternization."

Keelan grinned. "You would."

"You know, Tina has lots of friends who think you're super cute."

"I'm in love with Jacinda, Greg."

"Yeah, but she's, you know …"

"What?"

"Out there." Greg nodded his head towards the sunlight streaming through the skylights above the commons. "And you're in here. Besides, I think you should give our women a better chance. They're nice."

"*Our* women?"

"You know, the women in the CRC. The women like us."

"Like us?"

"You know. Fat."

"Oh god, you don't call them fat, do you?"

"Yes. I don't treat them any different from you. You're fat. I'm fat. Max is fat. Even if we're not *as fat* as the manatees, we're all here 'cause we're fat. The sooner you just accept that, the better. You have to stop with the denial."

"What do you mean?"

"I've been thinking about this for a while, Kee. You're an unhappy guy, brother. And I think it's because you have an ideal that you're trying to live up to. You have a vision of what your life should be, but in the attempt to achieve that goal, you're missing the day-to-day of your life as it is. You're living for some future, more perfect moment. But what if it never comes? What if an asteroid comes crashing through the CRC tonight and you die never really having lived?"

It was easily the most insightful and philosophical thing that Greg had ever asked him. And rather than be angry, it touched Keelan.

"I think Tina is having a good effect on you, man. That was fucking deep."

"Tina is definitely having a good effect on me. On certain parts more than others, if you get my drift."

"Oh, Greg, come on. I don't need to know the details ..."

"Seriously, she is insatiable. I remember reading somewhere that fat people make better lovers because they're more sensual. It stands to reason, right? I mean, if you like the sensual overload of food, then why not the sensual overload of sex?" Greg asked.

"I don't think that follows."

"Well, it does for Tina. She's crazy for giving head."

"Greg!"

Now Keelan had that image in his mind, and he was dreading having to talk with Tina the next time he saw her. And truth be told, he was intrigued, perhaps even a little upset with himself at missing the chance to experience that particular pleasure himself. But he loved Jacinda. He shouldn't be thinking about that, right?

"Sorry, but it's true. And I reciprocate, of course."

"Greg!"

"Sorry, but it's … you know, good. Gotta share, brother."

"Fine, you've shared. Now, can we move on?"

"You're a prude!"

"No, I'm not. But I have to live here with you people. I can't imagine you … like that and still have polite conversations."

"Screw polite conversations," Greg said. "The reason we're in here is because of fucking polite conversations. The reason that they can pick on fat people is because they don't like the visceral realities of fat. The idea of it makes them queasy. It's uncomfortable."

"Greg, what the hell are you talking about? And who is they?"

"Them. The *normies*. People who aren't fat."

"Greg, dude. You can't do that. We can't make this an us-or-them issue. We have to make people of a normal weight realize that we haven't necessarily chosen to be fat, and that it could happen to –"

"Not fucking likely," Greg interjected. "People don't think that way. People look at the world, and they see themselves as special somehow. They don't look at a fat guy and say, 'That poor dude. That could be me.' They don't. Really. They don't see someone who is living on the streets and think, *That could happen to me.* They think: *What did that guy do to fuck up so badly and end up like that? He's probably a drunk or a junkie.* They don't look at their lives objectively for a second and say to themselves, 'Boy I'm lucky I was born white, into a stable family with good income and I'm sure lucky I didn't get any of fat Aunt Serena's genes.' They think: *I'm special. I deserve all this.*"

"I disagree. We can change minds. Affective change is possible. Look at how society views homosexuality or depression. It can change. Slowly. Painfully. But we can get people to think differently about things. It's just that – right now – picking on fat people is the last acceptable prejudice," Keelan said.

"I dunno," Greg said. "Being black isn't so great. Or indigenous. Or any colour other than white. I think we have a different philosophy on a couple of fronts. You're all about optimism and hope. I know you think that's going to make you happier, but real happiness is right now. It's all about accepting the world as it is. I've learned it the hard way. When I was a kid, it was all about my skin colour. But I learned I couldn't change that, but my weight, well I could, right? But to what end? I'll still be fuckin' black. And somewhat proud about it now. Better to accept the world as it is, and find my happiness where I can."

"I can't think that way," Keelan said.

"If you don't, you're going to while away your life, never enjoying the pleasures that are in front of you. You'll live with hope, sure, but in denial of life. Not to mention how cruel it is to Jacinda. You love her, right?"

"Yes," Keelan said.

"Well, if you really love her, then the best thing you could do for her is to let her be free. Let her find someone that she can be with. We're all worm food, dude, and every moment you spend doing something for later is a moment you've lost. I spent all of my twenties not knowing that, but I've smartened up now."

"I can't think that way …"

"That's probably true. Look, I didn't mean to be this heavy."

"Ha. Funny."

"What? Oh, fuck you, man. I wasn't making a pun."

"Sorry. I thought you were trying to *lighten* the mood." Keelan grinned.

"Ugh." Greg looked thoughtful for a moment. "Don't you just want to forget all this philosophy and *chew the fat* instead?"

Keelan laughed and said, "Sure. Now tell me all about these women who think I'm sexy."

"I didn't say sexy, I said cute. And there's a lot of them …"

MYTH

Artificial Sweeteners Are a Great Weight-Loss Tool

It's a great idea – cut the empty calories you're getting from sugar by replacing them with artificial sweeteners. Unfortunately, mother nature turns out to be a complete bitch, once again.

Researchers from the Weizmann Institute of Science say gut bacteria transformed in subjects who consumed artificial sweeteners. This led to glucose intolerance, a precursor to diabetes and a condition that makes it easier to *gain* weight. So there are two things to take away from this study: you may want to reconsider your addiction to Diet Coke.

The other? Try not to be disgusted by the fact your gastrointestinal system is *just swimming* with single-celled organisms.

14

Chapter 5 – Fatheart

Brittany was cross.

There was no getting around it, Keelan realized; she was upset. Miffed and verging on pissed. Keelan had somehow managed to gain two pounds.

Personally, he blamed Greg and his new philosophy that was one part hedonism and one part carpe diem. Since their talk the week before, Keelan had stopped denying himself the little pleasures: he'd started drinking coffee again, even putting – gasp – a little sugar in it. And the other night, when Max had appeared at his door with a bag of salt and vinegar kettle-cooked ships, Keelan had had some. Truth be told, if Max hadn't been there also trying to eat them, he would have inhaled the whole bag. And he didn't stop himself from eating the things that he knew would be problematic. He'd yet to let any bread pass his lips, but he'd had the mashed potatoes on offer the night before at dinner.

He'd continued his exercise regime as usual, but those little things added up. The reality was that the two pounds were probably mostly water weight, but it was the first time in months that the number had increased. And Brittany was not happy.

"I'm pissed," Brittany admitted. "How is this possible, Kee? You've been doing *so* well."

"I'm sorry, Brittany, but I've just been a little – challenged lately."

"Challenged? How so? Don't you want to get out of here?"

"But they adjusted the numbers. If they hadn't, I'd be out."

"Tough!" Brittany shouted. "So they changed the rules. You still can do it!"

This was a new side of Brittany. She was usually just enthusiastic. Cloyingly so.

"What have you been eating? Have you been eating bread?"

"No! *Never!*" Keelan said. It was a huge lie. If they ever decided to serve blueberry fritters at Timmy's, he would totally scarf one down. It would call to him like a giant sugary purple-goo-filled siren, urging him to wreck his ship of denial in one glorious, glazed carbfest.

Brittany started to shake. "I know it's not easy, Kee, but you have to be strong."

"What do you mean it's not easy? You're not fat."

"No! God, of course not, but my BMI is up to 18.4!"

"That's good, isn't it?"

"I've gained five pounds since Weight Winners took over!"

"But isn't 18 on the lower end of the normal scale?"

"I used to be 17.3! I was *special*. Gorgeous!"

"You still are gorgeous, Brittany. Really."

Brittany started sobbing and trying to explain at the same time. It was hard for Keelan to make out, but it sounded like she was blaming the CRC for her weight gain. "It … it … be-be-cause … [sob] this … place … is … so [sob] … rolls of fat …"

Keelan grabbed a tissue from the nearby dispenser and gave it to her. The gesture brought her around and she dabbed the mascara running from her eyes.

"But you're so much skinnier than everyone else here, you really shouldn't get upset about a few pounds."

"I'm sorry," Brittany said. "That was very unprofessional."

"It's okay. I know these can be fraught issues, especially for women."

"Oh, you have NO idea," Brittany said. "I'm just glad I don't have to see any of my classmates looking like this. I would just DIE."

"You don't think that's an unhealthy attitude too? I mean, as far as I understand the literature, being underweight is more dangerous than being overweight."

"Even being slightly obese can be better, in some cases," Brittany whispered. She dabbed at her eyes and looked around her, as though making sure nobody could hear them. They were in a separate room and the door was closed, so Keelan wondered why she even looked. "It's true, though I shouldn't say that to you. You're still on the obese side of the equation, but not by much. Six more pounds gets you under 30." She smiled weakly.

"But that doesn't get me out of here, does it?"

"No, that will take fourteen pounds. But you can do it. You've already lost more than fourteen!"

"I've lost twenty pounds, almost exactly!" Keelan cried. "It has taken me more than two years, and I'm still only halfway to the goal. At least you can leave this place, Brittany. I have to stay. I have to stay here with all the other fat bastards and breathe in the stink. Why is it so stinky all of a sudden? Have I reached some kind of crisis point? Some Rubicon of hyper-failure that is affecting my sense of smell as well as my self-esteem?"

"Oh, I know why it stinks; it's because of the air conditioners."

"What, aren't they working?"

"Yes, they're working, but they've been retrofitting things. The new commandant has some ideas about how they can make more profits."

This was all news to Keelan. "What the hell is a commandant? And who was the old one, let alone the new one?"

"Oh, damn. I wasn't supposed to say anything about that either. I'm all over the place today, Kee. Please forgive me. And please. Oh, god, please don't say anything about the commandant, okay? I might get in trouble."

Keelan wondered if that would be such a terrible thing. But he was actually feeling a bit sorry for her. She looked so miserable, despite her model-like cheekbones and her razor-sharp hips. At least he assumed they were razor sharp. Judging from her raised collarbones, he figured there wouldn't be much more padding down there either.

Perhaps sensing his drift of thoughts, Brittany said, "Now, let's get you back on track, shall we?"

But Keelan was defeated. If hyper-thin Brittany, who had an entire education and all of her self-worth wrapped up in keeping unhealthily thin, could not manage it, what hope was there for him?

There was none.

The conversation with Greg ran through his mind. He was just fooling himself. He was lying to himself, to Jacinda, to everyone. Max kept saying they were never going to let them out. Now that cynical thought was – for Max – a reason to lose weight and somehow beat the system. For Keelan, who had been pouring his being into the goal for so long, that was just another reason to let himself feel a modicum of freedom. What if he just gave up?

Would quitting be that bad?

"Kee?"

"Oh, sorry," Keelan said. "I wandered off for a while."

"Look, I know it seems bleak. But you really can lose the weight. All the science is behind you on this. All you have to do is restrict your intake of calories and keep up your exercise routine. You won't be able to work out any more, because you won't – frankly – have the energy. Unless we could change your diet plan, but that's not an option."

"Why not?"

"The corporation won't allow us to put anyone on a special diet anymore. You can, of course, choose anything from the menu in the restaurant, and they are all Weight Winner-approved meals. But I'm starting to think that Tyrell's approach was right. I've been doing some more research since they fired him, and I suspect he's onto something."

"Remind me, what was it?"

"High nutrient-value foods. That's the secret. You eat small amounts of foods that are pure, whole, and filled with nutrition. That way you can fool your body into thinking it's getting enough so that it doesn't go into starvation mode while you reduce calories," Brittany said.

"So let's do it."

"No, there's no way I can order that kind of meal plan. First, you'd have to have five small meals a day, and the restaurant is only open for three mealtimes. Then there's the expense. Blueberries, walnuts, fresh fruits, and veggies … it all adds up, and the cost would be exorbitant."

"But so what? We're here to lose the weight, right? That's all that matters," Kee said.

"Sure. And if you ate like that, your health would really

improve too. But Weight Winners …"

"What?"

"Look. The corporation is not going to underwrite those costs. The commandant made that clear at the Profitability Retreat."

"The what?"

"Oh, I shouldn't say anything."

"Spill it, Brittany, or I'll tell the commandant you blabbed about his Profiteering Retreat."

"Profitability."

"Same thing, right?"

"Okay, he outlined his plan for making as much profit as possible during the Weight Winners oversight of the CRC facilities."

"Is there an end date?"

"Yes, apparently. Weight Winners Canada seems to think it's only a matter of time. It might take five years, it might take ten, but the Liberals will win an election sometime and they'll give the contract to one of their corporate buddies."

"Right. Because nobody ever renationalizes anything, do they?"

Brittany looked confused.

"They wouldn't put it back in the public sphere," Kee explained.

"Oooh. Anyway, they've got big plans to make as much profit as possible before they lose the franchise, and throwing cash at high-quality foods that may work for your dieting goals probably won't be one of them."

"Colour me shocked that a large corporation is putting their profits ahead of individual welfare," Keelan said.

So that was it. There really was no hope.

He wasn't going to be able to lose the weight. Greg was right that he should just accept it. He would be happier.

Except, he'd have to give up the dream of being with Jacinda. But if that was all it was – a dream – wasn't it also a lie? If he really loved her, wouldn't it be better if he just let her go? She could still have a happy and normal life outside the CRC. If they clung to their delusion, that Keelan could lose the weight and get out, they would both be miserable. And then the wretchedness of what he had to do struck him: not only did he have to accept that he was going to spend his life in the damned CRC, he was going to have to break up with the woman he loved so that she could be with another man.

It was the only thing he could do if he really loved her.

Which, he realized as his great, fat-wrapped heart began to break, he did.

QUOTE

"The twentieth century has been characterized by three developments of great political importance: The growth of democracy, the growth of corporate power, and the growth of corporate propaganda as a means of protecting corporate power against democracy."

~Alex Carey

Chapter 6 – Hark, What Light in Yonder Skype Window Breaks?

Jacinda was in her sexiest nightie and in bed, her laptop open in front of her crossed legs. A glass of Chardonnay sat on her nightstand while she logged into Skype and waited for that magical, pulse-like tone to sound. A sound that had certain effects of a personal and lubricatory nature – effects that were embarrassing on the occasions when she had to use Skype for professional reasons. A Pavlovian response of the loins. She smiled in anticipation of Keelan's call. He was always so sweet, so gentle, so very understanding of how she felt. And he had a wicked, sensual imagination that was perfect for "Skypie-time", as they called it.

The tone sounded, and she allowed herself a delicious moment before she clicked on the answer button.

Immediately, her body responded to her lover's body language. She sat up. The luxurious sensuality of the moment was over in an instant when she took him in. He sat hunched at his little desk, his eyes dark. He was fully dressed. So something was definitely up, and it wasn't his libido.

"What happened?" she asked.

"I have …" Keelan paused for a moment, and he closed his eyes. "I've come to a decision."

"What decision?"

"I think we should break up."

"What?" Her eyes began to well up with tears, and Jacinda felt a little light-headed, as though Keelan had just administered some kind of aural anesthetic. "What do you mean, Kee?"

"Jacinda, I don't want to do this – but, but there's no way I'm ever going to get out of here."

"Yes, you will, Kee! I know you will. What happened?"

"I gained a couple of pounds."

"That's just a little setback, lover. You can lose them again. And more. I believe in you. I know you can do it."

"But I can't. And even if I could, they aren't going to let me go. None of us. We're too valuable in here now. Before, when it was just the government, there was no benefit to keeping us in here, except for getting all the fatties off the street, of course."

"That's not why they passed the law –"

"Sure," Keelan said. "That's the story."

"But … okay, even if you're right. I think you're being overly cynical, but even so, they still can't keep you in there if you lose the weight."

"I won't lose it. Or it will take me years, at this rate. And my best guess is they will simply lower the BMI again. I can see it now. Even if they lower it to 28, that would still mean they're letting us go while we're overweight. They can sell that."

"Kee, do you know how many people out in the world are overweight?"

"Tons," he said.

Jacinda smiled and said, "That's weak, but at least you're joking."

"I'm not, though, Jacinda! I have to do this. It's the only way you can have a normal life. If we don't end it, you're going to spend your life waiting for me to get out of here. The Fatness is not going to let me go. And I don't know, who am I kidding? You're totally out of my league."

"That's ridiculous," Jacinda said. Her mother's voice said, somewhere in her subconscious, *He's right. You should listen to him. He's offering you an out.*

"It's not ridiculous. It's totally 'diculous."

"That's not a word, goofy boy."

"I know. I was trying to lighten the mood, Jacs. I *am* breaking up with you. It's the only realistic thing to do. I've thought about it. I believe it. It's true. I'm stuck. You're not. I don't want to drag you down with me. I won't! I care about you too much. Besides, Greg says there's lots of women in here who think I'm cute. I'll be okay."

Jacinda felt an icy hand grab her heart. Was this another Ballard situation? *How could that even happen?*

"Is there someone else?" she asked.

"No! How could you ask that?"

"You just said there's buttloads of heavyset women ready to fuck your brains out in there. Is that what this is about, Keelan. Sex?"

"No!"

Jacinda was angry now. The icy hand had fingers of pure fiery rage and they flared into light.

"Do you have any idea the shit I've been taking because of you? My mother thinks I'm insane, and I'm going to be fired."

"I'm sorry," Keelan said. "I never wanted those things. I want you to be happy."

"You want me to be happy so you're breaking up with me?"

"Yes!"

"That doesn't make any sense! It's the opposite of what you should do. You should fight for me!"

"I have been. I have. I've lost. It's …" Keelan started to cry, very softly. And the flames in her chest extinguished as though deprived of all oxygen.

She felt a little out of breath, and the dizziness returned. He was telling the truth; she knew it. He was done, and he was trying to do the right thing by her. And the ruthless part of her that spoke with her mother's voice said, *Let him go. It's your chance to get out scot-free. You can be free.*

It was all true, she understood, but deep down, she didn't care about logic or what was sensible.

"Don't break up with me because you're trying to save me, Kee. Do it because you don't want to be with me, but not because of some noble idea that it's what you should do. I *hate it* when men make my decisions for me. If I get tired of waiting for you, I'll say so. But it will not happen. I love you, you sweet, beautiful man."

Kee's will was already ravaged, she could see, and he caved under this argument. As tears ran, he said, "I just don't know … I don't think I could take it if you ever did change your mind. I think it would be better for us to end it now, and we could have some beautiful memories. We've had how many nights together?"

"Six," Jacinda replied. There were six nights they'd been able to spend together and she desperately wanted a lifetime more. But she was willing to take whatever she could get. "There's an easy solution."

"No, there's not. Even if you paid for my health care, they won't let me out."

"What?"

"I checked into it. They've rewritten the guidelines so that once someone is admitted to a CRC, they cannot leave until they reach 29 BMI."

"That's ridiculous."

"I know, my love, but that's the law."

"Maybe for now, but that is going to change."

"How?"

"Well, in case you've forgotten, I'm a lawyer, and you are a charismatic spokesperson if you set your mind to it. As far as I'm concerned, we still live in a democracy, and we can change a law we don't like!"

"I know what Max would say to that."

"Well, you know what Max can do with his absurdism and cynicism."

"I've just run out of hope, Jacinda."

She smiled at him, and she wished that she could reach through the Internet and hug him. Just hold him and let him feel her reality. But that was not an option, so she just whispered to him, "I have enough hope for both of us, Kee."

FACT

Willpower and Other Unknowns

First, a couple of definitions. Self-control is the ability to set goals for yourself. Willpower is what enables you to reach those goals. So you may set the goal of losing fourteen more pounds so that you can escape the Fatness, but it will take willpower to allow you to do that.

There are some studies that show willpower is a limited resource, like muscle energy or the ability to listen to your grandmother tell you how long she waited in line at the pharmacy to buy her "unmentionables" for the umpteenth time. They call this *ego depletion*, though I'd describe the latter case as *ennui*. However, a Stanford University study indicates that willpower depends more on your *concept* of how willpower works. If you believe it is an unlimited resource, you are not going to get tired out by using it.

In any case, you *really* don't want to ask granny what she means by "unmentionables".

15

Chapter 7 – O Captain, No. Captain, NO!

The commons was definitely changing. Weight Winners Canada had decided – sensibly – that it was unlikely the population of CRC-17 was ever going to need the bleachers so they could watch their own intramural sports teams play basketball, floor hockey, and heavyset dodgeball. This was because the sports coordinator – a sad young (possibly bulimic) woman who had also recently graduated from the Helmuth kinesiology program – had been unable to get enough people interested in playing any of these sports to form a single team, yet alone a league. With this dream dead, and the prospect of the PM returning to do another drug-induced press announcement there implausible (the PM's staff still had to be on the lookout for the occasional flash of truth from their boss first thing in the morning, and on those days all public appearances were cancelled), Weight Winners thought they might do something with the space. One side of the gymnasium had already lost its bleachers and a renovation was under way.

While one set of stands remained, the new manager of CRC-17 was going to use them to hold a public announcement about changes to the institution. Half the bleachers were enough. The attendance was thin. (Er, sparse.) Keelan and Max were there. Greg and Tina also showed up, and the four sat near the back of the stands.

There was a little stage set up with a microphone, and without fanfare, a small impeccably dressed man strode to the stage, his arms moving in rhythm with his legs, as though he was marching. His eyes were dark, verging on black as seen from their seats. His hair was white, and he had a salt-and-pepper mustache almost wide and thick enough to be called a pornstache, but not quite. He turned on the microphone and began to speak.

"Good morning, ladies and gentlemen, I am the new commandant of this facility, Calorie Reduction Centre 17, also known as the Uxford County Facility. I believe a few of you wags may even call this place the Fatness'." He did not smile as he said this, but a few people laughed anyway.

"That is going to end today. From now on, if I hear anyone call this place the Fatness or the FUX –" Max giggled at this "– there will be repercussions. You may call me Commandant McGrath, or Captain McGrath if you prefer to be more informal. Prior to running the successful and groundbreaking Camp Fitness program for Weight Winners America, I was a captain in the US Army. I take discipline seriously. I believe – I know – that discipline is your key to winning this Battle of the Bulge you are currently losing." McGrath waited for a moment, and Keelan wondered if he was hoping for a laugh.

He looked around and he could see bored annoyance on most people's faces, but Max seemed to be excited by the commandant's speech. He was actually sitting on the edge of his seat.

"This is a battle I want you to win. Weight Winners wants you to win. We will be assigning you all new exercise and diet programs in the coming weeks to enable you to win. Victory is possible. I have seen it myself. In the crucible of battle, discipline is the fire that melts fat."

"Oh, that's good," Max said. "The crucible of battle. Will they be giving us weapons? I hope they give us weapons."

"But," McGrath continued, "we also recognize that your surroundings must be normalized. I'm told – by psychologists and other *scientists* – that it will be difficult to instill this discipline in such a sterile and institutional place. And so, we will begin the process of making this facility more like what you'd see in the outside world. Behind me will be the first of a few stores in a new mall, so that you can do some shopping when you feel like it. Yes, you heard me correctly. Shopping. We will also build a small movie theatre into the space once occupied by our meeting rooms. And in phase two, the space you're sitting in now will be taken up by more shops and a few off-hours eating facilities. The food available there will all be at your cost, but it will be nutritious and it will fit within your diet plans."

He looked about the room and made eye contact with Max,

who seemed to be the only one who was actively listening.

"Some of you may be thinking that you cannot afford these new luxuries, to which I say, Weight Winners has a new program that will help you lose your weight while you provide valuable services within the CRC. Please talk with your new discipline advisors about this income-producing option when they are assigned to you."

"Discipline advisors," Max whispered to Keelan. "Is that what I hope it is?"

"No, Max, I doubt there's going to be a corporate-sponsored dominatrix assigned to you," Keelan whispered back.

"Finally, I want to say from a personal perspective that I understand how difficult it can be to lose weight and keep it off. I was a chubby kid. I was picked on my whole life until I learned the value of discipline and I took off the weight. I had the luxury of joining the US Army to do this. They helped me lose and keep off the weight. Now I want to pass along the wisdom of that fine institution and allow you to meet your weight-loss goals so that you can join society again as men and women I will be proud to call Weight Winner graduates."

Captain McGrath saluted, and there was a polite round of applause, except for Max, who was standing on his feet, clapping and whistling like a maniac. McGrath threw Max a confused glance and left the stage.

Max continued to applaud even after McGrath had left the room.

What McGrath had not said in his "inspirational" speech was that the CRC was going to see – and feel – a few other major changes as well. First, Weight Winners hired DarkRain – an American "security" company – to provide guards for the institution. They seemed more like mercenaries than rent-a-cops, but even Max admitted they had cool uniforms: all-black, with really impressive high-tech body armour designed to stop rounds from an assault rifle and protect them from explosive devices. On duty they wore helmets that looked like giant black suppositories – the faceplates were incredibly reflective, and talking to one of them was a bit like having a conversation with a shadowy doppelganger of Darth Vader. (The amplification their sub-vocal mics gave their voices reinforced this impression.) Their armaments included a variety of assault shotguns, automatic weapons (mostly Tek 9s and other submachine guns), and pistols, of course. Lots and lots of pistols. The DarkRain Corporation was famous for their pistol bonus system, and employees were allowed to wear as many pistols on duty as they wanted. It was one of the ways they could express their individuality and, when wearing their helmets, the only way you could tell one merc from another – apart from name tags stitched onto their body armour in dark grey lettering.

It seemed a little like overkill, even for a notorious bunch of rioting fatties like the ones at CRC-17.

The next big change was announced in a CRC-wide email they received early the next morning, before Keelan was normally up. He was awake because his room seemed exceptionally warm, and his body's sweating had roused him. Keelan read the email in his pajama bottoms as he toweled off:

To: Client #6623
Time: 4:10 a.m.
Subject Line: Get Grooving!

Dear Keelan Cavanaugh,

Research shows that temperature is a key factor in weight loss. Thus Weight Winners Canada has investigated and instituted our new Move-n-Groove™ atmosphere regulation process, which will take effect immediately.

Move-n-Groove™ will help you reach your weight-loss goals faster, with less active effort than a traditional exercise-only regimen.

How will this work? Your rooms will no longer be air-conditioned or heated from the hours of 4:10 a.m. to 8:40 p.m. This means that you will be able to get a good night's sleep in perfect comfort, but otherwise, your room will stay at the ambient temperature of the building. This will encourage you to move more in the colder months, and though it may encourage a feeling of lassitude in the warm summer months, research shows that higher temperatures encourage more calorie burning by the body. Add movement to either situation, and your weight-loss goals will be groovin'!

The exercise rooms, restaurant, and of course, the mall will all be air-conditioned and heated, and you can, of course, use them at your leisure. In addition the Move-n-Groove™ system will allow you to purchase Temperature Credits from Weight Winners, which you can spend on additional hours of cooling or heating in your room.

If you would like to purchase Temperature Credits, or need to join our new Work-n-Weigh™ income program to earn Temperature Credits, please ask your discipline advisor.

Client #6623 Data Insert
Your Discipline Advisor (DA): Daniel Starkey, Weight Winners Associate.
Your DA appointment time: 3:15 p.m.
Place: Consult Bay 12, CRC-17

Thank you for your time, and happy weight loss!

Lucian "Captain" McGrath
Commandant, Calorie Reduction Centre 17

Weight Winners Canada

Well, that's just great, Keelan thought. He clicked on the weather channel to see what the forecast was for the day. A high of 26 degrees Celsius, with a humidity that would make it feel like 34. It was May 12 and the summer had yet to begin.

His nose twitched with annoyance and, perhaps, anticipation.

QUOTE

"What's in a name? That which we call a rose by any other name would smell as sweet."

~William Shakespeare, *Romeo & Juliet*

Chapter 8 – Pungencies

Take a large number of overweight people, contain them in a small space with air that does not circulate well, and then turn up the heat. Observers will discover a number of things, the most immediately obvious of which is there is a smell. For Keelan, he thought of it as That Smell. Caps didn't really do it justice, he believed, thinking like a web designer for the first time in many months.

"I would use all caps or small caps to describe it," Keelan said to Max while they waited in line for the restaurant.

"What?" Max asked. He seemed sleepier than usual, and drips of sweat beaded on his forehead and ran down his temple.

"THAT SMELL," Keelan said. "I don't know how much more I can take."

"Ah." Max nodded. "Well, there's bound to be some effects if you raise the ambient temperature in an enclosed space filled with a population of people with hyperactive apocrine glands and way more adipose tissue than the skinny set."

"Huh?"

"The sweat glands that produce tasty proteins all sit under our arms, in our groins, the feet – and guess what the bacteria that live in those dark, moist places like to eat? That's what causes the smell, *compadre*. Our chubby brethren don't handle the heat well – especially the men – so we sweat more. The bacteria chow down and excrete smelly byproduct. Add in our limited access to the shower facilities – I get by with one shower a day, and sometimes I offend myself – and you have a recipe for what you call THAT SMELL."

"I'm sorry I mentioned it," Kee admitted.

"If only we could convince everyone to depilate themselves," Max said. "That would help."

"Dep-what now?"

"Depilate. Remove the hair. The hair down around those regions gives the stench real staying power," Max said. "Hmmm. That's worth considering. We could have shaving parties!"

"Oh, lord," Kee muttered. "What have I done?"

"Well, it would help. I think we also might convince the powers that be to allow our real problem cases to get some medical help. Oh, or *they could turn the AC back on!*" Max shouted towards the front of the line and the entrance to the Slender Taste, the new name of the "restaurant", where there would presumably be some employee of Weight Winners Canada to hear.

Two DarkRain guards sauntered down the line towards Max and Kee.

"Shit. Quiet, Max. You're bringing the heat down on us," Kee said.

"Sometimes I find your penchant for punning a peck inappropriate."

"Also, angry alliteration," Kee quipped.

Max rolled his eyes, and the DarkRain security staff halted next to Max and Kee.

"Y'all have a problem here?" a guard asked. From the pearl-handled revolver he had in a sling in a shoulder holster, Kee recognized the guard as a kid from Tennessee named Billy.

"Hi, Billy," Kee said. "No problem. Just getting a bit frustrated with the wait. We'll be quiet."

"You better be," the other security guard growled. His name was Chet, and he sported three additional pistols to his DarkRain gear: a pair of revolvers slung in hip holsters, and a small Beretta strapped to the outside of his right leg. Kee couldn't understand the point of that. Surely a leg gun was better if hidden? From what Kee could discern, Chet was the kind of guy who enjoyed kicking puppies and drowning kittens. It did not necessarily follow that because he liked guns he enjoyed kicking puppies and drowning kittens, but Kee did make note of the strong correlation.

As there were no puppies or kittens available, Max had just made them targets of Chet.

"Well, no worries. We'll be quiet as church mice from now on," Kee said. "Won't we, Max?"

Kee held his breath. There was no telling what Max was going to say. He was pretty sure that he would not provoke a confrontation. As much as he liked and admired Max, Kee would never have put physical courage high on his list of attributes. But prison can change a man. There was also the second thing that happens when you put a lot of overweight people in a confined area and turn up the temperature – people get testy.

"Just call me Mickey," Max said, his voice dripping with sarcasm.

"What?" Chet said, puffing up his chest and taking a step towards Max.

"Mickey Mouse," Max said. "The only mouse that popped to mind when confronted by clearly superior firepower and clearly inferior right supramarginal gyrus."

"What did you say?" Chet got even closer to Max – so close, in fact, that his Kevlar-coated gut was jutting against Max's unarmoured flab.

"He was saying you're stupid, Chet," Billy suggested.

"That's not true," Max said. "I said your right supramarginal gyrus was inferior. Possibly underdeveloped because of your childhood, or, more likely, just because of your genetic make-up. In any case, you've made the most of a bad situation and found a career where a puny right supramarginal gyrus would not be an impediment. I'd say it helps you do a better job, at least as far as your DarkRain masters are concerned.

"In fact," Max continued, "I bet that your other cognitive functions are just fine, and your intelligence, while at best average, is unaffected by this underdeveloped region of your cerebral cortex. After all, it is only the part of the brain that allows us to regulate our ego and feel compassion. And what use is that to a gun-toting neo-Nazi with, one suspects, equally miniscule male generative organs?"

Kee couldn't help himself. He laughed.

In fact, half of the people in the line laughed, even though they were concerned that one of their own was about to get his head blown off by Chet.

Chet confirmed this suspicion and pulled out one of his

revolvers. The laughter died.

"Whoa," Billy said, "I think this guy is a douche too, but you can't kill him, man. You'll get fired."

"He said—"

"I said you had a little dick, in case you didn't understand what I said before. Though, I repeat, I don't think you're stupid," Max said.

Kee had to revise his opinion of Max. The mad doctor seemed to be completely unafraid. He was calm, even though Chet was pushing the barrel of the gun into his cheek. The rivulets of sweat running down his face belied the calm though.

"Chet, put the gun down," Billy repeated. "Don't make me draw on you. I can't let you kill any of these fat fuckers. We'd both lose our jobs."

"He said I had a little dick," Chet said.

"He's probably just in love with you," Billy said. "Aren't you, you fat fucker?"

"Quite the opposite," Max replied. He said, slowly, "Penguin. Penis."

If a pistol hadn't been drilling into Max's face, Kee would have laughed again. Miraculously, Chet laughed.

"This guy is crazy!"

"He is," Kee confirmed. "I can absolutely verify that."

"Come on," Chet said to Billy as he holstered his hand cannon. "Let's leave this loser alone."

"Alliterative alligator," Max said as they walked away. "Crypto-fascist crocodile."

Chet poked Max in the chest and whispered something into Max's ear.

"You can't do that again," Kee said. "Or I am not going to hang out with you anymore. What's the point in getting Chet to kill you?"

"Please tell me someone got video of that," Max said.

A couple of hands in the queue went up, and Max sighed. "That's why, Kee. We need to push these people back any way we can."

Kee sniffed. "That is a crazy plan. And you, my friend, are going to need another shower today. Your armpit buddies just went nuts."

"Copious sweating will do that," Max said.

"I thought you were pretty cool under pressure there, Max."

"I was terrified. And pancake roulette," he said over his shoulder as he approached the people who had been videoing the exchange. While Kee held their place in the lunch line, Max talked with them.

He returned a few minutes later.

"They've agreed to post them on YouTube. So, that should be interesting."

"Uh-huh. We'll see if anything comes of it," Kee said. "I'm more interested to see what's on the menu today."

"Of course you are."

When they got to the front of the line, a whole new pungency assaulted their noses. The stench of body odour had just increased tenfold. It was as though the jockstraps of a thousand hockey players had been fermenting in a hermetically sealed hockey bag left in the trunk of a Ford Pinto during a Texas heatwave in the 1970s, and kept simmering at that temperature, only to be flown back to Canada and released on the unsuspecting denizens of CRC-17. It was beyond awful.

"It'll just be a minute, gents," the greeter said. Kee was shocked to see that it was Brittany.

"Brittany? What are you doing in the cafeteria?"

"It's called the Slender Taste now. And I've been reassigned," she said. She hadn't looked worse. Her face was drawn and bloodless. Kee thought she must have lost the five pounds she'd been so worried about, and then some. Of course, it might have just been the unrelenting pong coming from the cafeteria.

"Why?"

"They've reassigned most of the calorie supervisors, at least until we can get the discipline advisor training. And even then, there's no guarantee we'll get to work with patients anymore. Sorry. Clients … Clients?" Brittany thought for a moment. "Yes.

Clients."

"Not customers?" Max asked.

"No, Health Canada is the customer. You are the clients."

"I see," Kee said. "Well, I'm sorry to hear you're not going to be working with me anymore. And congrats on losing that five pounds."

"It was eight," Brittany said, a weak smile on her face. "I just put myself on the Freedom Fries diet for a bit. It really did the trick! Well, that and the new Move-n-Groove™ policy."

"How so?"

"I don't feel much like eating these days," Brittany admitted. "I have no idea how anyone is still in here." She looked about her and whispered to Kee, "The smell is awful."

"Agreed," Keelan said. "I thought it would be better here. Isn't it air-conditioned?"

"Oh yes, but that won't scrub out the smell of hoagie."

"Hoagie?" Max asked.

"Today's special. Meatball onion hoagie."

Normally the word *meatball* in anything would have Kee salivating, but the word *hoagie* and its overwhelming similarity to That Smell killed it for him. Was this a clever ploy by Weight Winners? To serve something he'd actually want to eat, but make its scent profile worse than the BO of the Fatness in summer?

A nearby table received their lunch, steam rising off the sandwiches with what Kee saw as stink lines drawn on a cartoon. The fresh waft of hoagie hit them, and Brittany gagged a little bit.

"Sorry," Brittany said. "That was unprofessional."

"No problem," Kee said.

"I don't know what's wrong with you two," Max said. "That sandwich smells delicious. Can I have yours if you don't want it, Keelan?"

And then Brittany threw up.

FACT

Meat Your BO

As Max mentioned, it's the proteins those apocrine glands produce that cause all the stench of body odour – glands that don't develop until puberty, which is why kids don't need to use deodorant.

But those proteins seem to double up when you eat meat. A 2006 Czech study showed that meat-eating males produced sweat that was more offensive, nasty and "unattractive" to females than the perspiration of their vegetarian counterparts. So what is a cishet male to do if he wants to attract a cishet female and not give up the pleasures of animal flesh?

This may seem like a radical suggestion, but he could still wash.
16

Chapter 9 – Boot Camp for Fatties

Consult Bay 12 had changed from the last time Kee had been there to see Brittany, his ex-calorie supervisor.

The ambient temperature was quite a bit higher, because of the Move-n-Groove™ system. The friendly decorations that Brittany had festooned the space with were gone. There was no educational literature, no kitschy motivational posters of cute kittens hanging from clotheslines that said, "Hang in there." Even the family and friend photographs on the little desk were gone.

In fact, the desk was gone.

The chairs were gone.

All that remained was a small table covered in black cloth and an array of instruments that reminded Kee of a dentist's office. A Nazi dentist. With anger issues and a jones for drilling into nerves. There was an array of shiny electronic devices, calipers, and what looked to be a small scalpel.

He looked around for Laurence Olivier. But he was not there. Kee was about to meet his new discipline advisor, Daniel Starkey, who was standing beside the small table. He looked perfectly nice. He had blond hair parted down the middle. He was wearing a pair of horn-rimmed glasses, and under his scientist's lab coat, he had on a white dress shirt and black tie. His trousers were pressed with military precision and his black patent leather shoes were shiny. So shiny.

"Please close the door and disrobe, Mr. Cavanaugh," he said to Kee.

"Uh, hi," Kee replied, closing the door. "Uh, what?"

"I'm Daniel Starkey, your discipline advisor. We will begin with a thorough measurement of your body to give us a baseline to work from, and we'll do some fitness tests in the Discipline Lab."

Kee checked the table again – no, there were no whips or chains or anything else that might connect the words he'd just heard with the requests he'd just received.

"Okay, Doc," Kee said. "But normally I like to be romanced a bit first."

"I do not have a doctorate. I do have a master's degree in mass communications, and I have undergone Weight Winner's intensive discipline advisory certification process. Now, disrobe so that we can begin."

"So you have no medical training at all?"

"I did not say that. The DAC instruction includes courses in physiology, endocrinology, nutrition, fitness, and some other psychological training that is useful in helping motivate our clients to be more disciplined."

"Is it legal?"

"I assume so," Starkey said, and smiled. His smile was about as sinister as a smile could be, unless it was on NAZI dentist revving his drill at the same time. "Now let's get started. The sooner we get the baseline established, the faster we'll get you out of here."

Kee hoped he meant the Fatness, so he took off his clothes. He left his boxer briefs on, which was apparently acceptable to Starkey.

The discipline advisor proceeded to measure Kee's body with the calipers, measuring tape, and at the end he had Kee stand on the scales to get an accurate body weight. He wrote down all the measurements on a clipboard, and when he had them all, he made his calculations.

"Can I put my clothes back on?"

"No," Starkey said, working out some math.

"Why not?"

"It's the start of your training."

"O-kay."

Kee stood there uncomfortably while Starkey worked on his measurements. By Kee's quick mental assessment, his body weight – 220 – put him at about 30.7 BMI. Still a long way from the 29 he'd need to get out. On the other hand, if he thought of it in terms of pounds, it wasn't so bad. It was only 12 pounds. Twelve wasn't so bad. He could just take it one pound at a time.

He snorted. That wasn't going to help. He'd been working on

it now for nearly three years.

"Well, this is interesting," Starkey said. "As you no doubt know, you are obese according to the BMI chart, but the good news is that your body fat percentage is only about 25%, which isn't too high. If we can shave that down by another 5%, that would get you into the healthy range for your age. So we definitely have something to work with here."

"Yeah?" Kee said. He'd heard this kind of talk before, even if it was nice to hear something positive.

"Yes, absolutely. You clearly are working out – your muscle density is pretty good. I'll need to take you out to the gym to do some fitness testing now, but I'd say the initial prospects are excellent. So let's go, shall we?"

"Let me just put my clothes on."

"Oh no, just underwear is fine. You may want to put your socks and trainers back on."

"What?"

"I'm going to wire you up the yin yang anyway."

"Um, I don't really feel comfortable traipsing around in my underwear and a pair of shoes, you know."

"Undoubtedly, but this will help. It's all part of our DP."

"Uh," Kee said, "what does that stand for?"

"Discipline Process™."

"'Cause you know it has another meaning, right? One that in context of being mostly naked in a gym might cause some of your patients –"

"Clients."

"Clients, right. It might cause your clients, particularly the feminine-gendered ones, a modicum of anxiety."

"All part of the DP™," Starkey said.

Luckily, the hallway to the Diagnostic Gym, which was the one that denizens of the Fatness only had access to while they were being tortured by their calorie supervisors, doctors, kinesiologists, and now, apparently, discipline advisors, was not full of people. Kee wasn't completely naked, but he felt that way. He was glad he'd worn his black undies.

The gym itself was depressingly full. There were six other "clients" and six other discipline advisors. They were easy to tell apart. One group was wearing white scientist's smocks, and the other group was covered with sensors, sweat, and what could only be described as shame. At least the female patients had been allowed to wear their bras in addition to their panties. It didn't really help.

Starkey brought Kee over to one corner of the room where the sensors, wires, and belts that held the wires and receivers together were. He put sticky pads on Kee and attached the electrodes.

"Sorry 'bout how low-tech this is," Starkey said. "New clients are having subdermal implants for all their measuring needs, but we're told that the consent form you filled out when you came into the CRC does not allow us to retrofit you."

"Subdermal? Retro-what?"

"Yes, all the measuring devices are implanted under the skin so that we don't have to spend time mucking about with pads and the sensor belts and so on. Plus we can monitor your biological functions continuously, as can you. It's like those fitness monitors you can wear around your wrist, but much more complex and helpful. There's even an option to have blood measurements if you don't mind paying for the extra implant. Would you be interested? This is a high level of service, but it should enable you to have real-time data on your weight-loss goals. If you want to sign up for our MeasureMore™ program, just let me know. In fact, I should have mentioned before that you can sign up for a number of programs with me. I can outline them all to you when we're done in here."

Kee was actually at a loss for words.

"Okay," Starkey said. "That does it for the sensors. Just let me connect the electrodes and we can get you on the treadmill."

Kee saw there were four in use at the moment. He vaguely recognized all the "clients", but he didn't know anyone well. There were two men and four women in the room. The men were both younger than Kee and quite a bit over the 30 BMI. *Manatees,* definitely. So were the women, but Kee didn't look at them too closely, whether from a sense of solidarity or a sense of decorum, he could not say. The women were all on the treadmills, and they were all sweating and panting as their discipline advisors put them through their paces. Needless to say, there was a lot of jiggling, but, again, Kee tried not to be mesmerized – or excited – by it. One of the men had failed at this activity, and it was fairly obvious.

Again, Kee opted not to look. He kept his eyes down as much as practicable.

"This sure has been a busy time for us," Starkey said. "We're doing baselines on everyone in the facility and giving them a chance for a fresh start. Some of the long-timers need it; I see from your previous, uh, helper that you have been consistently working at your weight-loss goal."

"Helper?" Keelan interrupted. "My old calorie supervisor was Brittany, and at least she had a degree in kinesiology."

"Of course. It's not her efforts, but yours that count. And they are a good sign, Mr. Cavanaugh. Now, let me get you set up here, and we can begin to test your fitness. I'm going to stand next to the treadmill here and do a stress test. That's a test to see how long it takes to get you up to a certain heart rate. Do tell me if you feel uncomfortable at any time."

"I already do," Kee said. "I'd like some clothes."

"Ha ha, Mr. Cavanaugh. Very funny."

"No, I'm serious," Kee said. "Why are we doing these tests half-naked? It seems like you're trying to humiliate us."

"Here we go," Starkey said, ignoring Kee's question.

The treadmill started slowly. Kee had been working out and getting lots of cardio – he still could jog under the Health Canada regime, when they could go outside and use the track around the facility – so it wasn't difficult. His body started to sweat a bit, even though he wasn't really puffing.

Kee looked around and saw that there were cameras in all corners of the room. They seemed to be on.

"What are the cameras for?"

"Oh, they are recording you. Most people don't notice them."

"Why are they taking video of us?"

"You'll see."

Kee didn't like the sound of that. The two men were now doing some kind of strength testing, and the women were reaching the end of their stress tests. The door opened, and the commandant of the CRC walked in, along with two DarkRain guards. They stared at the men and women working out.

"Disgusting!" he shouted. "You are disgusting human beings! How could you let yourself get into such a state?" The two guards laughed.

Kee's face burned with shame. He couldn't help but notice that the woman on the treadmill next to him started to sob. Combined with the exertion on the treadmill, it overwhelmed her. She collapsed. Her discipline advisor caught her and prevented her from hurting herself. Kee jumped off the treadmill and helped the discipline advisor get the woman to her feet. She was a mess. She was weeping uncontrollably, slick with sweat, and starting to hyperventilate. Kee's shame turned to rage.

"You should be ashamed of yourself!" Kee shouted at McGrath. "What kind of bullshit is this? Are you trying to hurt people?"

"Shut your face, you sack of lard," McGrath screamed back at Kee. "How dare you speak to your commandant like that? If you want to talk to me like that, you have to be a real person. Not some bloated freak!" He spun on his heel and left the room, the two guards sniggering behind him.

Starkey watched Kee and said, "I'm afraid we'll have to begin the stress test again."

"Fuck your stress test," Kee said. He started ripping the sensors off his skin.

"I wouldn't advise that," Starkey said. "If you don't work with a discipline advisor on your weight-loss goals, you will have to reach a lower BMI to be released. It's the only way we can be sure you won't reoffend."

"Reoffend?" Kee stopped pulling the sensors off.

"Put your weight back on. Studies clearly show it is easy for the obese to lose some weight, but put it all back on."

"How is that an offense?"

"It's an offense to decency. To your own person. You must learn discipline. It's the only way to get out of here."

"And all this?" Kee motioned to the cameras, the woman who had just collapsed.

"We're breaking you down so we can build you up. Now, put the sensors back on, you fat bastard. We're doing the stress test."

Kee wondered what would happen if he punched Starkey in the nose. He wasn't a very big man, and Kee knew he could hurt him.

As if hearing his thoughts, Starkey said, "You should know that if you strike your DA, that will also mean an additional point loss on your BMI goal. Another eight pounds for an even twenty. Your journey to self-restraint and discipline begins here. For others it will happen in other ways, but we knew that for a small segment of you it would begin in this room. For others, it will happen at the public shaming."

"Public shaming?"

"When we air the videos. They'll be viewable tonight. For a fee, but a surprising number of people have already signed up."

Kee didn't hit him. And it *was* the start of something new.

He was going to get out – and he was going to burn this system to the ground. Starkey increased the speed of the treadmill, and Kee started panting. Once he caught his breath, he was going to burn this system to the ground.

Part IV

"The orchard walls are high and hard to climb, And the place death, considering who thou art"

~William Shakespeare, *Romeo & Juliet*

Chapter 1 – Farting Is Such Sweet Sorrow

Jacinda turned off her computer, tears running down her face. Kee had just broken up with her again. It was the third time now that he'd tried. He was breaking up with her because he loved her, he said, both other times. The first time had been easy to change his mind. The second was even easier:

"I don't want you to wait for me," he had said.

"I'll decide what I want to do," she'd replied.

"Fine," he had said. "But it feels like I'm never getting out of here."

"You will. I am working on a case of wrongful imprisonment."

"I love you," he had said.

It had all been so romantic …

But this time was different. There was something new in Kee's voice – a hardness, an edge that he'd never had before. She didn't like the sound. It wasn't him. This time, the script had been almost the same:

"I don't want you to wait for me."

"I'll decide what I want to do. You know how I feel about that, Kee."

"But my opinion counts too, doesn't it? And I can't live with myself, knowing that you're out there wasting your life on a hopeless fatty."

"What? No, you're not hopeless, and you're not a fatty. Pleasantly plump. And last night you still had hope."

"Last night I did, but all I have left now …" He trailed off. "We can talk some more tomorrow, but I need to go to bed and think about what happens next in here. Things have to change."

"So we'll talk tomorrow."

"I love you, Jacinda, but I can't live like this."

"I love you too, Kee. Don't give up on us."

"I'm not, but hope isn't enough."

"Let's not decide anything now, okay?" she asked.

"Okay, but I have to be realistic. One of us has to be ..."

When he turned off the Skype connection, the sound of those words rang in her ears. She decided that he was right. One of them had to change enough so they could be together. And it was taking Kee too long to lose the weight. She believed he could, but she also believed that it was not going to be very easy. Weight Winners Canada was going to do everything it could to keep as many of its prisoners as they could.

Ballard had shared their business plan with her. It included building more facilities and increasing the number of people in them. They were lobbying to reduce the official BMI of obesity from 30 to 29.

Without consciously doing it, Jacinda found herself in front of the fridge. She pulled on the freezer door, grabbed the emergency Häagen-Dazs, and cracked the lid. Normally, the emergency ice cream was coated with a thick layer of hoar frost that had to be scooped off and thrown away. But that had changed of late, and this was her third such container of Rocky Road in as many weeks. It was half-empty, and she polished it off standing there in front of the freezer. The cold air flowed over her face and chest, giving her goose pimples in the warm summer evening. As she ate, the compressor of the fridge played counterpoint to the sound of her scraping the bottom of the cardboard container. Somewhere outside people walked by, having a conversation in a volume that was right for a busy street in the middle of the day, but not in a residential neighbourhood at midnight.

"They will get away with it if we fuckin' let them!" one of the voices said loudly.

She didn't hear the reply and nodded her head. *They are getting away with it*, she thought. She finished the last morsel of ice cream and immediately felt what she thought of as Häagen-Loss: the end of her ice cream coupled with a special kind of remorse about eating it all in one sitting.

And of course, she'd forgotten to take the pills that made the lactose intolerance less offensive. Jacinda returned to her bed, which was empty, though it wouldn't be for long.

There was trouble brewing.

While Jacinda slept in the redolence of her post-emergency ice cream flatulence, Chris Ballard had just finished servicing Melissa Handle at her lake house.

The bedroom was dark except for the refracted glow of a few security lights in the front, and a view of the Milky Way over the dark waters of Lake Huron. The beach grass was black in the night, and there was barely enough light to make out the form of Handle in the bed. Ballard was standing next to the wall-spanning window and taking in the view, naked. While he appreciated the view, the stars, and the feeling of just-fucked contentment, he was restless. He was an emptiness that no amount of food, sex, or money could fill. Inside him was an existential void. A black hole that sat at the core of his body's galaxy, around which all the molecules, like star systems, swirled and eventually died. Ballard was not thinking *these* thoughts. He was thinking that he wanted more. After all the work his firm had done, it wasn't right that his clients would get to run the CRCs. It occurred to him for the first time that essentially, he was in a service industry – would you like some fries with that? – and he wanted more.

Why shouldn't he control the CRCs? It would mean that he might have to undermine his relationship with Handle, which was a sad thought, but a necessary one.

"Well, I'm as happy as a dead hog in the sunshine," she said to Ballard. "Why are you up?"

"Just thinking," Ballard replied. "This is some place."

"You betcha. Bought it when they said I'd have to move to Canada. They say Mitt Romney has a place down the beach a spell."

"Well, then it must be nice," Ballard said.

"Was that sarcastic?" Handle asked. "It's hard to tell with you Canadians sometimes."

"It was," Ballard confirmed. "The fact that a failed presidential candidate owns a place nearby does not make this view any better."

"So you say, but it improves the value of the real estate. Now, come on back to bed. Let's shoot out the lights again."

Ballard grinned and said, "I need a bit more time."

"That doesn't mean I do. There's extra stock options in it for you." As he crawled back into bed with her, she said, "You are just naturally horizontal, aren't you, bad boy?"

"Only when it comes to you," Ballard said.

She laughed. "Right."

"That was definitely sarcasm," Ballard said as he kissed the inside of her thigh. "But I don't mind."

Not everything about the service industry was bad.

The next morning Jacinda woke feeling terrible. Her ice cream binge had resulted in a troubled sleep and even more troubling dreams. In them, she and Kee had been separated by a deep, fast-running river. It wasn't a wide river, but there were rapids that swirled with white water, and the roar of it made it impossible to hear one another. It was clear to her that Kee desperately wanted to get to her side, but she tried to tell him to stay where it was safe. He didn't listen, and he jumped from his bank to a large boulder that stood above the torrent. For a terrible moment, he swayed on the top, looking like he was going to fall. But he righted himself and made the leap to the next biggest rock, which was flatter and lower and so an easy jump. But there was no going back now. The next jump would be the hardest – the rock in the middle of the river was just barely showing above the white water. And it would be slippery and wet. Kee made the leap and landed perfectly on top.

"I love you," he cried above the roar of the rapids. "Wait!"

He made the next jump, and there was just one more rock to get to until he was on her side. But as he jumped, the rock moved. Almost as though it had a will of its own. He missed it completely, landing in the raging water – in the dream, she could hear him shout, "Be happy!"

His face was pushed under the water, and he was gone. And as it goes in the way of dreams, the rapids calmed, and the water changed colour from tormented blue and white to an almost Mediterranean aquamarine. And she went to the water's edge and looked into the surface, which was now as calm and still as a pond, and she could see a woman with a double chin and jowly cheeks looking back at her.

And in the mirror-like river, she could see that it was her.

QUOTE

"Being slim is the new elitism. Thinness today says that you are richer, smarter and more successful than the overweight masses."

-David Zinczenko

Chapter 2 – The Persistence of Penury

The next morning Kee was up with the dawn and blearily put on work clothes. He'd purchased them from the Manliness Hut in CRC-17's new mall the day before, right after he'd decided to join the small number of people who were earning credit for working on the grounds around the institution. He was still angry. But he was going to do something about it, he vowed. He also recognized that he was going slowly crazy.

Keelan was shocked that most people in the Fatness seemed to be content without the opportunity to get outside. It had been several months since Weight Winners Canada took over stewardship of the CRCs, and they'd yet to provide a way for their clients to exercise outdoors. They claimed this was because they needed security fencing and so on, but Keelan suspected they were just introducing new – and expensive – ways for their clients to spend money indoors. Where people got the money, Keelan didn't know. Sure, some people had jobs that they could work remotely, and some people – like Max – had enough savings they could dip into it whenever they wanted. And there were probably folks like Keelan, who had parents or relatives they could borrow the money from. Keelan knew his folks would send him whatever he needed. During his weekly call to his parents, his mom had admitted they regretted not paying for his health care and keeping him out of the CRC. But Keelan hadn't wanted to be a burden on them. They had their own worries, and he thought he could take care of it. If he could go back in time, though, he would have asked.

So he had joined the Work-n-Weigh™ program. The idea behind it was that inmates could improve the grounds, beef up security, and do whatever manual labour the company needed at low-to-no cost to the corporation. For the workers, they earned what was essentially store credit for all the Weight Winners Canada programs and they could be used in the mall as well.

(Personally, Keelan was going to spend most of it on extra showers and more AC in his room, but he might spring for more fresh vegetables too.)

Kee was pleased to see Greg waiting to join the work crew that morning.

"I'm surprised you're here," he said.

"I can use the credits." Greg beamed. "And besides, it's a beautiful day to be outside, even if it is digging ditches."

The crew consisted of Kee, Greg, three other young guys that Keelan didn't know very well, and the hard-faced, sharp-tongued friend of Tina's. She and Greg actually seemed friendly, and Kee nudged him. "What's her name?"

"Interested?" Greg grinned.

"Just being friendly."

"Barbara," Greg said, "this is my friend Keelan."

"Oh, I know who Keelan is," Barbara said.

"Nice to meet you too," Keelan replied.

And the DarkRain security detail arrived, and they explained the security protocols for working outside. There were two of them set to guard the work detail – Keelan was relieved to see neither Billy nor Chet were involved. They were armed with shotguns loaded with beanbag ammo. "We will shoot you if you attempt to escape," the head security guard said, as though he felt nothing about the idea. "These are supposed to be non-lethal, but if we hit you in the head … So, don't make problems."

A discipline advisor Keelan didn't know explained that they would be, indeed, digging; they were making post holes for a new security fence. There was a contractor already at work outside and they would help his men with the work.

They opened the doors, and Keelan got his first chance to experience the outside since his last overnight at Jacinda's place. It was a glorious July day, warm, but not too hot. A cooling north-west breeze made it even nicer, and, as the DarkRain security people escorted them to the area where the contractor was waiting, Keelan was glad of his decision.

CRC-17 was actually set up in a perfect location, on top of

a ridgeline north of Landon. It had fine views both north and south, but they were too far away to see the city. The land had been owned by a horse rancher at one point and purchased by the government for the facility. The initial vision had been that the CRC would not feel like a prison but more like a summer camp. At the bottom of the hill to the south was a large pond for swimming and diving, and there was an old racetrack where the owner of the ranch had trained his harness-racing horses. Originally, the government had planned to turn the racetrack into a place where the patients of CRC-17 could run. And before Weight Winners took over, Keelan and a number of others *had* used it for jogging.

Weight Winners Canada was going to put those early plans into effect and charge its "clients" for the privilege of using the new facilities.

The contractor was a nice guy named Joe, and he had a few workers already planting the new fence. He was in his mid-fifties and probably about as borderline obese as Keelan was. It was clear that most of his extra weight was being contained in a standard-issue beer belly. Joe seemed a bit uncomfortable with the working arrangements, but he was affable and explained their tasks clearly and efficiently. Essentially, they were just going to be digging post holes. They had a couple of tools Keelan had never seen before – some kind of cool hole-digging spade, a clamshell digger for grabbing loose dirt, and a big pole of some kind to use for breaking up the hard stuff and tamping things down. There were a couple of reticulating saws on hand too, to cut through roots and stuff.

They broke the inmates into two teams – one DarkRain security guy went with each group to ensure nobody made a run for it – and got to work. Keelan, Greg, and Barbara were teamed up and they worked together well. Barbara was a bit sharp-tongued for Keelan's liking – she never said anything without there being an edge of sarcasm to it – but she worked hard. She worked harder than Greg, truth be told, but they all pitched in, gaining satisfaction at digging the post holes. When they finished one, Joe would come by, measure its depth and width, and give them a big wide smile. "That's hella good digging," he'd say, and they'd go onto the next one.

At lunchtime, Brittany came out with their Weight Winners lunches and an extra treat of watermelon. Keelan thought that she might have lost even more weight since the last time he'd seen her, and she seemed even more unhappy than before. But the good spirits of the work crews were infectious. And she stayed for a while, chatting with them.

"This is great." Keelan smiled and said to Greg, "Wouldn't a cold beer at the end of the workday be even better?"

"I would kill for a beer," Barbara interjected as she savagely speared some hard clay to break it up with the pole. She was quite powerful. "An ice-cold Bud would be perfect."

"Or a Stella," Keelan said. "I love that beer."

"Ah, that's a sissy beer," Barbara said, "but each to their own."

"I'd have a plain old Canadian," Greg said. His voice sounded wistful.

"You should be worried about the calorie load of beer," Brittany said to them, overhearing the conversation as she packed up the lunch things. "But I think you've burned off way more than one beer's worth of calories anyway today. You're working hard and it's hot." She left and Keelan thought he might have seen her talking with Joe before she headed back into the CRC.

The afternoon flew by and they were all feeling famished when Joe came by to measure their last post hole. "Great work," he said. "I was wondering if you'd like to join me and the rest of the crew for a beer. We sometimes have one together on the worksite."

When they got there, they saw all of their favourite brands, and Keelan wished away all the terrible things he'd ever said or thought about Brittany. She was a real human being after all. Everyone except for the security detail grabbed a beer. They hung back away from the group, observing.

As they cracked open their brewskies, Joe said to Keelan, "I wasn't sure this would work very well, but you folks are fit and strong. Fitter and stronger than me, anyway."

"What do you mean?"

"Oh, I was under the impression that everyone in the CRC was grossly overweight. I didn't think you'd be able to handle the heat, let alone dig all those post holes. I'd be happy to have you guys continue working with us if you want."

"Sure," Keelan said. "It's nice being outside."

"And I can't pay you, but the facility does, right?"

"Sort of," Keelan said. He explained the voucher system for things like air conditioning and better quality food.

Joe was quiet at that. He patted his belly. "So I guess I made the right choice paying for my own health care?"

"You sure did, Joe. I wish I'd opted for that."

Even Greg, who had come to an equilibrium with the idea that he was never going to leave the Fatness, nodded his head.

"It strikes me as unfair," Joe said. "I mean, I really shouldn't be using your labour at all, but if you enjoy it …"

"Yes, we do," Keelan said, and added, "I do anyway. I don't speak for everyone."

"Maybe you should," Greg said. "You're getting better at stringing sentences together, and on the TV you looked good."

"I looked like a sweaty whale," Keelan quipped.

"No, you were fine," Barbara said. It was the nicest thing she'd ever said to Keelan. Maybe to anyone.

"I didn't just mean the unpaid labour," Joe said. "The whole thing strikes me as a bit unfair. If I understand what you were saying earlier, you can't leave now even if you are willing to pay for your own health care. That's not right. You guys didn't break the law or anything."

"Just the Law of Thermodynamics," Keelan said. When nobody laughed and most of the people just looked confused, he said, "You know, 'cause we can't lose weight as easily as calories in, calories out?"

"I take it back," Greg said. "You're not getting better at stringing sentences together."

They laughed at that, but Joe returned to the subject. "Is there anything you'd like me to do?"

"Yes, let people know. Ask your MP to get rid of the Fat Act."

Keelan noticed one of the DarkRain security guards walk away and say something on his radio. He had a brief conversation and came back. "Okay, time to wrap it up, folks. We need to get you back into the CRC stat."

"Really?" Joe said. "I thought we might have time for one more."

"No. Thanks for doing this for our clients though," the security guard said. "We know it wasn't part of our contract."

"Not everything has to be in a contract," Joe said. "Some things are just, just, decency, you know?"

"Yes, sir. Let's go, people."

"So there it is, Joe," Keelan whispered as they left. "That's what is going on in the CRCs. This one, anyway."

MYTH

Is There Really an Obesity Epidemic?

There's a strong argument to be made that the so-called obesity epidemic is an example of moral panic: that is, an intense feeling expressed by the media that menaces the moral order. Other examples of moral panic would include the War on Drugs and the mind-melting dangers of video games (and for an earlier generation, comic books). A classic example of moral panic is the idea that playing Dungeons and Dragons would turn you into a Satanist. (Many have played D&D for years without sacrificing any creature – living or dead – to the Dark Lord.)

The idea that obesity *causes* diseases like diabetes, heart failure, etc., is based on a flawed 2004 CDC report, which was sloppy science. It confused co-relation with causation. But the media picked up on it, and this gave the myth even more power. Does this mean that it's healthy to be fat? Probably not, but a lot of that depends on individual genetics, lifestyle, and other factors that we don't even understand yet.

So when someone asks you if there's an obesity epidemic, you can safely answer: "Hail Satan."

17

Chapter 3 – MooTube

Keelan checked the video again. Ever since it had been posted online, he'd been watching to see what kind of traffic the clip of Max's near-death experience with Chet was getting. Not much, as it turned out. Even though the quality of the video was actually pretty good. It was framed nicely, horizontally orientated, and it picked up right after the point that Max had initially insulted the security guard.

It included everything from that point on, including the startling visual image of Chet drilling the barrel of his pistol into Max's flabby face.

It was upsetting, actually. As he watched it again, Keelan was disturbed to think Chet continued to wander the halls of the Fatness with all that hardware, just waiting to lose his shit and shoot some fat motherfucker.

Chet had even visited Max's cell once. He didn't do anything but stand menacingly outside the door. Keelan hoped that Max understood he couldn't push him too far again. Next time he might snap.

He refreshed the page to watch the video one more time, and the view counter had suddenly gone up from 65 views – probably half of those were Keelan – to 12,542.

Maybe it was going viral?

But it was time to get to work. Joe and the gang were putting in the fence poles today and pouring concrete to hold them up.

He returned that evening, dirty but happy after a hard day's work. Their early success had encouraged even more inmates of the Fatness to join the work program, so the fence was being built quickly. It wasn't as special as it had been the first day, but Keelan continued to enjoy being outside and doing something productive. Even if it meant he was building a fence designed to keep him trapped in CRC-17 forever. He didn't care. He peeled off his dirty work clothes and went for a shower. Now that he was earning Weight Winner Credits™ on a regular basis, he could easily afford a shower whenever he wanted.

When he got back from the facilities, refreshed, and now feeling quite hungry, he thought he'd check the video again. He was astonished to see it now had ninety thousand views. The comments were filled too, though some were hardly edifying, including such gems as:

"Yo, fat boy almost got his head blown off!"

"Yeah, shoot all the fatties."

"He's in a fitness protection program."

However, the vast majority of comments were questions about the behaviour of Chet and whether the video was a hoax or not. Keelan replied to these, explaining that he was the guy standing next to Max, and the video accurately portrayed the events of that morning. He was immediately bombarded by a bunch of replies that were ... well, pretty hateful actually, mostly about his weight, but quite a few about his sexual orientation, and a few about his politics. (He'd been wearing his Richard Sneer T-shirt, which showed a headshot of the prime minister and said "I'm a Dick".) Funny, he had been feeling pretty good about himself – all the hard work outside had helped him to lose three pounds that week, which put him just under the 30 BMI number for the first time in years. (Not that it would get him out of the Fatness. He'd need to lose almost another ten pounds to get under 29.) He noticed there was a little pull-down icon, which he clicked on. It allowed him to report spam or abuse, so he did.

A reply to his comment said, "Hi, Keelan – I hope you remember me, Serena Lee. The reporter who blew open the Heavy Hitters story? Would you be willing to talk to me about this incident? And could you put me in contact with Max?"

Keelan still had Serena's email address, so he wrote her back there. "I'd be happy to chat with you. The man being threatened by the DarkRain security guard is Maximilian Tundra, and you can contact him at mtundra-time@happymail.com. The name of the security guy with the guns and the anger management issue is Chet, and his partner is named Billy. I'm sorry, I don't know their last names. But the commandant of CRC-17, where this happened, is Lucian McGrath. I'm sure you can find the best way to contact him."

Serena Lee was now an expert on the CRCs and was excited there was another juicy story to mine.

"I don't see what the interest would be," Keelan said. They were talking over Skype, in Keelan's room. "Outing one bully in the lunch line isn't going to save the world. It will probably save me some sleep and possibly save Max a beating though."

"Let's talk about the incident first, okay?"

So they talked about what happened. Keelan thought she was verifying the video at first, but he could detect another line to the questions. She wanted to know if the attitude of Chet was representative of the attitude of Weight Winners.

"I think Weight Winners is mostly here to make as much money as they can, but their employees seem to believe they can help us. I've lost nearly five pounds since they took over. But I lost much more under the Canada Corrections regime."

"Regime is a good word, isn't it?" Serena asked.

"It is. When Sneer won the election, everyone was thrilled, because he said he would dismantle the 'socialism gone bad' in here. But he just sold us to Weight Winners. It's like when Britain took over Quebec after the Seven Years' War, except imagine they just outsourced running the province to the Hudson's Bay Company."

"That's some serious CanCon," Serena quipped.

"Sorry. Stretching for a comparison."

"Basically he privatized the CRCs. He did it with some other things too. And more is coming."

"Well, it has made things worse and better."

"How better?"

"At least now I have a reason to work outside. They're using us as manual labour to build the new fence. It's ironic, I know, to be building enhancements to my own prison. But it has been good to be outside a little bit. And there's no questioning the fact that the coffee and the food is better if you have the wherewithal to pay for it."

"What?"

"Oh yes, there are many ways you can be upsold in here, Serena. Food, showers, heating and cooling. They even have trademarked most of these schemes," Keelan said, and went on to explain the various incentive systems and ways these "luxuries" could be paid for.

"It sounds like they're not missing any opportunity to make money off you guys."

"Of course not. It's what corporations are made to do. They are the polar bears of the economy. Sure, they look all loveable and fluffy from their advertising, but once they have you in their claws, don't expect cuddles."

Serena laughed. "That's quotable."

Keelan sighed. "You know who else you could talk to, Serena? My girlfriend, Jacinda Williams, has a lot more background information about the CRCs than I do. I can only really tell you what is going on around me. I know you worked well together when you did the Heavy Hitters story."

"I'll contact her, but I think I'll need to talk to you again."

"Sure, but she can give you some more specific details. And obviously, Weight Winners has their own view of things too."

"Well, of course. And I will make this a fair and balanced piece. First though, I have to clear the story with my producers. It may seem like an incident of bullying, but there is something bigger going on here."

"Pun intended?"

"No, I'm sorry about that. But I was going to make a pun about finding the clip on MooTube."

"Ha," Keelan said. "Seriously, LOL."

"Sorry. I'm just being honest. Do you think you'd be willing to get your friend Max to talk to me?"

"Sure. But I should warn you, he's a bit weird."

"Don't worry, weird is in my wheelhouse."

"As long as you don't mention penguins, you should be fine."

FACT

Why Your Labels Lie

The author can tell you for a fact he knows his waist isn't thirty-two inches, but that's the size jeans he buys.

That's because the maker of his jeans understands that if he has to buy an accurately sized pair, he just won't. In fact, he'll resent them for it so badly, he'd walk around in ragged burlap before he purchased their evil, smelly, truth-telling jeans. Researchers from the University of British Columbia and Florida University showed that smaller label sizes increased the self-esteem of buyers. Conversely, larger labels reduced consumer's self-esteem, and that negative feeling got transferred to the product. Brands create these "vanity labels" so we buy more.

This explains how tiny women can now purchase clothes that are sized below zero, and still be alive.

18

Chapter 4 – This Booty Was Made for Walkin'

Her Chanel suit was not cooperating.

Jacinda had tried to zip up the skirt several times, and no matter how much torque she put into the pull, it wouldn't go up to the top. She had a stylish belt that would work if it went over top of her skirt, so conceivably she could let the belt cover up the gap at the top, but there were two risks. The first was that the zipper would unzip during a meeting or something, and the skirt would fall down around her ankles after she got up to shake a client's hand. The second was that she would start to normalize this kind of behaviour. Her mother's voice rang in her head: "This is a sign, sweetums. Just a sign. You can still turn it all around."

Of course, she hadn't foreseen the third, most deadly problem: the belt didn't really fit properly either. The belt-with-Chanel plan thus had a fatal, aesthetically damaging flaw. Besides, the skirt was really too tight. It showed the bulge of her tummy, and it was just … humiliating. There was no better word for it.

Right then, she thought. *Fuck the Chanel suit.* The skirt was tossed into the pile of other clothes that were not fitting properly that morning.

She was probably just retaining water. She did have a lot of wine the night before. And more EIC (emergency ice cream).

Could she work from home that morning? No, she had a meeting with Ballard. Could she cancel? She was tempted, but she wanted to outline her plan for setting up a new non-profit division of Ballard, Ballard and Bones, which could oversee their pro bono work, and under which, she planned to develop an NGO that would advocate for the end of the CRC system. She knew that the firm was in bed – quite literally – with Weight Winners, but she also had a good argument for why they should set up the non-profit: he owed her.

It was one of the plans she was developing for how to get Keelan out of CRC-17. She was more optimistic about her human rights case, but they took a long time to develop. And she didn't want it to be her only shot.

The figure looking back at her from the mirror was not her. There was no way it could be her. Her face had shifted from slightly cherubic to just short of jowly. There was no other way to put it. And though she didn't mind the extra heft of her cleavage, there was no getting around that tummy. The flat abs that she'd had most of her life were gone. There was now a slight, rounded … disgusting mound of flesh there. And she dare not turn around to get another look at her butt. It was just too much to consider.

She attacked her closet with the suicidal élan of a doughboy going over the top.

At work, she kept her head down, but nobody commented on the ancient pants suit that she'd ended up settling on – it was out of style by a few years, but commodious and black, both of which helped her feel a little less balloon-like. She knew it didn't matter. Most of the people in her office were at least slightly overweight. The long hours sitting in front of computers and at meetings almost guaranteed it. Except for the people with the right genetics, or what seemed to her like superhuman willpowers, the majority of people in the country were overweight. But not Chris Ballard. He looked just as trim and beautiful as always; he was definitely going grey, and there was the hint of dark circles under his eyes as she came into his office for their meeting.

"Hi, Jacs. So you've got some big ideas, right?"

"Yes, yes, I do, Chris. I think you're going to like them."

"Sure, but before we start … what's happening to you?"

"I'm sorry?"

"You look – what's with the outfit?"

"Oh, just problems with my dry-cleaner's."

"Uh-huh. Well, you can take off the jacket."

"I'm fine."

"Suit yourself. But you look hot. As in, warm. You look warm."

"I'm okay."

"Sure?" He had already taken off his jacket. He loosened his tie. "Before you get started, I'd like to ask you something."

"What?"

"How much weight have you gained since you started dating that guy? You know, the blimp in the prison?"

"I don't see how that is any concern of yours."

"You'd think that, sure. But I am concerned about you, Jacs. You were a player. You had so much potential, but lately ... I don't know. You're hostile to me – your mentor – and you don't seem to have the best interests of the firm in mind. I think this blubber friend of yours is a problem. I think you need a little vitamin B."

"I get plenty of vitamin B," she replied, and realized he meant vitamin Ballard.

He smirked at her.

"I'm actually here because I *do* have the best interests of the firm in mind. I've got a proposal I'd like to go over with you."

Ballard sighed and said, "Okay. Fine, if you don't want to play. Let's work."

She outlined her proposed non-profit division of BBB, and he waited for her to finish her presentation before saying, "No. Never going to happen."

"Why not?"

"First of all, I'm not interested in advocating for fat fucks like your boyfriend, okay? I frankly resent that you think I'd want to do something so asinine. We already have a contract with Weight Winners Canada. They are our clients. We can't work against their interests, which your non-profit would clearly do. And secondly, though it is none of your business, I anticipate that we will be expanding our interests in the Calorie Reduction Centres as time goes on, not trying to shut them down. Why do you think I had you doing all that groundwork to begin with? So Weight Winners could land the contract."

"But they're American."

"Of course – which meant we had all that paying work to set up their Canadian subsidiary. A bonus, as far as I was concerned."

"Why Weight Winners?"

"I like them. Their attitude. They want people to defeat fat, not just minimize it like the other company."

"Weight Watchers doesn't do that."

"Ah, they're all about meetings and they're just not aggressive enough about it."

"But they've been more successful, long-term."

"We'll see. Weight Winners has the CRCs now. Let's give them a chance."

"But they're not fair. They're violating the human rights of the people living there. We have rules against unlawful incarceration in this country."

"Maybe, but we should have rules about ass width too!" Ballard said through clenched teeth. "What part of 'no' aren't you getting?"

Jacinda was quiet for a moment as she composed herself. When Ballard had mentioned butt size, her face had gone a bright shade of scarlet. She hated that her face had betrayed her like that – it wasn't as horrible a betrayal as her bum doubling in size over the past year, but it was the final straw. She was not going to allow herself to cry. She said, as calmly as she could manage, "What do you mean by that?" Her voice quavered with emotion, even though she willed it not to.

Ballard smirked again. "I mean that you aren't really getting me here, Jacs. I've always liked you, but this version of you is not that attractive. Your booty, especially. It's widening. It's unsightly. It does not reflect well upon the firm."

"You realize that you can't say that to me."

"I can, and I did. And now, we're going to end this conversation," Ballard said. He stood up. "And let's end this relationship too, Ms. Williams. I'm afraid the firm of Ballard, Ballard and Bones does not need your services any more. I will be happy to write a letter of recommendation for you, but our interests are clearly diverging. I would like to end this amicably."

"So you're firing me because of my weight? I just want to be clear on this."

"Of course not. We're letting you go because your legal counsel is no longer required here. Your interests are counter to those of the firm. The fact that your butt looks like it needs its own postal code is an unfortunate fact that I happened to observe concurrently. There was no causation."

Jacinda stood up and said, "Goodbye. I hope your partner is up for the heat I'm about to bring. I don't think he is, but it will be fun to see."

Ballard's smile deepened. "You're not going to sue us."

"Of course I am. And I'm going to win quite easily too."

As she walked out, Jacinda took off her jacket – she had been rather warm in it – and looked about the offices of Ballard, Ballard, and Bones, and she felt strange. Like she could breathe again after being under water for years. Years and years. Ballard's executive assistant smiled at her and said, "Don't listen to him. You look fabulous."

QUOTE

"I've always thought Marilyn Monroe looked fabulous, but I'd kill myself if I was that fat …"

~Elizabeth Hurley

Chapter 5 – The First Casualty Is Facenook

Captain McGrath called for a "camp" meeting the day after Keelan's interview with Serena Lee.

As usual, the announcement was thinly attended by the folks of CRC-17. Most of them were going about their day, shopping in the mall, spending credits in the Slender Taste, or just avoiding the heat in their rooms. The people that were attending the meeting were largely there because they could not afford to have extra air conditioning in their rooms during the day, so they were hanging out in one of the few places where there was still publicly available (free) AC. This wouldn't last for long. The stands were due to be removed that week to make room for phase two of the mall. Phase one was doing tremendously, particularly the Frozn Yoga Hut, which featured yoga classes and complimentary frozen yoghurt for a competitively priced $150/month. (The yoga classes were there mostly for Health Canada cover, Keelan had been told by Brittany, who was now teaching there. If the authorities ever did an audit, every calorie had to be compensated for with some kind of calorie-burning activity.)

As usual, the announcement was simultaneously recorded and also put on the CRC-wide audio. It reminded Keelan of the morning announcements in high school by the principal, except there had always been the hope that he would leave high school. Even if some days it felt like the hell would never end.

Keelan felt his anger return again. The last time he had seen the commandant was when the martinet had interrupted Keelan's fitness test to make fun of him. Keelan had felt like tearing the place apart, but, since then, he'd been a model of restraint and "discipline". That said, if he was ever put in a room with McGrath, the old army captain was going to need his combat training.

"I'm afraid I have some rather unfortunate news," McGrath began. "We will be suspending Internet access for the foreseeable future as we rewire the building and set up our own Weight Winners Net access. The new system will allow you to send emails and you will be able to receive any content you like from the web, but you will not be able to upload anything."

This nugget was greeted with shock. McGrath had no idea that he was talking to a room full of people who were basically addicted to the Internet. Their contact with the outside world was largely because they had access to social media. They had cute names for all of them: MooTube, Facenook, Skitter, and other such sites were how they felt some kind of connection to the world at large. Keelan knew that Greg practically lived on Facenook – he was constantly commenting on photos, news stories, and he loved playing some kind of weird game that was about "happy" horticulture. (Keelan didn't care for online games, so he never really asked about it.)

"You can't do that!" someone shouted. Keelan looked around. It wasn't Greg, but it was someone equally involved. "What about my blog? My blog will die!"

"We can, and we must control the flow of information from this theatre," McGrath said.

This just confused a lot of people.

"This theatre of operations," McGrath explained. "We cannot have things like this video escaping anymore. It looks very bad for the corporation."

"What video?" the death blogger asked.

"The one that makes us look bad. I will not have my soldiers held up for ridicule. You folks need to learn a little respect."

Keelan was pretty sure this was about the video of Max being assaulted by Chet. "What about your security detail, sir? Shouldn't they have a little more restraint? Isn't the video just a good reminder for you?"

McGrath gave Keelan an icy stare. "This is not the kind of operation that requires civilian oversight."

"Uh, I think it is the definition of an operation that requires oversight," Keelan replied. "You do have to follow the law, right?"

"This camp meeting is over!"

"Why *camp*?" the blogger asked. "Why is he calling this a *camp*? This is about as far from fucking *camp* as it gets. It's like … oh, a prisoner-of-war camp. Is that what you mean? Or is it a concentration camp?"

But McGrath was already off the stage and making his way for the safety of the administrative offices. It hardly mattered, because the audience already had their smartphones out and were typing a few last, desperate updates to their loved ones before they lost access to the Net. Keelan was doing the same, though the content of his message was less mushy than he would have wanted. He was telling Jacinda what they were about to do.

She didn't reply right away, so he sent a quick text to Serena Lee, who called him right back.

"Are they cutting your cell service too?"

"The captain didn't say, but it stands to reason. There's not much point in cancelling the Internet via one hardline and letting it in over the airwaves."

"Well, this may help the story. The video is up to nearly a million hits now – that's in less than a week, so I think it's fair to say it has gone viral. I'm going to pitch the story to *Vice* – they have the resources we'll need to do the research – but I need you to promise you won't talk to anyone else, okay?"

"Sure, not that anyone is going to be able to talk to me anyway. And have you connected with Jacinda yet? She has lots of other thoughts about the illegality of this system. She's a lawyer, did I mention that?"

"Pretty much every time we've talked."

"Sorry."

"No, hey, I get it. She's hot, she's smart, and she's dating you, so you're proud."

Keelan was about to interrupt her and tell her that wasn't true. He wasn't proud, was he? He admitted to himself that he was. He didn't really understand why she loved him, but he was glad she did. Kee was glad she'd refused his attempts to break up, because he knew Jacinda was going to save him. He was trapped in this system, but she was his way out. He wanted to tell this to Serena, but the line went dead.

And the disconnection of the people of CRC-17 was accomplished. They were now absolutely alone.

The first few moments were quite surreal. The small crowd of inmates who'd attended the captain's speech were all using their smartphones at the same time. Some, like Keelan, had sent a quick text or made a call; some were updating their Facenook pages, hoping for a few last meaningless interactions on that platform before they disappeared, electronically, from it. And then they stopped updating. The phones said they could not connect. It was over. A collective moan emanated from the small crowd. An unintentional sigh of muted existential outrage.

"Why?" the moan seemed to say. "Why take even this small morsel of pleasure from us?"

People thumbed at their phones helplessly. A few had tears in their eyes. Some held their heads, and Keelan wondered if this was some kind of sick part of the Weight Winners Discipline Process™. It seemed to Keelan that the commandant and his lackeys had done an excellent job of tearing their psyches down. This last step seemed like a particular coup – taking away any last vestiges of their connection to the outside world, loved ones, friends, and so on. Surely they were finished with the demolition work?

As the death blogger wept openly, hiccupping with emotion, he was almost afraid to see what the reconstruction phase was going to look like.

FACT

Is Obesity the Worst Thing?

Because it's so obvious, people tend to concentrate on fat, even when excess fat may be no danger to health. Civilians and doctors both suffer from this bias.

But research from Dr. Ulf Ekelund at the University of Cambridge – and many other contributors – shows that inactivity may be much more of a problem to health outcomes than obesity. In fact, their research showed that even small increases in physical activity, say twenty minutes of walking per day, could greatly reduce the chances of premature death. And comparing causes of premature death, physical inactivity caused *twice the morbidity* that obesity did. Of course, being both active and losing weight would be more beneficial than either alone.

One thing is for sure: Dr. Ulf Ekelund may be a good name for an obesity researcher, but it's an even better moniker for a Bond villain.

19

Chapter 6 – The Pleasures of Purple Prose

It was a shock for Jacinda to realize that she didn't have any friends in town. She'd been working at Ballard, Ballard and Bones for nearly ten years, and, apparently, she hadn't built much of a network for herself in Landon. She had some old high school friends in Toronto, and she kept in touch with a few of her friends from law school, but none of them lived in Landon. And whatever happened to her friends from her undergraduate days at Yale?

So on her first day of her new life, post-BBB, she spent a good solid three hours researching people on Facenook – she'd started using all of Keelan's cutesy terms for social media of late. She didn't want to think of it as stalking, but it was similar to stalking. She managed to find four people from Yale whom she could legitimately call friends and connect with them on the social media site. At least, she sent invitations to connect. Perhaps she was wrong and she'd never really been friends with them at all. She sent Prods to those friends she hadn't talked to recently, whom she'd already had in her list. The whole social media thing had kind of passed her by, somehow. She'd been so busy in law school that she'd just stopped paying any kind of serious attention; apart from notices from her classmates about law school parties and study sessions, she'd hardly used the site. And she certainly didn't spend any time on Skitter or any other social media platform. There was just too much to do, and she had nothing to tell the world at large. And her tiny network of Chris Ballard, her mother, and a few colleagues at work seemed sufficient. Since she'd met Keelan, his presence had replaced all of those slots.

But Keelan had been strangely silent the night before, and her attempts to Skype him had been rebuffed. It was like he wasn't even there. Maybe he was finally going to actually break up with her after all the threats? The dream she'd had about Keelan trying to cross the raging river returned to her with all its vividness, and she shuddered as she remembered the image of herself all jowly and fat.

She felt like getting some emergency ice cream, but she was all out. So instead, she really threw herself into Facenook. Apparently the network let one share links, news stories, thoughts, videos – all kinds of stuff. That seemed interesting to Jacinda, as she tried to distract herself from the quantum state of her mind: it seemed to exhibit all the properties of reflecting on Keelan and their relationship, when it wasn't focused on ice cream. And of course, the reality was that until she was conscious of her mind's state, it had the qualities of both. Keelan-ice cream. Ice-cream Keelan.

She tried Skype again, but clearly Keelan was not online. Perhaps he was working outside. The last time they'd talked, the last time he'd tried to break up with her again, he'd mentioned that he was going to volunteer for the Work-n-Weigh™ program to earn credits and help with his weight-loss efforts.

She got up from her computer and went to the freezer. There was still no ice cream in there. Should she get some?

Her computer dinged. "I got an acceptance!" she cried.

She chit-chatted online for a moment with the old friend. She was an acquaintance, actually. A girl from her sorority who had married a stockbroker and now lived in upstate New York in a giant house with their two kids. While they had this exchange, another request came in – a second acquaintance from her sorority, *beta beta cho beta beta doma ding dong*. She had a similar story, except she'd married a surgeon, and they lived in Boston. It was weird to think that some of her compatriots had already had their children. She'd always thought that she would have all that figured out by now. The husband. Kids. Maybe her mother was right, and she had spent too much time on her career. She'd definitely thrown too many years at the hard boundary of Christopher Ballard's solipsism.

Her quantum state vibrated for ice cream, and she found herself in front of the freezer before she remembered, *Right, I still need to get ice cream*. There was, however, a bottle of unopened wine in her pantry. That might be a suitable substitute.

After a couple of glasses of merlot, she didn't feel much worse about her old sorority sisters. She was happy for them, all married up and kid-making. She had vague notions that she'd like children someday, but unlike some women who just knew that motherhood was going to be their greatest experience, Jacinda wasn't enthusiastic.

As the merlot disappeared, so did the hours, and the good feelings.

At about five p.m., she noticed that she'd spent the whole day in her pajamas, drinking wine and fucking about on the social media site. She realized that she'd been lucky to be too busy to spend much time on it, because Facenook was clearly like the lonely uncle at family reunions – he will take up as much of your time as you give him, no questions asked. And unlike that situation, every moment you gave to the social media site was a shadow of real connection. She might be able to use it to help people, but after a bottle of merlot, it wasn't apparent to her how.

Her phone rang, and she started. She didn't recognize the number or name, Serena Lee, but she answered it.

"Hello?"

"Jacinda Williams? This is Serena Lee. Keelan Cavanaugh said I should talk to you about the situation in the CRCs."

"You talked to Keelan? How is he?"

"I talked to him two days ago, before they cut off communications to CRC-17."

"They what?"

"Ms. Williams, are you okay?"

"I'm sorry. I, uh –" Jacinda did not want to admit she was drunk to this total stranger. "I'm just waking up. I wasn't feeling well, so I, uh, had a nap?" *Perfect*, she thought.

"Well, I need to talk with you for some background on the CRCs. Keelan said your law firm was involved with both the SubOb committee and helping Weight Winners when they won the contract to run the sites?"

"That is true. Say, could we meet to talk about this?"

"Sure. How about now?"

"I'm sorry, I, uh," Jacinda stalled. Why couldn't she meet? "I have the flu, I think. If I'm feeling better tomorrow, why don't you come over here and we can chat?"

"Okay. Call me, please," Serena said. "And if you're not feeling better, maybe we can do it over Skype."

"Sure," Jacinda agreed, and hung up. Facenook pinged at her again, and she went back into the kitchen. She was pretty sure she had some cooking sherry in there somewhere.

She awoke the next morning with a terrible hangover, her mouth and eyes like cotton, and a slow crawling pain that crept up from the base of her neck, making its way into her brain as the morning progressed. But worse than the physical pain was the feeling that she had let herself down, quite badly, the day before. With a cringe, she remembered writing some comments on her old sorority sisters' Facenook pages ... something about being brood mares?

She couldn't stomach having a look. *Speaking of stomachs,* she thought, *what happened to mine?* After she'd finished off the bottle of cooking sherry, apparently she'd gotten the munchies. There was the remains of a large pepperoni pizza sitting in her kitchen. The slices had been torn out of it as though a shamble of zombies had decided massive amounts of carbs, cheese, and nitrates were a valid substitute for brains. No wonder her insides felt so tied up – there was enough mozzarella in there to kill her!

There was a yellow legal notepad beside the remains of the pizza, filled with writing. Apparently she'd only been able to find a purple pen, and her drunken writing looked like the ramblings of a madman. But the headline caught her attention: How to destroy Christopher Ballard.

A six-step plan was outlined in the following pages. It made for terrifying reading. Jacinda had no idea she'd harboured such deep-felt resentment towards him. But there was the kernel of a plan in there. The first step was one that she'd already threatened: sue Chris and the firm. It would make her a pariah amongst other law firms, but she'd already decided she was going to use her degree to help dismantle the CRC system, so who cared if other firms didn't want to hire her? Items two and three were also interesting, and potentially possible, but if she was successful in her suit against BBB, no doubt they would be hard to accomplish. But still, she felt inspired by her drunken self. Items four to six were … well, she had to admit they were appealing on a visceral level, but there was no way she would be actually willing to cut off any part of anyone's anatomy with garden shears. Those pages went into her shredder. But the first half of the plan was something to work with. And suing Ballard for sexual harassment and discrimination was going to be a slam dunk. She had hours of recordings that would help her case.

But first, she would have some digestive enzymes – it was unlikely to help, but that wad of cheese was not going to help her get anything done that day. And for the brainstem issues, some aspirin would just have to do. And then a shower, to wash away the stink of the previous day's bacchanalia.

Plus, she had to call that reporter back. If she was going to live happily ever after, she had to rescue Keelan too.

QUOTE

"The best measure of a man's honesty isn't his income tax return. It's the zero adjust on his bathroom scale."

~Arthur C. Clarke

Chapter 7 – Fortune Favours the Bald

After a week of no Internet, no phones, no contact with the outside world at all, the denizens of CRC-17 were getting cranky.

And Keelan was starting to lose it.

The last conversation he'd had with Jacinda was a quasi-break-up, and he was worried that she didn't know that he couldn't contact her, not that he wouldn't. The only thing they were getting was television, and CRC-17 was back in the news. Keelan was in the spotlight again; this time he was not standing at the centre of it – he was just at the edge.

The light was focused on the unlikely dyad of Chet and Max. Though they were more of a yin and yang thing, not a coupling of likes. On one side was the calm – apparently rational – Dr. Maximilian Tundra, and on the other, the intense – apparently psychotic – Corporal Chet Douglass (retired). Serena's *Vice* story had added context and colour to the viral video of Max and Chet's confrontation, but it was the video itself that had gathered the attention. Interest in the video might have faded, but Serena's reporting on the issue continued to keep it alive. The story had the same kind of interest in the United States engendered by the cocaine-fueled antics of Toronto's mayor. Late night talk shows had lots of fun with Chet's pistols, both metaphorical and literal, and Max's size and vocabulary.

Keelan could only imagine what the comment string on the MooTube video looked like now that the incident was politicized in the US too.

But the story was not a slam dunk for the inmates of the Fatness. Weight Winners Canada had a remarkably good media strategy. One was to cut off access of the media to the CRCs, and the other was to put the video into context. Max certainly didn't come out of it looking very good. They dragged out the details of how he'd lost his medical license because of his drug experimentation, and they made it look like he was a troublemaker.

Chet, ominously, had not been disciplined or let go, and he'd increased his nightly visits to Tundra's cell. So far he hadn't done anything except stand there and whistle for a while. Tundra was terrified of course, but he'd responded by throwing himself into his psychonautical-pharmaceutical "research".

It had been more than a week since he'd last talked to Jacinda, and Keelan was getting a little frantic. And more stressed. He'd managed to put on another pound despite the fact that he wasn't eating very well and was still working outside. They had finished the fence, and they were framing two new buildings. Perhaps it was stress. Perhaps it was the communal beer at the end of the day. The beer would only be two hundred calories max, so that shouldn't add up to a pound, but this just confirmed that it was not simple thermodynamics – calorie-in, calorie-out. Hormones were involved, and stress messed with them. He also wasn't sleeping well, and Tyrell had always said they were more important components of weight loss than exercise and food.

And then an important figure returned into this maelstrom of controversy and discontent: Colin Taggart.

He'd spent the previous six months in jail, working out the details of a plea bargain in which he would help the Crown prosecute Selwyn Seward and the other CRC directors. He also agreed to testify against some of his own lieutenants in the Heavy Hitters – the violent ones like John Carver and Wayne Falco, who had hurt people during the riots and in their frantic search for Keelan when he ratted them all out. (All this despite the fact that he was the head of the Heavy Hitters, but he'd had the wherewithal to pay for some excellent criminal attorneys.)

Of course, it was a much different Taggart. He was still bald and fat, but not as fat. Before his jail time Taggart's BMI was over 39, and after six months of no junk food, booze, or other inputs other than the carb-rich diet of jail, he'd lost quite a bit of weight. When Taggart walked through the mall, past the Timmy's where Keelan and Max were having their morning coffee, Keelan thought he'd probably lost at least twenty-five pounds – maybe thirty. And naturally, he wasn't riding his Rascal anymore.

"Keelan." Taggart smiled. "Nice to see you!"

"Really?"

"Of course. No hard feelings."

Max looked suspicious. "That doesn't seem likely."

"Seriously. I know that you were only doing what you thought was right. I know that you thought ratting us out would destroy the system. I might have done the same thing in your shoes," Taggart said. He put forward his hand and said, "Please, let's put it behind us."

Keelan shook his hand, feeling as suspicious as Max looked.

"Can I join you?"

"Sure," Keelan said. "You know Max."

"The famous Dr. Tundra. You naughty boy. How are you managing without the Heavy Hitters' supply of mescaline?"

"I'm managing," Max said. Keelan wondered how Max had kept up his supply. Keelan had certainly been unable to get his phentermine, a diet drug that was probably more dangerous than helpful anyway.

"Of course, you're a resourceful man. I like what you did in that video."

"Thanks," Max said. His voice was flat and Keelan knew that Max really didn't trust Taggart as far as he could throw him. (And given Taggart weighed nearly three hundred pounds, that wouldn't be far.)

"Look. I know you have no reason to trust me. But I was doing it all for the money. And the fun of being in charge, a bit. But mostly the money. And now all the money is going to Weight Winners, so I want to get out of here, just like you."

"Well, good luck," Max said.

"Max, come on," Keelan said. "I'm willing to put things behind us. But getting out of here seems unlikely. Even if you can get down to 29 bimmi – and I'm not saying you can't, but it is going to be a tough row to hoe – what's to prevent them from dropping it to 28. Or 27? It's in their interest to keep us here. Paying for the extras when we can."

"Not to mention getting the suckers to work for free, like my good friend here," Max said, nodding to Kee.

"Ah, but that's where you're wrong," Taggart said. "They are in the business of making money, not depriving us of our freedom. What we need to do is make it so keeping us is more costly than losing us."

"That's what I said," Max said. He turned to Keelan. "Right? On the day when Chet nearly blew my head off?"

Keelan nodded.

"Then we have some common ground," Taggart said.

"Okay," Max said, "but how do we make it more expensive to keep us? We haven't come up with a single idea yet!"

Taggart ran his hand over his bald head and said, "Well, that's the problem, isn't it? But I think Max's stunt with the security guard is one avenue. How do we exploit it?"

"Yes, how?" Keelan said.

"I don't know that yet, but you need to get organized. *We* need to get organized, I mean. You've broken up my old organization, but that doesn't mean we can't make a new one."

"And what do you get out of it?" Max said, still suspicious.

"I want to get out of here, just like you. And if we can make a little money on the side, that would be a nice benefit."

"But the main goal has to be to get out of here," Keelan said. "If we do anything illegal, it should be motivated by that goal, not greed. I don't mind breaking the law if it's to resist this system, which, let's face it, is pretty unjust."

Taggart looked at him and said, "I know. You've got that juicy piece of ass you want to spend more time with. Some of us are motivated by love. Some by money."

"And some by ostrich pudding." Max nodded.

Quote

"A lean compromise is better than a fat lawsuit."

~George Herbert

Chapter 8 – Jeremiah Bones, Esquire at Law

As it turned out, her suit against Ballard was not the slam dunk she thought it might be. She believed that her recordings would be admissible, but unfortunately, the judge – a man, she noted – did not feel the same way. And she did have to hand it to Jeremiah Bones, the other partner at the firm of Ballard, Ballard and Bones. He was a wizard of some kind. He even looked like a wizard, with his distinguished white beard, white hair, and decked out in his black robes. He lacked a wand and the floppy hat of a Hogwarts' headmaster, but he could certainly achieve magic in the courtroom.

How Bones had managed to get the case tried so quickly was a feat of high sorcery indeed. He'd clearly called in some kind of favour, which meant that Jacinda didn't have as much time to prepare for the trial as she'd hoped.

Still, she'd drawn a good jury, and she'd managed to convince a number of other young women at the firm to testify on her behalf. Plus, she suspected that Bones's heart was not really in the case. She knew for a fact that he had grown to despise his younger partner. She'd once heard a rumour that he had only agreed to take him on because of Christopher's father, Valence Ballard III, who had been a great friend and co-founder of the firm.

And so, they were in a conference room at the Landon courthouse, resplendent with threadbare furniture from the '70s; the aesthetic fit perfectly with the Stalinist architecture of the entire edifice. She felt a bit uncomfortable, as Ballard was going to join them at the meeting. Without a network of friends, nor the wherewithal to hire her own team, Jacinda had elected to be her own advocate. (Which she knew was a bad idea, but she didn't have much choice.)

So far Ballard's overwhelming arrogance had not helped the firm's case too much, and Jacinda suspected that she was on her way to winning despite Bones and his legal legerdemain.

"It's actually just us lawyers," Bones said as he took a seat opposite her at the conference table.

"Where are the others?" Jacinda had asked. In addition to their magician, the firm had thrown no fewer than four other junior lawyers at the case.

"I thought it might go better if it was just us grown-ups."

Jacinda smiled at the old man's compliment, but she wasn't taken in. He could charm the pants off Lucifer, she knew.

"That's nice. So are you willing to make a deal?"

"That's why I'm here. I want to offer you a sizeable settlement."

"What about your client?"

"I – unfortunately – am the client in this case too. How we got into this position, I'll never know, but that boy ..." Bones stopped himself from saying anything he was going to regret. He slid a piece of paper over to her and said, "I'd take it. We can't go any higher and keep the firm afloat – I know you won't necessarily believe me, but I do respect you, Jacinda. Any more and the firm goes under. I know you don't want to put everyone out of work."

Jacinda was torn, really. Part of her just wanted her time in front of the jury, making Ballard pay, but the old master really did know her. She didn't want to kill the firm. That thought was in her mind as she turned over the paper. It was a challenge not to show anything when she did. There were a lot of zeros on that paper. Enough that she would never have to work again, that could pay for Keelan's health care a hundred times over. Hell, it was enough to start her own firm if she wanted to.

"I want an apology too," she said.

Bones slid another piece of paper over to her. It was an envelope with a letter from Ballard.

She opened it and read.

"And you'll note that it is cc'd to the Ontario Bar Association," Bones added. "We'll only mail it if you agree to our terms."

"Which are?"

"Standard non-disclosure. No discussion of the settlement. The usual. Ballard just wants this to go away, and frankly, so do I. It's very bad for the firm."

"Okay. Let's sign it."

And so, Jacinda was a wealthy woman.

She now had options.

Ballard sat in another room, not far away, fuming. He looked out the windows of the courthouse. They were on the twelfth floor, so he could see a bit of the greenery of Landon, known for its tree-lined streets and parochial ways. But not *that* parochial. Even twenty years ago, there was no way Jacinda would have even thought of bringing that case, let alone scampered away with a third of the firm's capital.

Even worse, from Ballard's perspective, was the decision by Bones to retire. In fact, it had been a condition of having him do the defense. So he had to buy out the old courtroom sorcerer too, from his personal finances.

It was still hard to believe there was no way to win the lawsuit outright, but he did trust Bones. If he said there was a good chance they could lose it, he believed the old man. He wished now that he hadn't had Bones call in the favour to get the case heard so quickly. Their initial court date had been months and months away, and now that seemed preferable. But it was done. He'd lost that round.

So that left Ballard without enough money to buy up a controlling share of Weight Winners Canada. He was going to have to change his plans. He stared out at the horizon. There was a dark line of clouds approaching from the west, and no doubt Landon would be getting one of its signature summer storms. Landon's centre was just below the courthouse, at the fork of the Medway River, but the city was built in a giant bowl, essentially, with ancient glacial moraines surrounding it. That seemed to be a recipe for thunderstorms in the humidity.

He spotted a flash of lightning, and its distant heat reminded him of a time when he'd felt that kind of passion for Jacinda. Back when she'd started working for the firm, she was just so exciting and young …

Bones came back in the room and said, "Okay, it's done. She's signed the agreement, so the firm is safe, and you can get back to doing whatever it is you do."

"Why don't you like me, Bones?"

"I never liked your entitled attitude. You didn't hit a home run in life, kid. You started out on third."

"And you're old. Done"

"Maybe. But I predict you'll miss me. Anyway, it doesn't matter now. The firm's all yours, lad. Do with it what you will."

"And you don't care?"

"Of course I do. I built that with your dad, and I'm proud of it. But this latest incident has shown me that it's time to do something else. I may start my own little boutique firm. Do a bit of pro bono work in addition to taking some of your best clients."

"What? You can't do that!"

"Hey, there's no non-compete clause in our partnership agreement. You probably thought I was going to retire, didn't you, you arrogant little shit?"

Ballard's mouth was agape. It was one of those rare instances when he didn't have something clever or crippling to say.

"Don't be too upset, Chris. I just saved you a ton of grief with that case. She was going to clean you out if you hadn't settled. You know, I may just see if she's looking for work."

Ballard sneered and said, "You're welcome to my sloppy seconds."

Jeremiah Bones, Esquire, just laughed and nodded towards the window. "Storm's coming, boy."

FACT

The Magic of Intervals

Many believe that long sessions of cardio are the best way to burn calories and so increase weight loss. But research from the University of New South Wales showed that short, intense bursts of activity can be more effective.

The researchers had patients do twenty-minute sessions on exercise bikes, pedaling as fast as they could for eight seconds, followed by twelve seconds of moderate spinning. Over a twelve-week period the participants lost almost 5 pounds of fat and gained 2.5 pounds of muscle – about the same as if they had done seven hours of jogging per week.

Plus they didn't have to spend any time cramming themselves into running tights that, frankly, can be a bit of a fire hazard.

20

Chapter 9 – Extreme Electric Exercise™

A month had passed without Internet. This lack of contact with the real world coincided with a late August heatwave. Though Canadians are known for complaining about our savage winters, we like to complain about summers too. A place like Landon, Ontario, is not so unusual in a sixty-degree (Celsius) variance between the coldest winter day and the warmest summer day. But what that swing doesn't cover is the concept of wind chill and, on the far summery end, humidity.

And Landon – the whole eastern region of North America – was getting some humidity. Fish trying to evolve were crawling out of their watery homes, sampling the air, and saying, "Ew. And what's THAT SMELL?"

Ugh. THAT SMELL! Keelan thought to himself most mornings. He'd been paying for extra air conditioning in his cell, which made sleeping at least possible. It was still warm and humid, but not feculent, at least. But as soon as he slid open his cell door, the unrelenting pong of CRC-17 at 32 degrees Celsius – 40 with humidex – would smack him in the nose like a boxing glove made out of fish guts, rancid pork fat, and some kind of sickly sweet tone that he thought of as "sugar-coated leprosy". It was Gagarrific™. Or it least it would be as soon as Weight Winners thought of a way to make money by trademarking the notion.

The simmering anger of everyone locked into the place was kept in check by their obesity and general torpor. It was just too hot to start a riot over the lack of connection with the outside world, the paucity of cool air, and the continued attempts by the discipline advisors to "break down their slave-to-their-gluttony mentalities". Never mind that half of the population was now skipping at least one meal. It was just too hot to eat. The only places where there was any relief were the mall and the swimming pool; for the people fit enough to work outside and make extra cash there was the option of turning up the feeble AC in their rooms.

That, of course, was when the facility had any power at all. The entire grid was feeling the effects of the heatwave, and there were rolling brownouts on a regular basis. The only parts of the CRC that were reliably cool were the mall, the admin offices, and the infirmary. Everything else was conditional on, first, power and, secondly, the ability to pay for extra AC.

Keelan arrived at the mall, where he was going to have his morning coffee with Max, Greg, and now, Taggart.

Max was already there, handing out pamphlets.

"I know this sounds extreme, but in order to keep things under control, I recommend the cold showers. They are a bit bracing, but you'll feel so much nicer after you sluice off some of your sweat. Plus, you can use some soap against those apocrine glands. If you really want to reduce your own smell, I'd also recommend shaving your armpits and genitals," he was saying to a large bear of a man waiting in the Timmy's line.

"What if I like my smell?"

"I'm thinking about the public good, here," Max said.

"Do you shave your genitals?"

"Of course," Max said. There was a bizarre note of pride in his voice.

"Weird. Kinda kinky too. Let me know if you need help next time."

"Well, some parts are hard to get at, but … wait, are you suggesting what I think you're suggesting, sir?"

The bear grinned at him. "I'll be gentle."

"I'm sure. But perhaps we can keep this a practical medical activity? Anyway, here is a pamphlet with a few tips."

The bear watched Max walk away with new interest as he clutched Max's pamphlet.

"Is he still watching me?" Max asked as he joined Kee at the end of the coffee line.

"Oh, yeah. Everyone else too. Where did you get those things?"

"I made them when the power was still on. I have a printer in my room, and I had a sheaf of paper. I slid one under every door in my hallway, and I thought I'd get more chance to explain it here."

"And how has it been going?"

"Well, that's the longest conversation I've had. Most of the women I talk to are quite offended." Max looked around him and whispered, "But really, they smell just as much as the men do. I know it's not right to say so, but it's true."

"They smell in different ways. I think the fat boys are winning the stench race though."

"To each their own."

Before Taggart or Greg could join them, the intercom snapped on and the commandant's voice said, "Good morning, folks. It's with great pride that I announce our latest technique for helping you reach a healthy weight. It's called Extreme Electric Exercise™ and we believe it will help you shed those unwanted pounds. Not only will you be helping yourself, you'll be helping your friends, family, and neighbours. Your discipline advisor will be in touch regarding your fitness level to determine if you are healthy enough to partake of this newest Weight Winners innovation. If you are fit enough, participation is mandatory. Also, during brownouts, supplementary air conditioning will not be available in the rooms. Thank you for your attention."

Max looked about and said, "I'd better distribute the rest of these. This place is going to be unbearable if there's even less AC."

"Give me a few," Kee said. "I'll help."

Daniel Starkey informed Kee that naturally he would be eligible for the Extreme Electric Exercise™ plan, but as he was already working outside, he would be given a time slot outside of the regular work day.

"What's your preference, before you head out to work with Joe or after you're done for the day? Each inmate has a two-hour quota."

"Quota of what?"

"The triple-E, of course. I think this is one of the best programs Weight Winners has ever come up with."

"You're not going to electrocute people, are you?"

"Don't be ridiculous. We would never torture you – you're our clients. Without you, there is no Weight Winners Canada."

"Yes, that's definitely occurred to many of us. Can we do a weigh-in while I'm here?"

It turned out that Keelan had lost the two pounds he'd recently gained, so he was back on the right track, at least.

"So how extreme is this exercise?" Keelan asked.

"Well, it's intended to get your heart rate into the training zone and keep it there for two hours."

"What part of the zone? What percentage?"

"Sorry, I forget that you are one of our more educated clients when it comes to the science of weight loss. Yes, yes, indeed you're a rarity, Mr. Cavanaugh. You know, I almost suspect you could lose your extra weight even without our help. So any other questions?"

"Just the one you didn't answer. What *range* of the training zone?"

"In point of fact, it does not say," Starkey said as he consulted his clipboard. "But I imagine it will be in the lower end of the range for someone as fit as you."

"Okay. I guess the morning, then. Can I do my time before breakfast?"

"Of course! I'm going to slot you in for 5:30-7:30 a.m."

"What?"

"Well, you did say before breakfast."

"5:30 in the morning? I'll be a frickin' zombie."

"Don't worry, I don't think it will affect your progress."

"I *know* it will. Getting decent sleep is one of the most important factors in weight loss. You should know that!"

"It's not a necessary component of the Discipline Process."

"Is *science* part of the Discipline Process?"

"Only our own trademarked science. So report to Hall A at 5:30 a.m."

"Where the fuck is Hall A?"

"You know the outbuildings they were constructing last week?

The one that says Hall A."

"Yes, I helped build them. I have to say, I'm surprised you're letting people go outside."

"With the security fence in place, DarkRain thinks it's safe to allow small numbers of you outside the walls. Isn't that great news?"

"Oh, just peachy. Small numbers of us can go outside. What a treat."

His alarm was ungodly. There was no other way to describe it. Keelan had never been a morning person, but this was just ... he'd probably fallen asleep at 1:00 a.m. despite his best efforts to get to bed early to compensate for the 5:00 a.m. wake-up. He rolled out of bed and put on his exercise clothes, which were frankly disgusting – the power shortages had made it difficult to get laundry done. He'd tried to wash things by hand, but it just didn't do the job on his industrial-strength sweat. He did his best to ignore his own pong as he made his way through the CRC, which was eerily quiet.

Since he'd been working outside already, Keelan already had a security card. The security detail checked him out of the building and said, "Just make sure you swipe in as soon as you get to Hall A. You'll see the card reader at the door."

Outside, the air was still oppressive, but the predawn light was hopeful. He could hear the sound of crickets and frogs, and though the air had the slight chemical smell it had all during the heatwave, he thought that under the oppressive tones he smelled a note of the fall. That made him smile. The fall was always his favourite season. The crisp air, the return of the students on campus where he (no longer) worked, the changing of the leaves. The air was always cleaner and bluer in the fall, and he would more than welcome it this year.

He watched the light brighten for a few moments in the east and wondered what Jacinda was doing. He hoped she was still asleep, but he had to admit, there was something beautiful about the day's beginning.

He swiped in at Hall A, which had all the aesthetics of an

Ikea warehouse without the distractions of a pile of Fnoogs or Plurpers. He'd helped frame it, though he didn't have any of the skills to help with other parts of the construction. Both buildings had gone up quickly, and as he walked inside, he could see why. There was not much to it. The walls were still unfinished – that was on the job docket for the week, and Keelan suspected he might be helping with putting in the insulation and drywall.

The room was filled with exercise bikes hooked up to what Keelan imagined was some kind of … electrical thingy.

He was a bit early, so there was only one other inmate there, a woman he vaguely recognized from the Friday night dances. There was also one of the discipline advisors on hand.

"What is that?"

"I believe it's called a capacitor. It stores electricity."

"Okay. Why?"

"It's part of our Extreme Electric Exercise regime. You clients are going to start generating all of our power. Isn't that exciting?"

"Extremely," Keelan drawled. "It's electrifying."

"Why don't you get started? You can leave after you've done your two hours. If you want to see what your heart rate is doing, just put both hands on the silver parts of the handlebars, and it will show you on the little screen. But don't keep them there. That will draw power away from the capacitor."

Keelan got on the bike and started pedaling.

"Oh, you'll have to go much harder than that," the DA said.

"Why?"

"You need to generate two hundred watts."

"Um, is that a lot?"

"Not really. About enough to run a TV. But you'll probably need all two hours to make it. If you don't, there is a slight penalty, but if you exceed the two hundred, there are, of course, Weight Winner Rewards™ to be earned."

"Of course," Keelan said, pedaling harder. "When do I know I've reached two hundred?"

"That light will go on, and then you're done."

Others arrived for their shift, and the revolution began.

FACT

Sleep Less and Gain More

Sleep deprivation may be contributing to the increase in obesity rates, and research shows that getting a good night's sleep is critical to weight control.

When we don't get enough sleep, our hormones get out of whack, and we feel a need to eat more to compensate for our low energy levels. One study at the University of Colorado demonstrated that decreasing sleep by just a few hours a few nights in a row resulted in an average weight gain of two pounds.

Plus, let's face it: sleeping is awesome.

21

Chapter 10 – Sustain & Sustainability

Jacinda had been awake, sitting on her deck in the backyard, drinking coffee and preparing for her day.

The sunrise had caught her attention too, despite how busy she was and the morning news. Sometime after 6 a.m. the day brightened, and the intimation of reds and yellows started to appear in the east. By 6:30 the sky was a bit eerie, but beautiful. She wondered how Keelan was doing. She'd been trying to get word to him for the past two weeks, but so far none of her efforts had succeeded. She was starting to feel as though this forced separation was the universe's way of testing her resolve. Did she really love him, or was he just a distraction from her destined perfect life, as both her mother and Christopher Ballard thought?

Events were moving quickly. The morning's business news was filled with her ex-boss-slash-lover's antics. He'd sold all of his stock, let go of Weight Winners Canada, and taken on Greatlife Fitness as a client. He was now sitting as the chair of the board. Greatlife was a local success story. They owned fitness studios across Canada and had ambitions to be the largest fitness company in the world. It was a client that he'd been courting for some time, and his success with getting Weight Winners Canada set up so quickly was probably one of the reasons he got them as a client. That, and their obvious desire to take over the Calorie Reduction Centres.

Frankly, they seemed a better fit to run the centres. Their emphasis was on fitness first, not some of the bizarre notions of discipline and psychological-focused solutions to obesity. She couldn't help but be skeptical of Ballard's take on the viral video of Max nearly getting his head blown off by the DarkRain guard.

"It's not in the interests of the Canadian health system to have such clearly American values driving the process of helping to cure our country's obese. Gun culture, their so-called Discipline Process™, and the monetary incentives for weight loss, these are American notions. They lack the compassion of our own system. So we need a made-in-Canada solution to our obesity epidemic, and I believe that Greatlife Fitness has the approach that will make our country the healthiest in the world," he said.

The article explained that Ballard was petitioning the government to review the terms of their contract with Weight Winners Canada (which Ballard knew intimately, of course, as he'd had a hand in writing it.)

It all smacked of insider trading to Jacinda, but, clearly, Ballard had insulated himself from that by divesting himself of the client, their stock, and presumably the lovely Texan president, Melissa Handle. She wondered how that conversation had gone.

Jacinda had no desire to help Weight Winners Canada, but, at the same time, she felt as though the enemy of her enemy was, in some sense, her friend. She thought of Keelan stuck in CRC-17, and she realized – with horror – that her real enemy might be Weight Winners. Or perhaps it was the government of Canada, which was ultimately responsible for the whole mess. She thought about that for a moment and made some more notes for her meeting with her board later that day.

It was the first meeting of the group, and she was excited, which was why she was up so early. She'd taken some of the money from Ballard's settlement and immediately set up the non-governmental organization. Keelan's Hope had one goal, which was to dismantle the CRC system.

Even more exciting, she was set to meet with Jed Bones, who had agreed to act as their legal counsel. He was even willing to do it pro bono.

She just wished she could tell Keelan about it all, but that would come soon. She had also petitioned the federal government for access to the CRCs. She had the signatures of thousands of people from around Canada who had been unable to talk to their loved ones for four weeks. It was clearly unjust.

She finished writing her notes for the board meeting and began to prepare for her other big meeting of the day, with the reporter Serena Lee. She hoped that a bit more attention on the unfairness of the system would put enough pressure on Health Canada to force Weight Winners to open up the lines of communication again.

As the sun came up, her eyes teared up with the thought of seeing Keelan again. She missed him. *There, I miss him*, she thought. *I'm not crying just because of some whim. I do love him.*

But before she could tell him again, there was a lot of work to do.

A week later, Christopher Ballard sat in Ottawa, at Health Canada, waiting for the minister to arrive so that he could make his pitch: Greatlife Fitness should take over the CRCs.

He was excited about his chances. George Welland was an old buddy from his Upper Canada College days, where he'd gone to school as a boy, and he'd always followed Ballard's lead. Ballard was sure that he'd kick it up to the Prime Minister's Office. Ballard was already planning his campaign with the PM.

His media campaign had borne fruit, and he'd been unexpectedly helped by Jacinda's own efforts to talk to her boyfriend – that was how he saw her efforts anyway. She was motivated by some misguided sense of duty, or perhaps even love. He shook his head. She'd shown so much promise. And she'd been so good in the sack. He thought wistfully about her for a moment. Since he'd let Weight Winners Canada go as a client and started his campaign, he had not exactly been Melissa Handle's favourite person. (Even if they had still met once for some furious hate sex.)

He needed to focus. He was feeling confident that he had a good case. His polling data showed Canadians now felt that a truly Canadian company should be running the centres. Of course, his data also showed that support for the scheme was failing even more than support of Weight Winners, because the CRCs were seen as expensive, ineffective, and cruel. Un-Canadian, in fact. Most of the citizens who'd answered the poll said they thought the whole thing was a bad idea and should be scrapped. There were some interesting sidebars in there though. People who were more likely to vote Conservative liked the idea that the obese should not be allowed to have free health care, and they liked that the CRCs were a way to address that issue. If the system could be fixed and made more affordable, they would continue to support them. So, in addition to his proposal that Greatlife take over the contract, he had a memo about some of the ways in which the company proposed to streamline the operation so that it cost the federal government even less.

It was an exciting document.

An assistant arrived to take him to George. There was no one else in his room. George got up, smiling, and shook Ballard's hand. "Ballard, you old reprobate."

Ballard smiled.

"So, I'm going to keep this meeting short, Chris," the minister said before Ballard could even begin his presentation.

"I know you've got high hopes for that Landon fitness company of yours, but we're not going to change providers in the middle of their contract."

"But, George," Ballard interrupted, "you've got lots of reasons to let them go. I've got a detailed memo on the legal –"

"I'm going to stop you right there, Chris, ol' buddy. The PM is a good friend of Melissa's, and more than that, they've proposed a deal to us that we – frankly – just can't refuse, and I doubt your little company down there in Landon can match it."

That shut Ballard up. Did he detect a patronizing note in George's tone?

"Yep, they've sewn it up good, despite all the PR nightmares. They've got a fix for that, by the by. And the deal, is just, well, really great."

"What is the deal?" Ballard couldn't help himself, even though he should tactically be changing the direction of the meeting.

"Well, first they're completely separating themselves from Weight Winners America. As of today, they'll be a true made-in-Canada company, so that argument won't fly anymore. And Melissa has agreed to step down as president so a Canadian can take over. They've got this peach of a doctor from Vancouver to take over. You should see her résumé. It'll make you cream your pants. And finally – and this is really the thing that sold us on their restructuring – they are not going to cost the Canadian taxpayer a single beaver-loving nickel."

"What?" Ballard said. He had a horrible pain running up his arm. And his head was swimming. What was his old school chum telling him?

"Yep. They've got a plan to make the CRCs totally self-sufficient. It's not going to be easy, but they've already begun. Do you know they have those fat fuckers running on treadmills to generate their own power?"

Ballard wanted to make some kind of observation about George's own size, which was in extra-extra-large territory, but he was distracted by the shooting pains in his arm, the weird sensation in his chest. He wanted to say that this was all just a tactic by Melissa Handle – there was no way they could make the CRCs self-sufficient unless they charged the inmates for being there. And he realized that's what had George so excited. They'd found a way to do that?

His vision started to telescope in, and all he could see was George's bulbous nose – a nose he used to tweak in school. Didn't he used to tease him about his fat lips too? Yeah, cock-locking lips, he'd called them.

"You don't look so good, you old reprobate. Don't worry, I'm sure you'll find another scheme to hang your hat on."

"Urp," Ballard said as he fell off the chair.

"Ballard? Ballard?"

Part V

"The proof of the pudding is in the eating."

~Cervantes, *Don Quixote*

Chapter 1 – Smooth Operators

The stands were finally gone, and the commons now looked exactly like a mall. There were shops down both sides of what had been the largest open space in CRC-17. It was still the largest space, actually, even with the stores. In addition to the Frozn Yoga shop and the Manliness Hut, there were other clothing shops, including a Pineapple Republic, an outlet store, shoe stores, a store for exercise equipment (which seemed like bringing coals to Newcastle to Keelan), one of those stores where you could buy the crap they "only" sold on TV, and the ubiquitous pharmacy superstore: Consume-It!

But it was still the largest gathering place in the facility, and everyone still called it the commons, even if Weight Winners Canada had dubbed it – in what Keelan assumed was some well-educated marketing manager's flight of fancy – the Agora. (There was even a sign done up in some kind of fancy-but-legible script.)

To celebrate their new mandate with Health Canada and their "helpful" new approach to weight loss, Weight Winners Canada had a series of speakers coming to the Agora to do presentations all week. Kicking off this extravaganza was Dr. Molly Maguire, a petite, perfectly turned-out peach of a scientist, who had a solution for all their adipose ills.

Dr. Molly, as she was known, was a regular guest on one of the morning shows in the US, on which she would discuss the latest research on dieting, fitness, and other health-related issues. Everyone loved her. And now, she had taken everything she'd learned, and she'd put together a diet plan that she would guarantee – guarantee – even the most repugnant of *jabbas* could lose weight. In fact, the fatter you were, the better Dr. Molly's plan was.

She was an excellent presenter, and she had charisma, there was no doubting that. They'd set up a little stage at the top of the stairs that led from the administrative wing to the commons. And there was a giant screen hanging behind her, where the hallway to the admin area went, with a lovely PowerPoint presentation backing up her speech. The crowd was with her. All the porkers and manatees were hanging on her every word. She was telling them about her own weight troubles, how she'd tried every diet out there, but she'd found an answer: smoothies!

Smoothies. She said it about a dozen times a minute. Four smoothies a day, plus a regular lunch. Add in some exercise – moderate at first if you were out of shape, and more robust as you gained fitness. She guaranteed that it you stuck to this regime, you would lose the weight. And if you kept to it after you'd lost the weight, you would also keep the weight off.

She launched into a presentation of how many diets failed, and how many people just put all the weight back on after their diet was over. It was depressing. Keelan knew the stats. He *was* one of the stats. He'd lost thirty pounds – twice – before his rebound weight-gain had landed him in Porker Prison.

Everyone was rapt with attention.

She finished up by saying, "And for this week, you can sign up for a free trial of our Mollysmooth™ plan. The Slender Taste will serve your smoothies too and a moderate, regular lunch, for free. All I ask is you give it a try, and if you lose some weight this week, consider signing up for the Mollysmooth™ plan."

As she spoke, it seemed like the entire staff of CRC-17 appeared with trays of smoothies. There were chocolate, strawberry, HyperGrass, and banana flavours. They were delicious, and it was nice having their torturers, the discipline advisors and exercise technicians, put in the position of waitstaff.

"But how do we pay?" someone asked. Keelan thought it might have been Taggart. "We have no access to the outside world."

"Oh," Dr. Molly said, "I almost forgot. Access is being restored this week, and, by the end of the trial period, you should be able to wire in as much money as you need to your Weight Winners credit accounts. Or you can spend more time earning Work-n-Weigh™ credits, I believe."

That seemed to make everyone happy on two fronts. Keelan

took an experimental sip of his bright green HyperGrass smoothie. It was surprisingly good for something made out of lawn and snake oil.

Keelan continued to work with Joe and the construction team. They'd been pressing hard to finish a series of new outbuildings, which looked kind of industrial. At least the heatwave was over and the fall was beginning. Each morning he'd go do his two hours on the electrical generating project – though strictly speaking, he didn't see how it could be generating enough power to make it worthwhile – surely the equipment was too expensive to make it economical? But apparently CRC-17 was a pilot project in the CRC system. In addition to the discipline advisors talking about the AWFUL, he sometimes heard them whispering about something called the Vig. Keelan thought it was a betting term, but he wasn't sure. And whenever he asked Starkey about it, the DA just clamed up.

But after his session of Extreme Electric Exercise™ (Keelan had shaved his time down to one and a half hours to get to his mandated two hundred watts), he'd go outside and watch the sunrise. He would watch the colours in the sky, thinking of Jacinda. And he'd mull over their plan to leave the CRC behind.

Taggart and Keelan had been quite successful at reconstituting the Heavy Hitters, though this time it looked more like an activist group than a mafia. People were getting angry, even if the week of free smoothies had softened everyone's rhetoric.

Keelan, Max, Tina, and Taggart were meeting at the Timmy's after the workday to discuss their plans. Keelan had invited Greg to join their "steering committee", but he had suggested that Tina was a better choice. She was an experienced activist, having worked with a number of community groups before the Fat Act landed her in the CRC. She didn't have any family left and she was her only support, so there was no way she could afford to pay for her own health care.

It was a common story.

"I'm telling you this is class warfare at its most obvious," Max was saying while they waited for Taggart to show up.

"How so?" Kee wondered. "Everyone has the same options."

Tina looked at Kee as though he was naïve. Max wasn't so kind. "You're an idiot if you really think that. If you have enough wealth, you don't have to go into this place. I've heard there are people going into deep financial crisis to avoid coming in here. Those who've got the wherewithal can sidestep the same thing. That is the essence of class warfare. The more they can distract the middle class and persecute the economically dispossessed, the easier it is for them to perpetuate the system."

"But to what end?" Kee wondered. "I mean, it's not like this is going to help them!"

"Sure it is. Now instead of having people like Tina here advocating for subsidized housing, she's in here, effectively silenced. And the age range of the act is suspicious too, don't you think?"

"It does seem like the act discriminates there, but they have scientific reasons for doing that – it is much easier to change habits when you're young, and losing weight past the age of fifty is quite a bit more difficult," Kee replied.

"Yes," Max said, "and you think the fact that the older generations tend to be the ones who vote have no impact on this?"

"They voted for it because they knew it wouldn't affect them," Tina confirmed.

"But it would affect their kids," Kee said.

"And did that stop them? Has that stopped them from staying in their jobs well past retirement age? Has it stopped them from over-consuming? Do the Boomers have any pangs about the unsustainable nature of our economy?"

"Max, you know many have."

"But not the aggregate. Despite their self-serving rhetoric, the Boomers are the most selfish generation in a century," Max replied.

"They're one of the biggest generations," Kee said. "I think you're confusing size with motive."

"Well," Tina mollified, "we won't sort it out today. Where is Taggart?"

"Probably scheming," Max said. "His Flabometrics score is off the scale for shiftiness."

"Max!" Kee chided.

"I know, he's got clout and he's smart, but still, I don't think we can trust the guy."

"He wants out as badly as we do."

"I know. I know. But I don't trust him," Max said. "And the Flabometrics don't lie. Just watch his mendacious butt flab in motion."

"Has anyone had a brainstorm yet?" Tina asked, trying to change the subject. For two weeks now, they had been trying to come up with a scheme that would make it more costly to keep them in the Fatness, but it just wasn't coming to them. The system was designed to encourage Weight Winners to keep people trapped in the CRC, and to get more people incarcerated if possible. Especially now that they had a new business model that required the labour of the denizens of CRC-17.

"I think our only real hope is to get public opinion on our side and change the law," Tina said. This had been her position from the beginning, and Kee was with her in spirit. But from what he understood, it would be challenging to change the public's mind about the system. They were out of sight and out of mind.

Taggart finally arrived, looking pleased. "I think I've got it figured out," he said to everyone as he sat down heavily.

He slurped his coffee as everyone waited in anticipation.

"Well," Max said, "what is it?"

Taggart looked around and said in his best conspiratorial whisper, "How about a good old-fashioned prison break?"

"Sure," Max said. "But I'm going to need an awful lot of crazy glue."

QUOTE

"The history of the twentieth century was dominated by the struggle against totalitarian systems of state power. The twenty-first will no doubt be marked by a struggle to curtail excessive corporate power."

~Eric Schlosser, *Fast Food Nation: The Dark Side of the All-American Meal*

Chapter 2 – Burying the Greed

Jacinda had thought about not attending Ballard's funeral, but it seemed like she should. Even though their relationship had not ended well, she thought it would be good closure for her. Until she'd heard the news that he'd keeled over in his meeting with the Health minister, she'd always been somewhat worried about whatever revenge he was planning. She knew him well enough to know that there would be a scheme. He was predictable that way.

The massive coronary had not been so predictable, and it was hard to imagine. Jacinda – and most of Ballard's contemporaries – had always envied Ballard's seeming immortality and ever-youthfulness. His hair had only started turning grey that year, sometime after his fifty-eighth birthday. And he never seemed to gain weight, despite his love of pulled-pork sandwiches, beer, and classic (butter rich) French cuisine. But apparently he had been just another one of those thin guys who was a ticking time bomb.

Jed sat with her at the service; he did get up to deliver a short eulogy, which was polite and professional. None of the old partner's rancor showed at all, and if anything, a bit of sadness. She looked about at the small crowd of mourners. A couple of people from the firm, Jed and Jacinda, and surprisingly, Melissa Handle, the president of Weight Winners Canada. As the minister finished up his homily, all about the value of hard work and looking after others, Jed whispered to her, "You know he died intestate?"

"He didn't have a will?"

"Nope. It's quite a scandal. He's got no family left, so it looks like the government is going to get it all. I had to set up the damned service and pay for it myself."

Ballard would have hated that, she knew. And it almost made her laugh.

It was a glorious fall day – still warm enough to go without a coat. A light breeze made the gold and red maples shimmer as they lowered Ballard's casket in the ground. There was no wake planned after the service, and Jed gave Jacinda a hug.

"I'm going to re-establish the firm, and if you want to come back to work for me, I'd love you to," he said.

"I think I'll continue with the NGO. We're going to do good work."

"Well, I think we can give you some legal help if you need it. Pro bono of course."

"Thanks, Jed!"

"Keep punching, Jacinda. Keep punching."

Melissa Handle approached Jacinda as Jed left. "I guess that just leaves us ladies," she said. "My condolences, Miss Williams. I understood that you worked with Ballard for quite a long time."

Jacinda couldn't help but notice the emphasis Handle put on *worked*.

"I was surprised you're here. I didn't think you parted ways amicably."

"Well, we didn't. That boy had more twists than a pretzel factory."

Jacinda covered her mouth and stifled a laugh.

Handle nodded her head and said, "Still, he was one of God's creatures, and I learned a thing or two from him, so I owed him a final visit."

"That's nice," Jacinda said.

"Just the right thing. Though I tell you, I'm happy to see him get his comeuppance. The man was a snake."

"I hear you," Jacinda agreed.

"And greedy as Mammon. And vain. That man thought the sun rose to hear him crow. Still, he knew his way around the sheets."

Jacinda didn't think that was so true. She'd found Ballard a competent lover, but he seemed more concerned with his own performance and her perception of it than actually enjoying the moment. She couldn't help herself around him, but that wasn't because of any intrinsic knowledge he had in bed. She didn't reply. "Well, I'm sorry to see him go," Jacinda said. "He was a personality."

"He was definitely that." Handle smiled. "But I'm not sorry he's dead. It was the only way to bury his greed. He almost ruined me."

"He did that to most people. Well, I have to get going," Jacinda said.

"Oh, I was hoping we could jaw some more," Handle said.

"Really? About what?"

"Well, not to put too fine a point on it, but your little organization has got my ox in a ditch."

"Sorry?" Jacinda asked.

"You are a problem for us," Handle said. "Probably the most serious one we've got at the moment, though how I'm going to keep the shareholders happy with this new plan we're implementing ..."

"Plan?"

"Yes, they haven't made it public yet, but I'll tell you as a gesture of goodwill. We're going to start charging the costs of the system to the users of the system."

"You're going to make people *pay* to be incarcerated?"

"Oh, those terms are as ugly as homemade sin," Handle said. "They are not incarcerated. They are being treated for a medical problem."

"Well, that may be, but when they opted to go into the CRC, it was voluntary. Many are now being held against their will. Against the law, I would argue."

"Those are strong words, Miss Williams," Handle said. "Now, I know why you've got your tail up, and I think I may have a solution that will help both of us."

"My tail up?" Was this skinny, bottle-blond bitch making fun of her ass?

"Angry. Argumentative. I see why you're upset."

"Oh."

"A young fella, as I understand it. Keelan. You're in love with him and you can't be together. Just like Romeo and Juliet. It's sad enough to bring a tear to a glass eye."

"So?"

"Well, like I said, I have a solution. What if we let young Romeo out of our facility? He's doing very well. My understanding is that he's very close to getting under 30 BMI, or bimmi as those chubby scamps like to call it. I can see letting him go if you promise to get him under the mark and keep him there. Our company's reputation is on the line here, but I can see my way forward to making this deal if you cease and desist your public relations campaign against us."

"But we haven't even started yet."

"Oh, sure, but I'd be dumb as a barrel of hair if I didn't take this opportunity to draw your teeth."

"Wow," Jacinda replied. She wasn't sure what was more surprising: the offer to get Keelan out or Handle's inexhaustible supply of folksy Texas idioms.

"Yeah. I think after the years you spent with Mr. Fabulous there, now earning his reward under the dirt, you're due a bit of happiness. And I'd like to give it to you. I'll let Keelan out of the facility today as long as you both sign an agreement to never speak up against us."

"I can't even talk to him yet," Jacinda said. "You've still got the CRCs locked down."

"Oh, that's changing today. We're allowing limited communications. We're blocking big uploads, so no more videos can get out, but you'll be able to talk with him."

"Okay," Jacinda said. She had never intended to save everyone from the CRCs, even if they were manifestly unfair and illegal. That was someone else's problem. Her goal had always been to rescue Keelan so they could start their life together. *Is that a cop-out?* she wondered. No. She was just one person, and even though she had a plan, she knew it would take years to free everyone. And she just wasn't sure she could wait that long. She knew that Keelan couldn't. The last time they'd talked, he was already in a state of despair.

"Okay." Jacinda nodded her head. "Let's see the language of your agreement and get this done."

Handle beamed. "Well, that makes me so happy."

They shook hands, and as they walked away from the grave site, she imagined Ballard laughing at her.

MYTH

Fast Weight Loss Doesn't Last

A common idea amongst dieters is that it's better to lose weight slowly than quickly. There's a number of reasons for this, but one of them is that if you lose the weight quickly, you're unable to keep the weight off. This turns out to be problematic.

Australian researchers tested this idea by having dieters lose weight quickly and slowly. Then they came back three years later to see what happened. For the fast dieters, they'd regained 70.5 percent of their weight. The slow dieters regained 71.2 percent – a statistical wash. So it really doesn't matter how you lose the weight.

The really depressing takeaway for those of us trying to lose some pounds? Both groups gained more than two-thirds of their weight back, and the other third was still trying to deal with leftover loose skin.

22

Chapter 3 – Fortune's Drool

Jacinda had thought the conversation was going to be triumphant. Their happy ending. But it wasn't going well.

She'd called with the fabulous news that Weight Winners was willing to let Keelan out of the Fatness, and that she had rescued him. They were going to be able to be together, finally. But then Keelan said, "If you really love me, you won't ask me to leave."

"What are you talking about? What's happened to you?" Jacinda asked. After six weeks of not talking to Keelan, it seemed almost as though he was a different person. He'd certainly lost more weight – in fact, it seemed hard to believe he wasn't well under the 30 BMI range yet. He seemed more muscular, trim, and healthy. His colour was dark from working outside, and there was life in his eyes.

She liked that he was no longer depressed, but not what she was hearing.

"I can't go yet. I can't just leave everyone."

"But do you know what I've had to give up to get you this chance?"

"I can only imagine, Jacinda. How did you do it?"

Jacinda couldn't help herself. She burst into tears, and the entire story of leaving the law firm, suing Ballard, her encounter with Handle – they all just spilled out of her. She felt guilty about abandoning her plans to start the NGO. The board was still in place, but after that first meeting where they'd talked about mandate and goals, they had yet to meet a second time. As far as Jacinda was concerned, the organization had served its purpose – it got Keelan out of the Fatness. And now he refused to leave!

"How can you stay?"

"How can I leave?" Keelan replied. "They need me in here. I'm doing good work. I feel like, for the first time in my life, what I do and say actually has an impact on the world. I know that your work has always been like that, so you probably don't know what it's like to feel powerless, but that was how I was feeling. And now, I'm part of something bigger."

Jacinda said, "You're part of us. That is bigger. Isn't it enough?"

"I want it to be, but if I cut and run now, I'll always feel like a coward."

Jacinda cried again. He was making her feel even more guilty. These were all emotions she understood. The feeling of power-lessness. The idea of being part of something larger than oneself. The notion that she was abandoning a principle for her own ends. She wanted Keelan to hold her, but the Skype connection did not have that capability. She rallied her courage. She wiped at the tears in her eyes, and she smiled at him. He was forcing her to do what she knew to be the right thing too.

Maybe that is what relationships really are for, she thought; they're mirrors that show ourselves truthfully. No, more than that. A true relationship shows us our better selves, encourages us to strive to be the best we can, not out of guilt, but out of wanting to inspire the source of our love.

"I know you wanted to just be together, and I want it too. I want to leave this place and feel you in my arms. I want that, Jacinda. But I need to come to you with some semblance of –"

"Of what?"

"I don't know the right word for it. I wanted to say manhood, but that seems, I dunno, sexist or something. Pride? No, it's not pride that is driving me. Integrity, maybe? I need to feel, to prove, that you can depend on me, and wouldn't you always wonder if I just abandoned all my friends in here to be comfortable? I know it's a hard thing to ask. You've been so patient with me, but would you be willing to wait a bit longer?"

"There's no guarantee, though, Kee," Jacinda said. *Why did I say that?* she wondered. *Do I have to torture him for it?*

"I understand," Keelan said. "If you want to end it, I'd understand."

"No, that's not what I'm saying. I'm just saying that it's not going to be easy."

"Nothing worth doing ever is."

"So what is your plan?"

"My plan is your plan. You bring a case against the government for unlawful imprisonment. While you do that, we're going to have a hunger strike."

Jacinda laughed. "Really?"

"Hey, at the very least it may get me under 29 and I can get out legitimately. Though Max says they're never going to let us out."

"I love you," Jacinda said.

"Me too," Keelan replied. "At least we can Skype again. Now, have you got any thoughts about what else we could talk about?"

Despite feeling let down by the news, Jacinda still experienced a little thrill of excitement. "Whatever are you suggesting?"

Keelan waggled his eyebrows, and she laughed.

Taggart did not take the idea of doing a hunger strike very well.

"No. Prison break. It's the best way to get out."

"Seriously, now that we have a way to get news out of the Fatness again, we should be playing the PR card," Keelan said. "A hunger strike is the best way to do it."

"I've already started," Max said as he sipped his coffee.

"You can't drink coffee on a hunger strike, Max."

"Really?"

"No. Just water."

"Where do you get that?"

"I dunno," Keelan said, "it makes sense, doesn't it? It's all about protesting via denial."

"What about psychotropics?" Max asked.

"Definitely not," Keelan said.

"Oh." Max looked disappointed. "Then we can't start today. Besides, who says we can't have coffee? Is there some kind of hunger strike rulebook? Isn't a hunger strike basically a political fast?"

"I guess," Keelan said.

"Why no psychotropics? Shamans have been doing it since the Neolithic."

"This is beside the point!" Taggart shouted. "We need to do something, not deprive ourselves of food. Have you thought of the drool? There'll be pools of it everywhere."

"Drool?"

"Keelan, look around. These people are in here because they don't have the willpower to stop eating poutine and potato chips and donuts … and cheeseburgers! Goddamned cheeseburgers, kid! How are they going to manage a hunger strike?" Taggart asked.

"That's not true. Many of us are just big boned," Max said.

"Max, seriously. Look, Taggart, I know you think the prison break is the best bet, but this will work."

Taggart stood in the commandant's office, waiting for him to arrive.

McGrath came in, with two of his DarkRain guards in tow. They stood at ease by the door, and the martinet said, "Please sit, Mr. Taggart."

He tried not to groan as he did, but a little sound escaped his lips. He'd been standing there for nearly an hour, and his legs were killing him. He'd lost quite a bit of weight in prison, but not enough that standing still was fun. He was still a manatee, after all. Taggart tried to sit as upright as possible, while McGrath took his seat. The decorations in the office had changed from the days of Selwyn Seward. The plush chairs, big desk, and beautiful Group of Seven replicas had all disappeared, to be replaced by plain wooden chairs and a small desk, which seemed to have no purpose, as it was completely bare. Taggart imagined the drawer empty except for a few sheets of paper and a line of writing implements, ordered precisely by colour or perhaps length.

"I don't know what to make of you, Mr. Taggart. Let's start by saying you are a fat sack of moral turpitude, but, even so, one must work with the allies at hand, and, I will not lie, I need allies," McGrath said.

Taggart was hardly charmed, but he had a plan and he stuck

to it. "I must say you are not the kind of person I like to do business with either, Mr. McGrath, but we can't always choose our partners in crime."

"You may call me Captain McGrath, or Commandant."

Taggart smiled and said, "Okay, let's make that our first agreement. I'll call you Captain McGrath, and you will never again refer to my weight."

McGrath frowned. He looked at the DarkRain guards standing at ease and told them to leave. When they were gone, he stood at the window, looking over the changes he had overseen. There was now a secure fence surrounding the perimeter of the CRC property. There were two outbuildings, and the foundations for two more had been poured. In the distance, he could see Keelan and the other inmates helping with construction on the deck around the pond, which was going to be open for swimming next year.

"It's changing, isn't it?" Taggart said. "But you can't change people."

McGrath turned to face Taggart and said, "No, you can't. Not easily. But you can control them. And teach them self-control. Okay, I will never again refer to your weight issues. And you will be excused from the Discipline Process. Now, let's get to work, shall we?"

"Not quite," Taggart said. "I would like some concessions. I realize that you would never be able to allow me the freedom to run my, uh, enterprise as I did under the old regime, but I would like the freedom to leave the CRC on occasion – in secrecy, of course. And I'd like my creature comforts back, the ability to run my business from my room, and I'd like my criminal record expunged."

"Done. Though the latter may take some time. Now, can we get to work, Mr. Taggart?"

"Of course, Commandant."

"The first thing I want to know is what your organization is planning. I want you to keep me informed at all times; of course, we'll have to do so secretly. I'm working on a way for us to do that. I may also need you to sabotage whatever plans your group is making."

"That seems reasonable. Anything else?"

"Yes," McGrath said. "You have a criminal mind –"

"I like to think of it as a business mind unrestrained by convention."

"Ahem, I don't mean to disparage. Your … unconventional thinking is what we need. We have a problem, and I'm not quite sure what to do about it."

"Go on."

As McGrath explained the problem, Taggart's eyes widened, and he realized he should have asked for more concessions. *Perhaps later*, he thought as McGrath spelled out the issue …

Keelan had thirty other inmates of the CRC ready to try the hunger strike. They were all committed porkers. (He'd been hoping to get a few manatees too, but alas, none were willing to join them.)

Max volunteered to help look after their health, so he wasn't joining them in the strike itself. He had even brushed up on the topic to ensure he could give them better care than the kidney-threatening CRC quack, Dr. Fundarek. They were gathered in the pool, under the guise of hydrotherapy, to begin their preparations. Max, who had once been a doctor, was explaining how best to approach the strike.

"So it's important to realize what you're signing up for," Max said. "A hunger strike is extremely dangerous, even if you're fat. The lack of food can mess with all kinds of your systems, and it's especially hard on your kidneys. So the first thing I need you to do is to stop drinking coffee and smoking cigarettes. They might make you feel better, but they will kill you a lot faster."

"Seriously?" Greg asked. He drank at least six cups of coffee a day. "Okay, well, I'm out. I thought liquids were okay when I signed up for this."

"Yes, but only liquids that will support your health," Max

said. "You have to take this seriously. I thought coffee would be okay, but it turns out it isn't. No psychotropics either."

"Oh-kay," Greg said. "I'm not a regular acid dropper, so that isn't a problem. No coffee is a deal-breaker though."

Greg and several other people heaved themselves out of the pool, a wave rebounding off the walls as they did so. When the water had settled down, Max continued.

"Now, as far as I can tell, this is a good time to try this. We have nice weather outside, but it's not too hot. So that should help. It's extremely important that while you're fasting, you limit your activities as much as possible."

"What about sex?" Tina asked.

"Yes, that too. Anything that would exert you."

"What about some light exercise?" Keelan wondered.

"No, nothing like that. You'll have to stay as still as possible and marshal your resources. Your body is going to be under an intense amount of strain."

Tina and a dozen other people got out of the pool. Tina was blushing, and she whispered to Keelan, "Sorry, but I thought Greg and I would be able to fool around during the strike. I mean, life is too short!"

"Sure," Keelan said, his heart sinking. "I understand."

That left them with less than twenty. But still, enough people to make the point. Keelan looked at Max. "Okay, what else?"

"We're going to start this week by weaning you off food. No junk food, no crap. By the end of the week you'll only be eating vegetables and fruit. Keelan and I have enough credits that we will be able to supply everyone with those. Then we start fasting. I'll be dropping by your cells every day with some electrolytes, but I can't stress this enough – this is an extremely dangerous activity, even if you've got lots of fat to turn into energy. While your body does that, it produces something called ketones, which are toxic. It's why I'll want you drinking as much water as possible, to help you excrete it."

"How long until it becomes dangerous?" someone asked.

"About four weeks. Maybe longer for this group, as we have

more fat, but once we get to the point of burning about forty percent of our body mass, it becomes quite dangerous. I'd guess six weeks."

"Plus a week of veggies before?" Keelan asked.

"Yes, and I haven't talked about coming out of the fast. We'll have to be very careful about what you eat and how much as you recover."

"Okay," Keelan said.

The pool came alive with the sound of nearly twenty large people moving towards the edges.

"No, wait, we can do this!" Keelan said.

"No, we can't," Barbara said as she passed Keelan. She stopped and put a hand on his shoulder. "Look, I'm sorry, but this is a crazy plan. I'm not going to kill myself to make a political point, and I doubt that anyone would even care if a bunch of fat fuckers started to starve to death. They'd probably think it was hilarious."

"I certainly thought it was," Max said.

"What?" Keelan cried.

"It's hilarious. Absurd. A prison full of obese inmates not eating anything to protest a system that is purported to help them lose weight. It would be a PR nightmare."

"So why didn't you just say that?"

"I repeat: hilariously absurd," Max said.

Keelan joined the rest of the group and got out of the pool. "Fine, I was pruning up anyway."

"At least Taggart was wrong about the drool," Max said.

QUOTE

"It has always seemed strange to me … the things we admire in men, kindness and generosity, openness, honesty, understanding and feeling, are the concomitants of failure in our system. And those traits we detest, sharpness, greed, acquisitiveness, meanness, egotism and self-interest, are the traits of success. And while men admire the quality of the first they love the produce of the second."

~John Steinbeck

Chapter 4 – An NGO By Any Other Name Would Spell as Leet

After deciding it would be wrong to call her NGO *Keelan's Hope*, Jacinda still needed a name. They had a working group, a board of directors, and now, two employees, but they didn't have a catchy name yet. It was important, Jacinda realized, to capture the essence of the organization in a name, and there were some fine examples that inspired her: Greenpeace, *Médecins Sans Frontières*, and Amnesty International. Not necessarily all their tactics, but the boldness of their missions and their labels.

Jacinda was brainstorming with her new hires, Jeremy and Julie. Jeremy was a handsome young man with a communications master's and an undergrad in computer programming. Julie was in her mid-forties; she had burgundy hair and extensive experience with fund-raising. Keelan was with them virtually, his head projected on a screen in front of them. It made Keelan the centre of attention, and Jacinda found it very distracting. She kept staring at his eyes.

"J-Force?" Jeremy asked.

"'Cause of our names?" Julie replied.

Nods. Jacinda wrote it down on the sheet of paper. There was no judging during a brainstorming session. They'd been at it all day and had already gone through two sheets of really bad ideas.

"What about something that tackles the subject directly?" Keelan asked.

"FatFree!" Julie almost jumped out of her chair, she was so excited by this notion.

"FreeFat," Jeremy added. "But spelled leet-style. Like, Fr33F47!"

Jacinda wrote them all down. She noticed Keelan's eyebrow arch. *No judgement*, she thought.

"Canadian Obesity Freedom For Everyone Exactly," Keelan suggested.

Jacinda wrote it down. "C-O-F-F-E-E. Coffee?"

"I wouldn't mind one, sure."

Jacinda laughed.

"Free the Fatties," Keelan added.

"Fat-So?" Jeremy said.

The pen scratched, and Jacinda said, "How about something less clever, to do with health and justice? Canadians for Health and Justice? CHJ?"

"Liberty for our Fat Friends," Keelan said.

"The Human Liberty Project," Jeremy said.

"Canadian Justice for the Obese," Julie said.

"Justice for Obese Canadians, Eh?" Keelan said.

Jacinda wrote. "J-O-C-E?"

"Yeah, but spell Kanadians with a *K*."

"This is serious, Keelan!"

"I know, but it's not coming to me."

"Well, we have to have a name. Even if it's boring, we need to have something so I can write the charter!"

"What about the Canadian Council Against Fatism?" Keelan said.

"Canadians Against Fatism," Julie added.

"Canada Free of Fatism," Jeremy said.

"End Canadian Fatism," Keelan said.

Jacinda scribbled quickly.

"No, wait, how about Fatism Free Canada," Keelan said. "The FFC."

"That's good," Jeremy said. "I could see that in a logo. Of course, it may confuse all the Final Fantasy players out there."

Keelan laughed, his giant head shaking on the screen. "Well, we'll just have to live with that."

Taggart didn't do any of the work, but he did oversee the operation. It was late at night, and the only people awake were the DarkRain guards at the entranceway and his two helpers, Chet and Billy.

"I don't see why that fat fucker doesn't have to do this," Chet grumbled as he cut the sod.

"Captain's orders," Billy said. "C'mon, we just need to dig out the grass and we can use the backhoe for the hole."

"Fine."

It took them longer than they thought, and in the darkness it wasn't easy. When the grass was removed, Billy got the backhoe and drove across the property to the secluded spot they'd picked for the grave. It only took a little while to dig a big enough hole, and he left the engine running and the lights on while he and Chet tried to drag the body bag to the hole.

"Who was it anyway?" Chet asked. "I hope it wasn't that Tundra character. I want to do him myself someday."

"I dunno. Some manatee," Billy said.

They couldn't get the body out of the bag easily, so they just pushed the body and the container together. It flumped unceremoniously into the bottom of the whole. Taggart pointedly did not look.

"How'd he go?" Chet wondered.

"I think heart attack. From the electric generation. He was doing his shift on a treadmill and keeled over. Fundarek said they got the poor bastard to the infirmary, but he was already gone," Billy said.

"Why hide it?" Chet said. "I mean, shouldn't the government take care of this?"

"I don't think the commandant wants the attention right now," Billy replied.

"Come on, guys," Taggart said. "Let's finish this up. Someone could see the lights from the highway."

"Right," Billy agreed. He got back into the cab and pulled the earth over the makeshift grave. The two DarkRain guards replaced the turf as best they could, and panted while they stood there for a moment.

"What?" Taggart asked.

"Shouldn't we say something?" Billy asked.

"Don't see the point," Chet opined. "He's dead and gone."

"But —"

"Seriously. Ah, fuck, I've got mud all over Betty," Chet said, wiping dirt off one of his pearl-handled pistols.

"I'll say something," Taggart said. "Here lies the mortal remains of Bernie. He was a good customer and, from what I could tell, a nice man. He loved burgers a bit too much, but his weight doesn't matter anymore now."

"Easy for you to say," Chet griped. "You didn't have to lift him."

Jacinda did her name search the next day. Julie worked with a local graphic designer to help them develop their visual brand, and Jeremy set up the website. By the end of the week, they had enough to start work on fund-raising and their first campaign. They were going to do a modest media blitz describing the situation to Canadians and underscoring the essential inequity of the situation. People living in the CRCs were discriminated against because of their weight and their age. Only people between the ages of eighteen and fifty were targeted by the Health Canada law. The fact that Weight Winners Canada and Health Canada had taken away the option of leaving the system was illegal, the FFC would argue. In fact, once they'd started this publicity campaign, Jacinda intended to bring a case against the two organizations. At the very least, she felt that the treatment of the obese in the CRCs was an infringement of several rights guaranteed under the Canadian Charter of Rights and Freedoms, particularly article nine, which said that "Everyone has the right not to be arbitrarily detained or imprisoned".

But first, Jacinda would give Melissa Handle and her company a chance to rectify the situation on their own.

She had arranged to meet with Handle at the head offices of Weight Winners Canada, which occupied several floors near the top of Landon's tallest building, One Landon Place. She waited in the lobby of their two-floor spread, which was designed to impress. The open-concept offices had a huge vaulted space, and early-October morning light streamed in through the wall of glass like God looking good for his first date with an unsuspecting carpenter's wife. The inner walls of the space were tastefully decorated, and the entire offices were surprisingly devoid of corporate propaganda, except for a gold-plated Weight Winners Canada wordmark on the reception desk's forward face.

The receptionist said, "She'll see you now, Ms. Williams."

Handle's office was on the south side of the building, so the light wasn't quite as imposing there, but the room was just as aesthetically pleasing as the lobby. Handle got up from her minimalist steel-and-glass desk and shook Jacinda's hand. As usual, Handle was decked out in a classy skirt and jacket, which was reminiscent of Jacqueline Kennedy. Almost as though she'd stepped through some kind of door in time. Her hair wasn't quite as tall. Handle's outfit, her perfect blond hair, and white, white teeth were her armour. Jacinda reflected on her own outfit, which was a perfectly serviceable black pants suit that hid her giant butt and flabby arms, and realized that it was all about presentation. Despite being a one-time beauty pageant contestant, Handle wasn't exquisite. Jacinda had the sudden intimation that if so much attention was not paid to Handle's dress and make-up, she would appear rather normal. On the attractive end of the scale, but no more.

"So, Ms. Williams, can this visit signal a change of heart? I see you've gone ahead and registered a group you call Fatism Free Canada, and I read your charter, but my sincere hope is that you've just done that as a bargaining ploy. Perhaps you want some recompense for your boyfriend as well as his freedom? Because that would be fine in my books," Handle said.

"Really?" Jacinda wondered.

"Absolutely. Look, Jacinda – may I call you Jacinda? I see us as kind of sisters. We've both endured that stewed skunk Ballard, and I'm thrilled that you've found true love. It's a rare thing in this world, especially for us working girls. Women of power, I mean. So I want to help you achieve that, but I can't let you interfere with my business."

"My apologies, but I can't just fold like that," Jacinda said. *Damn, that's fucking Canadian,* she thought. Be tough.

"That's a sorry thing," Handle replied.

"Look, I appreciate the offer, but this is not just about me and Keelan. He refuses to leave until people have the ability to opt out of the system again, at least. If you could change that policy, then we could have a deal, right here and now."

"I can't do that, sweetie," Handle said. Her smile was brilliant and so false.

"Why not? It's how the act was originally drawn up, and I for one think it is the least legal part of it all. And I'm sure we'll find other issues as well —"

"Meaning what?" Handle interrupted.

"I don't know yet; we'll see what the court has to say, but I'm sure you don't want the expense of all that."

"We couldn't afford to just let everyone go who wants to. Our new agreement with your lovely president wouldn't work if we allowed it. Too many people would leave, even if they did have to pay for their own upkeep."

"Prime minister. And you probably have your contract with the Government of Canada. And if you think he's lovely, I think you're nuts," Jacinda said.

The smile disappeared.

"Look, I'm trying to be polite, but it just won't work if you keep acting like a stuck-up little bitch in heat," Handle said.

"Don't try to out-polite me, you Texan trollop, we invented politeness in Canada!"

"Slut!"

"Hypocrite," Jacinda rejoined.

"Whore," Handle said.

"Profiteer," Jacinda said, and added, "though you probably see that as a good thing."

"Bitch."

"You said that already. Shall I get you a thesaurus, you ignorant bottom-feeding cunt?"

Handle smiled. She was having trouble maintaining the insipid grin, but years of training for beauty pageants propped it up. "Well, thanks for dropping by. I'll give you a minute to leave before I call security, just 'cause I was raised to be a lady."

Jacinda didn't smile back; she just said, "See you in court."

"I hope you've got more money than Mammon, because that's what I've got, you snippy little bitch."

"That won't be a problem," Jacinda replied. She turned and left before Handle even had a chance to ask her why.

QUOTE

"Sacred cows make the best hamburger."

~Mark Twain

Chapter 5 – The Trouble with Taggart

"The trouble with Taggart is that I don't trust his fat," Max said. They were walking to the pool for a late-afternoon swim. It was the only form of regular exercise that Max would agree to do, and Keelan liked to encourage his friend. Besides, Keelan felt the swimming helped ease his muscles after a long day working with Joe and his construction crew. They had just finished framing another set of outbuildings that day, and he was sore.

"Max, we're all fat," Keelan reminded his strange, trying, and possibly insane friend.

"But there's something about his fatness. He's got a shifty paunch. And his pudge is just downright insincere."

"What?"

"I mean, you're fat, but just barely. Actually, are you still fat? When did they last weigh you?"

Keelan was grateful to get away from the insane topic of Taggart's untrustworthy adipose tissue. "Nothing official, but my own scale tells me I cracked it," Keelan said.

"Really?"

"Yes, as of this morning I weigh exactly 211 pounds, which means my bimmi is 29.5 – a full half-point under the obese range. I'm overweight!"

"That's … that's wonderful, Kee! I'm so happy for you."

Keelan reflected that a person who had never struggled with obesity, someone watching this scene from the outside world, would be baffled by the conversation. How could he be so happy – overjoyed, really – to be overweight? It had taken him three years and countless attempts, but he'd lost the weight that got him in the CRC in the first place. Now he just needed to lose a bit more and he could officially leave. Four pounds would put him just under 29. Call it five to be safe – and there was always the vagaries of the human body. Weight could vary by five pounds from day to day, based on many factors. Ironically, working out could cause it, though in the long run the time spent lifting weights was probably one of the reasons he'd been successful. The

stairs down to the Jack LaLane Memorial Pool ran off a corridor
that was perpendicular to the mall.

"Thanks, Max, but we both know they won't let me go."

"Yeah, I suspect. You still have to get underneath the 29 bimmi threshold, and I wouldn't be surprised if they lower it again.
But it's goddamned impressive. I know how hard it is to do, and
in this place, it's even harder."

"Well, I'm not leaving. At least not until we have a chance
to get everyone physically out of this CRC. I need to prove to
Jacinda that I can be a hero."

"That's noble of you, but stupid," Max said. "You should get
out when you can. Be with the normie you love. Besides, you can
probably be of way more help on the outside."

"I'll think about it," Keelan said, "but –"

"Shhh. Look, there he goes." They stopped at the entrance to
the corridor and watched as Taggart slouched by. He was heading
up the stairs towards the administrative and diagnostic wing,
which Weight Winners Canada had renamed the "Discipline
Centre". Max followed him at a distance. The mall was filled with
stout shoppers, and it was easy to avoid being detected by Taggart.

"His time away has not improved the mendacious nature
of his blubber. I'd give him a rating of 6.4 on my Flabometrics
scale," Max said.

"Okay," Keelan said. He really wanted to change the topic,
because when Max started sounding really crazy, it made him sad.
"What do you think Taggart is up to?"

"I think he's up to something," Max said.

"It could be perfectly innocent. He could be meeting with his
discipline advisor, his DA."

Max snorted derisively. Whether because he didn't believe
Keelan's premise, or because of the term *discipline advisor*, Keelan
could not tell. "Let's follow him. Look, he's almost hauled his
gargantuan ass up the stairs. Let's see where he goes."

Keelan knew enough not to argue, so they tailed their co-con-
spirator up the stairs and down the hallway towards the administrative offices and the torture chambers where the DAs worked.

"You really shouldn't be making pejorative remarks about his weight, Max. I mean, you're obese too."

"Yeah, but I'm just a porker. He's a fucking manatee. A *shifty* manatee."

Keelan gave up the argument, and they just followed Taggart, who was clearly unaware he was being tailed. In the upper level there were fewer people, so Max and Keelan would have been easy to spot. Taggart walked into the discipline labs.

"Let's follow him in," Max suggested.

"He's probably just meeting with his discipline advisor."

"What if it's just a cover?" Max said.

"It could be," Keelan admitted. "It's how I would arrange it."

"Okay, let's go."

They walked to the discipline labs, and at the entrance were met by Daniel Starkey. "Hello, you fat fuckers." He smiled.

"Screw you, fascist," Max said.

"Why have you heaved your disgusting flab up here? Do you have appointments?"

"No," Keelan said. "And I thought we were past the break-down stage. Aren't we building yet?"

"Maybe I can for you, Mr. Cavanaugh, but not this corpulent reprobate."

"I resemble that comment." Max grinned. "Fishy, fishy eyebrows." He waggled his hand in front of Starkey's face and sang a little impromptu song:

> Fishy, fishy eyebrows,
> they called him fishy eyebrow face,
> fishy, stinky fascist,
> he wants to play with his sticky mace.

Keelan couldn't help himself; he started to laugh out loud as Max repeated this doggerel and added a little faux-Irish step dance to the hand waggling. He laughed even harder as Starkey's face turned as red as some of his victims after he made them strip and jiggle on the elliptical machine.

Starkey, starkey, starkers
He gets off when he sees us starkers
Fishy, fishy, barkers,
He's a nosey parker!

Starkey was so red in the face Keelan thought he'd pass out, but he still managed to say, "If you don't have an appointment, you have to leave."

"And if we don't, Mr. Fishface?" Max asked, continuing his step dance.

"I'm calling security. I think Chet may still be on duty too."

That ended Max's dance. Keelan was still laughing, but he said, "Okay, we'll go."

As they made their way back to the commons, Keelan's eyes were still watering. "That was hilarious."

"What, the part when we found out Taggart is betraying us, or the part where Starkey threatened me with Mr. Psycho, Chet?"

"No, the part where your hands kind of did that weird counterpoint to your step-dancing. And Starkey was just freaked out —" Keelan laughed again.

Greg found them as they made their way to Timmy's, and said, "Hey, have either of you guys seen Bernie?"

"Who's Bernie?"

"You don't know Bernie? Burger Bernie, we used to call him back when the Heavy Hitters still brought in the Mickey Dees. Nobody has seen him for days."

"Oh yeah, I know him. That's weird, is he sick?" Keelan said.

"Yeah, we should look into that," Max agreed.

"I've checked with Fundarek, but he wouldn't tell me anything," Greg said.

"Odd."

"Why don't you talk to his discipline advisor? Do you know who it was?" Keelan asked.

"No, but I'll find out. Some of the other guys knew Bernie well. I'll get back to you later."

MYTH

The BMI Bummer

Here's the reality – the BMI tables are a tool, and a flawed one at that, when it comes to predicting death rates cause by obesity.

Numerous long-term epidemiological studies have shown that being underweight according to the BMI tables, i.e., 20 or less, is less healthy than being overweight, i.e., BMI of 25–29. In fact, a number of studies show that being overweight and even obese (30 or higher) can lead to above-average lifespans compared with those in the low end of the "normal" range. So why even use the BMI table? Is it because the term Body Mass Index sounds cool?

Ironically, it's because of laziness.

23

Chapter 6 – Jabbas

Keelan wondered what had happened to Greg.

They'd been framing for most of the month, but now that was done, and while the plumbing and electrical guys did their thing, he was helping to clean up the worksite and do other scut work until they were ready to start putting in insulation and drywall. If nothing else, he was learning valuable skills – hell, if he couldn't find web work after he was done being a pudgy prisoner, he might try the construction field. Perhaps a combination of the two – he could keep his hand in on the web side of things, plus get the exercise and outdoor work of construction.

Outdoor work seemed less appealing as the weather changed. It was the first cold morning of the fall, and he made a mental note to buy some insulated work gloves and warmer work fatigues at the Manliness Hut. Keelan watched steam rising off the electrical building in the cold morning air. It reminded him of the heat escaping a cowshed in the winter.

Two contradictory thoughts occurred to him at that moment. One was the obvious. To Weight Winners Canada, that was what the denizens of the CRCs were – cattle. They weren't human beings anymore; they were units. They were chattels to be worked to make electricity, milked of their dreams and dollars in the mall, and metaphorically slaughtered to feed the rapacious appetite of the corporation that owned them. At the same time, Keelan couldn't stop himself from thinking that it was quite wasteful, all the sweaty energy that was literally evaporating through the roof of the building. He wondered if there was a way to capture it and feed it back into the system. Not that he was going to help Weight Winners make any more out of his labour.

Greg appeared over the rise, flanked by Billy and psycho Chet. Actually, it was more like they were frog-marching him. Not that they could, really. Even if he was fat, Greg was a big dude, and both the DarkRain guards were little guys, comparatively.

"Wander away from the worksite again, and I'll fucking *do* you," Chet shouted at Greg.

"Fine. I just went for a walk. What's the big deal?"

"You're here to work, not *dick* around," Chet continued. He pulled out Betty and waved it vaguely at Greg, who got very quiet.

"Fine," Greg said. "Be cool, man."

Billy put his hand on Chet's arm and said, "You can't keep doing that. What if someone saw?"

Chet growled and holstered his pistol.

When they were gone, Keelan said, "You okay?"

"Yeah. That guy doesn't scare me. I was just wandering down to the woods. I saw some tire tracks and I wondered what was going on there."

"What did you see?"

"Nothing. They rushed me back here before I could even get close."

"That's odd," Keelan said.

"Everything about this place is odd, Kee. Come on, these scraps aren't going to pick up themselves."

That evening, after Kee had gone for his swim with Max, he learned that two other inmates had disappeared. Just like Bernie, nobody knew what happened to them, except that they'd gone to the infirmary and never reappeared.

"Fundarek told me they were all in the hospital for tests," Greg said. "But why didn't he just tell me that to begin with, when I was asking about Bernie? It doesn't seem right."

"Hmm," Max said. "Well, there's another reason *never* to go to the infirmary. If you're sick, come and see me."

Taggart appeared and they all got quiet. Since they'd suspected him of colluding with the commandant, it was hard to trust him. At the same time, Keelan wanted to be able to feed Taggart false information, so they had to put up with him. They waited for a while for the rest of the Liberation Committee to arrive.

"So did you hear the news?" Taggart asked when they showed up. "Weight Winners says they need to find new 'efficiencies'.

Apparently they're going to put two to a room and double the populations. Except for CRC-17. Instead they're going to retrofit a whole wing so they can accommodate Class III obesity cases."

"Class III?"

"40 BMI and higher," Max said. He looked thoughtful.

"Well, Weight Winners doesn't want news of this escaping, so the ban on communication with the outside world is being reintroduced," Taggart said.

"How did you hear it?" Keelan wondered, at the same time noting that he would have to let Jacinda know as soon as the committee was done meeting. And if he was going to share a room, that would put a crimp on "Skype time" with her too. Assuming it was going to be allowed still.

"I've got sources," Taggart said. "One of them is Tundra's best buddy, Chet."

Max ignored him, lost in thought.

The Liberation Committee had a heated discussion about the changes. Some wanted to escape right away. Others wanted to use the confusion caused by the construction to make their break. Taggart was one of these, Keelan noted, and he didn't actually disagree. He suggested they use the work that was planned as a cover for their own efforts. Max was distracted, and Keelan asked him what he was thinking.

"It's wonderful, Kee. Just think of it. They're going to have all strata of the obese in one place. There's going to be *jabbas*."

"I don't think we should use that term anymore," Tina said. "I don't think it's right to use those terms at all." Keelan noted that he had never once heard Tina use the term *porker* or *manatee* either.

"No, it's helpful," Max said. "Particularly in my work on Flabometrics. Now I'm going to have a population of the extremely obese to study as well. Imagine how much I'll learn."

"It's not helpful," Kee agreed. "I didn't mind until now, because really, *porker* and *manatee* don't sound that different to me. But *jabba*? That is an image that's just too close to the bone."

"Pretty far from the bone, actually," Max said.

"Max!"

"Okay, fine," Max said. "I move that we encourage people to stop using these terms, even though as fat people we should be allowed to."

"Seconded," Tina said.

The committee was unanimous. And uncomfortable. They sat there for a moment looking at one another, and Keelan realized that he was the only one there who was technically not obese. Taggart was the biggest of all of them, but Tina was a close second. He stopped himself. Tina was right. Ranking levels of fatness was just not helpful. If they did this to themselves, how could they expect people outside of the Fatness to see them as people? Not that they were going to get a chance to speak with anyone outside for a while. They'd gotten that message loud and clear.

Keelan thought about Jacinda. She was going to be apoplectic. She was going to be angry with him for not leaving the CRC when she made the chance, but he felt now, more than ever, he had made the right decision. He was going to help everyone escape. "I would like all of us to join the work crews so that we can see what opportunities there are, and so we can steal the tools we're going to need to escape."

"What tools?" Taggart said. "What's our plan? Specifically?"

Keelan arched Max a look that said, *See, he wants specifics to sell to McGrath.* "We can figure that out tomorrow. I want everyone to promise. You're going to volunteer, right?"

Barbara was already working on Joe's crew, so she'd just have to transfer. The rest of them – Tina, Max, and Taggart – looked uncomfortable. "Come on, I know it's going to be hard, but we need this. And we need to recruit more. Tina? Max?"

They nodded in agreement, and Taggart did too, reluctantly. Max looked into the distance and said, "This will really interfere with my work on Flabometrics."

"Max!"

"Fine. I'll work for our oppressors, but only because it's going to pinch their hippo."

FACT

Hippos Aren't Funny

A hippopotamus can weigh up to eight thousand pounds and run at roughly eighteen mph. (Humans top out at twenty-three mph, but that's, like, Olympic sprinters.) They are extremely cranky (hippos, not sprinters) and often attack for no reason.

Hippos are considered the most dangerous animal in Africa and kill roughly 2,900 people annually. Way more than any other mammal (except for humans, of course).

And they *really* don't like cracks about their weight.

24

Chapter 7 – This Holy Shrine, This Gentle Spin

She had the dream again. She was watching Keelan try to cross the raging river, hopping from stone to stone while the torrent roiled below him. Each leap brought him closer to her. She could see the concentration in his eyes as he gauged the distance, the wetness of the stone, its shape and angle. And in the logic of dreams, her point of view changed from moment to moment, more a feeling than a vision, and she could see the cords of muscles in his legs tense as he prepared his jump. She shouted at him not to try. It was too dangerous. She didn't want to lose him. But she loved him and she ached to be with him.

It was a dream, and she could communicate her longing telepathically. But the dream always ended the same. The final gap was too much, and even with his maximum effort, he could not make it. The bank she stood on seemed to quiver and move, and he would fall short, landing in the white water without even a sound, and he would be gone. And in the dream, the river always turned to glass after he was gone and she was left with a feeling of emptiness. She always looked at her reflection in the mirror, and she was always fat.

He'd made it to the last stone and readied his fatal jump. "No," she cried, "don't do it! Wait for me to find a way to save you."

But Keelan didn't wait. The look in his eyes when he made that jump was so filled with love and longing. It made her warm, thrilled her. He jumped and crashed into her, grabbing her to keep himself stable and upright. She raised her lips to his and they kissed, a sweet sin that was a PG stand-in for all the naughty things they'd get up to in bed. The kiss lasted long moments, and the longer it went, the more she knew there was something wrong. She opened her eyes to see the corpse-white face of Christopher Ballard smirking at her.

She screamed and mercifully awoke.

It had been two weeks since Weight Winners Canada had shut off access to CRC-17 again, and the strain was starting to wear Jacinda down. She had a cough that she just couldn't shake, and her appetite had waned. The only good thing about the situation was that she wasn't gaining any more weight, though she recognized it was not a healthy way to do it.

She'd petitioned the courts to speed up the process with her various lawsuits, but that just wasn't happening. Even with Jed's help, she wasn't going to be able to accelerate any of the cases she was funding: one with the Ontario Human Rights Tribunal, two with the government of Canada, a class action suit and a constitutional argument, and she had a class action suit against Weight Winners Canada too. It was going to take months and months to make an argument, and it didn't help that she couldn't talk to any of her clients in the CRCs; she had a plan for that though.

The good news was that fund-raising was going well. They had begun their campaign with at least some tangible support. They got it from an unexpected quarter, Greatlife Fitness. The Landon corporation did not think it was reasonable that people should be forced to stay in the CRCs if they did not want to. And so they donated to Fatism Free Canada's "Calorie Free" campaign, which centred on the unconstitutional treatment of Keelan and all the others like him. This gave them the resources to hire one of the best PR firms in the region to help build momentum against the CRC program, and Weight Winners in particular. Before they had taken over, there was general acceptance of the Fat Act amongst Canadians. But the corporate philosophy was just antithetical to Canadian values, the PR firm argued.

And a grassroots campaign was already under way. Friends and family of people in the CRCs were telling their stories online, explaining how long it had been since they'd seen their fathers, mothers, brothers, sisters, best friends … the people they loved. Everybody knew someone who was incarcerated. When the option of leaving, of paying for one's own health care had been there, it seemed like a kindness to force people to lose weight. It was for their own good.

But that had changed.

Jacinda was attending one of the first taping sessions for the national media campaign. They were interviewing Keelan's old trainer, Tyrell Taylor, who had gained national prominence after the news stories about corruption under the old Corrections Canada regime was released. Tyrell looked as fit and happy as he always had, but there was a new tone to his voice; it was tempered by simmering anger.

"Weight Winners is making the mistake that so many have made before. Instead of concentrating on the biochemistry and easy-to-manage psychology that will help anyone live a healthier lifestyle, they are focusing on the old myth of discipline. People who are overweight do not lack discipline. That's not the problem. They don't have the information they need to lose their extra pounds. They don't have the support they need. And the so-called 'calorie reduction' centres just make it worse. People can only make these kinds of changes when they're motivated to do so for positive reasons. You can't force it," he said.

"Why not?" the producer asked.

"Because stress is a significant factor here. We don't understand all the mechanisms yet, but we're learning more. It's not just about calories in and calories out. Stress causes the body to react, and our bodies are evolved for homeostasis." He smiled for the camera and went on to explain: "That's just a fancy word that means our bodies don't like change. If they're overweight, the body tries to keep it that way."

Jacinda was sorry that Keelan hadn't been able to work with Tyrell for longer. He might have been able to get out before Weight Winners had taken over. But she wasn't sure this was going to help. It was too scientific and complicated. She had a lot more faith in making people outside of the CRC system feel like it was working against them too. She stopped the taping and whispered to the producer, "He's great. Photogenic, smart, and the compassion oozes off him, but he sounds too smart. What he's saying is just too complicated. See if you could get something … simpler."

"Thanks, Dr. Taylor," the producer said.

"Actually, it's Mr. Taylor. I don't have my doctorate yet."

"Oh. Well, thanks, I guess. Can we come at this from another angle? What would you tell a child about this whole thing?"

"Oh, that's easy: The best way to be healthy is eat lots of fruits and vegetables – like eating a rainbow – move your body and get good sleep. And don't be mean to other people because they're different from you!"

"Will that last one help you lose weight?"

"No, but it will make you a better person."

QUOTE

"I dreamed: I am the fish whose flesh is eaten, and because I am fat, it is good."

~Philip K. Dick

Chapter 8 – Death Is Amorous

Keelan watched as the DarkRain guards closed the gate behind the truck, and looked away to the west. The low ridge in that direction was actually a glacial moraine, he remembered from his high school geography class. A mound of earth and massive stones pushed forward by the advance, and then the melting, of a wall of ice a mile high. The moraine was clad in colours, now fading with the October winds, as the shimmering yellow poplar and jaunty red maple leaves blew away. Just a week before, the old mound of dirt had been a riot of colour on a sunny day, and now it was faded, leeched of vibrancy. Like a cosmic Photoshopper had taken a desaturation tool to the world.

Now the forest was thinning. He could see some strange mounds under the edge of it, and he wondered what they were, but he knew the guards wouldn't let him check it out. They had been careful to make sure everyone stuck to their worksite. It made stealing tools harder, but they'd managed.

The wind picked up and swirled dried leaves at his feet.

Keelan loved the fall. He sometimes wondered why. Everything was dying. Maybe that was why he enjoyed the season so much. It was honest about things. Not some lie like the spring, no soporific heat of summer, but it had the honesty to say that, yes, this is the end, as you too will end.

It made him horny.

"Keelan? Come on, we're burning daylight," Joe said.

He sighed and returned to his work. He and the crew was unloading a flatbed truck with the last of the equipment for the jabbas – *No*, he corrected himself. *The new inmates.*

They had already arrived and were in their new digs. The equipment was specialized lifting equipment and medical sensors for the most recent arrivals to CRC-17. Some were so obese that they needed to be monitored, and there was always the difficulty of getting them back to their wards after surgery. The inmates were so heavy that immediate surgery was their only hope of getting their weight under control. Instead of cutting off a leg to get under 30 bimmi, these poor souls were getting bariatric bypasses on a daily basis. That is, if they could afford it.

It made him seethe, to think that Weight Winners was holding them hostage. They could only get the surgery if they had enough savings to pay for it; otherwise, they were stuck in their wards – there were eight beds to a room – until they either died or managed to lose enough weight so that they could get mobile. Presumably at that point they could do what Keelan and some of the other patients were doing: providing free labour to Weight Winners in exchange for "credits". Earn enough credits, and they could get the surgery. Of course, the idea that they were going to lose the hundreds of pounds they would need to was ludicrous.

Thinking about the situation certainly reduced his carnal desires. He missed Jacinda. He missed the smell of her. He was having trouble remembering her face, the sound of her voice. It had been weeks now since he'd even seen her on Skype. He sometimes regretted his decision to stay, but the escape plan was going well. He tried not to look at the fence, the weak spot where he knew he could use the wire cutters he'd squirreled away to get it open in seconds. That was the real escape plan. Through the fence.

What the committee had been planning, and working on, was a tunnel, right out of the main buildings. He and his "crew" had been working on it and providing evidence of its progress by elaborate misdirection. Getting some people to smuggle dirt out of the CRC and to hide it outside. Max had even taken to bouncing and catching a baseball in his room.

Many prisoners were now working on the grounds, preparing fields for a spring planting, or working in the greenhouses that Keelan had helped build. The new Weight Winner fee structure was now high enough that most people couldn't cover the costs with their government stipend, and they had to work. It was all part of Weight Winners' plan to make as much profit as possible off their fatted calves. Not that they would be fat forever. Keelan had lost another three pounds and was nearing the 28 bimmi mark. He would be able to earn freedom through the system at this rate. Two more pounds. Heck, he could probably get weighed at the end of a long day doing manual labour, and the loss of water weight would put him under that. He could leave a free man any time he wanted.

But he was going to stay and help everyone get out. At least, as many people as they could.

The fake tunnel was simply a ruse for Taggart's benefit. They were sure he'd sold them out, and they were just waiting for their moment to make their break.

It was going to happen soon. It had to. He couldn't wait much longer. He needed to see Jacinda. To kiss her lips. To begin their life together before it faded away like the colours of fall.

That evening, after work and his swim with Max, Brittany knocked on his door. Max was unconscious, "exploring" his psyche. Since the return of Taggart to the CRC, Kee had noticed that Max was back on his regimen of psychotropic drugs – mostly mescaline – in the evenings.

"Hi, Brittany," Kee said. "What's up? Slumming?"

Brittany looked haunted, but not as skinny as she once had been while she was working in the cafeteria. Running the Frozn Yoga had been good for her, as she got to lead people in yoga routines (even if they were only mostly there for the low-fat frozen yoghurt they got after the workout.) The arrival of the Type 3 obesity inmates had shaken her, though she couldn't admit it to anyone.

"No, I'm just making a delivery."

"Really? Do I want to know where you're hiding the yoghurt?"

She smiled. "Oh, you. No, it's a gift from Jacinda. You have to promise to be very careful that nobody sees you using it, okay?"

"What the hell is it?" Keelan tried to see what she was holding behind her back. "Some kind of sex toy?"

"Depends on how inventive you are, I suppose," Brittany joked, and handed him a smartphone. "Jacinda says hi. She looks tired, but good. She's got some new power suits that really flatter her, uh, figure," Brittany said, some of her sorority sister returning to her voice. "But you can see that for yourself."

Keelan was overwhelmed. Tears formed in his eyes, but he managed to blink them away. "Thanks, Brittany. I mean, you have been so …"

"Just remember to eat healthy and keep off that weight. You look great, you know."

"For a fat bastard."

"You're under 30 now, so I can't say that. You're just overweight, and you know what, that's okay. You're healthy."

Keelan was floored, and he just waved goodbye mutely as she left.

He found the storage closet where Max hid his drug paraphernalia, and he knew it was about as secure a spot as he could find inside. He couldn't wait until the next day, and he hoped he'd get reception in there. The blue light of the phone illuminated the tiny room, making it feel like a crypt, but he did not care. He tapped on the Skype app and connected. And she was there, held in his hand like a tiny talisman that could stave off the cold inevitability of entropy.

"Hey, kiddo," she said. "I've been waiting for your call. What took you so long?"

"Oh, you know, I've been keeping myself busy. Planning a prison break, that kind of thing," he quipped.

"God, I missed you," Jacinda said.

"I want to kiss your lips."

"All of them, I hope," she said.

Keelan smiled lasciviously and nodded his head. She took off her sweater and winked at him, which was actually kind of hard to see on the little smartphone screen. He got the gist and looked around. He propped a stepladder against the door handle and started to take off his pants.

"Wait. First, you have to tell me about this prison break," Jacinda said.

FACT

Why Your Brain Is "Lovin' It"

Our brains light up like a crack pipe when we bathe our stomachs in salt, sugar and fat. Refined sugars, in particular, have been identified for their addictive properties and have the same hallmarks of craving, binging and withdrawal. Add to this the low cost of fast food, the convenience, and the fact that most of us have limited impulse control, and certain companies have us where they want us.

There's also some research that shows brands can have Pavlovian-type effects on our brains. Like the dogs starting to salivate because they heard the metronome, we can get all juicy just after hearing a jingle. Or seeing the golden arches. And what about the smell? Smell has a direct route to your hippocampus, where your memories reside. Just smelling those fries can recall all the wonderful memories you have of your mother taking you to the burger joint when you were a kid.

Unless, of course, your mother was terrified of clowns, in which case the company mascot probably kept you away from the place entirely.

25

Chapter 9 – Living Off the Fat of the Brand

Max was tripping again. He had been since they doubled up the cells. He was sharing with Keelan, but that didn't make him any less uncomfortable or claustrophobic, it seemed.

"Max, you have to stop. I need your help," he said.

Max was sitting cross-legged on his bunk – their beds had been replaced with bunks to make room in the cells for two. Max had dosed himself with mescaline not long before. His eyes were closed, and he was meditating. Keelan knew he was conscious and aware. At least he hadn't thrown up again.

Keelan was sitting at the end of Max's bunk, hoping to reach him.

"I'll be exploring at least another ten hours, Kee. This adventure is just starting." Max opened his eyes, and Keelan was worried to see the pupils didn't focus on him, but just beyond him somewhere in the space behind him, but in the room. "Oh my," Max said.

Gooseflesh on the back of Keelan's neck made him shiver. Or perhaps the shiver came first. In any event, it was clear that someone else, some*thing* else, was in the tiny room with them.

"What?"

"They are upset with you. Especially the clown."

"The clown?"

"You know, Ronald."

A feeling of dread ripped through Keelan. He'd never told Max about his hallucinations. He'd only ever mentioned it to Brittany and he knew she would never have said anything to another patient about him.

"What's he saying?"

"He's pissed. He's angry. You know, when he gets angry, his teeth get sharper and a little elongated. If I wasn't so centred, he'd be terrifying. Maybe it's okay because he knows that I still love him. I do, Keelan. I really do. My mother used to take us there

– my sister and me – when we were little kids. It was always as a special treat, at least at first, but it became a more regular thing, like maybe once a week. But it was the best, Keelan. The fries, especially. They were so good back then. I dunno, maybe they changed the recipe or something, or maybe it was something to do with my young taste buds, but they – wait – he has a message for you."

"What is it?"

"He says you'll come back. They always do. Oh, and the other guy is here too. He's hilarious."

"Other guy?" Keelan knew what was coming, but he didn't want it to be true. "What other guy?"

"The Colonel, of course. I don't remember him talking like Foghorn Leghorn though. That's ... whew, I'm really out there this time, Keelan. The clown has a flick knife."

"A switchblade?"

"Yep. He's telling the Colonel to shut the fuck up about his herbs and spices. He's all, like, 'We both know it's mostly salt. And fat. And just enough sugar to hit the bliss point.' I don't care for this vision," Max said. He closed his eyes and opened them up again. The eyes widened, and his focus was on Keelan now. "They're both still there, fuming. Do you want me to tell them anything?"

"Tell them I'm never going back. I've lost this weight, and I'm never going back."

There was an uncomfortable pause while Max waited for something.

"Finally, they've stopped laughing. They think you're a scream, but they are leaving."

"That's good, Max." Keelan was quiet for a moment. He wasn't sure what just happened there. Had Max tapped into his subconscious somehow, or were they sharing one? It didn't matter.

"Oh shit, no, the clown is back. He's ... he's ... I think that's Bernie's leg."

"What?"

"He's chewing on Bernie's leg. He said he found it in the forest."

Keelan's ears started ringing. Since Bernie's disappearance, six other inmates had similarly vanished. The story was that they were sent away to the hospital for observation and treatment, but you'd think that some of them would have gotten better by now. Keelan wondered about those mounds he'd seen at the edge of the forest. He thought about how careful the guards were to keep them at their worksites. He had a horrible thought. What if Weight Winners was killing inmates and burying them in the forest? It would certainly be a "win-win" for the corporation if they were never caught. They'd still get the government funding for the inmates, but never have to pay to support them …

"Look, we need to get out soon," Keelan said with urgency. "I have an idea, and I want you to think about it."

"What's that?"

"Is there some way we could, uh, drug the security guys the day we decide to make our break for it? Without hurting any-body, of course."

Max grinned like a happy Buddha. "Poppin' Fresh has a few ideas."

FACT

Nature Will Castigate Those Who Don't Masticate

There was once a Victorian loon named Horace Fletcher, who suggested that food must be chewed to the point that it was liquefied and absorbed through involuntary swallowing, not actual conscious swallowing. Bizarrely, he felt that even liquids should be chewed too, "Just in case."

Dubbed "The Great Masticator", Fletcher promised that even horrible morally corrupt gluttons could become wise and intelligent through the use of their teeth, and like many of our modern diet fads, he had a following. Fletcherizing, as it became known, was adopted by presidents and poets alike. Franz Kafka's father had to eat behind a newspaper, so horrifying was the excessive chewing of his son. In the early part of the twentieth century, it was almost adopted as the US national health policy.

And it was only marginally less creepy than John Harvey Kellog's infamous yoghurt enemas.

Chapter 10 – Chewing it Over

Taggart finished his meeting with the commandant and felt uneasy. He'd been able to recover some of his previous power as the leader of the Heavy Hitters, but it was precarious. Too much of it depended on the whim of Weight Winners and, in particular, the old army captain, Lucian McGrath, who'd proved more wily in business matters than Taggart had expected. Taggart had to admit to himself, he'd been outmaneuvered on several fronts.

If nothing else, Taggart was totally complicit with the scheme Weight Winners was running now across many of the CRCs – whenever someone died, they simply kept the death a secret, kept collecting the money from the government, and saved money on upkeep and housing. So if it ever came to light, Taggart literally knew where the bodies were buried. And he had to admit that he felt some guilt about it. Not the deaths, but the idea that friends and loved ones would never know.

And Taggart was intelligent enough to realize there was a slippery slope. For example, some of his fellow "co-conspirators" on the Liberation Committee were being watched – if they ever became truly inconvenient, would people start disappearing from their cells?

His information had kept the commandant calm though. Progress on the escape tunnel was going slowly. It would not be ready till spring at the earliest.

He walked through the commons, waving at people as he went. When he'd been in charge of the Heavy Hitters, he'd felt powerful. Since he'd joined Keelan and the others, he'd felt like he was liked for the first time in his life. This didn't do anything to assuage his disquiet. In fact, it made him want to check on the tunnel again, just to be sure his report to McGrath was accurate.

Six months at least, to finish the digging, and then to wait for the ground to thaw.

Jacinda had just finished her talk with the private investigator she'd hired to do surveillance of CRC-17. In addition to checking out their proposed escape route and getting dossiers on everyone who worked at the CRC, she'd also had the detective look into Keelan's fears.

Her Skype chimed. Her body didn't react like it usually did, even though she knew it was Keelan. He was in the custodial closet again, and his face looked eldritch in the blue glow of the screen.

"Did you find out anything?"

"Sorry, Keelan. The detective tried using a drone to take pictures, but it's too hard to tell. He'll have to get in to inspect the ground himself. Unless we have a lot more money to throw at it."

"Okay," Keelan said. He was more subdued than usual.

"What's up?"

"Nothing."

"Please don't lie to me, Kee. You know I can't take it."

"Chet was outside our room again last night. That's three times this week."

"Shit," Jacinda said.

"I think he may be getting ready to make his move. You know he hardly ever leaves the CRC? People keep shouting at him on the street when they recognize him. It's just making it worse."

"You have to escape soon. Are you ready?"

"No, but I don't think Max has long. Chet's going to kill him, especially if I'm right. If there's a way to get rid of his body, there's almost nothing stopping him."

"So you're in danger too. He can't leave a witness. So, when do you go?" Jacinda repeated. "I need to know so that I can arrange the buses and other transportation, and the media, of course."

"Maybe the day after tomorrow?"

"Babe, you need to be sure. Can you get it done by then?"

"I think so. Max has the drugs. Taggart actually helped him get them into the CRC, if you can believe that. Greg, Tina, and Barbara also know the plan. They have a communication scheme worked out so we can get all the inmates out who can move. I'm afraid we'll have to leave the people in the Class III wing behind."

"Kee, you've done the best you can. And think of it this way: we'll have hundreds of stories that will back up what we've been saying all along. It will bring the whole thing down, and everyone will benefit."

"I hope you're right. Okay, I'll call you before bedtime tomorrow to let you know we're a go. Love you."

"Love you too," Jacinda said. "Be safe."

The escape plan was set, but Keelan couldn't sleep. They were ready in the CRC, and Jacinda was going to meet them outside in the morning. She'd organized buses to pick them up to take them back to Landon, where a fleet of taxis would whisk people wherever they wanted to go – home, the airport, or straight to their local member of Parliament to complain about their illegal treatment in the CRC.

They both hoped that many would be willing to tell their stories on camera, or to Serena Lee, who had agreed to cover the event; then Fatism Free Canada could begin the media campaign that would eventually free all the other obese people trapped in the prison their bodies, their government, and Weight Winners Canada had made for them.

The wild card was Taggart. As far as he – and everyone else – knew, their plan was to use a tunnel they had been digging under the inside wall of the CRC. The real plan was wildly simple. They were going to walk out the front door and flee through the fence that Keelan had helped build.

First thing in the morning, before he'd done his time generating power for Weight Winners, he would run out to the fence, use a pair of wire cutters to open it up and sew it back together again with some clear fishing line. It would be invisible to everything except a close inspection, which nobody had ever done. While he did that, Max was going to dose all the coffee makers and electric kettles in the DarkRain and administration lounges with a special treat. If any of the security guards went to Timmy's for their morning java, or tea, or any drink at all, Tina, who was on staff there, would do the same. Max had assured Keelan that his "treat" was not going to hurt anyone, but he worried about that. If someone died because of a drug overdose or interaction caused by it, there would be hell to pay. Tina and Max also had a "special" surprise for the DarkRain guards that would "move things along". Keelan didn't really want to know, but Tina had promised that nobody would be hurt by it, so he said okay.

Max had also promised a backup dosing option. This worried Keelan.

"It will be fine," Max said. "Go to sleep."

"Sorry," Keelan said. He still wasn't used to sharing a room. Especially with such a freak. Before the new living arrangements, he'd had no idea how often Max was taking drugs to help him "explore his mind".

"Poppin' Fresh says goodnight too. He really misses you, you know."

"Tell him I'll have a croissant when I get out, but just the one."

"You've made him so happy."

There was an ominous pause.

"But?"

"The clown is really angry with you. He says he has healthy choices now. You should really check them out when you get free."

There was a knock on their plastic door, and they could see the shadow of a figure.

"Who is it?"

"Mickey Mouse," a voice said.

"Chet?" Keelan asked.

"None other. Just want you ladies to know that I'm watching you. I've seen you looking at the woods. I've seen you both skulking around. I know that you're up to something."

Max looked quite terrified, but he said, "Cool. I'd prefer if you killed me with Veronica though. I always had a sweet spot for blondes."

"Oh, I don't think I'll use either," Chet said. "Too much noise."

Keelan grabbed the hammer that he'd snuck into their room, and quietly got out of bed to stand by the door. He held it in his hand, tense. The moment stretched into minutes, and then the shadow moved away. Keelan stood there for about half an hour, waiting. Slowly, he relaxed and sighed.

"Well, I bet we'll be awake for a while," Max said. "Let's talk about all the cheeseburgers I'm going to eat tomorrow."

"How about you explain to me what's with the drugs?"

"I'm just trying to understand the universe, but I may have to give it up. The clown keeps coming back, and he's kind of ruining it all. Besides, I'm not really learning anything as much as escaping."

"And tomorrow we'll escape for real, so what's the point?"

"Walrus gumboot, of course."

QUOTE

"If you grow up fat, you have to try harder."

~Kevin Smith

Chapter 11 – Operation Endomorph

It was still dark when Keelan made his way out to the fence to cut a hole in it. The wire snips were like ice in his hands. Steam rose off his body like he'd just emerged from the bowels of hell. He'd just finished his morning ride – the last one he'd ever have to take to generate power for Weight Winners – and the cold November air was bracing. He quickly cut a hole in the fence and used a length of nylon wire to lace it back together.

His work here was really just a backup. If Max's plan to dose all the security guards with – whatever he was dosing them with – worked, they could all just walk out the main gate. Keelan was worried that not everyone would get a high enough dosage from their morning coffee or tea to be affected. And he was especially concerned about the DarkRain guys who didn't have coffee or tea. What about them? Max had told him he would take care of it, but he refused to "spoil the surprise".

So there were wild cards. Their plan for Taggart, and the amount of surveillance McGrath and his cronies had on them all too. They didn't really know how closely they were being watched. Keelan looked around in the predawn gloom. They weren't out there watching him now; that was for certain.

He was exhausted. After the visit from Chet, he'd been unable to fall asleep, and when he finally felt like he could, Max was thoroughly unconscious. He hadn't thought it was safe enough for both of them to be out of it, so he stood watch until it was time to get up for his Extreme Electric Exercise™. He got Max up first and handed him the hammer. "You're on watch now, John. *Koo-koo-ka-ju.*"

Keelan noted the main gate seemed to be unguarded as well. So the only real impediments were the two guards at the exit of the main CRC building and the electronic control on the gate. Barbara already had a remote control for the gate – she'd stolen it from one of Joe's crew last night, and it wouldn't be missed until they were gone.

The sun was still half an hour from rising, but at least the sky was lightening. In the east, Keelan could make out the angry red of a troubling sunrise – the kind they warn sailors about. But even if there was bad weather, Jacinda would have buses ready for them just down at the highway.

He went inside, where the two DarkRain guards were anxiously waiting for their shift change.

"Trouble?" Keelan said.

"They're late. Again."

"Who?"

"Our relief. It's ridiculous. We're not allowed to leave unless they're here, but they're always late."

"Well, there's nobody around. You probably *could* leave."

"Yeah," the one guard said. "Besides, I'm already on a double shift. They can't do this to us."

"You can't just leave your post!" the other guard said. Keelan didn't know their names. Weight Winners seemed to be moving the guards around from CRC to CRC quite a bit – *Probably so they don't become too friendly with any of their charges*, Keelan thought. The latest additions in CRC-17 were as bedecked with pistols as the last group, even if they seemed a little more reasonable.

"Frank, seriously. I want to go home, have a sleep, and watch some football with my boys," the first guard said.

"Fine. You go and I'll wait for the shift change."

"Want me to get you a coffee or something?" Keelan asked.

"Would you mind?"

"My pleasure." Keelan grinned like a chubby demon about to chomp into a donut filled with creamed Bavarians. He made his way down to the Timmy's, where he ordered "a special coffee" from Tina. As he was walking back, he saw Brittany opening up the Frozn Yoga.

"Hey, Brittany, a quick bit of advice for today – avoid all coffee, tea, and baked goods," Keelan said.

Brittany looked shocked that he would even think she would allow baked goods to pass her lips.

"But seriously. No coffee or tea either."

"I don't drink coffee, but no green tea? How will I get through the day?"

"I'll get you one, but that will have to be it, okay?"

"So what's up?"

"You'll understand soon enough."

Keelan got her the tea, and she said, "Thanks. It's weird to be taking nutrition advice from you, but I'm glad to do it. Good luck today, with whatever you have going on."

He nodded and just said, "It's better that I don't tell you. But if I don't get a chance to chat with you later, I want to say thanks. Even if you did torture me with celery, I know your heart's in the right place, Brittany. And I think you could probably do much better going into business for yourself."

Brittany smiled and waved as Keelan brought his "special" coffee up to the last remaining obstacle to his freedom.

The coffee wasn't needed. The new shift was already in place and sipping on the brew made by their own devil, Maximilian Tundra. They were already acting strangely.

Keelan approached them and said good morning.

"I feel weird," said the guard. "Do you feel weird?"

"Y'all weird all the time, buddy. What, do you – wait, did you see that?"

"See what?" Keelan thought he might be slurring his words.

"It looked like a big chicken running down the hallway." The second guard stuck his head out the door and saw Keelan. "Oh, it's you." His eyelids drooped a bit, and he was definitely slurring his words.

"I'm no poultry." Keelan smiled.

"I see it," the first screamed. "It's horrible! It's coming for revenge!" He tried to pull one of his pistols out, but he couldn't seem to get it out of his holster. His hand seemed to be stuck on the pistol grip too. He pulled frantically, but it was stuck. He used his left hand to try to pry it off, but that hand got stuck to his right. What had Max done?

"It'ssss gonnnaaa fuccccccsh," the guard slurred, and slumped to the ground, breathing rapidly.

"Shhhhet?" the other said, reaching for one of his own pistols. His hand got stuck too, and he collapsed.

Keelan shrugged and thought he might as well drag them into the surveillance room. He was careful not to touch their hands or get near any of the holsters. He could see some kind of liquid in there. Max. He laid them in the safety position, heads down in case they vomited from whatever Max had dosed them with, and then, for good measure, turned off all the cameras in the CRC.

Excellent, he thought, popping the lid off the coffee he'd been carrying and put down to drag the guards.

The intercom buzzed, and a voice said, "What the hell is going on down there, soldier? My feed has gone dark." Keelan recognized the voice of the commandant.

He toggled it and said, "Oh, just a malfunction. We'll have it fixed shortly, Captain."

"Good, now could you have someone bring me another one of those pastries? They're delicious."

"Pastries?"

"In the break room. I couldn't help myself. Had two, and I've got a hankering for another … belay that."

There was a moment of silence and then a moan. Then a sound. Somewhere between a high-pitched wail and a scream, and underneath that, in terrible counterpoint, a deep rumbling sound and a squishy, jet-like noise that was hard to interpret.

"Oh god!" McGrath shouted. "It's coming now!"

"Sir?" Keelan asked.

"Never mind, I –" The sound, it was best described as a liquid passing through a tiny opening quickly, repeated itself: "Ffffssssssssssssffffssff." It bubbled and frothed at the other end of the intercom, which then clicked off.

Ah, Keelan thought, realization dawning: Tina had laced the pastries with laxatives.

Keelan's next part of the plan was to alert everyone in B wing about the opportunity to escape. It went like a charm, but a surprising number of people refused to leave their cells. They didn't want to risk whatever penalties a failed attempt might mean.

"We won't fail! We're just going to walk out the front gate. Nobody will stop you, and there's buses waiting to take us to town. We need you to tell your story to the media!"

It went as smoothly as several pastries escaping a commandant under intense pressure. Between Max's drug and Tina's delivery of high-powered laxatives in tasty cakes, most of the morning shift had been thoroughly debilitated. Keelan got a small group of ex-Heavy Hitters together and took them to the DarkRain changing rooms, intending to make sure they were disarmed, but Max warned him not to touch their pistols or holsters, which were filled with industrial-strength epoxy.

Max shrugged. "I saw their lockers were just open, so I thought why not? Just in case anyone hallucinated while they were going under."

The Liberation Committee made sure everyone was lying in the safety position. They didn't want to go into the toilets. The sounds were both hilarious and terrifying, and Keelan was not keen on experiencing the smell. But they had to be sure nobody was going to die. It was very important that none of the guards or staff were physically injured.

After dealing with a particularly messy facility that serviced the discipline advisors, Max said, "Hey, where is Greg?"

"Yeah," Keelan said. "He was going to help us with this."

"And where's Taggart?" Max said.

Cold gripped his heart like a night in an unheated pool. "Shit."

They'd planned so well, but nobody had planned on Taggart. That was the trouble with Taggart. He was giant, but you could forget him. Kee asked Barbara to find someone to help make sure the rest of the guards were safe, and said, "Go for the gate, and don't wait for us. Jacinda will be at the highway, waiting with the buses."

"What about you and the freak?" Barbara asked.

"Don't wait for us!" Keelan said.

"Freak?" Max said. "Are you flirting with me, Babs?"

Barbara rolled her eyes and got back to work.

"Let's check out Greg's room first," Keelan suggested.

"Okay, but I may be missing my chance with Babs."

"She doesn't like people calling her Babs," Keelan said.

"Oh, I'll change her mind."

"Pharmaceutically?"

"No, with old-fashioned *pinniped* charm."

FACT

Does that Study Have a Seal of Approval?

In one of the most hilarious scientific papers ever written, John Ioannidis, an epidemiologist at the University of Ioannina School of Medicine in Greece, wrote that most scientific studies are wrong.

A large amount of research is flawed. Small sample sizes, research bias, poor design, and a host of errors in critical thinking can all lead to science that points in the wrong direction. The importance of a study is proved in its replication, by many researchers, over time. Then we can take a study seriously.

This would, of course, include not only that study itself, but every bit of research mentioned in this novel. Bam, irony, bitches!

Chapter 12 – A Sharp Sauce

Greg wasn't in his room, neither was his roomie, but their neighbour had opted to stay behind and he told Max and Keelan where to find him: at the commandant's office.

"Why would he be there?" Keelan wondered.

"Maybe that was the most logical place to find Taggart?"

Keelan nodded, and they ran in that direction – McGrath's office was in the administrative wing, almost on the opposite end of the CRC. By the time they reached the commons, Max was panting like a basset hound mistaken for a beagle: there was no danger to the fox at all. Keelan waved at Brittany as they passed the Frozn Yoga.

"Thanks for the warning!" Brittany shouted as they loped by.

Keelan was hanging back so that Max could keep pace, but they were slowing.

"Come on, Max, this could ruin the whole plan! Faster!"

"You're a –" he panted "– cruel bastard, making a fat old man run. They'll be burying me in the forest next."

They raced (walked) up the stairs and were met at the top by Billy and Chet.

Billy didn't look well. He didn't smell well, either. He'd clearly had both coffee and one of Tina's hyperlaxative Boston Creamers, but was trying to power through.

"Why?" Billy said. "So much … sauce."

"Stop right there, douchewagons!" Chet shouted.

A noise emanated from Billy, both front and back, and his eyes rolled up in his head. He went for his gun, but his hand got just as stuck as all the other guards' did. Not that it mattered. He was falling unconscious. Chet just watched as his compatriot keeled over.

"What did you do to Betty and Veronica?" he asked Max.

"Industrial epoxy in their holsters. Don't worry, the guns are ruined."

"Why, you fat fucker."

"Sociopath," Max replied. He seemed bored, almost, by the

confrontation.

"How come you're not, uh –"

"Shitting myself and acting like a lunatic?" Chet supplied.

"You're not shitting yourself, anyway," Max said. "You've always been a lunatic, so how could we tell?"

"Look, just because I don't have Betty and Veronica doesn't mean I can't fuck you up," Chet said.

Right, Keelan thought, *the leg gun*. Had Max accounted for that? Max looked worried, so obviously no.

"Chet, there's no upside to hurting us. Besides, we should put Billy into the safety position, just in case."

"You're not touching him, you homo."

"Then you should do it."

"I'm not touching him either. He's a mess," Chet said.

Billy came back to consciousness briefly and mumbled, "Wit's sweeting ... sauce. Sauce most sharp. Oh, the sauce ..."

"What did you do to him?" Chet accused Max.

"Drugged him. Don't worry. He'll be fine. His pants are a write-off, but that's Tina's doing, not mine."

"You're done," Chet said, taking a step backwards. "I'm going to take you both down now."

"Look, Chet, we don't want to fight you –" Keelan took a step forwards.

"Of course not, because I'll win."

Max took a step towards Chet too and started to flank him. Keelan thought Max was fumbling with something in his right hand.

"Because we don't want anyone to get hurt," Keelan said. "That's the most important thing."

"Then you're going to be disappointed," Chet said. He bent over to grab his leg gun, which Max had, indeed, forgotten to epoxy. Keelan didn't wait. He launched himself at Chet, hoping to pin his arms. He didn't want to hurt the guy, but he really didn't want to be shot. Chet had good reflexes and training. He sidestepped Keelan's rush and hip-checked him to the left. This left Chet open to Max, who came at him a moment after Keelan's rush. Chet was bent over and pulling the small pistol out of the holster on his lower leg when Max got to him and inserted a needle into Chet's neck. He depressed the plunger and Chet collapsed like a marionette that had had its strings cut. He panted heavily and the pistol rolled out of his hand. Max scooped it up and checked Chet's pulse.

"Woo, a little high there, my emotionally retarded friend," Max said.

Keelan stood up and asked, "What was that?"

"Horse tranquilizer. He'll be out for a while. Still, we'd better tie him up."

"Horse tranquilizer?" Keelan asked.

"I was saving it, just in case I got too excited."

They tied up Chet, put Billy in the safety position, and continued their trek to the commandant's office. There was no point in running anymore, given how Chet had delayed them. Keelan was shaking a bit, which Max noticed.

"Don't worry. It's just the adrenaline."

"Why are you okay?"

"Elephant seal soup, my good buddy. ESS."

Keelan was too worried to even chuckle. Tina appeared and said, "The front door is locked. We can't get it open."

"Not even with a crowbar?"

"We're working on it, but we're losing the window. Soon the next shift of guards will arrive," Tina said. "There's about forty of us waiting at the front door."

"Shit," Max said.

"Take my hammer," Keelan said. "Maybe this will help. Hey, is Greg with you?"

"No," Tina replied. "Is he okay?"

"We forgot about Taggart, but he didn't. Okay, you keep working on the door, and we'll find Greg, don't worry. But as soon as you get it open, you go, okay?"

"No, I'm not leaving without Greg," Tina said. "But I'll make sure everyone else is gone. Barbara's already got half the CRC out, so we're still going to be successful, right?"

Keelan nodded. The main goal was to get enough people out that word of their treatment could spread, so yes. But now that he'd done that, he wanted to get out too.

The office door was locked, which was too heavy to break down.

"Let me try this!" Max cried, pointing the gun at the door. He pulled the trigger and nothing happened.

"Is there a safety?"

Max looked confused and Keelan said, "There's probably a safety switch. Chet probably didn't have time to turn it off."

A moment later Max figured it out and fired a shot. Their ears rang, and Max saw that he'd missed the lock completely. He fired again. He hit the wall.

"Shit, Max. That's fucking loud!"

"Wait, one more," Max said, and fired again. Somehow, it hit the lock dead on. There was a spark, the lights flickered for a moment, and the door swung ajar.

There were raised voices coming from an interior door.

"You're dead now!" Taggart said.

"Fuck you!" Greg shouted.

They opened the door and saw Greg pinning Taggart on the floor.

"Keelan, thank god!" Greg cried. "I thought it was a guard."

"What the hell?" Kee asked.

"Taggart tried to warn the commandant, which, of course, didn't matter because he's out of it. He's in his bathroom there." Greg nodded his head to another doorway. "But Taggart locked down the CRC somehow."

"Taggart, what did you do?" Keelan said.

"What have *you* done?" Taggart said. "What happened to all the guards and staff?"

"Never mind that," Max said. "How do we unlock the door?"

"Why should I tell you?"

"Because you're part of the team," Keelan said. Greg gave Kee a look that basically said, *Are you out of your mind?*

"You expect me to believe that?"

"Sure. We thought you might be informing on us, but that became part of our plan. You helped keep McGrath and his goons out of the way while we went ahead with things. I know that wasn't your intention, but so what? Except for locking things down now, you've been a big help," Keelan said.

"What do you mean we don't care about his intentions?" Max said.

"Yeah!" Greg said while he pushed down a little harder on Taggart.

"Look, I'm just saying that what he did helped us. Think of all the people who are going to be helped by his actions. He might not have intended that, but that's what came out of it," Keelan said.

"But, but ..." Greg said.

"Utilitarian whammy!" Max said.

"Okay, so let's say I accept you're not angry," Taggart said. "What do I get?"

"You get to leave."

"But I don't want to leave."

"I don't think you have much choice. Either you help us or you get caught in the collateral damage," Kee said. "You do know where the bodies are buried, right?"

"Shit, you know?"

"I didn't, but now I do," Kee said. "You help us, and we'll help you."

"Okay, okay, let me up." Greg got off him, and Taggart went to McGrath's desk.

"He has a lockdown switch here. Okay, it's flipped and the door should unlock," Taggart said. "You really will help me?"

"Of course," Kee said. "Like I said, you were integral."

Max went over to Taggart and offered his hand. Taggart looked sheepish and shook it. And Max stuck another needle in Taggart's neck, depressing the plunger simultaneously. He kept Taggart from hurting himself as he collapsed, and he rolled him onto McGrath's desk. Max calmly checked Taggart's pulse and smiled at Kee.

"What the serious fuck, Max?"

"I'm more of a Kantian, not a utility guy," Max replied. He nodded at the unconscious form of Taggart. "Obviously."

"Huh?" Greg said.

"Intentions matter," Max said, "Just like my otter sandwich pie!"

"Please tell me that was the last of your syringes."

"Nope, got one more, just in case!"

"Just stay away from me with that shit, man," Greg said.

"I love you, Greg," Max said. "I would never Tundraize you."

By the time they got to the front door, practically everyone had left. Tina was so relieved to see Greg, she burst into tears. He kissed her, and she managed to say, "I would have stayed if you couldn't get out."

Keelan wiped a few tears from his eyes too, he was so moved. Max opened the door and shivered.

The day had gotten much colder and a few flakes of snow were swirling in the air. The four of them looked at one another, and the tears turned into giddy laughter. They were leaving. Finally. Max had been in and out of the CRC for more than five years. Greg was working on his fourth year, and Keelan was just a few months behind. Tina was in her third year, and all of them were heading into the unknown. None of them had jobs. But they didn't care. They laughed as the snow blew, and the cold November wind whipped away the stench of the Fatness.

"Let's Shammu this zoobidoo!" Max said, and started skipping towards the gates.

Tina and Greg kissed, and he realized, at that moment, that he not only loved Jacinda, but he loved the notion of love. He felt almost giddy as he watched his friends smooch. They took each other by the hand and walked for the gate.

"Come on, Kee, let's go," Greg said as they got to the gate. Keelan nodded and started to walk towards them.

Somewhere he could hear the sound of motors, and for a

horrible second, he thought it might be some DarkRain guards arriving for their shift early, but it was just a trick of the wind.

Keelan was the last person to leave the grounds. He had a look back at the CRC, the many outbuildings that he had helped build, and felt a strange melancholy. He'd spent just over three years in the institution. Three years and three months. He hated the place, so why should he feel sad?

He watched as his compatriots walked down the road towards the highway, some striding with purpose, some gazing at the dark grey clouds scudding overhead, the snow gathering. Most of the escapees were still obese. Some had managed to get close to the 30 BMI mark, and a few – like Keelan – were under 30 now. (Keelan was nearly at 28, in fact, which made him the only person who could have left earlier.) But by any measure – social, economic, body fat percentage – the experiment with the Calorie Reduction Centres was an epic failure.

He could see the long line of yellow school buses waiting to take them to a better place, he hoped. When he saw the figure of Jacinda running towards him, carrying a pizza, he knew that it would be. Possibly a place with waiters and crisp linen tablecloths.

After that, well, there was the question of dessert.

The End

AFTERWORD
Weight Is Not a Matter of Willpower

Most writers want you to read their novels untainted by backstory. So if you're one of those readers who just *has* to read the end of the book first, to see how the story concludes, you've flipped too far!

Go ahead and read the last chapter; just don't read this, please. And don't worry – I'm not judging you on spoiling the book. (Actually, there's research demonstrating it enhances the enjoyment of reading a story when you know how it ends. [27])

It should come to no surprise to you that I have been tormented by my weight throughout my life. A novel like this one has to come from somewhere. I was a chubby kid. A chubby pre-teen. And even when I had a golden era between the ages of fifteen and nineteen when I wasn't overweight, I felt fat. The damage had already been done. The template was set.

I feel fat *still*. Though at the moment I'm writing this, I am, despite Herculean efforts. I am what many call a "yo-yo" dieter. I lose weight, then gain it all back, plus a few pounds. I have dipped in and out of obese territory many times over the years.

In 2005 I read Paul Compos's book, *The Obesity Myth: Why America's Obsession with Weight Is Damaging to Your Health*. I would recommend it. It's currently out of print; you can find used copies fairly easily. Hell, write me and I'll mail you my copy if you promised to send it back!

In the book, Compos takes on the received wisdom that obesity equals unhealthiness. With clear prose and thorough research, he shows that our image of what is healthy drives this debate more than science. There's lots of research (and I mention it in this book) that it's quite possible to be overweight, even obese, and be healthy. The media's obsession with obesity is a kind of moral panic. It reinforces the terrible idea that it's okay to shame people for their weight. The idea behind this use of shame is that the negative feeling will help the fat person control themselves better, but the research on this shows that fat-shaming just makes it *harder* to control weight. [28]

I see the attack on obesity as a class issue: though society is in general getting heavier, it is the lower socio-economic strata of our community that suffers more from obesity.

I see it as a human rights issue. Up until the election of a certain president, I would have said it was the last acceptable prejudice. Few comedians are roasted for telling "your mamma so fat" jokes the way they are for stepping outside of other PC boundaries. It's well-demonstrated that fat people earn less, have fewer job and promotion opportunities, and are treated differently from other people. Teachers have said that it's the worst thing that could happen to a child. Fat-phobia is especially pernicious in the medical industry, where serious illnesses are not investigated or diagnosed, and instead, the patient is told to "lose some weight".

Thanks, doc, but I'm not sure how losing a few pounds is going to help my broken leg. Maybe we can treat that first?

I don't want to be too critical of medicine, because these attitudes are changing. Very slowly, but they're changing.

This obsession over weight is a women's issue too. An important one. It's critical to fight discrimination against fat people and to fix the distortions the media and society as a whole make of women's bodies. That said, I'd like to say that I didn't attempt to write from a fat woman's perspective in this book. (There are fat female characters, but there are no fat female protagonists.) There are other novels that do, and, frankly, tackle the angle better than I ever could. I just felt that I couldn't treat that perspective with enough reality to do it justice. Perhaps this was artistic cowardice, but I felt like I had plenty to cover without culturally appropriating fat femininity.

But Keelan still falls for a *normie*, right? Well, you got me there. This reflects reality too. Men – fat men in particular – are tremendously lucky that women are not as judgemental as men are, generally.

So this book began shortly after I read *The Obesity Myth*. At the time I was well over 30 BMI, and the topic spoke to me on a visceral level.

The book was not funny. It wasn't even close. It wasn't biting satire. It was just bitter.

So I let it sit. I finished *Marvellous Hairy*. I wrote *The Fridgularity*. I collected the nonsense flash fictions I had been writing on my blog for several years and released them as a collection called *Pirate Therapy and Other Cures*.

I tried to lose some weight again, and miraculously, with the help of two patient and talented personal trainers, I did. And for whatever reason (probably my obsession with losing weight, diet, and the minutia of my BMI) the book became possible to write. I was basically living out Keelan's struggle with weight loss, though I was able to control my stress levels and I didn't have to worry about Dr. Max "Tundraizing" me unexpectedly.

Luckily, I got the draft done that summer. I say luckily, because then my life got stress-y, and I started to put the weight back on. (Despite my earnest promises to my trainer, Tim, never to go over 29 BMI again. Sorry, Tim.) Soon, I'd regained all the weight I'd lost and then some. I crash dieted the next summer and took off twenty-five of the pounds I'd regained, so at least I could wear my non-fat pants again.

And then I regained it all again. Noticing a pattern?

So as I work on this afterword, I'm in the process of dieting. Again. I know it's not good for me, but my hope is that I can get under 30 BMI again before I release this book. I've lost twenty-five of the forty pounds I regained last year, so maybe. I might make it. But the point is, I shouldn't *have to* if I'm otherwise healthy.

But we don't live in that world yet.

I want it not just for Keelan, but for everyone.

Acknowledgements

This work would not exist without the generous assistance of many people. First I'd like to thank Paul F. Campos for his aforementioned *The Obesity Myth*. Special thanks also to Michael Moss for his bestseller *Salt, Sugar, Fat*, which helped me understand the food business better, and the work of Michael Pollan in general, but his 2008 book, *In Defense of Food: An Eater's Manifesto*, in particular. I'd recommend them all.

I've included some information for many of the articles referenced in the "interstitial" bits – the facts and myths. You can Google the quotes yourself. This is not a work of science, but fiction. Still, I hope I haven't distorted anything along the way. And if I have, my apologies to those writers and researchers. The important thing to remember is that science is a process, not a destination. Certainly, none of my ruminations on this should be taken as medical advice.

Thanks to my friends and loved ones who supported me throughout the writing of this book, especially to my long-suffering beta-readers, Jeff Black and Mike Rayner, and the other members of the Emily Chesley Reading Circle, whose feedback always helps at the early stages. Paul Suttie gets a special mention for reading a second draft of the book and giving me great suggestions that made this a better story. Great advice also came from my editor, Ronny Zoo, who has a dozen other names, which I also encourage you to Google for fun. Pauline Nolet did my proofing. I'm eternally grateful and relieved for her help, knowing how terrible I am at it. And how about the cover work, done by Taryn Dufault? Her designs are amazing. Anyone self-publishing would be doing themselves a favour by hiring all of these pros!

Any mistakes or errors in production are my own, or more likely, the fault of my publisher, Dr. Maximillian Tundra.

About the Author

Human-shaped, simian-obsessed, robot-fighting, pirate-hearted, storytelling junkie Mark A. Rayner is an award-winning writer of satirical and speculative fiction.

By day, Mark teaches his bemused students at the Faculty of Information and Media Studies (at Western University), how to construct social media campaigns and viable information architectures that will not become self-aware and destroy all humans. By night he is a writer of short stories, novels, squibs and other drivel. (Some pure, and some quite tainted with meaning.)

Many cheeseburgers were harmed in the making of this novel.

Photo by David Redmond

ENJOY THIS?

Join Mark's email list and he'll send you a free ebook only available from him directly!

All you have to do is sign up, and Mark will send you a copy of *Clown Apocalypse and Other Calamities*, his short collection of coulrophobic fiction: **markarayner.com/clown**

Endnotes

1   Michael Moss, "The Extraordinary Science of Addictive Junk Food," *New York Times*, February 20, 2013. Retrieved July 31, 2013. <http://www.nytimes.com/2013/02/24/magazine/the-extraordinary-science-of-junk-food.html >

2   "Gym, Health & Fitness Clubs in Canada Market Research Report | NAICS 71394CA |" IBIS World, Oct 2016. Retrieved Jan. 13, 2017 <https://www.ibisworld.ca/industry/gym-health-fitness-clubs.html>

Sarah G. Miller, "Fitness or Fatness: What's More Important?" LiveScience.com, Nov. 10, 2015. Retrieved Jan. 13, 2007 <http://www.livescience.com/52745-fitness-fatness-obesity-paradox.html>

3   Sarah Klein, "Fatty foods may cause cocaine-like addiction," CNN.com, March 30, 2010, Retrieved on June 10, 2013. <http://www.cnn.com/2010/HEALTH/03/28/fatty.foods.brain/index.html>

4   Patzer, Gordon L., PhD. *Looks: Why They Matter More Than You Ever Imagined*. New York: Amacom, 2008.
Perrett, David. *In Your Face: The New Science of Human Attraction*. New York, NY: Palgrave Macmillan, 2010.

5   Tony Edwards, "Drinking Doesn't Make You Fat." The Daily Mail. November 24, 2013. Retrieved on June 23, 2017. < http://www.dailymail.co.uk/femail/article-2512850/Drinking-doesnt-make-fat-A-startling-new-book-claims-nightly-glass-wine-wont-straight-hips.html>

6   Dr. Barnard, "Cheese and Obesity," Dr. Barnard's Blog, Physicians Committee for Responsible Medicine. January 24, 2012, Retrieved on January 7, 2015. <http://www.pcrm.org/media/blog/jan2012/cheese-and-obesity>

7   Julie Flaherty, "Is Being Fat Contagious?" *Tufts Now,* November 21, 2011, Retrieved January 6, 2015. <http://now.tufts.edu/articles/being-fat-contagious>

8   Mary Brophy Marcus, "'Hunger Hormones' May Drive Post-Dieting Weight Gain," *HealthDay,* October 26, 2011, Retrieved, Oct. 15, 2014. <http://consumer.healthday.com/vitamins-and-nutritional-information-27/dieting-to-lose-weight-health-news-195/hunger-hormones-may-drive-post-dieting-weight-gain-658270.html>

9   University of Adelaide. "Obese stomachs tell us diets are doomed to fail." *ScienceDaily,* September 16, 2013, Retrieved June 30, 2015. <www.sciencedaily.com/releases/2013/09/130916103352.htm>.

10   Denise Winterman, "History's Weirdest Fad Diets," *BBC News Magazine,* 1 January 2013, Retrieved September 18, 2013. <http://www.bbc.co.uk/news/magazine-20695743>

11   Rachel Moss, "Men With Bigger Bellies Make Better Lovers, Study Says," *The Huffington Post UK,* September 19, 2014, Retrieved, January 15, 2015. <http://www.huffingtonpost.co.uk/2014/09/24/sex-men-overweight-bmi-study_n_5871816.html>

12   Alice G. Walton, "Skipping Breakfast May Not Be Bad For Weight Loss After All," *Forbes,* June 5, 2014, Retrieved, January 15, 2015. <http://www.forbes.com/sites/alicegwalton/2014/06/05/skipping-breakfast-may-not-be-so-bad-for-weight-loss-study-finds/>

13   DiNicolantonio, James J.Lucan, Sean C.O'Keefe, James H. et al., "Is Coffee Harmful? If Looking for Longevity, Say Yes to the Coffee, No to the Sugar," *Mayo Clinic Proceedings,* Volume 89, Issue 4 , 576–577

14   Kenneth Chang, "Artificial

Sweeteners May Disrupt Body's Blood Sugar Controls," *New York Times,* September 17, 2014, Retrieved, November 18, 2014. <http://well.blogs.nytimes.com/2014/09/17/ artificial-sweeteners-may-disrupt-bodys-blood-sugar-controls/>

15   Tia Ghose, "Willpower Is All in Your Head, Study Suggests," *LiveScience,* August 19, 2013, Retrieved, January 16, 2015. <http://www.livescience.com/38980-willpower-is-not-a-finite-re-source.html>

16   Clark, Josh, "How does diet affect body odor?" *How-StuffWorks.com,* 24 September 2009, Retrieved, 14 May 2015. <http://health.howstuffworks.com/skin-care/information/ nutrition/diet-body-odor.htm>

17   Andrea Castillo, "Big Fat Lies: Public Choice, Cultural Bias, and the 'Obesity Epidemic, '" *The Umlat,* June 4, 2013, Retrieved, October 3, 2013. <http://theumlaut.com/2013/06/04/ big-fat-lies-public-choice-cultural-bias-and-the-obesity-epidemic/>

18   Roger Dooley, "The Psychology Of Vanity Sizing," Forbes, July 29, 2013, Retrieved, Jan. 20, 2015. <http://www.forbes.com/ sites/rogerdooley/2013/07/29/vanity-sizing/> Full disclosure: at the time of the final draft the author was back up to 34 waist ☹

19   Lisa Nainggolan, "Inactivity More Deadly Than Obesity, Large New Study Finds," *Medscape,* January 15, 2015, Retrieved, January 22, 2015. <http://www.medscape.com/ viewarticle/838209>

20   Nicky Phillips, "Forget the jog slog and fit in a sprint for maximum weight loss results," *The Sydney Morning Herald,* June 29, 2012, Retrieved, January 23, 2015. <http://www.smh.com. au/executive-style/fitness/forget-the-jog-slog-and-fit-in-a-sprint-for-maximum-weight-loss-results-20120628-215a4.html>

21   Anahad O'connor, "How Sleep Loss Adds to Weight Gain," *New York Times*, August 6, 2013, Retrieved,

January 23, 2015. <http://well.blogs.nytimes.com/2013/08/06/how-sleep-loss-adds-to-weight-gain>

22   Nicholas Bakalar, "A Weight Loss Belief Is Tested," *New York Times*, October 20, 2014, Retrieved, January 23, 2015. <http://well.blogs.nytimes.com/2014/10/20/lose-weight-quickly-or-slowly-research/>

23   Paul Campos, *The Obesity Myth*, (Penguin Books, New York, 2004) 12-14

24   "Are Hippos the Most Dangerous Animal?" The Straight Dope, December 6, 2000, Retrieved, January 23, 2015. <http://www.straightdope.com/columns/read/1862/are-hippos-the-most-dangerous-animal>

25   Joshua Gowin, PhD, "7 Things McDonald's Knows About Your Brain," *Psychology Today*, August 8, 2011, Retrieved, September 18, 2013. <http://www.psychologytoday.com/blog/you-illuminated/201108/7-reasons-we-cant-turn-down-fast-food>

26   Kurt Kleiner, "Most scientific papers are probably wrong," *The New Scientist*, August 30, 2005, Retrieved, June 1, 2015. <http://www.newscientist.com/article/dn7915-most-scientific-papers-are-probably-wrong.html>

27   Inga Kiderra, Spoiler Alert: Stories Are Not Spoiled by 'Spoilers', *UCSanDiego News Center*, August 10, 2011, Retrieved: June 23, 2017.
< http://ucsdnews.ucsd.edu/archive/newsrel/soc/2011_08spoilers.asp>

28   Perelman School of Medicine at the University of Pennsylvania. "Fat shaming linked to greater health risks." ScienceDaily. January 26, 2017, Retrieved: July 5, 2017. <www.sciencedaily.com/releases/2017/01/170126082024.htm>

MORE FROM
MARK A. RAYNER

The Fridgularity

Blake Given's web-enabled fridge has pulled the plug on the Internet, turning its owner's life – and the whole world – upside down.

Blake has modest ambitions for his life. He wants to have his job reclassified, so he can join the Creative Department of the advertising firm where he works. And he wants to go out with Daphne, one of the account execs at the same company. His fridge has other plans. All Blake knows is he's at the center of the Internet's disappearance, worldwide economic and religious chaos, and the possibility of a nuclear apocalypse — none of which is helping him with his career plans or love life.

The Fridgularity is the story of a reluctant prophet, Internet addicts in withdrawal and a kitchen appliance with delusions of grandeur.

"With plenty of humor and much more, "The Fridgularity" is an exciting, sci-fi view askew, highly recommended."   *-Midwest Book Review*

"If you're looking for a combination of humor, romance and a power hungry refrigerator, look no further than The Fridgularity, a very enjoyable read. 5 stars!"   *-IndieReader.com*

How to be a Magnificent Bastard

Want to become a hero to indie authors?

Those of us creating novels have the huge challenge of getting our work noticed. If you love an author, or a particular book, such as . . . ahem, *The Fatness* . . . consider helping them. There's two things that are easy to do and that help immensely.

1. Review the book and post it on Amazon

If you're only going to do one thing, this is probably the most helpful. Rankings on Amazon help create their algorithm that makes customer suggestions. And there are lots of other review sites you could join, such as Goodreads, Library Thing, Booklikes and so on. Post your reviews there too.

2. Tell your friends and family

Tweet it, post on your FB page, and blog about it, but think about the friends and family who would really enjoy the book. Send them a personalized note. (Or talk to them, if you're old school.) If there's a particular thing about it you know they'd enjoy, mention it.

On behalf of all idies, thanks for your support!